ME...
SH...

BY
CINDY DEES

AND

HER SHEIKH
PROTECTOR

BY
LINDA CONRAD

Harlequin (UK) policy is to use papers that are natural, renewable and recyclable products and made from wood grown in sustainable forests. The logging and manufacturing processes conform to the legal environmental regulations of the country of origin.

Printed and bound in Spain
by Blackprint CPI, Barcelona

MILLS & BOON

All the characters in this book have no existence outside the imagination of the author, and have no relation whatsoever to anyone bearing the same name or names. They are not even distantly inspired by any individual known or unknown to the author, and all the incidents are pure invention.

First published in Great Britain 2011
by Mills & Boon, an imprint of Harlequin (UK) Limited,
Eton House, 18-24 Paradise Road, Richmond, Surrey TW9 1SR

© Cynthia Dees 2010

ISBN: 978 0 263 88538 5

MEDUSA'S SHEIKH

BY
CINDY DEES

How could this book be dedicated to anyone other than my Middle Eastern Dance instructors over the years, women who preserve and share this ancient art form and make it new again? With each generation of dancers who are trained, the great sisterhood of women spanning the history of mankind expands and grows, and that's a beautiful thing. So thanks to Trudi, Isis, Vashti, Tambra, Karen B., Suhaila and so many other magnificent ladies.

Dance on!

Cindy Dees started flying aeroplanes while sitting in her dad's lap at the age of three and got a pilot's license before she got a driver's license. At the age of fifteen, she dropped out of high school and left the horse farm in Michigan where she grew up to attend the University of Michigan.

After earning a degree in Russian and East European Studies, she joined the US Air Force and became the youngest female pilot in its history. She flew supersonic jets, VIP airlift and the C-5 Galaxy, the world's largest airplane. She also worked part-time gathering intelligence. During her military career, she traveled to forty countries on five continents, was detained by the KGB and East German secret police, got shot at, flew in the first Gulf War, met her husband and amassed a lifetime's worth of war stories.

Her hobbies include professional Middle Eastern dancing, Japanese gardening and medieval re-enacting. She started writing on a one-dollar bet with her mother and was thrilled to win that bet with the publication of her first book in 2001. She loves to hear from readers and can be contacted at www.cindydees.com.

Chapter 1

Hakim El Aran, "Hake" to his British friends, took the flavored rose water and soda from the waitress. He sipped it before turning to his lawyer, Geoffrey Birch. "So, have you come up with a solution to my problem?"

The older man gave a noncommittal shrug. "Let's talk business after the show." He reached for a menu. "Food's excellent here, by the by."

"When did you develop a taste for Middle Eastern food?"

"Since I saw the entertainment that comes with it."

Amusement bordering on disbelief crept into Hake's voice. "You mean the belly dancer?" He had serious trouble picturing strait-laced Birch enjoying the gyrations of some half-naked female along with his dinner.

The lawyer explained earnestly, "This isn't just any belly dancer. It's Cassandra. She's amazing."

On cue, the overhead lights dimmed in the packed

restaurant, while Hake stared at his companion. Geoffrey lived and breathed for the law. Hake had never seen anyone or anything that could distract him from his work. But apparently, this Cassandra chick had pulled off the impossible. The woman's timing couldn't have been any worse.

Irked at the dancer sight unseen, Hake watched the center of the cavernous room, where five musicians sat on a raised platform behind a parquet stage. He'd traveled with his father since he was a small boy, and he'd seen the greatest belly dancers in the world from Cairo to California and back. He highly doubted some schlocky theme club in London had pulled in a top-flight performer. He braced himself for a travesty of actual Middle Eastern dance.

The overhead lights faded away to nothingness, and the background buzz quieted. Darkness, relieved only by the small candles at each table, cloaked the restaurant. The silence grew thick with anticipation. Scents of cumin and cinnamon swirled around Hake, accompanied by the musky tang of Turkish tobacco.

Middle Eastern music began to play almost subliminally quiet, gradually growing in volume. Hake was suddenly gripped by a sensation of approaching a giant bazaar from afar. It promised exotic sights and sounds, bright colors and a tangle of pungent odors. *Home.*

Not that he'd been home to Bhoukar in years. His work abroad for his father, and El Aran Industries, kept him on the move. Truth be told, he'd been avoiding going home most of that time. He was deep into prime marriageable age, and he had no interest in dealing with scheming aunties and the political jockeying of people trying to ally themselves to the powerful El Aran family. But the marriage trap was closing in on him fast. Hence, tonight's meeting with his attorney.

Into the restaurant's gloom, a lone spotlight illuminated. It cast a bright circle in the center of the stage, bathing the spot in harsh, desert brilliance. A haze of smoke wafted through the column of light. The music pulsed rhythmically, gaining power with every beat. Despite his cynicism, he had to admit a certain visceral excitement rose in his gut. Maybe it was the call of the desert to his half-Saracen blood.

A dancer glided into the shimmering mirage of light as if conjured from the heat and smoke. Slender and darkly, ravishingly beautiful, she wore a costume dripping with red, glittering beads that caressed her golden skin and glowed against her raven hair. Hake stared in appreciation. She looked the part at any rate.

Eyes closed, her arms open in sensual invitation, she swayed with the music. The melody caressed the dancer, a feather drawn across her skin with a loving hand. She shivered at its delicate touch. Something about her called to Hake, beguiling and beckoning him—something beyond the obvious sexual allure of a beautiful, scantily clad woman. She was the music and the music was her soul.

The outside world ceased to exist as he was drawn into her dance. The moment contained only the woman, the music and him. Her body glistened with a sheen of perspiration as she undulated for him, her movements an extension of the mysterious *taksim* melody twining about them both.

His avid gaze followed a ripple which started just below her ribs, traveling sinuously down her stomach to the top of the heavily fringed belt that rode low on her hips. The belly roll traveled back up her torso, leading his gaze to the plunging, crystal-encrusted bra that revealed a cleft of swelling softness.

Her figure was an exquisite hourglass of perfectly

toned muscle. As a nearly invisible hip vibration caused the dancer's fringe to quiver against her skin, he was struck by an urge to feel her doing that beneath him, gripping his male flesh in building ecstasy.

She sank slowly to the floor, her arms rolling elegantly, as if they rested on the surface of a gently swelling ocean. One movement flowed seamlessly into the next as the dancer rose again, invoking images of a snake rising charmed out of its basket—graceful, exotic and mesmerizing.

It was probably rude to stare at her as if he were intent upon devouring her, but he couldn't stop himself. She was stunning. Her control—of both her muscles and the moment—was exquisite. The drums quieted to an erotic throbbing and her head fell back, exposing the artful line of her throat. Potent sexuality poured off her along with the heat of her body, steamy and tangible in the restaurant's dim light.

Hake shifted uncomfortably, his body raging in response to the woman before him. Her smoky sensuality enveloped him like a silken veil. He felt a strange intimacy with the dancer, as if he knew her somehow, as if she were dancing just for him. He studied her sculpted features, the straight, narrow nose framed by wide, catlike eyes, the high cheekbones, the delicately defined jaw.

No wonder Geoffrey had gone loopy over her. Hake managed to wrest his gaze away from the dancer long enough to glance at his dinner companion. The attorney stared slack-jawed at the woman. Hake felt a little better as he scanned the crowded restaurant. Everyone, it seemed, was caught in her thrall. Even the waiters stood motionless by the kitchen doors, transfixed by the dancer's magic.

Effortlessly, spectacularly, she had woven a web around the room. She'd transported them all to a faraway fantasy of hot desert winds and the sumptuous splendors of a seraglio, to a place where women such as her existed solely for the pleasure of the men who owned them.

As drums joined the strains of dusty flute music, the tempo increased and the mood changed in an instant. The dancer's head snapped forward and her eyes flashed open, fiery with passion. As it so happened, she was facing Hake directly when she did it. Her gaze speared into him.

They both froze. She, too, seemed caught in the grip of a powerful, instinctive recognition. Something alive coiled between them, pulling them inexorably toward one another. Sudden knowing burst across him. *This woman was meant to be his.*

Buried somewhere in the back of his brain, a sarcastic internal voice commented that his family would just love it if he brought home a belly dancer he'd met in a tawdry joint in London. In conservative quarters of Middle Eastern culture, dancers were often viewed as barely one step above prostitutes. But insatiable need to have this woman, to mark her as his, overwhelmed all else.

For an endless, breathless moment, the music paused while the dancer stared at him, the connection between them naked in her gaze.

She was his.

Casey Chandler stared at the man in devastating shock. The music faded and the spotlights spun around the edges of her vision.

It was *him.*

Hakim El Aran.

The one face she emphatically didn't want to see here tonight. She was supposed to make contact with his lawyer, not with the suspect himself.

El Aran's intent gaze touched her physically, sliding across her skin like a lover's cajoling caress, willing her to come to him, threatening to strip away the layers of her deceit. All of a sudden, she felt naked. Exposed far beyond the skimpiness of her costume.

Her breathing faltered and betraying heat flared low in her abdomen. Sizzling awareness tingled in her toes and raced like lightning to the tips of her fingers. *Focus.* She was on the *job!* Men weren't supposed to have this effect on her when she was working. Particularly not this one. She'd been warned that he was a ladies' man. but she'd never dreamed he'd be like this.

She was a soldier, for goodness' sake. A trained Special Forces operative working undercover. Not a harem girl swept off her feet by the first come-hither glance some Arab prince threw at her. Although technically, he was Bhoukari, from the small principality nestled between Oman and Yemen. And technically, he was only a sheik— several dozen cousins away from being emir of Bhoukar. Still. She was not supposed to react to him like this!

Tell that to her body. Her flesh throbbed with need, tingling as if he were already drawing his fingers across her skin, already whispering for her to dance the oldest dance of all for him. He wasn't a ladies' man. He was a lady killer.

The drummer gave a sharp pop on his *tabla,* the ceramic drum perched between his knees, demanding her attention. Awareness of her surroundings returned abruptly. Good Lord. She'd stopped dancing cold in front of a restaurant full of people, in the middle of a song, no less. She threw an apologetic glance over her shoulder at the musicians and picked up the rhythm of the music with her finger cymbals.

She moved to the other side of the stage, carefully avoiding glancing in *his* direction. Thing was, to do the dance justice, she had to put her heart into her performance.

Share a little piece of her soul with the audience. It simply was not possible for her to dance and maintain military detachment simultaneously.

It was terribly dangerous for him to see her like this. The next time they met, he might recognize her. And that could be disastrous. One word from Hake to the wrong people and the whole mission would come crashing down around her.

While most of her mind concentrated on the performance, a tiny piece of it prayed desperately that she'd make it offstage before disaster struck. She had to think. Had to figure out what to do, how to respond, how to salvage the mission.

Panic tickled the edges of her consciousness, but blessedly, her training and the performer within her knew how to cope. She concentrated on breathing, then on moving her feet, and then on relaxing her shoulders. The show continued, but her mind ran unchecked, leaping from one disjointed thought to another.

Why, oh why, did he have to show up now? She was a week at most from convincing Birch to hand over the evidence on the El Aran empire. Should she still try to talk to Birch tonight? Or maybe she should delay until the next time he showed up here. Except that could be days or weeks from now. Did she dare wait that long? The Medusas' other intelligence sources were hinting that there might not be much time left before Hake and his father made the sale of nuclear production equipment to an unnamed buyer.

Could she skip the attorney and play the son directly? Did she dare?

It would be a dangerous gambit. By all accounts, Hake was smart, suspicious and wary of women. But then, why wouldn't he be? Available, gorgeous females went into mass feeding frenzies any time he went out in public. It must really suck for him, being a billionaire, single, handsome and under the age of forty.

No, it wouldn't work. She'd never get close enough to him to find out what he was up to. And frankly, she'd be damned if she'd throw herself at any man, mission or no mission. The only way for a seduction of Hake El Aran to work would be for him to approach her. And that wasn't going to happen in this lifetime.

The rest of the show passed in a blur. She was vaguely aware of the audience's enthusiastic applause, the Middle Eastern customers shouting, *"Aiwa, habibi!"* Technically, it meant "Yes, darling," but a better translation was probably "Yeah, baby!"

She made her exit, gliding through the kitchen doors. The minute they swung shut behind her, she picked up her skirts and fled down the long hallway to her dressing room. She collapsed onto the stool at her makeup table and stared at her reflection in the lighted mirror. Beneath her airbrushed tan, she was pale as a ghost. She pressed icy palms to her cheeks.

What the hell had happened to her out there? As the Brits like to put it, the guy'd gobsmacked her but good. One look from Hake El Aran and she was a mess. *Get a grip. You're a trained killer.* Not that she'd been out on all that many missions, but she wasn't a complete idiot. Except when it came to hunky sheiks, apparently.

He made her feel like a…a woman. And in her world, that was emphatically not a good thing. She was the job. The next military mission to save the world. She did not do girly stuff, particularly if it involved emotions, swooning over men, or—heaven forbid—makeup. The sexy costume and heavy, cat-eyed stage makeup she wore tonight, notwithstanding. That stuff was all a disguise. None of it was *her*.

Then why was she such a basket case all of a sudden? Where were her vaunted Medusa nerves of steel? Bizarre how she was as calm as a cucumber when someone was shooting at her. But let Hake El Aran turn on the charm, and she fell completely apart.

She'd been shocked, and frankly, none too pleased, when her boss, Lt. Colonel Vanessa Blake, had briefed her on this mission and the need for her skill as a Middle Eastern dancer. She'd always done it for the exercise, not because she wanted to be Mata Hari someday. But like she'd verified for Vanessa, it took years, decades even, to train a world-class Middle Eastern dancer. Furthermore, it was not an art that could be faked in front of a knowledgeable audience. Hence her being here. Half-naked, slathered in makeup, perfume and hair spray, dancing in a nightclub.

None of this was real. She was just bait. Darned successful bait, it turned out. She'd been trying to net the minnow but had hooked the shark, apparently.

In her defense, she hadn't been expecting Hake, nor for him to look at her like that. Plus, when she danced she let down her emotional defenses. Like it or not, to do the dance justice she had to tap heavily into her feminine side. One thing she knew for sure, she could never, ever confess her reaction to Hake to her teammates. They'd never let her hear the end of it.

Faced with the horrifying truth that she was desperately attracted to the man she was supposed to take down, only one question remained: if she actually managed to reel in the shark, what on earth was she going to do with him?

Chapter 2

Hake contemplated Birch, who sipped at a tiny glass of arrack, the potent, licorice-flavored liqueur of the Middle East. He noted Geoffrey's flush, the subtle shifting in his seat, the uncharacteristic silence. Hake's mouth twitched in amusement. The dancer had seriously affected the poor man. He took pity and laid down his napkin beside his plate.

"When you called, you said you'd researched my situation. Have you figured out a way to deal with it?"

The attorney leaned forward, abruptly serious, abruptly at work. "You realize, of course, that this conversation is completely off the record. I'll deny any knowledge of it if you repeat a word of it."

Hake leaned forward, equally serious. "Cut the lawyer crap. It's me you're talking to, old friend. You've known my father since before I was born and watched me grow up. You know I won't say anything."

"Yes, but I am counsel to your father as well, and you're asking me to advise you against him. It's a blatant conflict of interest to involve myself in a dispute between the two of you."

"Fine. I have duly noted that this conversation is off the record."

The attorney's shoulders relaxed fractionally.

"So tell me, Geoffrey, hypothetically of course, if you weren't my father's attorney and represented only me, what would you advise me to do? Is he within his rights to insist I get married before he'll release my trust fund to me?"

"More or less."

"Don't equivocate. Yes or no?"

"Marriage is not stipulated in the terms of the trust, but there is a clause stating that your father must approve the release of the funds. In reality, he can set whatever conditions he wants before he'll give you that approval."

Hake's jaw tightened into the rippling mass of tension that never failed to make people around him jumpy on the rare occasions it occurred. Although quiet, his voice vibrated with fury. "What the hell am I supposed to do?"

"I'd suggest, my dear boy, that you start looking for a wife. Although I do have to ask, why do you want your trust released to you? You have millions in other funds. Money that you've earned for yourself."

In truth, it was the principle of the thing getting under his skin. He didn't like the idea of anyone else having control over him in any way. "So I've got to do the wife thing, huh?" Hake remarked grimly.

"It wouldn't be the end of the world. You might even discover you like it."

"You're a fine one to talk. I don't see you breaking your neck racing to the altar."

Geoffrey grinned unrepentantly. "Nobody's forcing me

into it. Frankly, I think your father secretly detests lawyers. He doesn't want to encourage us to reproduce."

"Lucky dog."

Geoffrey smiled and glanced over at the stage where Cassandra had performed. Hake was startled by an urge to grit his teeth in response. "Has my father indicated how soon he expects me to marry?"

"My impression is that he'd like the matter settled within a year."

"A year?" Hake echoed in dismay. If his old man wanted him to marry, Hake suspected there wasn't going to be a whole hell of a lot he could do to stop it. But the thought infuriated him. He was thirty-five years old, had already made his own millions, and was his own man, dammit. It was high time his father recognized that he was an adult, full-grown and capable of running his own life, including marrying or not marrying. Personally, he voted for the not-marrying option. There were so many beautiful women out there. Why be in any rush to close the door on them all?

Geoffrey asked, "Are you seeing anyone right now?"

Hake kept his expression bland. He'd lay odds his father had instructed the lawyer to ask that question. He answered vaguely, "I see a few women here and there."

He dated any number of women casually, but none held his attention for long. At the end of the day, they were all pretty much the same. They wanted the same things, were impressed by the same things, reacted the same way in most situations. Although he enjoyed having a beautiful one around for decoration and taking advantage of the pleasures one could offer, he didn't particularly *need* women. And that was the main reason he'd never married. Why saddle himself with someone who would ultimately become an inconvenience?

"Hake, now may be your only chance to choose your

own wife before your father gets involved and chooses one for you. I hate to say it, but if I were you, I'd start hunting for a nice girl who doesn't make you crazy. You know as well as I do your father's not going to budge on this."

Hake restrained an urge to swear.

Birch continued, "I never thought I'd hear myself say this, but if I were you, I might seriously consider finding a woman who will agree to be your wife in return for… some sort of compensation."

"You're saying I should *buy* a wife? You don't think I can get a woman to agree to marry me on my own merits?" Hake was genuinely shocked. He literally had to fight off women. He didn't need to buy one. Hell, all he had to do was hold out a diamond ring and they'd be falling over each other to snatch it.

Geoffrey squirmed uncomfortably. "I was thinking more along the lines of…a marriage of…convenience. Something mutually beneficial to both of you."

Hake sat back in his chair, flabbergasted. "You're joking."

"You could dictate the conditions of the relationship to your liking. After she produces an heir, you might want the freedom to maintain…discreet liaisons…on the side, maybe separate residences for the two of you, that sort of thing."

"What am I supposed to do? Walk up to…" Hake cast around for a suitably outrageous example "…say, that dancer we just saw, and ask her to marry me? I'll put her up in the lap of luxury forever in return for her marrying me, making a baby or two, and then leaving me the hell alone for the rest of my life? You've lost your mind!"

Geoffrey shrugged and grinned. "You're right. Forget I mentioned it. It was a ridiculous notion." He picked up his glass. "A toast. To bachelorhood."

Hake matched the lawyer's grin and clinked glasses with Geoffrey. "To bachelorhood."

Maneuvering awkwardly in the small space of her dressing room, Casey removed the heavy, beaded costume and hung it up to dry. Wrapped in a thin cotton robe, she fanned herself until she cooled down and then began repairing her stage makeup. Despite all of it being heavy-duty and waterproof, it was simply not possible to keep makeup entirely in place as she sweated profusely over the course of a forty-five-minute show. There was no getting around it. Belly dancing was strenuous stuff.

She sipped at a bottle of water to rehydrate before the next show in about an hour. Right before she went on, she would eat a tablespoon of peanut butter. She needed the calories and protein to get through another forty-five minutes of aerobic exertion. On performance days, she didn't eat after breakfast and wouldn't eat again until after her second and final show. A large meal would make her stomach stick out and not have the smooth, sinuous line customers associated with Middle Eastern dancers.

She had some time to spare before she needed to put on her next costume. Idly, she unlocked her equipment bag and checked her service pistol, ammunition clips and various other tools of the Special Forces trade that she currently had stowed along with spare finger cymbals, music CDs and safety pins.

Out of habit, she checked her cell phone for messages. None. Her headquarters, H.O.T. Watch Ops, was aware of this show. Heck, knowing that gang, they had a surveillance camera somewhere in the restaurant. She could just picture the cave full of analysts and Special Forces operatives getting a cheap thrill watching her dance. She hoped they all were too uncomfortable to stand up straight. It would serve them right.

She glanced in the mirror and met her own cold, cynical gaze with a certain relief. "Welcome back, Captain Chandler," she muttered. Who was she kidding? A special operator like her could never land a man like Hake El Aran. He'd take one look into her hard-edged gaze and run screaming.

It wasn't that she hated men. Far from it. It was just that she was entirely realistic about her inadequacies when it came to dealing with all things pertaining to men. She didn't do the girly thing well, she didn't do the girl-boy thing well either. Take Hake, for example. The guy was smoking-hot and she definitely felt intense attraction to him. But the idea of acting on her impulses struck terror into her heart.

Nope, a direct approach to the El Aran heir definitely was out of the question. She would continue with the original plan and focus her attention upon the manufacturing empire's much more gullible attorney. It wasn't as if she was asking Birch to violate attorney-client privilege. She was merely urging him to assist in a vital, joint undercover operation between the United States and Great Britain by giving them advance notice of the timing of a business deal.

Geoffrey Birch was an honorable and patriotic man. He would do the right thing for Crown and country. This mission would be a piece of cake. And then she'd get on with her regularly scheduled life and Hake El Aran could get on with whatever it was that he did.

"Miss Cassandra?" one of the waiters called through her door. "A man. He wishes to meet you."

"You know my policy on that, Ismael. I don't chat up the patrons and I don't allow men in my dressing room."

"He is most insistent, ma'am. He offered me a thousand pounds to introduce him to you." A pause. "I could really use the money. My wife is pregnant—"

Oh, for crying out loud. A thousand pounds? She tried to guess which one it was. The restaurant had been packed with middle-aged, successful-looking businessmen. No telling which one had made the outrageous offer. And frankly, she wasn't the slightest bit curious to find out. Men were all pretty much the same around belly dancers. They thought they could take liberties and make offensive suggestions because they'd seen a girl half-naked and sharing her most sensual self with him…and everyone else in the joint. But that last bit always seemed to escape the pushy patrons.

She did hate to cost the waiter that much cash, though. Her gaze glittered with irritation in the mirror. She called out, "Fine. Tell him he can buy me a drink after my second show. But make sure he pays up first."

Ismael called back his enthusiastic thanks, and she was alone again. She remembered now why she'd never pursued a full-time career as a dancer. She adored the music, and there was nothing quite like the exhilaration of feeling the rhythms of it moving through her, shaping her body and freeing her soul to fly. It was just that she couldn't deal with the men. Good thing she worked with all women on Medusa Team Two.

When Geoffrey excused himself to go to the loo, Hake had a quiet word with the maître d'. A wad of cash changed hands and Hake leaned back more relaxed than he'd been since that dancer had shocked him to his toes earlier.

Birch returned to the table. Hake announced jovially, "Well, old man, you and I both have plenty of work to do tomorrow. What say we call it a night?"

Geoffrey looked wistfully at the empty stage and nodded reluctantly. "Yes, of course. You're right. Too bad Cassandra didn't come out to say hello to the patrons tonight."

Hake's mouth turned down sardonically. "If I were her, I might not show myself either. With the state she got this crowd worked up into, she'd run a real risk of being assaulted."

Geoffrey smiled, a tight, smug little smile. "Indeed. And besides, there are so many better ways to make contact with a woman than mugging her in a place like this."

Hake's gaze snapped to his lawyer. Now what did the old bird mean by that? Did the man actually have aspirations of meeting the divine Cassandra and having her for himself? A stab of something sharp and unpleasant speared through Hake's gut. What was that all about? How odd.

He escorted the attorney from the restaurant and hailed a cab for the man. As soon as the black taxi had disappeared around the corner, Hake turned and headed back into the restaurant. The maître d' had been more than happy to hold his table for him—for a hefty tip, of course. Hake ordered himself a drink and sat back to anticipate the return of Cassandra to grace the stage and perform for him.

Casey peeked out of the kitchen moments before the lights were to dim, startled at how many patrons from the first show were still in the restaurant. And then she caught sight of *him*. Hake was still out there. By himself now, but squarely facing the stage and nursing a drink.

Butterflies leaped in her stomach. Usually, she experienced no stage fright at all. Yet the idea of Hake watching her again, observing every nuance of her body, made her all but hyperventilate. She glanced down at her costume, gold and skimpy and beaded from head to toe. In keeping with the later show, this costume showed more leg and cleavage and her arms were completely bare except for matching snake bracelets clasping her upper arms. She swore under her breath. She could really go for a set of full camouflage clothing right about now.

"Ready, Cassandra?" the manager murmured, startling her.

"Uh, yes. I guess so."

"Knock 'em dead, love. Not that you don't always. My receipts triple on the nights you dance."

She smiled gratefully at the manager, who was in on her secret identity and the reason for it. They'd needed him to shuffle the dancers' schedules around to accommodate adding Casey to the rotation, and he'd initially been reluctant, Scotland Yard request or no. It had threatened to turn into an ugly stalemate until she'd diplomatically suggested that maybe an audition for the man was in order. Of course, once she'd danced for him, he'd been more than happy to give her the coveted Saturday night shows.

The restaurant went black. The musicians started playing so softly she could barely hear them. She closed her eyes, let the exotic chords wash over her and through her, and Casey Chandler, former FBI agent and current Special Forces operative, retreated. Cassandra, the desert seductress, took over. *It's a disguise. Just a disguise.*

Without Birch present, Hake allowed himself to truly appreciate Cassandra's second show. If possible, it was even more sultry and alluring than the first. She really was an accomplished dancer. As fine as any he'd ever seen. They'd go crazy over her in Cairo, the global capital of belly dancing.

She aroused him so intensely that it would be a while before he could leave the table without embarrassing himself.

After the show, he kept an eagle eye on the kitchen from

whence she would emerge. He'd already ascertained from a helpful waiter that she was not married and, furthermore, never arrived or left the restaurant in the company of a gentleman. Fierce satisfaction coursed through him at that news. Nonetheless, Hake was determined not to let anyone else move in on her. And no way was he letting her slip past him and duck the drink she'd agreed to let him buy her. He wanted her and he planned to have her for himself. End of discussion.

Chapter 3

A hush fell over the cavernous interior of H.O.T. Watch headquarters and the nearly three dozen intelligence analysts, communications experts and Special Forces operatives clustered in the giant underground facility to watch Cassandra's second set in the nightclub. When it ended, Beau Breckenridge, one of the lead duty controllers murmured, "Whoa. That girl sure can dance."

The six women standing beside him all snorted, but the commander of the entire Medusa Project, Lt. Colonel Vanessa Blake, was the one to answer. "She's a Medusa. We do a thing well or we don't do it at all. I wouldn't have suggested her for this mission if I didn't know she was good."

Breckenridge grinned. "How long did it take her to learn to dance like that?"

Alexandra Rios, known to her teammates as Tarantula,

answered, "She says she's been at it for close to twenty years."

Naraya El Saad, the Medusa's resident mathematician and genius at large, piped up in her cultured accent, "Trust me. It's taken every bit of twenty years to achieve that level of mastery. I danced a bit when I was a little girl and what she does is a great deal harder than it looks."

Beau stared at the reserved Middle Eastern woman. "You can dance like that?"

Naraya laughed. "No, not even close. That's why she got sent on this mission and not me. The op called for a professional dancer, not an enthusiastic but untalented amateur."

Navy Commander Brady Hathaway, the man in charge of the bunker tonight, interrupted, "And speaking of the mission, what are we going to do about Hake El Aran? Not only has he seen Scorpion, but he's just spent the past hour studying her in excruciating detail. Is she blown or do we proceed with the operation? Thoughts, ladies?"

Vanessa, aka Viper, frowned. "It took us a great deal of maneuvering to get my operative placed close to the El Aran empire. Marat El Aran is an extremely cagey and cautious man. I don't think we have time to establish another undercover operator before the deal goes down, do we?"

Hathaway looked over at Beau, who replied, "Our source says the sale is set to happen within the month."

Vanessa asked grimly, "Any word yet on exactly who the buyer is?"

Beau shook his head. "Nope. That's why we need your girl. We need her to find out who and where and when so we can stop the deal before some terrorist group gets its hands on the capacity to manufacture precision nuclear weapon parts."

The Medusas traded long, silent looks among themselves, then Vanessa spoke for all of them. "I think we should leave her in place. It's a calculated risk, but the stakes are too high to do any less. If her contact ends up being Hake El Aran himself, so be it."

Beau glanced back up at the jumbo screen and the image of Hake El Aran shifting in his seat and staring at the door from which Scorpion would emerge shortly. "I wish your girl luck," he muttered. "Lord knows she's gonna need it to deal with him. He's infamous for hating government officials and loving the ladies."

Casey finished stripping off the heavy stage makeup and replaced it with more appropriate personal makeup. God bless Roxi—the Medusa's fashion stylist turned commando—wherever she was tonight. The woman was magic with cosmetics, hair and fashion and had put her through a crash course in all of the above before this mission.

Casey checked to make sure her purse was zipped, her pistol tucked into its hidden compartment. The purse was cleverly padded so someone touching the bag wouldn't see or feel the weapon nested inside. As she slung the strap over her shoulder, she felt the telltale vibration of her cell phone within it. She dug it out. "Hello?"

"Scorpion. Viper here. We noticed the wrinkle sitting stage left tonight."

Casey winced. So, H.O.T. Watch *did* have a camera in the restaurant. "Did the boys enjoy the show?"

Vanessa laughed. "Oh, yeah. You completely silenced them. Not a single wisecrack out of the lot of them. Never thought I'd see the day. Congratulations."

"Cool. Any advice on removing wrinkles?" Casey asked.

"We've talked it over and agree that you should feel free to pursue that avenue if you think it might turn out to be profitable. But it's your call whether or not you think it has potential."

Casey stared at her reflection in the mirror. She was suddenly a bit pale. She was greenlighted to pursue Hake El Aran himself? Her first impulse was to run far away and hide from the man and his aggressive sensuality.

He'd been sending her vibes so charged with sexual promise during the show that she'd had trouble keeping her knees from buckling. The heat he'd aroused in her had practically incinerated the stage. She'd never danced that intensely before, and the audience hadn't missed it. The crowd had been all but drooling collectively by the time the show ended. It was why she'd dawdled backstage afterward. She was hoping most of the patrons left before she had to go out and face them.

Not to mention she dreaded facing her thousand-pound paying patron after that steamy performance. It was one thing to put on a girly act from a distance and behind the protection of a costume and makeup. But it was another thing entirely to keep up the act face-to-face with a man, one-on-one. She never had been comfortable around men, but in this persona, she would be expected to be perfectly at ease with the whole beautiful-woman-who-men-fawn-over-all-the-time thing. She admitted it. She was a big fat chicken.

"You still there?" Vanessa asked in her ear.

"Yes, I'm here. Thinking. It's a bold idea to go directly for the El Aran heir. Risky."

"Agreed. Is it worth the risk?"

Keeping nuclear weapons out of the hands of terrorists? Unfortunately, that one was a no-brainer. It was worth a whole lot more than flirting with some guy who might be more than she could handle. Strike that. Who no doubt *would* be more than she could handle. But that was just her tough luck. She was Medusa and she had a job to do.

"You and I both know the answer to that question," she replied grimly.

Her boss asked soberly, "Can you handle it, Scorpion?"

Dammit. Was it that obvious to her teammates that she was completely ill at ease with herself as a woman and with men in general? She sighed. "I guess I'll just have to."

Vanessa chuckled. "Hey, it could be worse. He's yummy. Have fun."

"Whatever," Casey scowled. "Oh, and next time could you let me know when I'm on *Candid Camera?*"

"Sorry about that. I thought it might make you self-conscious, so I didn't mention it. I promise I'll tell you next time."

"Thanks."

"Good luck. I know you can do this."

Casey disconnected the call glumly. She could do something all right. But she wasn't at all sure it would include succeeding on the mission. If she was lucky, Hake was long gone from the restaurant and would never be back. The issue of dealing with him directly would be moot.

The waiter, Ismael, spoke outside her door. "The customer's waiting for you, Miss Cassandra. He's on the last stool at the far end of the bar."

"Got it. Did he pay you?"

"Yes, and a hundred extra because he was so pleased that I talked you into it."

Casey smiled gamely at the young man. At least one person was going home happy tonight. She took a deep breath, squared her shoulders and stepped out into the restaurant. She headed resolutely for the bar. One drink, a polite-but-firm refusal of the patron's advances and she'd be out of here.

She stopped in her tracks, staring at the last stool on the end. Ohcrap, ohcrap, ohcrap. The patron was Hake El Aran.

Hake's breath hitched when he caught sight of Cassandra walking toward him. Her dress was black, sleeveless, simple and sexy as hell. He'd expected the usual model's catwalk while she strutted her stuff for him, but was startled to see her striding forward confidently, athletically even. Odd.

She frowned when she spotted him, which startled him. Disappointed that he wasn't someone else? What was there to frown about? He was a good-looking man, well-educated, heir to a giant manufacturing empire and richer than one man had a right to be. There was no arrogance in the knowledge…it was just a fact.

"Good evening, Mister…" Cassandra said cautiously.

"El Aran. But you can call me Hake." Huh. She was American, judging by the accent. He hadn't expected that. She slid onto the bar stool beside him, her gaze roving around the room keenly. "Worried about something?" he murmured.

Her gaze snapped back to him. "No. Why do you ask?"

"You were searching for someone."

She looked at him in momentary noncomprehension. Then, "Oh, that's just a habit of mine. I like to know what and who is around me."

"Does that come from being afraid of free-handed patrons when you dance?"

She smiled, a tight little thing that stemmed from confidence and maybe a hint of disdain. "No, I'm not afraid of any patron. I can take care of myself, thank you."

Startled, he studied her anew. Was there more to this dancer than met the eye? Intrigued, he leaned forward. "Tell me about yourself."

She gazed at him levelly. "I agreed to have a drink with you, not share my life story."

"Ah, but I paid dearly for that drink. I think I've purchased a little more than just polite conversation, don't you?"

She gazed pointedly at the empty napkin in front of her by way of response. He laughed and signaled over the bartender. "Get the lady a..." He looked over her.

"A bottle of water and a club soda with a twist of lime," she finished.

"Nothing stronger than that?" he blurted.

"Were you hoping to get me drunk and take advantage of me, perchance?" she retorted.

Prickly, she was. But he supposed he couldn't blame her. She must get sick of men trying to crawl all over her. He grinned and murmured, "I don't usually have to get women drunk to get them in my bed."

She inhaled a sharp, satisfying little breath. So, she wasn't totally unaffected by him after all. His male ego felt much better and he settled in to be patient. The hunt was an art form at which he happened to excel.

When she opened the bottle of water and drank the whole thing down, he grinned. "Thirsty were you?"

She picked up the club soda and took a daintier sip of it. "I can lose up to ten pounds of water weight during a single show."

"You must be in pretty good shape to do that night in and night out."

Her eyes glinted with humor. "I've been known to work out a bit," she commented drily.

"It shows," he replied.

Her eyebrows shot up and he thought that was veiled disapproval in her gaze.

"Oh, come now. Surely you know how perfect a body you have. You're toned from head to foot."

She merely shrugged. He looked for some indication that she was offended or playing coy but saw neither. Strange. Most women craved hearing men tell them how beautiful and desirable they were. She seemed…disinterested in the subject.

"What do you like to talk about?" he asked.

She studied him for a long moment. "Do you seriously care? We both know what you want from me, and intellectually stimulating conversation is not it."

Direct, this beautiful creature. As stunning as she'd been in her stage makeup, he was coming to the conclusion he liked her better like this. Her skin was flawless, her natural coloring more delicate without the heavy makeup. Her eyes were rounder and bluer without the eyeliner, too. Softer. Yet more remote, somehow.

He swirled his brandy and took a slow, appreciative sip. Then he surprised himself by answering, "Actually, yes. I do care what you like to talk about. Tell me."

"Why?"

"I find you intriguing."

She leaned close to him and murmured gently, "That's what they all say, Mr. El Aran."

He recoiled, stung. She was lumping him with every other lounge lizard who'd ever come on to her? How dared she? He wasn't some common bloke looking to bed the closest hot female he could land. He frowned. All right. So his end goal might be the same in principle, but he was imminently more sophisticated in how he went about getting it than most men.

On the heels of his disgruntlement came a flare of

something sharp and hot in his gut. Foreign. What *was* that? He took several more sips of his drink before he put a name to it. Attraction. He was intensely interested in this woman and the challenge she posed. He *would* find a way to have her. That decision reaffirmed after talking to her, he turned his attention to achieving his goal.

"What do you like to do in your free time?" he asked.

She gave the question the same consideration she had all his other questions so far. "I'm not accustomed to having much free time, so that's hard to answer. I like all sorts of things, I suppose. Reading. Traveling. Pretty much any activity having to do with water."

"Do you sail?"

"Yes."

"Water ski?"

"Yes."

"Snow ski?"

She nodded. That might even be a hint of a smile in her eyes.

"What do you read?"

"Everything. Anything."

Encouraged by the roll he was on in getting her to share information, he continued his rapid-fire questions. "Fiction or nonfiction?"

"Both."

"London or Paris?"

"Mmm. Tough. I love them both."

"Beaches or mountains?"

"Gorgeous natural scenery in any form," she equivocated.

"Fair enough. Steak or seafood?"

"Steak."

"Milk chocolate or dark?"

"Dark."

He made a mental note of that. "Favorite color of rose?"

"Red."

He grinned. "Of course. The color of passion. Quiet dinner for two or a big party?"

"The quiet dinner. I get my fill of loud crowds dancing."

"Bottom or top?"

She froze. Gave him a cool, level look that made it clear he'd just crossed the line and she didn't appreciate it. The sharp pull of this startling woman intensified. He couldn't remember the last time a female had set a boundary with him like that. Mostly, they tripped all over themselves to offer him whatever he wanted.

"Sorry," he said forthrightly.

She nodded, accepting his apology matter-of-factly. Now *that* was decidedly not typical of any female he'd ever known. Who *was* this woman?

"Where do you come from?" he asked, burning with curiosity to know more about her.

"America."

"I could tell that from the accent. America's a big place. Where, specifically, do you call home?"

"My family moved around a lot when I was a kid."

"Brothers and sisters?"

"I prefer to live in the moment and not discuss my background."

He considered that rather cryptic nonanswer. Didn't want to talk about her past, eh? He could fix that. Geoffrey's law firm had an entire team of private investigators who could tell him everything he ever wanted to know about Cassandra's life.

"Another club soda?" he asked.

"No, thank you. I believe you only paid for the one drink."

"What is it about me you find so distasteful?" he burst out.

Her right eyebrow arched slightly. "I don't find you distasteful, Mr. El Aran."

"Call me Hake," he all but snapped in his frustration at his failure to dazzle her.

She answered blandly, "I don't find you distasteful, Hake."

How did she manage to make him feel so stupid for his outburst like that? He took a deep breath. She was unpredictable, that was all. She didn't respond to anything like he expected her to. It was as if she was onto his game and determined to disrupt his usual pattern of the hunt. She was succeeding, too. He had no idea how to proceed with getting her into his bed at this point.

"What's your last name?" he asked in a certain desperation.

She smiled wryly. "I believe the correct answer to that one is, whatever you want it to be…Hake."

He rolled his eyes. "You're an exasperating woman, Cassandra."

She smiled in genuine amusement as if that had been her goal all along. Minx! "What am I going to do with you?" he muttered.

"That's easy," she replied lightly. "Nothing at all."

He looked at her directly, capturing her light gaze with his own dark one. "I think not, clever Cassandra. That's the one thing I'm definitely not going to settle for. You can fight me or tease me or try to run away from me, but I guarantee you I'm not going to settle for *nothing* from you."

Chapter 4

Casey mentally gulped. Beneath her devil-may-care exterior, she felt way over her head. She was definitely tempting fate to tangle with this man. His technique when it came to sweeping a girl off her feet was darned near perfect. Heck, it was hard to even look at him without getting a little breathless. There was handsome, and then there was drop-dead gorgeous. Hake fell somewhere beyond the latter. His eyes and hair were dark, but his skin reflected his mother's Caucasian heritage and bone structure.

And then there was the way he looked at her. Intently. With total focus. As if she was the most important person in the world. It was a heady thing to have this man's undivided attention. His verbal repartee was nothing to sneeze at either. He had her ducking and dodging like a prizefighter. But her instincts told her not to reveal herself to this man lest he take advantage of the smallest opening and strip her soul bare.

She expected someone in H.O.T. Watch Ops could read lips, assuming the gang there didn't have an audio feed of this conversation somehow. They must be in transports of ecstasy over how the encounter was going. She hadn't set out to play hard to get, but she couldn't help herself. She felt like a mouse being stalked by a tiger. Her years of Medusa training had taken over and she'd reflexively scrambled to deflect the predator coming after her. Just her luck, the tactic had made him even more eager to snare her.

From an operational perspective, that was fantastic. But from a personal one…the danger was almost more than she could face calmly. She sensed that this man had enormous power to hurt her. He would get inside her guard, and as sure as the sun rose and set, he'd break her heart.

She had to get away from him. She still had Geoffrey Birch. She didn't need this lethal man to complete her mission. She started to push back from the bar. "Thank you for the drink, but—"

It wasn't Hake who cut her off. Rather, it was her stomach. Growling loudly.

Her companion grinned. "Hungry?"

She shrugged, embarrassed. "I can't eat for twelve hours or so before I dance."

"And here I've been keeping you from your dinner!" he exclaimed. "How rude of me. Let me make it up and take you to dinner."

"No, thank you—"

He interrupted briskly. "I'm not taking no for an answer." He pulled out his cell phone, punched a button and spoke into it briefly. "My car will be around front momentarily." He tossed down a hefty tip for the bartender and reached courteously for her elbow. "Shall we?"

"I'm not having dinner with you!"

"Why not? You're hungry. I'm hungry. We both have to eat. Why not do it together?"

She couldn't very well confess that she was freaked out by all his questions and curiosity—and sheer male presence. While she tried to come up with a suitable answer, he steered her to the front door of the club. The night was damp and cool and shocked her into action.

"Hake. You can't do this. I don't want to—"

"Why not? You already said you don't find me distasteful. You're not afraid of me, are you? Afraid of how I make you feel, perhaps?"

He asked the latter with such obvious pleasure at the notion she couldn't admit he was exactly right. She was terrified of the things he did to her innards. She had no business whatsoever being attracted to him. He was a target. Nothing more.

"Here's the car," he announced cheerfully.

Calling the vehicle in front of her a car didn't do the glossy black Rolls-Royce any more justice than calling Hake handsome did for him. A uniformed chauffeur materialized in front of her, holding the back door open. "Mademoiselle," the man said politely.

To advance the mission, she had to go to dinner with Hake. This was just a job. Vanessa's doubtful question about whether or not she could handle it popped into her head, galling her. She *hated* the idea of being weak. She was a Medusa. She could handle one stinking meal with some hunky guy! The folks at H.O.T. Watch Ops would do back handsprings in delight if she went to dinner with the mark.

She smiled at the driver and stepped into the Rolls. It was as plush inside as it was outside. An elegant crystal bud vase was built into the armrest, and it held a single white rosebud.

"Champagne?" Hake murmured, reaching into the built in cooler.

"No, thank you." She never drank alcohol when she was armed and working. Besides, dealing with this man required every bit of her mental faculties.

He sighed. "You have nothing to be afraid of, Cassandra."

Given that she was trained in a dozen different methods of disabling him and probably twenty more ways of killing him, she would hardly call herself afraid. At least not of him directly. She was more afraid of herself. Of her reaction to him.

She slipped a hand into her purse and hit the speed-dial button that connected her to H.O.T. Watch Ops. Speaking loudly enough so the folks there could hear her over the smooth purr of the Rolls, she asked, "Where are we going for dinner?"

He smiled mysteriously. "It's a surprise."

She sighed. Oh, well. It had been worth a try. At least headquarters knew she would have dinner with the target. They could triangulate on the GPS unit in her cell phone if they wanted to see where she was going.

Hake leaned forward and opened the mini-refrigerator. He poured chilled water into a cut-crystal glass and held it out to her. "Here, my thirsty dancer."

She took the glass in silence. *His* dancer? The thought made her stomach tumble disconcertingly. *Stop that.* Not that her gut listened to her, of course.

"Is your dancing a safe topic?" he asked.

"I'll let you know," she replied cautiously.

He laughed quietly. "You are determined to lead me on a merry chase, aren't you?"

"I try."

The rest of the ride passed in silence. The Rolls headed

for the heart of London and took a street that ran along the Thames. The imposing medieval block of the Tower of London loomed across the river. And then the Rolls slowed and turned into a narrow, gated drive.

In a few minutes, the vehicle stopped. The chauffeur opened the door for her and Casey stepped out to see a pier with a half-dozen luxury yachts moored along its length. Hake held out his arm and she had no choice but to loop her fingers around his forearm.

The muscles beneath the fine wool suit were hard and sculpted. The guy worked out, did he? Her uncooperative stomach gave an appreciative flutter.

No surprise, he led her to the biggest, sleekest yacht of all. A white uniformed sailor, clearly also a highly trained bodyguard, welcomed Hake aboard. Casey recognized the sailor's relaxed, balanced stance as the same one she was trained to employ in high-threat security situations.

They passed two more crewmen on their way to the ship's expansive living room. Both men were as sharp as the first one. Of course, given Hake's wealth and prominence, it was no surprise he was surrounded by bodyguards of this caliber. Frankly, now that she thought about it, the biggest surprise was that these goons hadn't been with him at the restaurant.

She subtly slipped her hand in her purse and turned her phone on again. "What's this boat called?"

Hake grinned. "Don't call her a boat in the captain's presence unless you want a lecture. She's a yacht or a ship. And she's called the *Angelique*."

Mission accomplished. H.O.T. Watch's crack researchers would know where she was in two minutes, tops. She figured that in five more, they'd have satellite surveillance on her. Not that she needed the backup. She had things under control. At least for the moment.

A crewman came in and asked, "Are you ready to dine, sir?" At Hake's nod, the man laid a table for two. Hake spent the next few minutes giving her a tour of the salon, which held an impressive collection of art and baubles from around the world. Her host proved to have impressive expertise in both archaeology and art. In spite of herself, she wondered what else his wide-ranging education encompassed. She always had found smart men irresistible.

"Dinner is served," yet another crew member announced.

"How many people are on the *Angelique*'s crew?" she asked.

"Eleven at sea. Seventeen in port."

"Why the difference?"

"Security," he answered shortly. "My father insists upon it."

"He's probably right to insist," Casey commented before she stopped to think.

Hake whirled to stare at her. "You know who I am?"

Crap. She thought fast. Probably best to stick to the truth. "Of course, I know who you are. You're one of the most eligible bachelors in Europe. And with your… escapades…splashed all over the tabloids, it would be darn near impossible not to know who you are."

He rolled his eyes. "Don't believe most of what you read in the British gossip rags."

"The truth is worse?" she asked lightly.

Hake laughed. "If I were American, I'd plead the Fifth Amendment to that one."

She smiled. "I'll let you plead it…this time."

Hake waved off the crew member and held her chair for her himself. She brushed past him to take her seat and her pulse skittered at the proximity to him. Oh, Lord.

He smelled fabulous. His cologne was as smooth and sophisticated as he was.

Someone dimmed the lights in the salon, leaving only a pair of tall tapers between them for illumination. A low arrangement of a dozen red roses decorated the table. Was it just luck, or had he specifically ordered those flowers and his crew worked a miracle to get them at this time of night?

She looked down at her plate as the waiter uncovered it and had to smile. A gorgeous prime rib stared back up at her. "Your staff is really, really good," she commented wryly.

Hake merely smiled enigmatically at her and murmured, "Bon appétit."

The meal was delicious and the conversation enjoyable as they discussed everything from ballet to Formula 1 car racing—a hobby he'd given up recently at the worried urging of his family. Gradually, she found herself relaxing. It was just food and talk. She could handle those.

After a sumptuous dark chocolate mousse, she laid down her spoon with a sigh of contentment. "My compliments to the chef."

Hake nodded. "I'll pass them on."

She smiled over at him. "I have to confess, I've had a wonderful time. Although, I'm going to have to exercise for hours tomorrow to work that off." Thankfully, Hake didn't leap on that and suggest any lewd alternatives for working off the meal with him. She asked, "Would you have one of your men call me a cab, please?"

Hake looked stunned for a moment but recovered quickly. To his immense credit, he didn't argue or press her in any way to stay. He merely murmured, "No need for a cab. I'll have my driver take you home."

"I don't want to put him out," she protested. "It's very late."

Hake waved off her protest. "I insist. I'd worry about you making it home safely otherwise."

Right. As if she was in any danger. She highly doubted that too many people in London could hurt her in a one-on-one fight. She had to admit, though, another ride in that amazing Rolls would be fun. "All right," she acquiesced.

Hake walked her down the pier to the car a few minutes later. Although she was as nervous as a cat, he didn't even try to kiss her cheek good-night, and for that, she was grateful. Smart guy. Must have figured out his only chance was to go slow with her. Mental whiplash jerked her. His only chance? He had no chance at all with her. They were never going to be a couple or even hook up for a one-night stand. This was work.

"Thank you for a lovely evening," she murmured.

"Likewise. We must do it again soon."

Her toes curled at the prospect, but a frisson of alarm chattered down her spine. Too much more proximity to him and she'd be in grave danger of weakening.

She breathed a huge sigh of relief when she pulled away from the pier in his Rolls and his tall form faded into the night behind her. She gave an address to the driver and sat back to relish the plush seats and silky smooth ride.

The driver offered to walk her inside the apartment building but she turned him down firmly. She watched the vehicle until it had turned a corner up ahead and disappeared, then turned and flagged a taxi. She gave the driver, a grizzled Cockney fellow this time, her actual address and sat back for the long ride across London. She wasn't about to let Hake El Aran know where she was staying. After all, their relationship was going to end up being all about power and leverage if she didn't miss her guess.

Let him stew about how to get in touch with her again. He'd do it on her terms or not at all.

Chapter 5

Furious Hake leaned forward to glare at the pair of private investigators squirming in Geoffrey's office Monday afternoon. "What do you mean you've got nothing on her? Surely you managed to get her name at least!"

"I'm sorry, sir. The restaurant pays her in cash and she does business under a license in the name of Cassandra. Nothing more."

"My man told you where she lives from when he dropped her off. Couldn't you track her from that?"

Negative shakes of the P.I.s' heads. "False address. No woman matching her photograph lives in any apartment building for two blocks in any direction of the spot your man dropped her off."

Hake sat back, flabbergasted. The woman had well and truly hoodwinked him! She must be laughing her head off to have pulled the wool over his eyes like that. A part of him admired her clever evasion, but another was more determined than ever to solve the mystery of Cassandra. He knew one way to learn who she was. Ask the woman herself and don't let her off the hook until she told him what he wanted to know.

"When does she dance again?" he asked. "Did you at least find that out?"

The P.I.s looked relieved. "We did get that. This coming Saturday."

Five days until he could get to the bottom of this mystery. The wait would kill him. He tried not to look as if he was sulking, while Geoffrey dismissed the investigators and closed his office door behind them.

"Hake, you and I need to talk. I've got some news from your father."

When Geoffrey turned on the electronic white noise machine behind his desk to foil any possible listening devices, Hake sat up straight. Not many topics rated this level of caution from the attorney.

"The buyers have contacted your father and accepted his terms. The deal is a go."

"Excellent. What does he need me to do?" Hake replied, both appalled and relieved. He was appalled that he and his father were being forced into selling this equipment to likely terrorists and relieved that they might yet get out of this mess alive.

"Their agent will contact you here in London. Your father has one instruction for you—don't screw this up."

Hake snorted. "That goes without saying. Besides, I never screw up deals."

Geoffrey looked pained. "I really wish you two would reconsider this scheme. It's entirely too dangerous. There must be another way—"

Hake cut him off. "You have the affidavits from me

and my father on file, right? And copies elsewhere in safe deposit boxes?"

"Yes, yes. I followed all of your instructions to the letter. But as I've said before, I don't think a set of letters from you two stating that your intent is to identify these jokers and turn them over to the authorities once you have proof that they're trying to buy nuclear manufacturing equipment from you is going to hold up in court."

Hake sighed. They'd been over this before. "Geoffrey, my father and I are dead men if we refuse outright to do business with these people. They have the means and the mind-set to kill us simply because we know they exist. But no way is El Aran Industries selling precision milling machines to these madmen."

"Tell someone. Your own government. The Brits. The Americans. They'll help."

Mention of Americans sent Cassandra's lovely visage flashing through Hake's mind. Reluctantly, he pushed the image aside. "My father and I both agree that government bureaucracies would bumble around and mess up the deal. They'd end up getting us killed anyway. Better that we handle this on our own and turn over the bad guys when we have all the evidence we need to prove our innocence and good intentions."

"I don't like it," Geoffrey retorted heavily.

"Duly noted," Hake replied implacably. He didn't like it either, but what choice did they have? It was either appear to play ball with these terrorist, or be murdered. Personally, he richly appreciated being alive.

Hake spent much of the remainder of the week handling the paperwork associated with fabricating a state-of-the-art milling machine for an as-yet-unspecified buyer. He figured he would eventually have to come up with a fake entity to represent the real buyers. It would be the only way past the government regulators who closely watched such things. One step at a time, though. First he had to make contact with the terrorists and identify them. Then, he had to wait and see if they actually managed to come up with two million euros to pay for the machine.

Normally, he would've gone out and partied Friday night…and incidentally woken up Saturday morning to see himself on the front pages of the tabloids. But he was beat after a busy week of setting up the illegal deal and chose to go to the yacht to crash early and alone Friday evening.

He wasn't saving himself for Cassandra, dammit. He'd never limited himself to one woman, and he didn't plan to start now. He certainly didn't sit around mooning over some girl who hadn't even given him her name. He vowed grimly to have both her real name *and* a kiss from her tomorrow.

He dreamed of her that night. Hot, steamy imaginings that had him waking up at dawn grouchy and intensely uncomfortable. The woman was like a fever in his blood. He had to have her, and soon, so he could begin getting over her.

Cassandra was jumpy and irritable all day Saturday. It didn't help that her Medusa teammates had shown up in London the day before to help with the play of Hake El Aran. After her little disappearing act to his yacht last week, her superiors had decided that eyes-on, human surveillance backup was the way to go with this mission. Great. Just what she needed. People watching her every move with the guy. Even if they were her sisters-in-arms and constant comrades for the past two years. It felt like a hell of an invasion of her privacy.

Whoa. Check that. There was nothing private going on or about to go on between her and Hake El Aran.

Vanessa Blake had sent orders along with Monica Fabre, who in her previous life had been a very high-priced call girl, to give Casey any pointers she thought might be useful. Thankfully, the sum total of Monica's advice had been, "You're playing hard-to-get better than I ever could have. In my line of work the point was not to be hard to get. I don't know what to tell you other than keep doing what you're doing. Get the guy panting after you so hard he can't see straight. That's when he'll get careless and let slip with the information we need."

The idea of having Hake panting after her was both intimidating and scintillating. Problem was, she was likely to end up panting after him even worse than he would be after her. And then where would they be? She'd compromise the mission and blow a huge undercover investigation. If it went badly enough, terrorists could end up with the capability to manufacture their own nuclear weapons, for God's sake.

But still. Panting? Every time the thought crossed her mind, she got a little more tense and grouchy.

Some comedian at H.O.T. Watch had sent along a new costume for her with her teammates. She had no idea where they'd gotten it, but the thing was R-rated, pushing X-rated.

Casey unzipped the garment bag in her dressing room, wincing as she did so. The dress really was magnificent. Long-sleeved and floor-length, the gown was black and sheer in its entirety. It came with, in effect, a black bikini and bra for her to wear underneath. The only cover the thing afforded her was a serpent starting at her right shoulder, heavily beaded in tones of copper and gold. It wrapped around her strategically so she didn't look naked. But that was about all that could be said about its body coverage.

Clusters of long, beaded fringe were sewn randomly all over the dress. Whenever she shimmied in it, the entire gown seemed to quiver, the snake alive and flowing sinuously across her body. The costume was entirely gorgeous, and so sexy it embarrassed her to look at, let alone imagine herself wearing.

She was saving it for the late show. Meanwhile, she had to get through the first set. It would be strange dancing with an earbud in her ear. She'd given her teammates strict instructions not to bother her during her performance, however. They were only allowed to talk to her in a life-threatening emergency.

Her microphone pickup was tricky to hide. Belly dancing costumes weren't designed with battery packs and wires in mind. She ended up going with a microsize unit that clipped underneath her right bra strap. It poked her a little bit but was bearable. And thankfully, the unit laid flat enough that it didn't make her costume look weird. She only hoped her perspiration didn't knock the thing out. And she prayed she had no need of it during the course of the evening. Having to call for help at any point tonight would *not* be a good thing.

The hour-long contingency planning session just before she'd come over to the restaurant hadn't helped her nerves one bit. The Medusas had brainstormed everything they could think of that might go wrong during the evening and discussed what the best response to each crisis would be. While she understood the necessity, she really didn't relish talking about what if Hake tried to rape her, or what if he got drunk and passed out in bed with her. Besides, she had no intention of ending up in bed with him, drunk or otherwise.

Of course, her teammates had laughed uproariously when she'd asserted that. She scowled in recollection. Sometimes being part of such a close-knit group was a pain in the butt.

"Ten minutes," the restaurant manager announced through her dressing-room door.

She glanced at her watch. The restaurant had filled up early again tonight. The manager swore it was because people were packing the place to see her dance. She had a hard time crediting that explanation, however. She tilted her chin down and muttered to the microphone in her bra strap, "Is he here?"

"Just walked in," Alex replied. "And may I just say, nicely done, Scorpion."

Casey rolled her eyes. But butterflies were jumping around in her stomach and for some reason, she felt an impulse to check her makeup and hair.

Ten minutes until she would stand in front of him again, half-naked and baring her soul for him. A shiver ran across her skin that was all about anticipating his dark, smoky gaze caressing her and making her feel beautiful. The guy was truly dangerous.

She stretched carefully, going through a quick yoga routine, warming up her muscles and loosening her spine. Appearing boneless was more of a strain on the body than most people guessed. But compliments of her Special Forces training, muscular strength was not a problem. She just had to watch her flexibility. Blood began to flow and her body became warm and limber and supple. She was ready.

Then why was she so jittery and tense?

Because she was about to step out onto a stage and make love to a man in front of three hundred people.

* * *

Hake sucked in a sharp breath as she stepped out onstage. He'd forgotten just how stunning she was. He devoured the sight of her greedily, anticipating having that sinuous sexual intensity all to himself. When she finally opened her eyes after the opening *taksim* dance, she looked straight at him and flashed a private little smile that sent his blood pressure through the roof. Lord, that woman was incredible.

She moved off the stage and out into the audience, momentarily breaking her intimate connection with him. He followed her willowy form, jealously waiting for her to return and dance for him.

"Excuse me. May I sit with you?"

Startled, Hake looked up at the man speaking to him in Arabic. The man threw him a significant look that made Hake start. Here? Now? The contact for the terrorists wanted to talk about the sale of the milling machine? Hake gestured for the man to have a seat.

"You may call me Jabar."

Not a chance in hell that was the guy's real name. Hake nodded. "You already know who I am, of course."

"Of course," the man murmured with an ominous little smile that sent bugs crawling up Hake's spine.

"I'm afraid we're not likely to get much service from the waiters until the show's over or I'd offer you a drink," Hake murmured to the man in Arabic. "The girl's got the staff mesmerized."

"She's not half bad for an infidel whore."

Hake bristled but checked the reaction quickly. He dared not appear sympathetic to anything or anyone western around this man. He studied his guest. The man was perhaps forty-five years old, his body and face starting to sag. Most of his hair was gone, but he had a heavy, black five-o'clock shadow. His eyes…ah, his eyes were sharp. Didn't miss a thing.

Hake glanced up and noticed Cassandra looking at him from across the restaurant. She frowned and her glance slid to the man at his table and back to him, almost as if she were silently asking if everything was okay. He nodded slightly and gave her a little smile. She did an odd thing then, ducking her chin toward her right shoulder and mouthing something. Was that aimed at him or was she speaking to a patron near her, perhaps? He'd probably been looking at her long enough. No sense drawing his companion's attention to her any more than necessary.

He turned back to the man beside him. "I understand we have a mutual acquaintance, Jabar."

"Yes, we do. He passes along his greetings and hopes that everything goes well for you."

"Indeed, it does. My father's company made a significant sale this week and is hard at work preparing to make the delivery. It is always good to have plenty of work to do."

Jabar nodded. "Our friend has also been busy. Although, he has run into a snag in a business dealing of his own. It seems a seller has set an unreasonably high price for a product he very much wishes to procure."

Hake's gaze narrowed. The jerk was here to haggle over the price of the machine? He took a slow sip of his drink and reminded himself that his life rode on not pissing off this man. "In this weak global economy, El Aran Industries has made the decision to take no profit but merely cover the costs of production and paying our workers. My family has enough wealth and does not need more. It is the least we can do to assure our employees remain employed and our customers not only happy but in business."

Jabar leaned forward, studying him intently. "Truly? You sell your goods at cost?"

Hake met the man's eyes squarely. "Absolutely. It is the right thing to do, is it not?"

Jabar pursed his lips. "It is a wise decision. Very wise, indeed. But there is no margin that can be cut at all?"

Hake spread his hands open in apology. "None. I wish there were. But were we to sell our equipment below cost, it would surely attract the attention of government regulators. And we try to avoid upsetting them as much as possible. You understand."

Jabar nodded but didn't look happy. Not the answer he'd wanted. It was a calculated risk not to play ball with this guy's request for a price break. But Hake sensed that any show of weakness now would lead to further exploitation by the terrorists later. Hake did add in a conciliating tone. "When you next see our friend, by all means pass on my family's greetings and best wishes."

Jabar nodded once. If Hake was reading him correctly, the guy seemed to have relaxed fractionally. God willing, their business was concluded and the guy would leave now.

Sure enough, Jabar stood up, disregarding Cassandra, who was moving back toward the stage and about to pass by their table. She pulled up quickly but still brushed into the man. Jabar muttered a rather foul epithet at her in Arabic, which Hake sincerely hoped she didn't understand. As it was, he had to clench his teeth and hang on to his temper not to react to the insult.

Jabar stalked past her and Cassandra moved forward smoothly. As she passed Hake's chair, she murmured, "You all right?"

"Yes. You?" he replied.

She whirled out onto the stage, flourished her finger cymbals, and laughed in his direction. He'd take that as an "I'm fine."

The rest of the show passed in a blur. His thoughts were in turmoil from the visit by Jabar. He second- and third-guessed his refusal to bargain on the price and prayed he hadn't just gotten himself and his family killed. They were, indeed, selling the machine at cost, and he hadn't been lying that discounting the price beyond that would have drawn the attention of all the wrong kinds of people. This deal had to look just like any other deal El Aran Industries did every day.

Whether Cassandra sensed his distraction or not, he didn't know. But he did know she ended her show with a steamy number that she aimed squarely at him, much to the envy of most of the men in the crowd. If her intent was to recapture his full attention, the tactic worked spectacularly.

Casey had barely cleared the kitchen doors before she was on the radio with her teammates.

"Anyone get a picture of the guy who sat down with Hake?"

Roxi answered. "I got one. Sent it to H.O.T. Watch immediately. They haven't ID'd him yet."

"Let me know when they do," Casey replied. She continued, "Did someone follow that man out of here? Something wasn't right about him."

Alex's terse voice answered low, "Cho and I are on him. He left the restaurant, walked about a block east of there and entered the back of a step van parked on a side street. The vehicle has not moved since. Too bad we don't have a full surveillance setup. I'd love to hear the phone conversations emanating from that van right about now."

Monica answered tightly, "I'd like to have an infrared scanner and see what's going on inside that van. I don't like it at all."

Roxi piped up, "Maybe Hake's associate is relaying information to someone and then plans to come back in the restaurant and continue speaking with Hake."

Casey didn't like the sound of any of this. What had that man said to make Hake so tense, and why had the fellow left so abruptly? It had been clear that the guy wasn't happy with whatever Hake had said to him. But Hake had indicated to her that everything was okay. Maybe she was worrying too much about him.

That made her sit up straight and stare at herself in her dressing-room mirror. Since when did she have a personal interest in Hake's well-being? Irritated with herself, she went through her usual between-show ritual of drinking water, eating a tablespoon of peanut butter, repairing her makeup and stretching again.

"Ten minutes, Miss Cassandra," someone called through her door.

"Thank you," she called back. Time to don the risqué serpent gown and blow Hake's mind. She eased the garment over her head and smoothed it down her body. Its weight pulled the gown into a skin-hugging fit against her body. Wow. Nowhere to hide any flaws in this puppy. Thankfully, though, the high neck allowed her to thread a wire around from behind and nestle a microphone unobtrusively just inside the neckline of the gown. Not that she thought anyone would be looking at her neck in this thing.

In sudden inspiration, she reached for her hangers of veils and commenced wrapping three-yard-long lengths of rainbow-colored silk around herself and tucking in the ends to secure them. The traditional dance of the seven veils required the dancer to shed all her veils and end up naked. It was actually a burlesque tradition and not an ancient one belonging to folkloric Middle Eastern dance. But it would serve her purposes tonight. Hake wasn't going to know what had hit him when she was through with him.

She checked in one last time with her teammates. "Any I.D. on Hake's guest?"

"Nope," Alex replied. "No movement at the van either. No telling what the guy's doing in there. Cho moved in closer for a look, but there's a curtain behind the front seat and the back windows are painted over. She spent a few minutes under the van. But other than the fact that it's got a transmission leak, she learned nothing. All was quiet inside it."

Monica asked in alarm, "She's not still under the van, is she?"

Alex replied, "Negative. Cho's back with me."

"Okay, then," Casey replied. "It's about time for my show. Give me a warning if that man heads back to the restaurant even if I'm dancing."

"Worried about your guy?" Monica asked quietly.

"Honestly, yes. I've got a bad feeling about this."

Monica replied reassuringly, "We'll be right here. Roxi, Naraya and I will be at our table, and we've got a clear sight line on the front door. Alex and Cho will keep an eye on Hake's contact. You do your thing and don't worry. We've got you covered."

"And by the way," Naraya murmured, "your first show was wonderful. It's a pleasure to watch you dance."

Coming from a Middle Easterner, that was a fine compliment. Casey murmured, "Thanks. I needed that."

The manager knocked on her door. "It's time, Cassandra."

Time, indeed.

She glided through the darkened restaurant and stepped into the lone spotlight. The audience gasped appreciatively. They knew a veil dance was coming, and she enjoyed dancing for a knowledgeable crowd. She could really cut loose with the difficult, subtle stuff and be assured that they would get it.

The musicians—also not slow on the uptake—shifted immediately into a sexy melody perfect for seduction. She turned her back on Hake and began the slow striptease. Looking at him directly while she did this would have posed two problems: one, she didn't know if she could keep her composure and not lose her nerve; and two, this sort of dance was so provocative she risked embarrassing or offending Hake if she came on to him too strongly in public.

But when she got down to the last veil, a length of black silk wrapped around and around her body, she couldn't resist. She moved over to Hake and offered him the end of the veil. Then, as he held it, she began turning slowly away from him, revealing herself and the magnificent serpent gown to him by inches.

He got a look at the costume before anyone else, and his gaze blazed in response. He looked up at her and the promise was clear in his eyes. He planned to have her and there wasn't a damned thing she could do about it. Her insides quivered in response and anticipation leaped in her heart. Seriously? Was she really that attracted to him? Shock joined the desire zinging through her.

She'd expected a strong reaction from him, but she was blown away by the intensity of his response. Well, all right, then. She'd played with fire. What did she expect? His gaze raked down the costume and back up it again, and she all but moaned aloud.

He nodded slowly. Appreciatively. Possessively. And her knees went weak.

She registered vaguely that the rest of the restaurant was going wild, cheering and whistling and shouting

compliments at her in a half-dozen languages. She smiled
and held her arms out to them all. But she danced for Hake.
He was the one who lit the fire in her belly, the one who
made her limbs feel boneless and heavy, who made her
breasts ache and her body long for the weight of him.

The result of turning how he made her feel into dance
movements was incendiary. Even the musicians grinned
and nodded their approval at her as the energy climbed
higher and higher in the room. Money poured like water
onto the stage and a waiter had to be permanently stationed
at the corner of the stage with a push broom to sweep it
up. Not that she paid much attention to such things, but
thousands of dollars landed on the floor at her feet. Even
after she split it with the band, she would have a profitable
night. The women's shelter she donated her earnings to was
in for a windfall.

"Van's opening," Alex announced in her ear, throwing
abrupt cold water on her jubilant mood. "One man emerg-
ing. Late twenties. Middle Eastern at a glance. Five foot
nine. Medium build. Long black raincoat. Jeans. Black
tennis shoes. Heading west."

Crud. That was back toward the restaurant. Casey's
smile slipped a notch. She signaled the musicians to slow it
down and shift into a folk dance, its traditional movements
easy to do. She recruited women from the audience to stand
up and dance, freeing her to move around the place. What
the heck was going on with Hake's contacts?

"Here he comes," Monica murmured. "Just walked
in."

Casey maneuvered so she could spot the guy. No big
surprise, he looked around once and then headed straight
for Hake. Candlelight from a table he passed illuminated
his features. He looked as if he was about to kill someone.
His eyes were grim, focused. Dead. She looked down at the

guy's coat. It was a warm night out. No need for something that heavy. Unless...

Swearing under her breath, she moved fast, racing toward Hake. She cut across the stage, which gave her an advantage over the young man in the coat because he was forced to wend his way between the tables.

"What's wrong, Scorpion?" Monica bit out.

Casey spotted her three teammates rising, alarmed, from their table in the corner.

She opened her mouth to respond, but just then the man unbuttoned his coat. She saw what was beneath and took a running dive.

"Hake!" she screamed.

Chapter 6

Hake's mind went blank as Cassandra slammed into him, knocking both him and his chair over sideways and rolling him under a table all in one violent movement. They came to a stop just as a second impact hit, this one much bigger, much heavier. It flattened him like an elephant had stepped on him.

Brilliant light, heat, then deafening noise and flying debris, and then the first screams registered. His ears rang. Cassandra's weight was upon him. Her voice yelled urgently. Something about a perp. And a security perimeter. And then she was yelling at him over a cacophony of screams and shouts. "Hake! Are you hurt?"

"I don't think so. What the hell happened?"

"Bomb. C'mon. We've got to go."

"We have to call the police and help the wounded!" he retorted.

"There's no time to be a hero. We have to get you to safety before someone comes back to finish the job!"

"What job?"

"Killing you," she grunted as she pushed off him and into a crouch. "Stay low and stick by me," she yelled over the chaos. Sirens wailed nearby. And then a spray of water, cold and shocking, hit him from overhead. *Fire sprinklers.*

He sat up, looking around in disbelief at the demolished side of the restaurant. The back wall of the stage was obliterated. It looked as if a tornado had struck that one spot. The front of the club was damaged but not destroyed like the area immediately around him. What the hell? A bomb? Why wasn't he blown to bits along with everyone else in here? He opened his mouth to explain that she must be mistaken, but she cut him off urgently.

"Let's *go*." She dragged him to his feet, put her hand on the top of his head and hustled him toward the kitchen.

"The exit's that way—"

She interrupted. "Sniper may be waiting out front to pick you off. We'll use the back door."

She spun into the kitchen low and fast in a move that looked suspiciously military. She waved to him to follow her. And then a tall, elegant blonde woman materialized by his right elbow. He started, but before he could say anything, he became aware of another woman on his left. He lurched in surprise. "Who are you?"

Cassandra looked back impatiently. "They're with me."

With her? What the hell did that mean? He must be in shock because he had a hard time stringing coherent thoughts together. The four women—it turned out there was one behind him, too—all but shoved him through the kitchen, past screaming staff and waiters rushing around grabbing fire extinguishers and heading into the other room. He and his impromptu bodyguards burst out the back door.

The alley was far from quiet with sirens now wailing toward the club in earnest, but it was better than inside. The tall blonde took the lead as they neared the end of the alley. "Wheels this way," she bit out. The woman made some sort of hand signal to Cassandra, who did another hand signal back.

Hake frowned. His security team did stuff like that now and then. And then he was shoved into the back of a minivan, lying on the floor with Cassandra on top of him, while the other women looked out the windows and chattered back and forth about tails and threats and evasive maneuvers.

"Where to, Scorpion?" the blonde called back over her shoulder.

Cassandra replied, "The *Angelique*. The crew will augment our phalanx and it can be moved on short notice. See if H.O.T. Watch can call the captain and tell him to ready the ship to sail immediately."

"Good idea," one of the other women murmured.

What the hell was a hot watch? Hake turned his head, burning his cheek against the nylon carpet, but bringing himself face-to-face with Cassandra. "Who are you?" he demanded.

"Later. We've got to secure you first."

He glared. "Oh, we're definitely going to talk later. And tell the captain of the *Angelique* that Hake wishes him blue skies and fair weather."

"Is that a distress code?" she asked astutely.

He nodded tersely.

"Got that, Mantis?" Cassandra called.

"Affirmative," the blonde replied.

"Mantis? Scorpion? Are you women exterminators or something?" he asked. This whole evening was turning into a surreal nightmare.

"Something like that," Cassandra replied, flashing a wry smile. "Just relax and be patient with us a little while longer."

He commented blankly, "I planned to get horizontal with you tonight, but I didn't imagine it would be like this."

Her gaze snapped to his, wide and startled, vulnerable for a moment. And then she smiled faintly. "That would've been nice."

"The night's not over yet," he murmured back under his breath.

"No, but this is going to be a long one for me. We'll be debriefing till dawn. You, too, I imagine."

"Who do you work for?" he asked in sudden alarm. The deal! The terrorists! He couldn't blow this thing—the entire El Aran clan's safety was at stake!

"All in good time," she murmured soothingly.

"Stop the car. Let me out," he ordered.

She looked at him apologetically. "I'm sorry. I can't."

"You have to! You have no idea what's at stake here!"

"Tell me about it," she asked evenly.

"I can't. Let me out!"

"Hake. My employers need to talk with you."

"No!" he answered forcefully. "I'm not talking to anyone!" In fact, he'd probably already said too much in his panic and disorientation. He closed his mouth and subsided to wait out the ride. Once he was back on the *Angelique,* he'd regain control of this disaster somehow. Make it go away. He could only imagine the favors he was going to have to call in and the strings he was going to have to pull to fix this mess. But he had no choice. *Everything* depended on it.

The van turned a corner and then came to a stop.

"Scorpion, I need an I.D. on these guys," the blonde said sharply from the driver's seat. Cassandra lifted off him, and he registered missing her body pressed against his.

"Those are Hake's men. They're okay."

Hake started at the weapons being brandished around him. "Don't shoot my security team," he snapped. "They cost me a lot of money."

Cassandra held a hand down to him. "We're about to see if they're worth their salaries."

The back door of the van opened and the blonde was there, talking low and urgently with his men, who looked to be in minor shock at whatever the woman was saying. She finished speaking and his men nodded tersely. Then he was dragged out of the van and hustled onto the *Angelique* amid a tangle of weapons and big, tense bodies.

"Where's Cassandra?" he demanded, as he ducked into the salon.

"On the pier," one of his men replied. The guy spoke into the radio clipped to his collar. "We have the principal aboard. Cast off."

"Wait!" Hake ordered. "I want her on board."

"Sir, your security—"

"She knows what happened at the restaurant. And she owes me an explanation."

"But—"

"Do it," he snapped.

The security man nodded and turned on his heel. It was only a few seconds until he heard Cassandra's voice raised in protest. Didn't want to come with him? Avoiding him, was she? Well, that was just too damned bad. Someone had just tried to kill him and he bloody well wanted to know who. Plus, he might need the leverage with her employer to keep him or her from interfering with the sale.

He pushed past the security man blocking the doorway and stared down at her on the dock. He called out grimly, "If your employer wants a single shred of cooperation from me, you're boarding this ship right now, Cassandra."

The group of women glanced at each other in silent communication. And then, reluctantly, Cassandra stepped forward. One of the women grabbed a big duffel bag out of the van and shoved it at her. She took it as she stepped onto the gangplank. Poor girl looked as if she were marching to her own execution. Tough. He wanted answers and he wanted them now.

There was a flurry of activity as his crew stowed the gangplank, cast off and pulled away from the dock. And then one of his men was quietly urging him back inside and safely undercover. Cassandra approached him and he took her firmly by the elbow, steering her inside with him. "You and I need to have a conversation."

She looked at him for just a moment, her expression closed. Stubborn. Didn't want to talk, huh? Not his problem. "Have a seat, Cassandra. Or should I call you Scorpion?"

"I answer to either," she answered evenly.

"What's your real name?" he demanded.

"That's classified."

"Who are you? And those other women with you?"

When she merely shook her head at him, he tried, "Who do you work for?"

"I have to make a phone call. And then maybe I can answer your questions."

He weighed that. Had to ask for permission to tell him anything, did she? "You'll make the call here, where I can hear you."

She nodded and rummaged in her bag for a cell phone.

She dialed a lengthy number. Overseas call, then. "Scorpion here. I need to speak to Viper."

A short pause ensued, and then she began to speak. "I assume you've gotten an initial brief from the team? You know my location? Not surprisingly, he's demanding answers. What am I authorized to tell him?"

Hake waited impatiently as she listened, her expression grim.

"Understood, Viper." She stowed the phone and looked up at him.

"Well?" he demanded.

Casey took a deep breath. How on earth was she supposed to figure out whether or not Hake was in league with terrorists? She couldn't believe Vanessa Blake had told her to use her own best judgment and tell Hake whatever she thought he needed to know based on where his loyalties lay. It was one thing to have her boss trust her in theory, but it was another to be out here on a real-world op where real lives rested on whatever she thought best. Apparently, she'd officially entered the big leagues now.

She ventured a look at Hake. He was not a happy camper, and she couldn't blame him. His mood probably wasn't going to improve when she started interrogating him either. No help for it, though. "So, Hake. Who was that man who sat with you during the first show?"

He looked startled for an instant, but then his face shut down and his gaze narrowed. "Why do you ask?"

"Because it was his compatriot who walked in wearing that bomb vest and tried to blow you to smithereens."

"What?" Hake burst out. "How do you know that?"

"Two of my companions followed the first man out of the restaurant to a van a block from the restaurant. Bomb

Boy came out of the same van, walked up behind you and activated a shape charge at you."

"A shape charge?" he echoed.

She explained, "It's a bomb designed to blow its energy in a narrow, directed cone, rather than just a general area blast."

"I know what a shape charge is," he snapped. "But how do you know?"

She ignored the question. "Why did the first man send a second man to kill you? What did the two of you talk about?"

He ground out, "Tell me who you are."

"Answer my question first," she retorted.

Hake shook his head. It appeared they were at an impasse. A crewman stepped forward to interrupt the Mexican standoff. "What are your orders, sir?"

Hake blinked. "Take me into international waters. And when everything has calmed down, we could use a bite to eat. Whatever's easy for the chef to throw together."

Casey cursed under her breath. If he made it out of English territory, neither she nor the British government would have legal jurisdiction to tell Hake what to do. And clearly, he knew that. Not good. "Look, Hake. You don't trust me, and I'm having trouble trusting you at the moment. So, I'm going to tell you who I am and we'll see if that makes a difference."

He nodded tightly.

If he was in league with terrorists, he might attempt to harm her in the next few seconds. She made sure her cell phone was turned on inside the duffel and her hand resting on a pistol. She took a deep breath and spoke. "My name is Casey—you'll forgive me if I skip the last name for now—and I work for the United States government. We have reason to believe you and your father are doing a business deal with a terrorist entity, and I've been sent here to stop you."

Hake stared at her. His gaze widened in shock and then narrowed in…what was that? Speculation? Irritation? Calculation? She wished she knew him better to read that look.

"You're a spy?" he finally asked.

"Not exactly. Think of me as more of a…soldier."

That made him laugh once, shortly, in disbelief. Not that she cared one way or another if he believed her or not. It didn't make any difference to her mission. The good news was that in response to the revelation, he hadn't ordered his men to lock her up or blow her brains out.

"Okay, your turn," she said expectantly.

He looked at her a long time. A shadow of the desire he'd roused in her back at the restaurant flitted through her mind. She'd never been around a man who could do this to her with a mere look. It bordered on scary.

Eventually, he sighed and said, "My family is being blackmailed into selling a piece of sophisticated manu-facturing equipment to an anonymous, but highly sus-picious, buyer."

"Do you have any idea who this buyer is?"

"No. That man who sat with me in the restaurant was my first direct contact with the buyers."

"How are the buyers blackmailing you?"

"They've threatened to kill everyone in my family if we don't do the deal. And after tonight's episode, I'm inclined to believe them."

She leaned forward. "Did you refuse to do the deal this evening? Is that why they sent a bomber after you?"

He snorted. "They tried to haggle on the price, but I refused to come down on it. If we did, it would make various governments, including yours, suspicious. Although that is a moot point now, isn't it?"

She frowned sharply. The terrorists must figure the son was expendable and that killing Hake would ensure Papa El Aran's cooperation. She pulled out her cell phone and dialed H.O.T. Watch. Vanessa Blake answered the call.

Casey didn't mince words. "We need to get surveillance and security on Marat El Aran ASAP. The buyer tried to kill Hake to scare Daddy into playing nice. If they can't kill the son, they may go after the father next."

"Got it," Vanessa replied tersely. "How much did you have to tell Hake to get him to cooperate?"

Casey laughed shortly. "I haven't secured that yet. I may have to spill it all, though."

"Don't compromise the Medusa Project," Vanessa warned.

"Understood."

"I leave it in your capable hands, then. Do what you have to. Get the son to help us and find out exactly how much he knows. We'll contact the father as well. Tonight's attack pretty much negated the idea of standing off and waiting for the deal to go down so we can snatch both the terrorists and the El Aran people."

"Hake says the family's being blackmailed into the sale."

"I'll be sure to ask Marat about that."

Casey started. Vanessa was going to lead the team herself? Wow. She only went out on the most crucial and difficult missions in person ever since she'd given birth to her daughter, Caroline, last year.

Vanessa was speaking. "...know where you're sailing?"

"Hake ordered the captain to take us into international waters. I'll let you know when we have a destination."

"Stay in touch."

"Wilco," Casey murmured.

She'd barely disconnected the phone before Hake demanded to know who she'd been talking to. He vibrated with masculine impatience, and something feminine within her thrilled to all that energy. Her reaction was damned annoying, in fact. "That was my boss," she said rather more sourly than his question warranted.

"And?"

She shrugged. "And what? Now you tell me everything you know about these terrorists and my people try to catch them."

Hake shook his head. "Can't risk it. You government types always foul things up and my family will be the ones to pay the price—with their lives. El Aran Industries goes through with this deal as planned and you'll tell your people to stay the hell out of the way."

She considered for a moment, then said, "I hope that's merely your opening gambit, because if it's your final offer, you're about to be very disappointed."

His eyes glittered with anger. Didn't like being threatened, did he? She couldn't blame him. "How's that?" he ground out.

"If you refuse to cooperate with me and my people, you're going to find yourself under arrest, the deal halted and whatever consequences the terrorists threatened coming true against your family."

"You wouldn't," he growled.

She looked him square in the eye and answered low and even, "Try me."

Chapter 7

Casey watched warily as Hake leaped up off the sofa and paced the salon. He reminded her of a seriously riled panther. He snarled, "So that's it, then? I cooperate with you or you throw my entire family to the wolves?"

She took no pleasure in defeating him. Not like this. "Terrorists cannot be allowed to get their hands on that machine. At all costs—including my life, yours and even your family's—the deal must be stopped."

Hake burst out, "My father and I don't want this bunch to have the machine either. We were going to sabotage it so it can't achieve the precision someone would need to fabricate, say, a nuclear trigger."

Casey's eyebrows rose. "Can that be done in a way the buyers can't spot easily?"

Grim humor glinted in his dark gaze. "We expect they'll manufacture faulty parts for six to twelve months before they figure it out. And by then, they'll have burned most of their raw resources."

"Why didn't you contact the British government or your own about all this?"

"Same reason I didn't contact yours. Governments mess things up. They have security leaks and are bogged down with bureaucracy and bungle delicate negotiations."

"We kept you alive tonight, didn't we?"

He stopped pacing abruptly to study her intently. "And you and your friends would be who again?"

"Government agents who are neither prone to security leaks nor bungling delicate negotiations."

"What do you want from me?" he asked directly.

She answered equally directly. "Your full cooperation."

"Not happening," he bit out.

She shrugged. "Nonetheless, my mission remains to stop this deal. I'll succeed with or without your help."

"You can't stop it!" he exclaimed. "My family's lives ride on it going through!"

She sighed. "What if my people were to set up heavy surveillance around the deal to apprehend the buyers?"

"Do I have any say in what you and your people do?"

He sounded bitter. Not that she blamed him. She'd be terribly tense if her family's necks were on the line, too. "No," she answered truthfully. "You don't."

"I can always tell my captain to stay in international water for the next few weeks until the deal is done."

"And throw responsibility for the whole mess onto your father's shoulders?" she said reproachfully. "I think not."

He scowled. She was right and he knew it. He wouldn't leave his father in the lurch like that. She watched in silence as he paced the salon. It turned out he was gorgeous from every angle.

Eventually, he dropped onto the sofa beside her. He asked, "If you hadn't seen that guy and tackled me like that, I'd have been blown to bits, wouldn't I?"

"Probably." They'd been lucky that the restaurant's tables were old and heavy and made of solid wood. That fact alone had likely saved both of their lives.

He reached over and took her hands in his. He looked her directly in the eye. "Thank you," he said simply.

"You're welcome." Their gazes met and touched in a moment of naked honesty. They were *alive*. Such a simple thing but so very precious. He reached up slowly with one hand to touch her cheek, a light touch, just the tips of his fingers trailing across her cheekbone and tracing the line of her jaw. A shiver passed through her, and a single errant thought filled her mind. *Do that again.*

He murmured, "A woman who can dance like you shouldn't also be some sort of superspy."

"Why not?" she murmured back. His gaze was mesmerizing, probing hers with an intelligence that made her worry about how much he was seeing of her.

"It's too much. You're intimidating."

"Me? Intimidating?" She laughed shortly. "You're the intimidating one. All this wealth and success, your perfect looks, brilliant mind, smooth sophistication... I'm just a soldier."

"You have no idea what other people see when they look at you, do you?" he asked, surprised.

"Same thing I see every morning in the mirror," she replied a shade defensively.

"I highly doubt that. I see a beautiful, sensual woman who, for some reason, chooses to pretend to herself that she is neither beautiful nor sensual."

What the heck was she supposed to say in response to something like that? At a loss, she demanded, "And I suppose you don't see movie-star good looks in your mirror every morning?"

He shrugged. "I take no credit for my looks. They're merely the luck of the genetic draw."

She just shook her head. Their worlds were so different that she could hardly imagine his. She suspected he'd be incapable of comprehending hers any better.

Hake startled her by asking, "Now what?"

She replied gently, "Now you tell me everything."

"No, I think this is the part where *you* tell *me* everything. Who are you and who do you work for?"

She sighed. She had to do something to cut the tension between them. Get him to relax and open up to her. It was probably time for some of that pesky boy-girl stuff. If she was lucky, he'd loosen up after nothing more than some pleasant conversation. "I can't tell you anything about me or my employer. It's classified."

"Give me a hint."

"I'm probably the only belly dancer you've ever seen who's been known to pack a Glock 9 mm pistol while she dances."

"You can hide a gun under those skimpy costumes?" She nodded and he laughed in disbelief. "If only I'd known. You'd have been even sexier to watch."

Okay. Time to change the subject. She tried to sound casual when she replied but failed miserably when she croaked, "Tell me something about you I'd never guess."

"I hate the idea of getting married, but my father's trying to force me to do it."

She grinned. "I have no trouble guessing that about you. Tell me something that will surprise me."

"I hate having my picture taken."

"Really? Why would *you* hate pictures? You're gorg—" She broke off.

"Thank you," he murmured in reply to her unfinished compliment. "Being judged for one's looks gets old much faster than you might imagine, however."

"I wouldn't know," she replied.

"Oh, come now," he retorted. "Surely you know how beautiful you are. And just as surely people judge you based on your looks all the time."

"I don't look like this most of the time," she replied drily.

"How do you usually look?"

"Well, I rarely wear makeup. I'm more likely to have mud or camouflage paint all over my face. And I never wear dresses or sparkly clothes."

"I'll look forward to seeing you *au naturel*."

Her gaze snapped to his. Did he mean merely without makeup, or was he referring to seeing her undressed altogether?

He moved on smoothly. "Tell me something surprising about you."

"I used to be a librarian."

His brows lifted. "I confess, I find that hard to picture."

"I was a research librarian, in fact." She omitted the bit about working for the FBI. It had always been her private joke that she was a belly-dancing librarian. She'd never dreamed her longtime hobby would come in handy on a mission. She glanced over at Hake, who was studying her with the kind of focus and intensity that threatened to make a girl feel darned special. She looked away, embarrassed.

"I have twelve sisters," he said unexpectedly.

"Good Lord!" she exclaimed. "My sympathies to you."

He laughed. "I knew a whole lot about girls early because of them. But if you ever tell anyone they used to dress me up like a doll and curl my hair and put makeup on me, I'll deny it to my dying breath."

"Are there pictures?" She laughed. "I'd pay a lot to see those."

"You and a whole bunch of tabloids," he grumbled.

"You don't like being rich and famous very much, do you?" she asked.

"The rich part is admittedly nice. The fame I can do without. But unfortunately in my case, they came as a package."

She nodded in understanding. "Anonymity is critical to my work. I hate public attention of any kind."

"How do you dance in front of crowds, then?"

"I mostly pretend they're not there. Unless someone like you is in the audi—" She broke off, appalled by what she'd just let slip.

He grinned but the expression faded fast. "You won't want to hang out with me for long, then, will you?"

The question startled her. Hang out with him? As in to date him? Good grief. Her mind stumbled hard enough over that concept that it took her a moment to move on to the rest of his comment. He was right. She could in no way afford to come under scrutiny. Reporters would dig into every facet of her life and identity. And although the U.S. military had covered those tracks very well, her lack of a past would raise red flags. Or worse, someone might actually find something on her.

She looked up at Hake and caught his grim look. His features smoothed out immediately and he said lightly, "Well, at least we have tonight."

Alarm exploded inside her. What exactly did he have in mind? She stammered, "Y-you're right. I don't have much time to debrief you. We really need to get busy with that."

"As tempting as it is to make a snappy comment about what you mean by debriefing, I'll refrain," he commented drily. Heat climbed her cheeks tellingly, but thankfully he moved on casually. "I don't know about you, but I'm hungry."

He was stalling. But it was his boat and his crew, and there wasn't a whole heck of a lot she could do to force him to talk if he didn't want to. She sighed. "Fine. Let's eat. And then we'll talk."

He shot her a stubborn look. So, it was going to be like that, was it? She'd just have to do what the Medusas always did. They used brains and creativity to circumvent any situation where they could not resort to brute force. And sometimes they—reluctantly—resorted to girlie stuff. Like flirting with the target over a simple but tasty midnight dinner.

She felt exceedingly weird smiling at him around mouthfuls of croissant sandwich and casting come-hither glances over the cranberry relish. But he seemed to relax as the meal progressed. No matter that she felt uncomfortably squirmy low in her belly and aching for something she had no intention of putting a name to.

It was Hake's turn to dawdle over the meal tonight, avoiding the inevitable conversation to follow, and it amused Casey. After dinner, he moved to stand over by a large bank of picture windows. A stunning view of moonlit English countryside slid past outside.

"It looks like a magical dream," Casey murmured.

"Mmm. An enchanted world," he agreed. "Like you. Too beautiful and elusive to be real."

He was the too-good-to-be-real one. It was hard to wrap her brain around a man like him actually existing. But then Hake touched her elbow, his hand warm and alive and entirely real. He murmured, "I promised myself I would kiss you tonight and, given our mutual brush with death earlier, I'm not inclined to delay much longer lest I never get a chance to do it."

Her stomach and her toes curled into tight knots of anticipation. Her gut warned her in near panic that this was *not* part of the mission. But if kissing Hake would get him to spill his guts, she probably ought to do it…for the good of the mission, of course.

She replied reluctantly, "Kissing is probably not a great idea if we're going to have to work together."

"All the more reason to do it and get it out of the way," he replied in a silky voice that vibrated through her with sexual intensity. "Then we can both relax and quit wondering what it would be like."

"Hake—"

He moved swiftly, drawing her up against him, his mouth swooping down to capture hers before either one of them could come up with any more good reasons not to do it.

Her first reaction was relief. Shockingly, she *was* glad to have the suspended sense of anticipation out of the way. But then…oh, my…a raft of other sensations flooded her. His big, hard body plastered against hers. His warm, wine-flavored lips moving on hers. His hand slipping under her hair, tilting her head to just the right angle.

And then the sheer charisma of the man, all his charm and attractiveness and confidence rolled over her and through her. His thumb toyed with a soft spot just behind her ear as his lips opened her mouth and the kiss grew deeper. More intimate. A hot merlot invasion that was druggingly delicious. His free hand drifted down her back sending electric pulses shooting up and down her spine until she felt hot and boneless all over.

It was a revelation. So much for the theory that she had

no desire to be a girly girl. She was loving every minute of being exactly that in his arms. Worse, she realized her hands had crept over his shoulders and around his neck and that she was pulling his head down to hers as eagerly as he was pulling her to him. This was not happening!

But as sure as she was standing there, her entire body strained forward, pressing into him as if she would become a part of him. She tore her mouth away from his and was appalled to realize she was panting. Hard. Okay, so she'd been lusting after him a whole lot more than she'd admitted to herself. But dang, that man could kiss!

Hake stared down at her, his eyes blazing spots of black fire in the shadows of his elegant face. He looked…shaken. And something warm and satisfied and entirely female unfolded deep inside her at the sight.

"I'm afraid we're going to have to do that again," he murmured.

"But…we can't…" she mumbled.

"Shouldn't and can't are entirely different creatures," he murmured as his mouth closed on hers once more.

Dammit, their second kiss was every bit as incendiary as their first one. More so. Worse, this time he settled into the thing, prepared to draw it out and savor it to the full extent of enjoyment for both of them. She'd never realized two people could kiss with their entire bodies. But as they pressed into one another, hands roaming and breath ragged, every inch of her burned with desire for this man.

He'd temporarily lost his mind. A man like him would never want a woman like her under normal circumstances. But she had to admit, it was a great fantasy while it lasted. Temptation insinuated itself into her consciousness. When in her life was a man like this ever going to kiss her just so again? This was a once-in-a-lifetime opportunity.

And it wasn't as if she was forcing the guy to come on to

her. He was in this purely of his own free will. Of course, he'd also just narrowly missed being blown to bits and was probably half out of his head with shock. She was a bad, bad person for considering taking him up on his offer in his state.

But then he drew her down to the sofa, his hands stripping the shreds of her gown off her shoulders and baring her skin to his mouth. Fireworks exploded inside her head and lower, deep in her abdomen. Oh, yes. She seriously wanted this man.

And then the flawless logic of the hopelessly-in-lust kicked in. They were both adults. If they wanted to have sex, it was nobody's business but theirs, right? They both knew the score. They would scratch the itch and move on like two civilized people.

Except there was nothing civilized in how she felt right now. And she had a sick feeling that he would be hard to move on from. This was the kind of man she could fall for—was falling for. She wasn't as worldly as he was. She hadn't spent most of her adult life jumping in and out of casual affairs flung across the front pages of the tabloids. She'd only had two serious relationships and both of them had ended badly.

But by his own admission, Hake wanted nothing to do with settling down. The fact that his father was pushing him to marry surely made Hake more stubborn on the subject. And why should the guy settle down? Every beautiful, available woman on several continents was throwing herself at him. The man lived in a gourmet candy store. Why should he settle on a plain old chocolate bar like her?

Reluctantly, she pulled away from him. Her entire body felt the loss of his heat and vitality. "I'm sorry, Hake, but this isn't going to work. I'm a Hershey bar, you see."

"Excuse me?" he asked, confused.

"Your life is a Belgian chocolate store with a hundred varieties of gourmet truffle."

His hands slid up her arms, raising goose bumps in their wake and he cupped her face as he drew nearer. "You'll have to explain that to me later. After we've had our fill of each other."

"I can't do this, Hake. Really."

"Because you're a Hershey bar?"

"Exactly."

He stared at her in what looked suspiciously like sexual frustration. "What on earth are you talking about?"

"I'm plain. Simple. I don't do the whole female seductress thing. Exotic, beautiful women of every flavor throw themselves at your feet for the sampling every day. I can't possibly be as captivating or interesting."

"But my favorite brand of chocolate is Hershey."

"You've never had a Hershey bar in your entire privileged life," she accused.

"Hence the novelty and appeal of it, my dear."

She shook her head. "I don't do casual relationships."

He answered lightly, "Then we're in luck. I don't do relationships at all."

That made her pull back sharply. "All the more reason not to do this."

He sighed and shoved a hand through his hair, standing it up all over his head but still managing to look like a picture straight out of an Italian fashion magazine. "I don't know what's happening between us. Hell, I don't even know your last name. But I know I haven't been this intrigued by a woman in…as long as I can remember."

"Chandler."

"I beg your pardon?" he said shortly. Poor guy sounded almost in pain.

"Chandler. That's my last name."

A slow smile unfolded on his face. "See. That wasn't so hard. Chandler. That's a sophisticated-sounding name."

She shrugged, embarrassed by how exposed she suddenly felt. He'd taken away the anonymous soldier persona she'd been hiding behind. "I'm not a sophisticated kind of girl."

He snorted. "You're more complex, and more fascinating I might add, than just about anyone I've ever met. I find you mesmerizing."

"And here I thought it was because you like watching me shimmy around half-naked."

"That, too." He laughed. "You're an extraordinary dancer, by the way."

"Thank you."

They looked at each other for several long, charged seconds.

"Don't do it," she warned.

"How are you planning to stop me?" he asked as he closed the distance between them.

"Well, I could hurt you in about a hundred different ways or just kill you," she murmured.

"But you won't," he murmured back, his hands coming up to cup her face where he'd left off before.

"What makes you so sure?" she muttered.

"Because you like how I make you feel. You want me as much as I want you."

"I do n—"

He pressed light fingers to her lips. "Don't lie to me. I hate it when women lie."

"I hate it when anyone lies," she retorted.

He smiled. "Touché."

They stared at one another, stalemated yet again.

"Help me out here, Hake. I'm going to have to report

to my superiors in the morning, and I've got to have more than you kiss like a god."

He grinned broadly. "A god, huh?"

"Work with me," she all but begged. "Give me something on that man who talked to you in the restaurant. Or better, give me what you've got on the people who approached you and your father."

He stared at her for a long time. She didn't for a minute underestimate how intelligent or calculating a man he was. His personal financial success was ample testament to both.

"Fine," he sighed. "But on one condition."

"What's that?"

"Come to bed with me."

Chapter 8

Hake waited tensely for Casey-Cassandra-Scorpion's answer. He was stunned to admit it, but his desire to make love with this woman only grew the more he got to know her. Who'd have guessed a confident, take-charge soldier lurked under all that organza and beading? An utterly fascinating combination of tough and tender.

"No deal," she said promptly.

"Then I tell you nothing," he retorted just as quickly.

"You don't seem to understand your position, Hake. I could arrest you for obstruction of justice and conspiracy to commit acts of terrorism."

She was hiding behind her soldier persona. He knew women far too well to be snowed by her act, however. He could all but taste the desire dripping off her. "Casey, Casey," he sighed. "Do you know yourself so little?"

"What are you talking about?" she demanded nervously.

He moved slowly, giving her every opportunity to prove him wrong and pull away. But as he'd expected, she did not. A combination of innocence and deadly experience swam in her wary gaze, drawing him to her more powerfully than an aphrodisiac.

"Let me show you," he said. Moving in slow motion, he drew her into his arms. She tensed, and he paused, waiting until she finally relaxed. He kissed his way across her collarbone and up her neck. He couldn't resist a little nibble of her earlobe, but he softened it with whispered word of how beautiful she was. By gradual degrees she went warm and liquid in his arms. The sensation exhilarated him. He wasn't generally fond of seducing innocents, but this woman lit a fire in his blood that was nigh uncontrollable.

Her arms looped around his neck and her body melted like warm chocolate against him. His eyes drifted closed as he savored her lithe curves in his arms.

She said sweetly against his lips, "You have…" a soft kiss "…the right to remain silent…"

He jerked back, startled. "What are you doing?"

"Reading you your rights. It's a required legal procedure in America. I don't know if we're still in British waters or not, so I went with my own country's recitation of legal rights while I arrest you."

"By what authority?"

"By mine. I'm a commissioned military officer, and as such, I have the right to arrest you. If you'll turn around and place your hands behind your back while I get out my handcuffs…"

Stunned, he stared at her. She didn't sound the slightest bit playful about that handcuff offer. "What the hell—" he started.

"I'm not joking, Hake. You're under arrest."

"And then what?"

"Then I'm commandeering your vessel and ordering the captain to go back to London so you can be put in jail."

"You can't!"

"I am."

Sonofa— For the second time tonight, he felt completely disoriented. First, someone tried to blow him up, and now this. She actually planned to arrest him! It wasn't his fault those people had approached him and tried to force him to sell them a precision milling machine. And it wasn't his fault they'd tried to kill him. None of this was fair.

"Why am I the bad guy all of a sudden?" he demanded. "I've done nothing wrong. I'm not a terrorist."

"But you are obstructing an investigation of terrorists. And that's a felony."

He rolled his eyes. "I'm trying to protect my family."

"Fine. Then go to jail and protect them all you like from there." She added grimly, "If you can."

He scowled at her, supremely frustrated.

"Or," she continued implacably, "you can let me help you. I have resources at my disposal you've never dreamed of. And contrary to your opinion, my team has never failed on a mission."

"There's a first time for everything, and I can't afford for this to be yours to fail," he snapped.

She stared at him with something akin to sorrow in her gaze. "Do you seriously think these terrorists will let your family live even if you do sell them the milling machine? They'll blackmail the El Arans until you don't have anything else they want, and then they'll kill you all. Your family is dead men—and women—walking. Particularly after you had the gall to live through tonight's attempt to kill you. You've embarrassed them."

"So by saving my life tonight, you killed us all?" he asked incredulously.

She shook her head. "Your family is rich, powerful, connected to governments and to the global business community. You represent everything they hate. They were already planning to come after your family."

He sat down heavily on the sofa, swearing under his breath. She was right. Horror rolled through him as he absorbed that truth. He looked up at her bleakly. "What do you need from me?"

She sat down beside him and said simply, "Tell me everything."

"And you'll tell me everything in return? Let me participate in all operations?" A stubborn look flickered through her eyes and he added desperately, "They're my family, for God's sake."

She sighed. Nodded. "All right. But promise me if I ever give you a direct order you'll follow it instantly and without question."

That sent his eyebrows up.

She added, "You're a civilian. I'm a trained Special Forces operative. I need to know you'll do what I tell you to if you're about to die."

Special Forces? Her? His mind locked up in disbelief. Surely not. Although she certainly had the nerves of steel down cold. Yet again, this woman had knocked him completely off balance. He nodded shortly. "Deal."

"Start at the beginning," she urged gently.

He sighed and began talking. She listened intently, without interruption. At the end of his recitation she asked a million questions and typed copious notes on a laptop computer that emerged from her duffel bag. Finally, an eternity later, she hit several buttons and nodded in satisfaction.

"Done," she announced.

"What is?"

"My report to my headquarters. They'll sift through everything you gave me and no doubt will have a bunch of questions of their own. But we've probably got a few hours to catch a nap before they contact me."

He felt like a washcloth that had been wrung out and hung up to dry. He also felt unexpectedly lonely. And vulnerable. Perhaps it had taken this long for the reality of how close he'd come to dying earlier to sink in. And for the reality that his family was in just as much danger to hit him.

"What are your people going to do to protect my family?" he asked.

"Your family already has an extensive personal security team, does it not?"

"We do, but it didn't do me a bit of good at the restaurant."

"You also didn't have your guards with you. I have faith you won't make that mistake again anytime soon. I'm sure by now my people have been in contact with your father and made it clear to him that no El Aran is to set foot outside without a full contingent of bodyguards. It would be best for your family to sequester itself somewhere safe, like your family's compound in Bhoukar, until this operation is concluded."

He felt slightly better, but his gut still rumbled warningly at the idea of his family's lives depending on agents of any government.

She changed subjects abruptly. "This milling machine you're selling the terrorists is big and heavy, I assume?"

He snorted. "It weighs several tons. We'll need a crane to lift it."

She commented thoughtfully, "They'll likely want to move it by ship, then."

"You're planning to give them the machine?" he asked, surprised.

"If we can't catch them by any other means, we'll have to go through with the deal. We'll use your suggestion and sabotage the thing. And, of course, we'll put tracking devices on it—" She broke off abruptly, a look of dismay crossing her face.

"What?" he asked sharply.

"Has your crew swept this vessel for tracking devices recently?" she asked tightly.

"I have no idea."

"Ask. Now."

He leaned over and pressed the intercom button. "Captain Soderling, have you checked the *Angelique* recently for tracking devices put here by someone interested in following us?"

"Not in the past week, sir," a deep voice answered in alarm. "Do you have reason to believe there is such a device aboard?"

Casey leaned forward to speak and Hake pressed the button for her. "Captain, as soon as it's feasible for you to do so, I need you to have your men comb every inch of this ship. You'll need to drop anchor, deploy divers and inspect the hull as well. And if you find a device, *don't* disable it. Is that understood?"

"Mr. El Aran?" the captain asked. Hake grinned. The man didn't know what to make of one of the boss's female guests giving orders. Especially an order like that.

"Do as the lady says, Jürgen."

"Roger, sir. I'll wake the crew and get started on it right away."

As the ship halted and men commenced crawling over it from stem to stern, Hake put in a ship-to-shore call to his father to make sure the El Arans had been warned.

Casey spent the time typing her personal report detailing the night's activities for her superiors.

Hake never did get through to his father. He left urgent messages at every contact number he had and then prayed the reason the phones weren't being answered was because the El Aran security team had already gone into lockdown. When the worry became too much for him, he broke down and asked Casey, "Do your people have some sort of status report on my family? Are they safe?"

She looked up from her computer surprised. "I'll ask." She made a quick call while he fretted. In a matter of seconds, she smiled reassuringly at him. "They're fine. The whole clan has gathered at your palace in Bhoukar and is under heavy security."

He sagged, relieved.

"Do you really live in a palace?" she asked.

"No. I live in a flat in London. But the family seat could probably be called a palace without exaggerating."

She just shook her head.

The ship's crew made their way through the salon just then, tearing the place completely apart before putting it back together again. As they moved on to other parts of the ship, Hake asked Casey ruefully, "Do you cause this much chaos everywhere you go?"

She smiled wearily. "On most missions, we slip in, do our thing and slip out without anyone ever knowing we were there. In a perfect world we're quiet and invisible. So, no. This is not a typical mission."

"Who is we?" he asked curiously. "I was not aware that your country had more than one belly-dancing commando in its service."

She laughed. "When you put it that way, it does sound a little strange, doesn't it?"

He frowned. She was smoothly ducking the question. "Who are you?" he persisted.

"I can't answer that. My unit is highly classified."

"I told you everything. I think I've earned a little information back—"

"Sir!" One of the crewmen burst into the salon. "We found it!"

Hake leaped to his feet quickly, but Casey beat him off the sofa. "Show us," he demanded.

The two of them followed the sailor down to the yacht's engine compartment. In the very rear of the vessel where the propeller screw exited to the water was a small metal object that looked like a radio transmitter. Casey examined it and then announced, "GPS unit. They can track us anywhere in the world."

"Shall we remove it?" the sailor asked.

She shook her head. "Not yet. And keep looking. They probably have more than one device aboard. I would if I were them."

Hake was amused by the incredulous looks his men threw her way when she wasn't looking. He knew the feeling. She appeared so soft and harmless but spoke like a trained killer. The woman could really quit knocking him off his feet like this. He didn't know what to expect from her next.

And sure enough, she surprised him when she spoke again. "It's nearly daylight. Why don't you lie down and try to get a little sleep, Hake? Once my superiors start working you over, you may not get another chance to rest for a while."

The ship's security chief, a Swiss fellow named Tomas, piped up. "And you would be who, ma'am?"

She smiled pleasantly at the man. "I'm not at liberty to divulge that information."

"Do you work with that woman on the dock? The one who told me how to do my job?"

Hake watched with interest as Casey fielded that minor grenade. "You'll have to forgive my teammate if she stepped on your toes. We'd just pulled Hake out of a bombing and were tense about getting him undercover. My colleague didn't know who you were and I'd had no chance to brief her. She only wanted to make sure Mr. El Aran was safe, same as you."

Tomas looked mostly mollified, particularly when Casey added, "Maybe later this morning we could discuss your ideas on where we should stash Hake to maximize your security team's effectiveness."

"Hey!" Hake objected. "I'm not getting stashed anywhere. I'm participating in whatever happens!"

Casey and Tomas traded downright friendly looks of commiseration with one another. The crew continued searching the ship, and Hake showed Casey to the lower deck staterooms, which had already been searched.

Hake paused in the narrow passage. "Do you want your own room, or for security reasons, would you like to be closer to me?"

She looked up at him, worry momentarily winking in her gaze. Afraid to bunk in with him, was she? Smart girl. But then amusement flared in his gut. She'd thrown herself in front of bomb and bullied him into cooperating without batting an eyelash. But sleeping with him scared her? He added lightly with just a hint of a dare in his voice, "You can take the bed. I'll take the couch."

"You'll do no such thing," she declared. "You sleep and I'll stand guard."

He snorted. "There's no way I'm going to sleep if you're hovering over me like some protective, UZI-toting mother hen."

She retorted drily, "I don't like shooting UZIs. They climb too much when you go full automatic with them."

He just shook his head and opened the door to his suite for her. He was shocked when she actually stepped inside ahead of him. A frisson of pleasure skated over his skin. She was going to stay with him, then, was she? Starting just inside the door, she worked her way counterclockwise around the luxurious space, examining it minutely from floor to ceiling. "What are you doing?" he asked.

"It's called a security sweep. I'm looking for listening devices, cameras and hiding places for possible assailants."

"This is a yacht. Every inch is used carefully. Space for bad guys to hide in is extremely limited."

"Nonetheless, I'm personally searching your room."

He waited patiently until she finished her sweep. "So, are you brave enough to sleep in the same bed with me?" He pointedly left out any promises to behave himself.

Her gaze narrowed. "Is that a challenge?"

He grinned. "If that's what it takes to get you in my bed, absolutely."

"In that case, I accept."

Chapter 9

Casey watched apprehensively as Hake disappeared into the bathroom. She might talk a good line, but inside her head a voice was screaming a big, fat, what-the-hell-are-you-doing at her. She was mature enough not to have to accept every stupid dare someone flung at her. And sleeping with Hake was definitely stupid. Thrilling, but stupid. Apparently, being a sensible Hershey bar didn't necessarily equate to making sensible decisions.

The bathroom door opened and Hake emerged wearing a pair of silk pajama bottoms—and nothing else. His bare chest, bronze and perfect, made her gulp. Any number of reactions to the sight came to her mind, most of which ran along the lines of *hubba hubba*. He was much larger and more muscular than a person noticed at first with him. His tailored suits and sheer charisma had a way of distracting a person from the size and raw power of the man.

"There are towels, toothbrushes, shampoo and robes

in the bathroom," he said, gesturing over his shoulder. "I think there's skin-care stuff and some cosmetics, too."

She'd bet. It was probably standard procedure on this vessel to be prepared for female guests sorely lacking in luggage or toiletries. As Hake threw back the covers and started to climb into bed, she fled for the bathroom.

She scrubbed off the remnants of her stage makeup and studied herself in the mirror. Seeing her like this would be the end of Hake's infatuation with her. The soldier was fully revealed now that the glamorous dancer's mask was gone. Oh, well. She'd warned him. He would see her as she really was as soon as she stepped through that door.

Funny, but part of her was reluctant to break the spell of her Cassandra persona between them. Had she actually been enjoying pretending to be beautiful and exotic and desirable? What on earth was wrong with her? She hadn't worn makeup in something like two years before this mission came along. She lived in combat boots and fatigues, often filthy and nearly always toting lethal weapons, which she had used on more than one occasion, thank you very much.

As regret ignored her arguments and stabbed at her anyway, she insisted to herself it was for the best this way. She had a mission to do, and she held no illusions that working with Hake would be easy. He was smart, stubborn and used to being in charge. Kind of like her, in fact, which was exactly why he was bound to drive her crazy.

She sighed and pulled on the tank top and skimpy shorts she found folded neatly on the bathroom counter. Discretion being the better part of valor, she left her bra on under the top. Thus girded to step back into battle with Hake, she opened the bathroom door.

The lights were off and the stateroom was pitch-black. Good thing she'd already memorized its layout. She made her way to the far side of the bed and slipped beneath a fluffy down comforter. The stupidity of agreeing to get into bed with a lady killer like Hake struck her full-force, and she went as stiff as a board.

"Are you all right?" His voice floated out of the inky darkness close by.

"Why do you ask?" she gritted out.

"It feels like you're on the verge of bolting."

"I am not."

He asked mildly, "Tell me, Casey. Why did you panic when I kissed you before?"

"I didn't panic!"

"Then why did you feel obliged to interrupt an inspired kiss, if I do say so myself, by trying to arrest me?"

"I was doing my job."

The bed shifted, and it felt as if he might have turned to face her and propped himself up on an elbow. He said gently, "You were hiding behind your job. Are you that afraid of being the woman you are?"

The words jolted through her like lightning, singeing her from head to toe. Was she afraid of being a woman? Was that why she hid behind combat boots and rifles? Most of her teammates still went out on dates, still did their hair and put on makeup and sexy little dresses during their off hours. But not her. She was the job. Always the job.

She must have been quiet for too long because he murmured, "Come here."

"Why?" she asked cautiously.

"It'll be easier if I show you." A hand touched her hip and she jumped about a foot straight up in the air. Lord, she was tense.

He murmured easily enough, "I won't do anything you don't want. Say the word and I'll stop. You have my word of honor." His hand shifted to her elbow and he drew her lightly toward him. She tried to brace herself, but the boat was rocking slightly and chose that particular moment to roll toward him. She overbalanced and threw out her hands to catch herself. Acres of warm skin sprang up under her palms and she gasped in surprise.

Hake gave a tug on her wrists, pulling them out from under her, and she fell on top of him unceremoniously. "Sorry," she grunted. "Just being a klutz."

He fell silent for a moment, then asked reflectively, "Why are you so tense about having sex with me?"

"I'm tense about *not* having sex with you," she snapped.

His voice, rich with amusement, tickled her ear. "There's no need to worry about it not happening. It will."

"That's not what I meant—" She broke off. He knew that; he was teasing her. "You're incorrigible."

"Mmm. I've heard that before." His lips touched her temple lightly and she about jumped out of her skin. "What's the problem, Casey? Why not sit back, relax and let things unfold naturally between us?"

"Nothing's unfolding here."

His fingertips traced her shoulders lightly. "Would it be so terrible if something did?"

"It's just…wrong."

"What's wrong about making each other feel good? Exploring the attraction between us—and don't try to deny that it exists. I've been playing this game too long not to know sparks when I see them." She remained stubbornly silent and he continued. "You're a consenting adult, as am I. You're sensuous and passionate. Why not savor both? Here we are together and alone. We're even already in bed and half-undressed. All you'd have to do is let down your guard and it would be right there for us to enjoy."

He must be a deadly negotiator to sit across a conference table from. "It's not that simple," she replied stubbornly.

He relaxed beneath her, which she somehow found even more threatening than if he had continued to push his case. "What's not simple about this, Casey?"

He was asking for it. She took a deep breath and fired both barrels at him. "This may be simple for you. See a chick you want to bed. You go after her, get the prize and move on to the next attractive female who comes along. That's fine for you, but it's not how I operate. I want the real deal. A relationship and feelings and long-term commitment." She hesitated but then forced herself to press on. "I happen to be attracted to you, Hake, which means I want more—and won't settle for less than—an actual relationship."

He chuckled beneath her. "Here we go. The lady's thrown a set of conditions on the table. Let's negotiate and close this deal, then. What constitutes a relationship in your mind?"

She frowned. "Spending time together. Sharing personal stuff. Having feelings for each other."

"I'd say we've started doing all of those already," he replied. "Now all we have to do is sustain them."

"Ah, but here's the kicker," she added grimly. "There has to be a possibility of more." That would stop him in his tracks for sure.

"As in, say, marriage?" he asked. Abruptly all humor was absent from his voice.

Ha. That had gotten to him. But as the idea of marriage rose before her and thoroughly alarmed her, she surprised herself by being the first to temporize. "Well, a long-term commitment, if not actual marriage."

His voice floated out of the dark. "I think I can agree to that."

She froze, stunned. "I beg your pardon?"

"My father has decreed that I must marry within a year. I currently have no serious wifely prospects in mind, but as of this week, I'm officially open to the idea, like it or not."

"What about true love?" she asked, aghast. "Finding your soul mate?"

He shrugged, his chest moving against hers in a way that completely distracted her for a moment. She felt the turbulence of his thoughts, but he declined to answer. "What will you do?" she asked in a hush.

"I love my family. And if I haven't found my soul mate after all the women I've dated, I highly doubt I'm going to now. I will search for the least objectionable candidate I can find and marry her."

"I'm sorry," she whispered. She couldn't imagine what it must be like to be forced into something so important and personal by an outsider.

His hand smoothed over her hair. "You're kind to worry about me," he murmured. "But I don't deserve your concern. I really am a cad when it comes to women. I'm probably way overdue for a comeuppance."

"I don't know about that. You've been completely honest and forthright with me. And not every man affords women that courtesy."

"Don't try to make a hero out of me, Casey. You're the hero here. I'm the useless playboy."

She lifted up on her elbows to frown down at him. "The way I hear it, you've been spectacularly successful in your own right."

"In business, perhaps. In love, not so much."

"Why's that?" she asked. "What inside you is keeping you from loving someone?"

"I haven't a clue," he answered soberly. "Care to take a stab at it?"

She answered thoughtfully, "My guess is you're afraid that women will love your wealth and fame and not *you*. I think you're secretly a romantic and don't want to get your heart broken, so you hold all women at arm's length emotionally."

"That's some theory you've got there," he mumbled.

"Does it ring true deep in your gut?" she pressed. If only she could see his face. She leaned across him and reached out, fumbling for the lamp on the nightstand.

"What are you doing?" he demanded.

"I want to see your face when you answer so I can read whether or not you're lying." The light flicked on and they both squinted in its glare. She stared down at him expectantly. "So, am I right?"

He exhaled hard. "Maybe."

Oh, yeah. He might be having trouble admitting it to himself, but all the signs were there. Who'd have guessed the big, bad playboy was such a softie inside? She spoke quietly, "I think you'll do fine with marriage. Just let your wife see this side of you and you'll find happiness."

He snorted. "And where am I going to find a woman I can trust with these feelings?"

"You mean besides me?" she commented wryly.

His gaze snapped to hers. As she watched, his eyes widened and then darkened. Alarm started buzzing in her own gut. "What?" she finally asked as he continued to stare at her.

"You are a woman, aren't you?" he asked, apparently speaking mostly to himself.

She laughed. "Last time I checked."

"I'm serious," he retorted.

"So am I."

Reluctant humor shone in his gaze. "You certainly can give back anything I dish at you, can't you?"

She blinked down at him, not sure what he meant. "I guess so. It kind of comes with the territory when you're a woman working in a male-dominated world."

He shook his head in what looked like disbelief. "A belly-dancing commando. Who'd have guessed you'd turn out to be so wise?"

Right. As if her life was a shining example of smart decisions, particularly when it came to love. Casey made a face. "I may be a lot of things, but I highly doubt wise is one of them."

His fingers traced a line across her shoulder and under the hair at the back of her neck while his thumb caressed her neck lightly. "You underestimate yourself. I think you're a rather brilliant Hershey bar."

She laughed, and maybe that was why she was surprised when his lips touched hers. Her humor evaporated in a nanosecond, leaving her equal parts shocked and nervous. What was happening between them?

But then, even that fled her mind as his mouth moved across hers. She'd never heard of a man tasting so good—dark like coffee, with a bite like whiskey, but sweet as well, like vanilla. She sipped of him to her heart's content, and he was generous, opening himself to her explorations and not rushing her. His teeth were smooth and even, his lips firm and warm. And his tongue was ever so clever, dancing lightly with hers.

His hands were not idle while they kissed, stroking along the undersides of her arms and down her ribs to her hips, raising goose bumps from her hairline to the tips of her toes. Eventually, she tore her mouth away from his and pushed herself up to a sitting position, straddling his waist with her thighs. She had to get control of this situation. Of herself.

Except, somehow, she wasn't in control at all. His hands trailed lightly down her body starting at her neck, down the valley between her breasts and across her belly. She shivered, craving more. A sound of need escaped her, stunning her. She had no memory of consciously making a decision about him, but apparently she had.

"You know my condition, right?" she murmured.

He nodded solemnly. "I can't promise you happily ever after, but I will give you everything I'm capable of in the meantime."

Was it enough for her? A real relationship…for a little while at least. It was as risky as heck. She was bound to get hurt, but the ride promised to be spectacular right up to the moment it crashed and burned. Hake was patient beneath her, waiting still and silent for her to wrestle it through. And that was probably what tipped the scales.

"This is insane," she mumbled.

"Indubitably." A dazzling smile lit his face. "Welcome to the asylum."

She just shook her head. But inside, the little voice in the back of her head was doing back flips of excited anticipation. She was really going to jump off the cliff and fly with Hake!

Getting their clothes off took a little maneuvering, but in a moment, Hake settled her back on top of him astride his hips, naked as the day she was born. He seemed in no hurry to proceed and merely looked at her, a slow smile spreading across his face.

"You're beautiful," he murmured.

It was hard for her to accept the compliment, especially from him, but she made herself let the words flow through her until she had absorbed them. "Thank you. You're pretty beautiful yourself."

He smiled as he reached up to tuck a strand of her hair behind her ear. "Come here, Casey. Let me show you just how beautiful you are to me."

She leaned forward until their mouths met. He reached out to turn off the light, and the last thing she saw before darkness enveloped them was Hake's gaze glowing with appreciation. Their joining was achingly slow and entirely perfect.

As the sensations piled one on top of another, each more delicious than the last, her body undulated in rhythm with the rocking of the boat beneath them. The twin movements amplified one another until everything was a tangle of limbs, a slide of hot skin on hot skin, a flurry of urgent kisses and gasped words of pleasure.

Hake surged over her, giving himself entirely to her and she to him. They rode the wave together until it crashed around them with an explosion behind her eyelids that all but rendered her blind and deaf. She cried out and Hake's hoarse cry mingled with hers as they surrendered to it together.

He rolled to his back and she collapsed on his shoulder, spent. His chest rose and fell hard, and perspiration slicked his skin against hers. He still smelled of coffee and whiskey and vanilla, but now a new note was added to the bouquet. Startled, she recognized her white orchid perfume on his skin.

A force moved within her, shifting and expanding before settling into a new place, deep in her heart. She liked the smell of herself on him. A lot. Nearly as much as she liked the feel of her body on his. Or her mouth on his. Or her hands on him.

His voice came out of the dark. "Thank you. I've never received a gift to compare."

"You probably say that to all your—"

He forestalled her, pressing a finger to her lips, as if he would protect the specialness of the moment. She subsided, letting the silence of it wash over her. They *had* shared something special.

But how special?

Special enough to hold his attention for a long time to come?

She forced the doubts out of her mind. There would be time enough tomorrow for regrets and recriminations. For tonight, it was enough to know she'd touched him as deeply as he'd touched her.

When she emerged from his shower the next morning, steamed to perfection, she was alarmed to see Hake talking on her cell phone.

"Ah, here she is," he said. "It was a pleasure speaking with you, Vanessa."

Casey's eyebrows shot up. He was already on a first-name basis with her boss? In minor shock, she took the cell phone he held out to her. "Hi, boss. I gather you met Hake."

Vanessa laughed. "Sounds like you're going to have your hands full with him. Good work talking him into cooperating with us. After I spoke with his father, I was skeptical of your chances. Marat seems to think his son is more than a little willful."

"That's a word for him," Casey replied drily.

"We got your message about the tracking devices. We concur with you—leave them in place. But in the meantime, we've got a problem. Rumors of Hake's death are rattling the European banking community. The British prime minister has asked the president of the United States to have us reveal that Hake is alive so there's not a nasty shock on the London Stock Exchange."

"But that'll expose him to the terrorists!" Casey protested.

Vanessa sighed. "I know. The good news is I think we can make lemonade out of this particular lemon."

"How's that?"

"If we have to show Hake anyway, why not use him as bait to draw out the terrorists? If we flaunt him loudly enough, they'll be honor-bound to make another try at him. I'll need you to work with his security team to protect him while we taunt the hostiles into showing themselves."

Casey winced. On the one hand, she loved the idea of getting to spend more time with Hake. But on the other hand, she purely hated the notion of using him as bait. "Have you decided when and where you want to put on this dog and pony show?" she asked in resignation.

Casey listened carefully as Vanessa described what had been arranged for them. Her boss finished with, "Got all that?"

"Yes, ma'am. We'll be ready."

"I'll relay the necessary instructions to Captain Soderling," Vanessa replied. "Get some rest. You're going to have a busy day tomorrow."

Now that was an understatement. She disconnected the call thoughtfully.

"What's up?" Hake asked from beside her.

"You and I are going on a little trip tonight."

"Oh, really? Where?"

Protocol dictated not upsetting the protectee. Except it felt weird not telling Hake everything. She knew it had been a bad idea to get involved with him! One night and already duty and obligation were clashing. She dodged carefully. "We've got a few hours to rest while my boss makes the arrangements. I'll fill you in once the details are finalized."

He studied her intently. "If I threaten to torture it out of you, will you tell me what's going on?"

She grinned down at him as he lounged beside her. "You can make all the threats you like, but you can't take me in a fight."

"You think not?" he asked. "When this is all over, we'll have to give it a go. I wrestled at Cambridge, you know."

"Let me know if you need me to lose intentionally to save your fragile ego."

"Don't you dare," he retorted, laughing.

"All right," she said mildly. "But I warned you."

He chuckled.

"What?" she demanded.

"You are completely unlike any other woman I've ever known."

"Is that good or bad?" The question was out of her mouth before she could suck it back behind her teeth.

He grinned widely. "I'll let you know when I've reached a verdict."

She stuck out her tongue, and he pulled her down to him. Their lips met. As their kiss spiraled out of control and it became clear that breakfast would have to wait for a while, Vanessa's parting words echoed in her ears. "Casey, stay out of trouble."

Right. No problem. A boy and girl thrown together in a life-threatening situation…tons of stress in need of burning off…a fancy yacht and a world-class playboy who kissed like a god…it all spelled *Trouble* with a capital *T*.

Chapter 10

Hake stared at Casey across the breakfast table. "Your government sent a bunch of *women* to Bhoukar to protect my family? Do you know *nothing* about my country?"

She smiled tightly. "Actually, we know quite a bit about it. We've run several successful missions in Bhoukar. In fact, we have a standing offer of both hospitality and military assistance from the emir any time we're in that part of the world."

His country's dyed-in-the-wool traditionalist leader supported a group of women soldiers? Hake felt his jaw sagging. "So, what's the plan?"

"We'll use the tracking devices on this ship to mislead the terrorists into believing we're sailing up the Irish coast. But meanwhile, you and I will head elsewhere. When we're in place, we'll spring the trap. With you as bait, of course."

"Of course." Hake sounded grim. Smart man.

She met his gaze equally grimly. "I don't like it any more than you do. Maybe less. But I've got direct orders from my superiors, and the stakes are huge. My hands are tied." She smiled lamely at him. "If everything goes well, we'll nab your terrorists and they'll never bother you or your family again."

"And if things don't go well?"

"Then people will die."

He shuddered at how matter-of-factly she said that. "Have you ever killed anyone?"

"Yes," she answered shortly, looking at a spot over his shoulder.

"How many?"

She made eye contact with him then. Her gaze was closed tight. "Do you seriously want me to answer that question?"

"Good point. Never mind." He sipped his coffee while he considered her. This was a first. He'd never been with a woman who was a killer. He probably should run screaming from her. But damned if she didn't fascinate him.

"Why do you do what you do?" he asked curiously.

She answered without hesitation, "Because I get satisfaction from knowing I'm making a real difference."

"You like your work, then?"

"I love it."

He nodded in understanding. He was passionate about his work, too, managing the El Aran financial empire. He loved the thrill of billion-dollar bets, outsmarting the next analyst, beating the odds. "How long do you plan to do this job?"

She pushed scrambled eggs around her plate thoughtfully. "As long as they'll have me or until I die."

That startled him. "Is mortality high in your line of work?"

"We've had a few close calls, but my team hasn't lost anyone." She added reluctantly, "Yet."

He nodded in commiseration. "In my world, deaths are inevitable, too."

Her lips twitched. "Banking is dangerous stuff, huh?"

"No. Being a jet-setting wild child is dangerous."

She commented under her breath, "You don't seem like much of a child to me."

He reached over to place his hand over hers. "Thanks. I generally prefer grown-up toys." He felt the shiver that passed through her. Such a responsive woman. "How long do you think this fishing expedition to draw out the bad guys will take?"

She shrugged. "It will depend on the terrorists and how fast they move in response to seeing you alive. A few days. Maybe a week."

One week with her. That wasn't long. Was it long enough to know if she was The One? Long enough to make a life-changing decision about the two of them? How in the hell was he supposed to figure that out in one lousy week?

"When will you know what our destination is?" he asked.

"I knew that last night. I just wanted you to get some decent rest before I made you all tense again."

That sent his eyebrows upward. A woman who could keep a secret? The surprises just kept on coming. "So, where are we going?"

"The French Riviera."

"You are aware that paparazzi crawl all over the Gold Coast, right? Because of my…notoriety…we won't be able to breathe without them on top of us."

"I believe that's the idea," Casey replied. "But never fear, your men and I will keep you safe—"

"You expect to be with me in a security capacity?" he interrupted.

"Yes."

"No, no. That won't do at all," he declared.

She stared at him. "Excuse me?"

"I don't need you as my bodyguard. I need you as my girlfriend."

"Come again?" she blurted.

"You heard me. If you're going to be with me, you have to be my girlfriend."

"You have a reputation for never doing relationships. It'll make the terrorists suspicious."

He shrugged. "I doubt they've studied my social habits that closely. And besides, think of the rumors it'll start. The press will go crazy if they think the most eligible bachelor in Europe is about to be landed."

That was definitely dismay on Casey's face.

He frowned. "You're the one who wanted a real relationship. Why the cold feet going public with it?"

She mumbled absently, "I have to make a call."

He watched, bemused, as she pulled out her cell phone.

"Vanessa. He wants to drag me around with him in front of the press as his girlfriend. They're going to want to know who I am. They'll dig—"

Ah. She was worried about her privacy. He snorted. She had no idea the invasion of it she was about to endure. He was loathe to warn her, though, lest she think better of being involved with him at all.

Casey said tightly into her phone, "You'll send me the dossier when it's built?" She hung up the phone after a murmured goodbye.

"What was that all about?" he asked.

"I can't exactly have the press digging into my life."

"Why? Are you an ax murderer?"

"No. After this mission I need to be able to disappear again and not be some sort of celebrity."

The idea of her disappearing from his life sent faint waves of nausea rolling through him. He didn't want to lose her. At least not like that, with no trace, as if she'd never been here. A week. He had one week to change their future.

Chapter 11

Casey grabbed onto the railing at her back as the big helicopter established a hover overhead. The French Puma helicopter was too big to land on the yacht's helipad, but they needed the big bird's extended range and lifting capability to get them to their destination.

"Are you sure this is going to work?" Hake shouted in her ear.

She grinned over at him. "I've done this a hundred times. Just remember what I said and do what I showed you."

"I know, I know. Keep my weight close to the rope and don't let go."

"When you get to the door, let the guy in the 'copter do all the work and maneuver you inside. Your job is to make like a sack of potatoes for him."

Hake nodded as a big, metal seat lowered toward them on a steel cable. His security chief, Tomas, rode up first. The seat came down again. "Your turn!" Casey shouted.

Hake threw her a devil-may-care smile that made her knees wobble and climbed onto the seat with effortless grace and power. She gave a thumbs up to the PJ hanging out the helicopter door on a harness, and in a rush of wind and salt spray, Hake was away.

It felt uncomfortable not being at his side, as if an umbilical cord between them was being stretched too far. The seat slithered back down toward her too fast. She jumped out of the way and steadied the heavy seat without bothering to scowl up at the PJ overhead. Men always tried to mess with the Medusas the first time they worked with the female Special Forces soldiers.

She climbed on the seat efficiently and gave a thumbs-up. As she'd expected, the PJ ran the hoist full-speed, yanking her into the air alarmingly fast. When she jerked to a stop beside the door, she waved off the PJ's hand, grabbed the hoist arm overhead and swung her feet up and out, flinging herself neatly into the helicopter's cargo bay and landing in a crouch.

She glanced over her shoulder at the gaping PJ and casually called him a less-than-polite name in flawless French. His sagging jaw turned into a grudging grin.

Tomas's men came up the hoist, followed by their gear. The helicopter's nose dipped and they sped away from the *Angelique,* leaving the vessel's sleek silhouette behind in the dark. The yacht would sail up the coast of Ireland, carrying its load of GPS tracking devices, and hopefully the suspicions of the terrorists, with it.

The working theory was the bigger the shock when the terrorists realized Hake was not only alive but flaunting that fact, the better the odds of infuriating them into attacking. Hence, the secret evacuation from the *Angelique.*

Hake was grinning and loving the ride strapped in the back of the big helicopter. As for her, she figured it was some sort of Pavlovian reflex to sleep in choppers because she was either heading into a tough mission or coming home exhausted from one. Her eyes drifted closed and she fell asleep in a matter of moments.

A kick on her foot jerked her back to consciousness some time later. The ocean had been replaced by dark farmland below the helicopter. And they were at low altitude and slowing down. They must be at Calais. She couldn't see the train station from this side of the bird, but it would be out there.

Sure enough, a few seconds later the helicopter's forward speed slowed to zero and a black hole of a landing pad came into sight below. The bird thudded to the ground and the scream of the engines cut off. Casey jumped out first and turned to steady Hake, but he didn't need the help. The man was as agile as a cat. He grinned at her as they jogged out from under the rotor blades and rounded the tail of the helicopter.

A long, sleek shape waited on the train tracks in front of them. The TGV, *Train à Grande Vitesse*. Also known as the French bullet train.

"We're headed for the last car," she murmured. "The one with all the window shades pulled and the lights off."

"Sounds romantic," Hake murmured. When she rolled her eyes, he amended. "You have to admit, it's very sexy and super-spyish to have a car on the TGV all to ourselves to sneak aboard and ride in secret."

She smiled widely at him. "What can I say? I have the world's best job."

Tomas and his men had formed a tight phalanx around her and Hake. As a group they ran to the train and piled aboard fast and quiet. Within thirty seconds of entering the train car, Casey thought she felt it ease into motion. She lifted the edge of a shade enough to verify that they were moving. Okay, that was cool. The TGV had been waiting just for them.

"How long will it take us to get to Nice?" Hake asked.

"Seven hours," Casey replied. "There's a private sleeping compartment at the back of the car. You might want to get some rest. It'll be morning when we get to Nice and Vanessa scheduled a press conference for you at the hotel shortly after we arrive."

"Efficient, isn't she?" Hake grumbled.

Casey smiled. "That's us. We waste no time getting to the point."

"Oh, I don't know about that," he drawled. "You took your time last night…to good effect, I might add."

And in a single sentence, the air between them was thick and charged with sexual vibes that hung as heavy as jungle vines. His gaze smoldered. "Come with me?" he murmured. She glanced doubtfully at Tomas and his men and Hake added, "They may as well get used to seeing you be my girlfriend now. We'll be going public soon enough."

His *girlfriend*. The word rattled through her, unfamiliar and thrilling, and hard to fathom.

"Please? I sleep better with a woman in my arms."

She laughed. "Now that's a great pickup line."

"But it's true."

"Oh, I believe you. That's what makes it such a great line."

As darkness enclosed them in the tiny compartment, Hake seemed to fill the entire space. It was odd and thrilling feeling so small and relatively weak around anyone. He stripped her clothes off by feel and she returned the favor, loving the texture of his body beneath her hands.

The bed was already folded down, and he laid her upon it gently. He stretched out beside her, and she did, indeed, cuddle up to him, more comfortable than anyone had a right to be. His chest rose and fell slowly beneath her ear and she reveled in being with him. They might not have forever, or even have long, but they had now. And now was pretty nice.

The train was nearly as smooth and powerful as Hake's lovemaking as the miles flew past. Eventually, they collapsed in each other's arms, sated and exhausted, and slept. When Hake finally shifted beneath her as dawn peeked around the window shades, she smiled up at him sleepily and was warmed to her toes by the easy smile he gave her back.

Tomas startled her by calling from the other side of the door, "We'll be arriving in approximately ten minutes, sir. Miss Casey's colleague, Vanessa, has confirmed that your hotel suite is ready. A limousine is waiting for us at the train station and French Special Forces will be driving the vehicle. They are also performing a security sweep of your accommodations as we speak."

"Thank you," Hake called back.

"My people didn't arrange for the limo or the security sweep," Casey muttered, alarmed.

Hake kissed the end of her nose lightly. "The El Aran name is not without a certain influence. I suspect my father made calls to a few friends in the French government."

Sometimes she forgot the guy was practically Bhoukari royalty. "Right. Well, I'd better freshen up a bit if I'm to look even vaguely worthy to be seen on your arm."

He laughed as she climbed out of the narrow bed. "No one will ever mistake you for arm fluff, my dear."

"Drat. I guess I'll have to try harder, then."

He grinned. "I can't wait to see this."

She made a face at him as she reached for her makeup

bag. She emerged from the tiny private bathroom just as the train was pulling into the station.

It was a strange sensation letting Tomas and his men sweep her along in their midst as if she was the one being protected. They were tall enough that she couldn't see a darned thing past them, which made her jumpy. A black limousine loomed in front of them and someone put a hand on her head to guide her inside.

Familiar, strong arms gathered her close in the dark interior. "There's my girl," Hake murmured.

She snuggled close to him with a sigh of pleasure. The ride to the hotel, a posh beachside resort, was all too short. They pulled into an underground loading dock and took a back elevator up to their penthouse suite, completely out of sight of the public. The message light was blinking on the phone in the living room when they arrived. Hake took the message and then passed the receiver to her. "It's for you."

Casey sat down beside him to listen to the message from Vanessa Blake, who ran through their schedule for the day—the press conference and then various television interviews with major news networks for most of the afternoon to talk to Hake about his close call with death. Vanessa ended with, "I'll leave tonight's itinerary to Hake to arrange. Far be it from me to tell the master how to play wildly and visibly. Oh, and Hornet arranged a little gift for you to help with the mission."

She glanced over at Hake. "Did you hear the bit about tonight?"

He grinned. "Aye, aye, captain. Wild and visible it is. Who's Hornet, by the way?"

"Roxi. She's the fashion stylist who helped me develop the Cassandra look."

"The woman is a goddess. Although she had an exquisite canvas to paint upon."

Casey smiled skeptically. "Careful or you'll give me a fat head."

"All women deserve to be spoiled a little. Good romance is in the details."

And apparently he had every last detail down to a fine science. One of Tomas's men came in to announce that the hotel laundry was steaming Hake's suit for the press conference. It would be back in ten minutes, and breakfast was on its way up.

Wow. They'd only been here a grand total of about two minutes. She asked Hake curiously, "Do all hotels race around trying to anticipate your every whim like this?"

He glanced up from the *London Times* the guard had handed him. "I suppose they do. I don't pay much attention to it."

She snorted. Why should he, when everything ran like a well-oiled machine around him, and his smallest need was met before he even knew he had it?

He rose to his feet and offered a hand down to her. "Breakfast, my dear?"

He read the financial sections of a half-dozen newspapers over the meal while she glanced through the world news. He ran once through the prepared statement H.O.T. Watch had worked up for him and faxed to the hotel.

"Do you need me to fire some practice questions at you to get you ready for the media?" Casey offered.

Hake grinned. "No, thanks. I deal with the worst elements of the press on a daily basis. Nothing these guys can throw at me will trip me up."

She wished she was that confident. After breakfast she

went into her bedroom to check out Roxi's gift. She didn't see anything out of the ordinary, other than an incredibly elegant room that she could never dream of affording on her own. She peeked in the bathroom—nothing. And then she opened the closet. The row of garment bags sent a thrill of delight down her spine. Oh, Lord. She was turning into a girly girl by the second.

Each bag had an index card pinned to it with instructions on when to wear it, how to accessorize the outfit and even instructions for what lingerie each required. She grinned. Roxi knew her too well.

She found a bag labeled "Press Conference." It held a gray, pin-striped suit that was nice, but looked about four sizes too small for her. Frowning, she took it into the bathroom and tried it on. The jacket turned out to be a cute, cropped cut and the skirt—what there was of it—was a mini that, along with the four-inch stilettos in the bag, made her legs look a mile long. Casey twisted her hair up into a loose French knot and secured it with the crystal-encrusted barrette that had been provided for the purpose. There were even hose and hoop earrings in the bag. The diagram of how to apply her makeup and what shades to wear in front of television cameras might have been insulting if she didn't know what a perfectionist Roxi was. Laughing, Casey pulled out her cell phone and dialed her teammate.

Roxi didn't bother to say hello but burst out, "Do you love it?"

"How could I not? Thanks, Rox. How did you arrange all this?"

"The hotel's concierge hooked me up with a local personal shopper. She took pictures of clothes in the stores and sent them to me, and I told her what to buy. Did she leave you instructions for everything? I told her you were totally fashion-challenged."

"I'm not that bad. I can do my own stage makeup now."

"Yes, but if you did that for daytime wear, you'd look like a very scary clown."

"Maybe you'd better fly down here and keep an eye on me, Mom."

Roxi laughed. "We'll be joining you in a day or two. Vanessa wants us to run standoff surveillance on you and your hunky boyfriend."

Casey winced. Yup, the gig would be up the moment her teammates watched her and Hake together. She lied and said, "I'll look forward to having you guys close by for support."

"Just be careful until we get there. These are seriously bad dudes we're messing with. You were lucky in London."

Thus sobered, Casey hung up the phone and stepped out into the living room. Hake glanced up from a faxed document and did a gratifying double take. He held out the papers and someone took them out of his hand as he strode over to her. He took both of her hands in his. "You look fantastic."

"You look pretty snazzy yourself," she replied shyly. His tailored suit lay across his shoulders without a single crease, the starched shirt pristine, the silk tie perfectly knotted.

"It's time for us to go, sir," Tomas announced.

Hake held out his arm to her with a smile. "Shall we?"

She slipped her hand into the crook of his elbow. "We shall."

Tomas and his men escorted them into a ballroom with

a stage set up across one end of it. Lights already blazed as reporters made preliminary reports. A buzz went up and all eyes—and cameras—turned on Hake.

Casey jolted. "Holy cow."

Hake murmured back, "This is nothing. Wait till a horde of paparazzi turns on us."

"Hoo yeah," she muttered.

Hake was as smooth and polished in front of the press as any politician. He read the statement expressing his condolences for those injured in the London bombing, thanked the local law enforcement, fire and medical crews who had responded to the incident and promised to do all he could to help the British government find and bring to justice those responsible for the bombing.

The questions, predictably, focused on how Hake had gotten out of the nightclub unharmed and where he'd been since. Casey was impressed at how adroitly he dodged the questions. As he'd promised, no mention of any female commandos was made. And then the question they'd all been waiting for came out of the crowd. A reporter shouted, "What do you plan to do now, Mr. El Aran?"

Hake turned toward the voice and fired off one of his patented bad-boy grins. "I nearly died in that blast. Now I plan to celebrate being alive as hard as I possibly can."

"Who's the girl?" another reporter shouted.

Hake blandly ignored the question as Vanessa and company had suggested. The more mystery surrounding Casey, the more media frenzy would be whipped up. She could only pray the cover story H.O.T. Watch had put in place for her would hold up to scrutiny.

Hake thanked the journalists and stepped down off the stage. Tomas had strategically placed her at the foot of the steps leading off the dais, and Hake headed straight for her. He dropped a kiss on her startled mouth. As he turned her loose, he murmured, "No turning back now. It's you and me, together all the way."

The two of them together? All the way? She liked the sound of that a whole lot more than she wanted to admit. And to think. The fun was just getting started. She gulped. What on God's green earth had she gotten herself into?

Chapter 12

Hake knew just the place. The French Riviera was known for its nightclubs, but one discotheque stood out from all the rest when it came to wild parties and high-end clientele: The Grotto. It was possible to get to the place by water and walk down its private pier to the club. Or there was the newcomer's traditional way of arriving. Seeing as he and Casey were supposed to be making a splash, he chose the latter.

As they stepped out of the limo in front of the sleepy little bar, Tomas looked at him questioningly. Hake muttered, "I wouldn't want to deprive her of the full experience."

Tomas shrugged. "It's your funeral, sir."

Casey glanced back and forth between them suspiciously. Hake ushered her into the dim joint. It was narrow and deep and crowded with bistro tables. She frowned up at him. "I thought we were going to a hopping nightclub."

He grinned back. "We're there."

Her frown deepened. "What's the joke?"

"No joke. Come with me." He couldn't keep a grin from playing at the corners of his mouth as he led her to the back of the club. "We have to separate for a moment, I'm afraid. If you'll step into the ladies' restroom, I'll head into the men's room with Tomas and the boys. We'll meet you after that."

As she stared in confusion, he swept into the men's room with his bodyguards. "Hurry, Tomas," Hake muttered. "I want to beat her downstairs."

"She's going to kill you," Tomas muttered back.

Hake grinned. "That's the beauty of it. She can't. She's under strict orders to act madly infatuated with me."

"I'm not saving you from her when you get back to the hotel. That woman scares me. And besides, you'll deserve it…sir."

Hake grinned at his guard and stepped over to the fire pole mounted in the corner. He slid through the hole in the floor and dropped easily onto the red velvet sofa below. A bell rang and a crowd of partiers applauded him as he sprawled on the cushions. He had to roll aside fast, though, because Tomas and his men weren't about to leave Hake unattended for long. Hake regained his feet, straightened his clothes, and turned to wait for Casey to join him on the pole from the ladies' room.

He should have known that landing in an unceremonious heap on a couch was not Casey's idea of a grand entrance. Her feet appeared through the gap in the ceiling. The bartender commenced ringing his bell to announce her arrival. Casey's red stiletto heels alone were naughty enough to set a guy's heart pounding.

Slowly, she twirled down the pole. Her shapely calves came into sight, then her knees and thighs. Her dress slid nearly up to her hips, and the crowd whistled and cat-called as she spun down, her legs gripping the pole in a way that made a man break out in a sweat.

She let go with one hand and leaned back, exposing her throat to everyone and nearly exposing her breasts as her low-cut dress pulled tight across her swelling chest. Eyes closed and a look of sexual ecstasy on her face, she slid slowly down the last dozen inches. The club drew a collective breath of appreciation, and then the place went wild.

She landed on her feet like the sofa was her own personal throne and held an imperious hand out to Hake. Grinning, he stepped forward and steadied her as she stepped down regally.

"Nice entrance," he murmured under the din. "In case I haven't mentioned it recently, your legs are perfect. In fact, all of you is just about perfect."

Her mouth smiled flirtatiously, but her eyes glinted an amused dare at him. "What next? Are we supposed to have a big fight and tear each other's clothes off by way of making up or something?"

He laughed. "Although that would undoubtedly land us on the pages of the tabloids, I think your spectacular entrance rather took care of that. Let's circulate a bit and make sure to run into, and then snub, all the undercover gossip columnists. They know I hate being splashed across the gossip rags, so if I tick them off, they should have a field day."

"You know who all these undercover reporters are?"

"If I told you a crazed terrorist was in this room, could you find him?"

She blinked. "I expect I could. It is my job, after all."

"There you have it. Spotting reporters is my field of expertise."

"Fair enough." She smiled bravely. "Lead on."

Oh, how he did want to lead her on. But not here. Not like this. She was the kind of woman who deserved better than being publicly flaunted like a cheap prize—or a very expensive one as the case might be. An image of his married sisters, safe in their homes with doting husbands, flashed through his head. Hake stopped cold, stunned.

The last thing he wanted was a traditional Bhoukari marriage with a traditional Bhoukari woman. But all of a sudden, he comprehended the concept of privacy in a relationship as a good thing. Not that he'd ever bothered to provide it for a woman before. He lived a fast, visible life, and any woman who wanted to be with him could deal with it.

Then why did he want to take off his suit coat and put it around Casey's shoulders? To gather her protectively close and take her someplace quiet where they could be alone… even if it was only to talk? Why were his teeth gnashing at the idea of every other male in this place ogling her like a piece of meat?

"I'm sorry, Casey," he murmured.

She threw him a perplexed look, but the dance music cranked up painfully loud just then, and they were swept along with the crowd out into the middle of the dance floor.

This was one place he didn't have to worry about Casey handling herself. The woman simply knew how to translate music to movement. Envious looks flew his way fast and furious from the men, and jealous looks from the female patrons shot Casey's way.

At one point he leaned forward to shout in her ear, "Having fun?"

"Yes! It's nice not to have to worry about giving everyone else a good show."

At least one of them was having fun. Maybe it was the

business of waiting for someone to try to kill him again that had him on edge. Or maybe it was his grossly mistaken expectation of being amused when the other men circled his woman like a pack of sharks. But tonight, he found himself clenching his jaw a lot and exhibiting an unusual tendency to touch Casey's arm or rest a hand on her back as they moved on and off the dance floor.

Long after he was ready to take a break from dancing and wet his throat, Casey finally nodded to him. He led her into the next room, which was ringed by a long bar and dotted with sofas.

"You've killed me, woman," Hake declared.

She laughed. "What we just did is not a fraction as strenuous as Middle Eastern dance. Are you admitting, then, that belly dancers are buff?"

"I concede the point." He toasted her with a bottle of water.

They chatted as best they could over the blaring music. At around midnight, the DJ thankfully backed down on the volume, and Casey was able to ask reasonably normally, "Why'd he turn down the noise attack?"

"The patrons need to start working their pickup lines," Hake answered in amusement.

"Seriously?" Casey asked in surprise, looking around.

"Yes."

"So. Is it customary for you to hit on the women or do they hit on you?"

He blinked at the frank question. "I suppose it's more of a mutual thing. I see a beautiful woman, she sees me. We meet, we talk, we—" He didn't know how to finish that sentence tastefully.

"Go back to your place for hot sex?" Casey supplied drily.

"When you put it like that, it sounds cheap. Boring."

"How would you put it?" she asked.

He stared at her for a stunned moment. "Now that I think about it, I suppose the whole business is rather cheap and boring."

Her eyebrows went up. She seemed almost as surprised as he felt. Since when was he tired of the playboy life?

Casey commented quietly, "I'm sorry to be cramping your style like this."

"On the contrary. You're enhancing my reputation spectacularly."

"And what, exactly, is that reputation?"

He leaned close and murmured, "I always go home with the most beautiful woman in the place."

Casey turned a critical eye on the rest of the club. "I don't know about that. The blonde in the corner is stunning. Maybe we should go set you up with her. Or maybe you prefer a more exotic look. Like that African woman—the tall, slender one with the incredible eyes. Or—"

"I'm already with the most beautiful woman in the place," he interrupted gently.

She shook her head. "I don't think so."

Hake captured Casey's ice-cold fingers to keep her from bolting from him. He asked, "What's going on? Are you panicking on me?"

She mumbled, "What do you mean?"

"I came with you. I'm leaving with you. Unless, of course, you want me to go flirt with one of those other women so you can get into a catfight and hit the tabloids that way."

"I'd accidentally kill someone. I'm not accustomed to holding back when I fight."

Hake laughed. "Duly noted."

Casey spoke in a businesslike fashion. "Okay, I've dirty

danced for you. And now you're holding my hand. What's next?"

"You don't have to sound like I'm about to extract your tooth with pliers. The idea is to relax. Have fun."

"No, the idea is to draw attention to you. To get your... friends...to show themselves."

He sighed. She'd lost the spirit of fun from earlier, apparently. She was going to hide behind the whole playing-soldier thing unless... Inspired, he murmured, "It's time for you to crawl onto my lap."

"I beg your pardon?" Casey looked alarmed.

"You need to drape yourself all over me. Imagine yourself tipsy, bordering on drunk enough to lose all inhibition. Trust me. It's how these transactions are conducted."

Reluctance in her eyes was replaced by grim determination. Didn't like mauling him in public, did she? They were in agreement on that score, then. Nonetheless, she leaned across him, ostensibly to set her drink on the end table beyond his elbow. And when she was physically draped across him, she glanced up. The sidelong look she gave him was so incendiary that he felt his clothing and various body parts catching on fire.

"Okay, I'm draped," she murmured. "Now what?"

"Uh—" he cleared his throat "—now we should probably kiss."

She leaned forward until her mouth was barely an inch from his. "Like this?" she whispered.

"Uh, yes. Exactly." And then her luscious mouth was on his, moving coaxingly, as if she thought he needed encouragement to go crazy for her. Her head tilted and she kissed him more aggressively. Her body pulsed forward, her chest coming up hard against his, her arm going around his neck wantonly.

Lights exploded inside his head and shock vibrated

through him. This was more than lust. More than man-sees-woman, man-wants-woman. This dug deep into his gut. Soul deep. The difference between a little buzz and a hopeless addiction. She flowed over him and through him like the finest wine, warm and spicy and complex.

Thankfully, she eventually came up gasping for air because he had no power to do so himself. He blinked, surprised to find himself in a dance club with people and noise and lights around him. Tomas was grinning like a Cheshire cat.

"Did I get it right?" Casey murmured low.

He laughed shortly. "If you got it much more right, you'd have killed me."

She smiled and slid coyly off his lap. If Casey wasn't an old pro at this game, she was, at a minimum, a hell of an actress. She fit into the party scene as if she was born to it. Meanwhile, he felt out of his depth. What in the hell had she done to him?

He was *still* flummoxed when, about an hour later, she leaned in close and murmured, "The patrons are starting to hook up. They'll be leaving soon. If you and I are going to make a grand exit, now's the time, while we still have a good audience."

His gut clenched. He ought to kiss her again. But he was suddenly terrified of doing so. What if that other kiss hadn't been temporary insanity? What if he was losing himself to her?

What was this? The great ladies' man, Hake El Aran, afraid? Of a simple kiss? Bah. He'd kissed so many women over the years he couldn't even begin to guess how many. Some of them had been pretty spectacular kissers, too. Casey had just surprised him. He hadn't expected her to throw herself into that earlier kiss with quite so much unbridled enthusiasm.

He leaned forward cautiously. She was just a woman. It would be just a kiss.

He drew her across his body to prove to himself that he could do so without losing control. Except as her softness and heat molded to him, he couldn't help relishing the sensation. He swore under his breath. Apparently, she was a fix of heroin and he an overdue junkie after all.

One kiss. And then he'd let her go.

Except when his lips touched hers, everything else evaporated, leaving only them in this magical place of pleasure and unslaked need. She tasted like coconut and rum—sweet and spicy. Dammit, she was as addictive as he remembered. It *hadn't* been his imagination! He speared his hands into her thick, silky hair and shamelessly drank from her, feeding on the taste and scent of her until his head spun madly. And then she all but ate him alive.

He couldn't think about anything but getting that dress off her and pulling her down on top of him while he plunged into her. His hand slipped under one of the garment's thin spaghetti straps while his other hand climbed her thigh, sliding under the hem of the slinky little dress. Ah, yes. Silken flesh. About to be naked and joined with him. His woman. Need to possess her pounded through him.

A throat cleared nearby. "Uh, boss?"

Hake tore his mouth away from Casey's long enough to glare at Tomas. He was about to turn back to making love to her when a bright mirror flash got in his eye. He swore to himself. He was in a nightclub. A very public nightclub. With an avid audience watching him and Casey all but devour each other.

Violent impulses ripped through him. "Later," he managed to grit out at her from between his clenched teeth. "When we're alone." He forced his hand to push the shoulder strap of her dress back up and smoothed her hem down her thigh before, through sheer dint of will, making himself set her aside.

He was not the kind of man who fell on any woman like a wild animal. Ever. But he literally shook with the effort of restraining himself. He put his hand on the small of her back and guided her toward the seaside exit. "Get us out of here," he managed to order Tomas.

The chilly night air cleared his head a little, and the long walk down the pier to the powerful speedboat his men had waiting made him feel a little more sane. But not much. Why was he so freaked out? They were already together. He'd even promised her he might consider marrying her. Was he really that big a commitment-phobe? Or was it something else? Was he developing *real* feelings for a woman? Was that what was messing with his head so badly?

No doubt about it. He'd lost his mind tonight. To a seductress sweeter than honey, hotter than fire and more mysterious than the rarest burgundy.

"Let's go back to the hotel, shall we, darling?" he murmured.

"Uh-huh." She sounded drugged, or perhaps so lost in lust she could hardly see straight. He felt a tiny bit better knowing he was not the only one so afflicted.

In a few minutes, they reached their hotel's pier. When they arrived at the penthouse, she kicked off her high heels and joined Tomas's men in sweeping the suite. It was disconcerting how quickly she shifted from sexy girlfriend to all-business soldier.

His head spun and he couldn't seem to clear it. He'd had very little to drink—he'd been far too busy enjoying Casey. It was one thing to talk hypothetically to her about a permanent relationship, but it was another thing entirely to see it starting to develop.

"Are you tired?" she murmured under her breath to him.

"Need to think," he mumbled. "You must be tired… Let you rest… See you in the morning…" He headed for the master bedroom, vaguely aware of Casey staring at him as he stumbled to his room. Someone closed the door behind him, and his bodyguards looked back and forth between him and the closed portal in amazement.

Frankly, he was pretty damned amazed himself. He couldn't remember the last time he'd had strong enough feelings for a woman to forgo sex in the name of honoring both her and those feelings.

Casey leaned against the closed door of her bedroom, unsure whether to sob in heartbreak or scream in fury. *One night.* That was his idea of a long-term relationship? One lousy night? Well, okay, one night, one train ride and one sexy date. Big diff.

And to think she'd been letting down her guard with him for real in the club, exploring her feminine side and discovering to her great shock that she enjoyed flirting with the right man.

She ought to be thanking her lucky stars that the jerk had dumped her this fast and hard before she really got emotionally invested in him. Right? Then why did she feel as if her stomach had just been used as a punching bag?

She stripped off her clingy little dress, threw on sweat pants and a sloppy T-shirt, scrubbed off her makeup and crawled into bed. And waited for relief from the grief and desire ricocheting through her body like out-of-control bullets.

She couldn't possibly have more than an infatuation for Hake after such a short time. This would pass in a day or two. It was just lust. A crush. None of this was real.

One thing she knew for sure: Hake El Aran had no idea

whatsoever of how to have a real relationship. She felt sorry for whoever his father forced him to marry. The poor girl was in for a miserable and loveless life.

As for her, she wanted more.

At least she hadn't made too huge a fool of herself in front of Hake's bodyguards. Sure she'd crawled all over Hake in the club, but they all knew that was just part of the act. The last thing she needed to do was have a torrid affair with Hake El Aran in front of his men. Word would get back to the Special Forces community in a heartbeat, and she would never hear the end of it. Yup. She'd dodged a bullet tonight.

Then why did she feel as if a bullet had torn right through the middle of her heart?

Chapter 13

Grumpy and tired the next morning, Casey dressed for exercise. She needed to do something physical and violent. Sleep—or a notable lack of it—had made two things clear to her. She'd definitely cared more for Hake than she'd realized. And just as definitely, she'd narrowly avoided destroying her reputation and career.

In that same vein, as satisfying as it would be to tear out Hake's eyeballs, she had a job to do. Terrorists to catch. She had to suck up her personal hurt feelings and go on with the mission. But from here on out, it would damned well be on her terms. Girding herself to face Hake, she stepped out of her room.

He had his nose buried in a newspaper and said little to her over breakfast, which was just fine with her. She ate a light meal, and then turned to Tomas. "So, am I going down to the gym to work out, or can you and your guys make me break a sweat?"

The bodyguards grinned as one. Tomas, dressed in jeans and a polo shirt, replied, "Thought you'd never ask. Full contact or just to the touch?"

She laughed. "What's the point if it's not full contact?"

Hake's newspaper came down. "What are you talking about?"

She answered breezily, "Nothing. Go back to your stock quotes."

The guards were already pushing the furniture out of the middle of the living room. "Street rules?" Tomas asked eagerly.

She nodded and stepped into the clear space. The Swiss man stepped forward and the two of them circled each other for a few moments, assessing one another. Then he lunged. She slipped to the side and dropped him like a rock with a blow to the back of the head as he charged past. It was classic Medusa strategy. Don't try to overpower a stronger opponent. Just don't be there when he attacked.

The other men stared. Tomas got up slowly, shaking his head. "I knew you'd be fast, but not that fast."

"Try again?" she asked him.

He nodded and settled into a fighting stance once more. This time he was cautious, focusing his efforts on wrapping his arms around her. It was a good tactic. Why chase her if he could make her stand still? But it still took him nearly ten minutes of grappling and lunging to finally subdue her. "Uncle," she announced good-naturedly from within a crushing bear hug.

Tomas grunted, "This is only a stalemate. As soon as I turn you loose, you'll be back at full strength. And in the meantime, I can't do anything else because it's taking all my energy to restrain you."

"If you had a partner you'd be okay," she pointed out.

"Still, that means I'd have to use two men to take you

out." Tomas turned her loose and she leaped to her feet and whipped around to face him all in one movement. He was ready for the attack, though, and mostly fended off the rain of blows she loosed on him.

"Hey!" Hake called sharply. "We've got places to go and be seen. Don't give the girlfriend a black eye!"

Tomas stopped fighting instantly, and it was only by dint of her excellent reflexes that she stopped her fist from plowing into the man's nose and breaking it. She turned to Hake, who scowled. She'd never seen him look that mad before, not even when he'd learned that terrorists had tried to kill him.

She answered tartly, "If I did get a black eye, you could always tell the paparazzi that you and I got carried away with rough sex. It would do wonders for your reputation as a bad boy."

His scowl deepened even more. He bit out angrily, "I don't hit women."

She took the towel one of the men offered her, wiping her face as she strolled over to him. "Good for you. I'd hate to have to break you in half."

He glared at her. "You know, it's not the slightest bit attractive to say things like that to a man."

She draped the towel over her shoulder. "Where is it written that women have to be wilting lilies to be attractive? Why should I pretend not to be strong and able to take care of myself so a man like you can feel macho and protective?"

He stared at her. "Don't you want a man to take care of you?"

She stared back. And then laughed shortly. "I can take care of myself."

"Then what's a man good for in your world?"

Maybe it was because he'd taken her by surprise, or

maybe it was because he'd pissed her off with his brush-off, or maybe it was because a tiny part of her did like the idea of a big, strong man looking out for her that she snapped, "In my experience, men are only good for one thing." She waggled her eyebrows suggestively, then continued, "And barring that, they're only good for decoration."

Hake stared at her in open shock. Apparently, having his philosophy about women thrown back in his face was like having a bucket of ice water dumped over his head. She snorted. That was just too darned bad.

She turned on her heel and marched into her room to take a shower. Only after spending a good long time under the soothing jets could she admit to herself that men—some men, at any rate—were good for other things. When they weren't being insecure about the girl doing too dangerous and manly a job, that was. Did the other Medusas get that from their men, or was it just her? Was she really a man-hater at heart? She'd never thought so, but now she wondered. Was *she* the problem?

Maybe love just wasn't in the cards for her. The idea of falling in love with someone else at the same time they happened to fall in love back was a minor miracle. Throw in a whacky career like hers and the odds went even higher against finding that perfect guy at the perfect moment.

It was all well and good to fantasize about a man like Hake El Aran. But one thing she knew for sure: he would never love anyone except himself, and surely not a woman like her.

Hake was losing his mind. Casey had pulled back from him abruptly and completely, and nothing he could say or do seemed to get through to her. Here he was, falling in love with the woman, and she acted as if she wanted nothing to do with him. Women were the most contrary and incomprehensible creatures on the planet!

The next several days settled into a steady and infuriating pattern. They avoided each other during the day. At night, he took her out to the sexiest, most crowded venues he could find. They all but made love to each other in public, and each time magic swept over them, transporting them to a special place where only the two of them existed. It was extraordinary. He fell in love a little more with her each night…and returned to their hotel room at dawn each morning where she retreated to her bedroom alone.

When he confronted her, she made lame excuses about not wanting to ruin her reputation, or she claimed to need to concentrate on the mission. The mission was to *be* his girlfriend, dammit, not just play-act it for a few hours each night! If she did deign to join him for a meal, she treated him with polite disdain as if they were total strangers. It was maddening.

Every trick of seduction he tried backfired more spectacularly than the last. He sent her a dozen red roses, and she gave them to the maid. He sent her ten dozen red roses, and she donated them to a local hospital. He sent her an expensive necklace, and he found out from one of the bodyguards that she'd returned it to the jeweler and donated the money to a women's shelter. He considered buying her something truly outrageous like a sports car or a jet, but in his heart he knew that wouldn't be any more effective than what he'd already tried.

Finally, in desperation, he went to Tomas. "Do you happen to have the phone number of the women Casey works with?" he asked his man.

Tomas was alarmed. "Is there a new threat I should know about, sir?"

Only to his sanity. He shook his head. "Nothing like that. It's personal."

Understanding lit the guard's eyes. "Ah. Do you want her boss or her best friend?"

How was it that his men knew who her best friend was and he didn't? He frowned. "The best friend."

"That would be Roxi. Here's her cell phone number."

Hake waited impatiently until it was a semi-civilized time to call someone in the United States, and then he dialed the woman's number.

"Hello?" a cautious voice answered at the other end.

"Hello. This is Hake El Aran."

"Is everything all right? Is Scorpion in trouble?" the woman asked in quick alarm.

"I'm the one in trouble," he replied grimly.

"What's happening?"

"I'm crashing and burning—"

"Say your location," she interrupted tersely. "I'll have emergency response en route immediately."

"No, no. I'm crashing and burning metaphorically."

"Excuse me?"

"I called you to get some advice. About Casey."

"Are we talking romantic advice here?" The woman sounded incredulous. Frankly, so was he that he was making this call.

"Well, yes," he admitted.

There was a long pause. Then a slow chuckle. Then an outright laugh. He endured it grimly, determined to figure out once and for all what had changed Casey's tune for the worse.

Finally the woman's mirth mostly subsided. "Striking out with our girl, are you?"

"In a word, yes."

"And you want my help getting through to her?"

"Yes," he bit out.

"Let me ask you this, Mr. El Aran. What makes you think you're good enough for her?"

His back stiffened. "I beg your pardon?" What was she talking about? Women all over the world were after him. He was a prime catch…wasn't he?

Her voice interrupted his indignant thoughts. "Why should I help you?"

The question startled him. "Because I want her."

"And you always get what you want?"

He didn't answer the question, stung.

"There's your first problem. Casey's not the type to go for arrogant men. She's a strong, independent woman. She wants a partner, not a lord and master."

"I don't boss her around—" he started.

"I'm sure you don't. She'd kick your butt if you tried."

He closed his eyes and took a deep breath. He would suffer through this humiliating conversation if it was the last thing he did. He was at his wit's end. "Tell me more about her."

"She's had exactly two boyfriends in her life that I'm aware of. She was engaged to both. One ultimately couldn't handle her being hired by the FBI. The other couldn't handle her becoming a soldier."

Hake frowned. Her career was so important to her that she'd sacrificed two men she loved for it? He'd had no idea. "What else?"

"Look. This is none of my business, Mr. El Aran. I trust her judgment. If she doesn't like you, she probably has a pretty good reason for it."

"But what reason?" he ground out, as much to himself as to the woman at the other end of the line. "She hasn't told me what it is."

"Have you asked her?" Roxi asked. "The women in our

unit can be a bit more direct than most. Too much of what we do is life-and-death stuff. We can't afford to pussyfoot around issues that come up."

He cringed at the idea of baring his soul to Casey. It went against everything he was. His life had been one long fight for privacy.

When he remained silent, Roxi said gently, "If you won't let her in, why should she let you in?"

Still he said nothing. Roxi made one last comment. "Casey is one of very few women working in an entirely male world. We all have had to fight tooth and nail to gain the respect of the men around us, to deserve and get equal treatment. If she's fought so hard to eliminate a double standard in her career, surely you can't expect her to abide by a double standard in matters of the heart."

He made a noncommittal sound, his mind running far ahead of the conversation at hand.

"Good luck, Mr. El Aran. I hope I've been of some assistance to you." The line went dead in his ear. He stared at the instrument for a long time.

He could accept Casey's career. And to his shock, he could even wrap his mind around making a long-term commitment to her. But she expected him to open his heart to her completely, with no reservations?

No way. He couldn't do it.

Casey was getting tired of the jet-set life. Quickly. The great clothes and fancy clubs were all starting to look the same. No wonder the celebrities in the tabloids always seemed so bored. They were. The late nights didn't agree with her, and waiting for someone to try to kill Hake grated on her nerves. And then there was the man himself. Fighting the jumble inside her of lust and simultaneous urge to kill him made thinking coherently a challenge.

But she knew not to give in to any of it. The more time she spent with him, the more obvious the man didn't have the first clue how to conduct an actual relationship.

She dragged herself out of bed at nearly noon yet again and dressed in a pale yellow dress that reminded her of something she might have worn to Easter church services as a little girl. According to Roxi and her French stylist pal, though, it was appropriate attire for the polo match she and Hake were slated to attend this afternoon. At least Hake had relented on the subject of playing in the match. He'd been determined to ride until his father was finally recruited to call and talk him out of it.

Hake had been surly ever since that call yesterday. Not that she blamed him. It would bug her to death if her father tried to control her life at her age.

She paused in front of her door, going through the daily ritual of girding herself to face Hake. His sheer beauty never failed to hit her like a sucker punch to the gut. She threw open the door and marched into the main room. Oh, Lord. He wore a white linen suit with the palest of pale blue shirts. His tie was pale blue and white striped. From head to toe, he looked like a royal prince. She gulped and hoped desperately that he didn't notice the check in her stride when she'd spotted him.

"Good morning," she murmured distantly.

"Good morning, Casey. How are you feeling today?" he asked mildly.

She started over the distinctly different note in his voice. It alarmed her. She felt much safer when he was all but humming with frustration. "I'm fine, thank you. And you?"

He nodded slowly. "Better."

"Better than what?" she asked cautiously.

"Hungry?" he asked, blatantly ignoring her question.

"I guess so."

"Would you like to dine out on the terrace? It's a lovely day."

What the heck was going on with him? He hadn't been this polite to her in days. "Uh, sure. If Tomas thinks it's safe."

"I already cleared brunch on the terrace with him. He muttered something incomprehensible about sight lines and high ground but declared it safe."

Casey smiled. Since the resort was one of the tallest buildings in the city, the penthouse would, indeed, be difficult to shoot at. Hake held open the door for her, and she slipped by him, concentrating with all her might on not reacting as she passed close to him.

She craved their nights on the town like she craved air to breathe. She counted the hours until she could let go of her precarious self-control and crawl all over him, kissing him and putting her hands on him and giving herself to him the way she wanted to.

Not here, she thought sharply. They weren't out in public. She had to behave until then. *Not yet.*

Check that. *Not ever.*

Hake seated her himself, forcing her to brush past him again. She was intimately familiar with his scent now, but it still sent a rush of excitement up her spine.

"I took the liberty of ordering up brunch for us," he said quietly. "I don't mean to presume, but I thought you might not want to wait for the meal to be prepared. If you don't like what I chose, by all means, feel free to order something else."

She gazed at him quizzically. "What are you up to?"

A faint frown crossed his face, but then his features settled back into patience. "I haven't been exactly good company the past few days, and I owe you an apology."

"You have a lot on your plate," she commented carefully.

"But that gives me no right to treat you badly. You're in as much danger as I am and certainly under as much pressure as I am."

She shrugged. "It's my job. I'm accustomed to functioning under high levels of stress."

"Tell me more about your work."

She frowned. "Why do you ask?"

"It's important to you. Therefore, I'm interested in it."

"What do you want to know?"

"Tell me about these women you work with."

Crud. Not territory she wanted to explore too deeply. "Some women work in the Special Forces. I'm one of them."

"What's that like? Do the men treat you all right?"

She laughed shortly. "What are you going to do? Beat them up if they don't?"

"If you need me to. But I suspect you could teach them a lesson all by yourself without any help from me."

She leaned back in her chair, studying him intently. Why the sudden and complete change in his attitude? Was this some new head game from him? A new and improved tactic to maneuver her back into his bed?

He leaned forward. "Casey, I'm sorry for whatever I've done to make you angry and uncomfortable. I know this business of publicly posing as my girlfriend has been difficult for you, but I wanted to tell you I think you've done a magnificent job."

She glanced down at the stack of gossip rags beside his plate. "How many did we make it into today?"

"All of them. We're the hottest gossip in Europe. They're starting to talk about your career as a dancer."

"Have they called me a stripper yet?" she asked drily.

He threw her a sympathetic glance. "A few have. Sorry."

"Why? It's exactly what we were hoping for. The more sensational your behavior, the more it'll infuriate our terrorists. Dating a stripper, and an American one no less, is quite a slap at the terrorists' extremist values."

"I hope you know I don't think of you that way."

She stared at him, startled. It dawned on her all of a sudden that she did think he saw her that way. Furthermore, it had been sticking in her craw for the past week or more. Was she starting to see herself as some kind of high-priced call girl, throwing herself at him indiscriminately every night?

He grimaced. "I can tell by your expression that you don't believe me. I really am sorry we have to…perform… the way we do in public." He added, "I won't deny that I enjoy our flirting. You, of all people, know exactly how much I enjoy it. I only wish we could be more private about it. It's disrespectful to you."

She shrugged, stunned. "It's the nature of the beast," she mumbled.

"For the record, I do respect you. I think you're smart and classy, and you deserve better than this. If only I could be the man to give it to you."

And with that salvo, he got up and left the table. She stared at his back in shock. What did that mean? Did he still want her for real? Or maybe he'd just told her he was giving up on trying to get her back into his bed. Common sense chose the latter.

Tears stung at the backs of her eyelids. All of the wildly inappropriate gifts and steamy flirting from him in the clubs might have driven her crazy, but at least she'd known that, at some level, he was interested in her. Who was she kidding? She was still the plain, boring person she'd always been.

She picked at her brunch listlessly but suddenly didn't feel much like eating. She retreated to her room and tried to study a map of the polo club, but it was all a blur. Her phone rang and she pounced on it desperate for a distraction.

"Hey, kid. It's me."

Roxi.

"How the heck are ya, Case?"

She'd known Roxi long enough to hear the false cheer in her friend's voice. Sure, the girl was always perky, but this was too much. "Why do you ask?" Casey asked cautiously.

"Just thinking about you. Did you get the dresses I sent over yesterday? I had to get those from Paris. I gotta say, you're getting expensive to dress. But we have to make each outfit more spectacular than the last if we want to keep the press's attention."

Casey frowned. "Something's up with Hake. He's acting weird."

"Weird how?"

"I think he's sick of me. I don't know if he's going to be able to keep up the boyfriend-girlfriend charade much longer. I think you need to warn the gang to start thinking up a Plan B."

Roxi laughed. "Not a chance."

"You should've seen him this morning," Casey said glumly. "He was all distant and polite. He wanted to talk about my job, of all things. It's the kiss of death, I tell you."

Roxi laughed harder. "Good for him."

"Excuse me?"

"The only kind of sick your boy is would be *lovesick*."

"Have you lost your mind?" Casey demanded.

"Chica, he called me yesterday, hat in hand, to ask for advice."

"About what?"

"About you, Einstein."

Casey's jaw fell open. "Oh, my God. What did you tell him?"

"I told him you don't like arrogant jerks, you take your career very seriously and you expect unconditional commitment from the men you commit to."

"No wonder he treated me like I had horns coming out of my head and a third eye in the middle of my forehead just now."

"Girlfriend, you've got him completely off balance. He doesn't know which end is coming or going."

Puh-lease. Hake off balance? Over her? Not in this lifetime. She forced herself into soldier mode and replied seriously, "I don't want him off balance. We need him alert and focused. I think our terrorists will strike soon. They've got to be gnashing their teeth at the shenanigans he and I have been up to."

"Any shenanigans happening off camera?"

Casey snorted. "No. I've been ducking and weaving like a prizefighter to keep it that way, though."

"Maybe you shouldn't dodge so hard. He sounds truly smitten with you."

"You don't know Hake El Aran. He snaps his fingers and women come running. I'm not about to be at his beck and call. The two of us would never work."

Roxi sighed. "Too bad. He seems like the kind of guy who, if he opened up to a woman, would be a heck of a catch."

"That's a big if. An impossible if. He'll never open up to anyone," Casey retorted. She didn't mean for the comment to sound bitter, but she feared it did.

"Well, hang in there, kiddo. And keep your chin up. No telling what'll happen."

Casey scowled. "In our line of work, we're supposed to anticipate events before they happen. And I'm seeing a big fat nothing in my future where Hake El Aran is concerned."

"You know what they say—love is blind."

"Ha. Hake is *so* not in love with me."

"Time will tell."

"Stuff it, Rox."

Laughing, her friend ended the call, leaving her scowling at herself in the mirror. She was *not* in love with Hake. Far from it. She wasn't even in *like* with him.

A quiet knock sounded upon her door. Hake's voice floated through the panel. "Casey, it's almost time to leave. Do you need a few more minutes?"

She checked her hair and makeup quickly. Both were fine. She opened the door to frown at Hake. Since when did he fetch her personally for their dates? He held out his arm to her gallantly.

Lovesick, huh? No way.

Chapter 14

Hake idly watched the polo ponies charging up and down the field. The match was actually a good one with a top Spanish team matched against the ever-powerful Argentineans. However, he couldn't seem to keep his mind on the action. His thoughts kept straying to the woman beside him.

She'd reacted with caution toward him at brunch, suspicious of his change in attitude. He supposed he couldn't blame her. If only he knew what she was thinking right now. But no such luck. The woman was a mystery.

How could Casey think that men were only good for one thing? Outrage at the notion soared through him yet again. He was intelligent. Highly educated. Successful. The kind of man any woman would be proud to have.

Sure, the irony of her observation wasn't lost on him. Casey treated him like he treated most—okay, all—women. But that was how the world worked. Men like him attracted a certain kind of woman, and the formula was always the same. Beautiful, ambitious woman seeks rich, handsome, successful man. She would give him all the sex and domestic backup for his career he needed, and in turn, he would provide a lavish lifestyle for her. There was nothing wrong with that, if everyone got what they wanted. Just because he hadn't entered into such an arrangement so far didn't mean it was a bad business model. He merely hadn't found the right woman yet.

A tiny voice in the back of his head suggested that the vast majority of the women he'd dated over the years would have been thrilled to live out that exact relationship model with him. He shoved the thought away, irritated.

What did Casey want anyway? True love? A soul mate? A man who would worship the ground she walked on? Well, she could look somewhere else, then, thank you very much. Women groveled for him. Not the other way around. *Liar, liar, pants on fire.*

Damn that little voice in the back of his head anyway. He *wasn't* missing any important point here! He liked his life just the way it was. He enjoyed the women in his life just the way they were. Except for the woman in his life right now. He wanted to understand her. To know her. To get what it was she expected of him. *But are you prepared to deliver what she wants?* All right, that little voice could shut up now.

When this cursed deal was done and his family safe once more, Casey would go her own way and he would get back to his life. And by then, his father would have forgotten all about this stupid business of forcing Hake to marry.

"Everything all right, Hake?" Casey murmured, leaning over and placing a hand high on his thigh, ostensibly to balance herself. The touch was intimate and possessive and set his blood on fire.

He forced a smile for her. "I'm fine. Enjoying yourself?"

"I had no idea polo was so rough, with the horses slamming into each other like that. It's like hockey, but on horseback."

He smiled. "That's an excellent analogy."

She leaned closer to him, and his arm naturally went around her shoulders. She snuggled against his side, and damned if she didn't feel exactly right there.

He murmured, "What would you like for dinner?"

She made a sound that could've been a laugh, or maybe half a sob. "Some privacy."

"Done," he answered promptly. Profound relief coursed through him. The idea of having Casey entirely to himself, to treat her the way she deserved to be treated for once, was a breath of fresh air to him. He glanced over his shoulder. "Tomas, Casey and I will be dining in, tonight. Could you ring up the hotel and have them prepare something special for two?"

"Of course, sir."

Hake did his best to ignore the grin on his security chief's face.

Tomas stood up. "I'm not getting cell phone coverage here. I'll be back in a moment."

A tiny frown crossed Casey's brow. She reached into her purse and pulled out her cell phone to check it. Her frown deepened. "Are you getting cell coverage, Hake?"

He fished out his phone and glanced at its face. "No. Why do you ask? We're probably just in a dead spot between towers."

"My phone works off satellites and so does Tomas's—"

And that was when all hell broke loose. An odd whoosh

sounded nearby, followed by four loud explosions so close together they sounded like a string of firecrackers but much, much louder. Glittering flecks of something flew in every direction. That was all Hake saw before Casey's weight threw him over backward in his chair. And then the screaming started. Horses and humans, men, women and children, all screaming. It was a horrible sound.

He didn't need to ask what was going on. He knew. It was the terrorists.

Casey rolled off him and bit out, "Injuries. Report!"

All but one of Tomas's men responded. Hake craned his head and looked up to see blood covering several of his bodyguards. But then Casey was snapping orders again. "Claude, Thierry, you're on Franz. Help him if he's alive. Get him to a hospital and see to your own wounds when you get there. The rest of you, on me and Hake. Let's go."

Franz had been sitting directly in front of Hake. Whatever had sliced the man to ribbons had been aimed at *him*. Cold horror washed over Hake. Just like the night of the restaurant bombing, Casey put a protective hand on top of his head and dragged him along in a half-crouching run. Tomas came up, panting, along his right side.

"Bounding fragmentation mines," the Swiss man grunted.

"I know," Casey replied. "I've run into them before."

Where in the hell had she run into something like that? The disjointed question stuck in Hake's head, probably some sort of mental buffer in lieu of the revulsion and shock trying to crowd their way into his mind.

"The limo?" Tomas bit out.

"No!" Casey answered sharply. "Hake's the target. It could blow. Into the city."

"On foot?" Tomas squawked.

"Will they expect that and be prepared for it?" Casey retorted.

"Good point. But we're down on men."

Hake thought he glimpsed a humorless grin flitting across Casey's face. "But not on women. As soon as we get beyond the terrorists' cell phone jamming, we'll have plenty of backup."

They ran in silence then. *Ran* being the operative word. He was huffing hard to keep up with the blistering pace Casey set. They sprinted the length of the huge polo field, past the barns and parking lot, and burst out onto a city street. Sirens began to wail. It was eerily reminiscent of that first attack in London.

"C'mon," Casey ordered. She moved in front of him, taking point as one of the other men slid in beside him. She continued to run at a breakneck pace, turning corners and crossing streets unexpectedly, making cars slam on their brakes and honk their horns. But always, she pressed forward, deeper into the heart of Nice. After maybe ten minutes, she gave a grunt of satisfaction and ducked into a bookstore. She raced toward the back of the place, startling several customers. She barged through a door marked Employees Only, and blessedly stopped.

Hake caught his breath while she rapidly dialed her cell phone. "Scorpion, here. The attack happened. The principal is unharmed and with me. We've got one man down, possibly dead. I left two men behind to render aid. I have five men with me and the principal. I need a safe house and quickest route from my current position. Request immediate backup from the Medusas."

Medusa? Hake frowned. The original man-hating woman with snakes for hair?

"Roger. Copy." And then Casey tucked her phone back

into her pocket. She shoved a wireless earphone into her left ear and gestured for them to move toward the rear exit.

"Where are we going?" Hake asked.

"Someplace safe. We'll hook up with my team there."

"These Medusas?" he asked curiously.

She gave him a sour look. "Yeah."

They ran for a few more minutes but didn't attract much attention in the growing chaos. Word of the attack was spreading fast across town, and the traffic had come to a standstill as emergency vehicles and bystanders made their way to the scene of the explosion.

Casey careened around a corner and ducked into a doorway without warning. She hustled him and the others inside and slammed the door shut. She spent several long minutes peering out the door's peephole. Finally, she announced, "We're clear."

Tomas and Hake traded relieved looks and the Swiss man muttered, "Damn, she's good. Where did you find her?"

"She found me," Hake grunted back.

"Hell, if you don't marry her, I will," Tomas commented under his breath. Hake wasn't sure he was supposed to have heard the comment and he chose not to respond. But his gut twisted hard at the notion of another man having Casey.

She took off again, racing up the stairs, gesturing them to follow. The woman's stamina amazed him. He kept up with her on pure adrenaline at this point. The attack hadn't gone at all as planned. The terrorists were supposed to show themselves when they tried to kill him, not leave anonymous land mines buried in a polo field to shred everyone indiscriminately.

Casey knocked on an apartment door on the fourth floor and it opened immediately. He and the others raced inside. He came to a halt in the middle of a living room that looked like a military surplus store. Weapons and electronic gadgets were neatly stacked all around the room. Several phones sat on the dining-room table, holding down the corners of a detailed map of Nice.

"Welcome to the snake den," a tall, blonde woman said drily.

"I know you!" Hake exclaimed. "You were in London. Told my men how to do their jobs!"

She held out her hand. "I'm Monica. Nice to meet you. Sorry it has to be under these circumstances."

Hake recognized the almost imperceptibly quick up and down she gave him, noting his brand of watch, the designer who did his suit. This woman was someone intimately familiar with his world. She knew the rules of engagement with men like him. But then the look was gone, replaced by grim focus.

"Early reports are that four bounding fragmentation mines were buried at the edge of the polo field," Monica said tersely. "At least ten dead. A hundred or more wounded. You guys were lucky to get out of there with only one man down."

"Any word on Franz?" Tomas asked quickly.

An Asian woman, who had a phone plastered to each ear across the room, answered, "He's at a hospital. Alive on arrival. Multiple severe lacerations and serious blood loss."

"Speaking of which—" the Asian woman stood up "—any injuries among you in need of a medic?"

"Who are you?" Hake asked.

"Cho. Medic."

Short on words, too, apparently. And then Casey's hands were on him, running over his limbs, across his belly, down his back. "Anything hurting?" she murmured.

He shook his head. "I'm fine. Yet again, your lightning-fast reflexes saved me."

"Franz took the brunt of the shrapnel meant for you. He's the one who should get the credit."

"I pray he lives so I can thank him," Hake replied quietly. Their gazes met in tense understanding. "Are you injured?"

She stopped for a moment, thinking. "No. I was behind Franz, too."

Several of the other men, however, had superficial wounds in need of care, and Cho set about cleaning and bandaging them.

Monica spoke up briskly, "What's the plan now?"

Casey sighed. "Well, that didn't work out the way we wanted. The terrorists outsmarted us and didn't show themselves. Only way we're going to get close to them, apparently, is to go through with the sale of the milling machine."

Monica shrugged. "At least we've got their psychology nailed. We thought we could provoke them to attack and we did. That's good, at any rate."

"Small consolation," Casey muttered. "Viper briefed yet?"

A compact brunette with a single, shocking red streak of hair over her right ear replied, "H.O.T. Watch is on the horn with her right now in Bhoukar. No attacks on the El Aran compound. So it wasn't a coordinated hit. This was definitely retaliation for Hake's antics."

"Which one are you?" Hake asked the punk rocker chick.

"Roxi," she replied. "Or you can call me Hornet."

Ah. The giver of excellent romantic advice. He made eye contact with her and nodded. She grinned back and then turned away quickly.

A beautiful, Persian-looking woman strolled out of another room. "Satellite imagery is chaotic. It'll take hours to I.D. everyone in the vicinity of the polo field. My guess is the mines were placed last night, or even earlier, and went off on timers. H.O.T. Watch is working on recovering telemetry from the past day or two that covers the polo grounds."

Casey made the introductions. "Hake, this is Naraya."

"What's her bug name?" he asked wryly.

Casey smiled. "Black Widow."

Hake nodded. "Any other dangerous insects I should know about?"

"Cho goes by Dragonfly and Monica's handle is Mantis. Tarantula is around somewhere. Her name's Alex, if you prefer."

Monica-Mantis murmured without looking up from the map of Nice, "Her turn to sleep."

Hake frowned. How could a person sleep through all this chaos? Although truth be told, the apartment was pretty quiet. He was the one in the chaotic state.

"Anyone thirsty?" Cho asked.

The women all grinned. He looked at Casey askance and she explained, "One of the symptoms of shock is pathological thirst."

Now that he thought about it, his mouth was as dry as cotton. He indicated he'd like a drink and added, "It's also a symptom of some woman running a guy all over town."

Casey smiled, holding out a two-liter water bottle to him. "That, too." He took it and cracked it open, promptly downing it in its entirety. Tomas and the other men had congregated around the table where Monica was briefing them. They looked rapt. Whether they were impressed with what she was saying or more impressed by the stunning woman delivering it, he couldn't tell.

"Would you like to rest, Hake?" Casey murmured. "There's a bedroom free at the moment."

"Show me where it is?" he murmured back.

Her gaze snapped up to his, but she merely commented, "This way."

He followed her down a long hallway which appeared to have no less than four bedrooms opening off it and a surprisingly large bathroom by French standards. She turned into the last room on the left and held the door for him. He passed by her and she pulled the door shut behind them both.

"You okay?" she asked.

"I'm rattled. It's not every day someone wants me dead bad enough to blow up a whole field full of people and animals to get me."

She sat down on the edge of the bed and picked up the TV remote on the nightstand. She turned on the television and he sat down beside her, numb, to watch the breaking news coverage. No mention was made of him, and that was just fine with him. The images of the polo field were bloody and hard to look at.

"How did we escape with so little harm?" he asked in disbelief.

She shrugged. "You weren't sitting on a horse unprotected, and you let Franz have the front-row seat you normally would have taken."

"I sat in the second row so I could be close to you," he commented, feeling a little detached from his body.

"I'm glad you did," she replied fervently.

"Any idea what's going to happen next with us?" he asked.

She looked up at him sharply, as if questioning how he meant that question. Frankly, he wasn't quite sure how he'd meant it. She chose to answer in a professional context rather than a personal one. "I expect we'll abandon the business of trying to draw an attack to you."

His stomach dropped like lead. "You're not going to leave me, are you?"

She blinked, startled. "I don't know what will happen next. My guess is a team will take you home to Bhoukar to join your family. It consolidates the security coverage, and I doubt the terrorists want to take out both you and your father simultaneously. They need someone alive with whom to do the deal."

"I haven't been to Bhoukar in years. I do not consider it my home," he replied woodenly.

"Nonetheless, I'm betting that's where you'll be headed next."

"When will we know?"

"There will be some sort of teleconference before long. Then as soon as transportation can be arranged, we'll move you."

"Are we looking at a day or two?" he asked grimly.

"More like an hour or two. If that much."

"What will you ladies do with all that gear in the living room?"

"We'll take it with us to wherever we end up going next, of course. We can have that stuff packed in a van in a few minutes."

He snorted. "I've never met a woman yet who can pack for anything in under an hour."

That made her grin. "We can pack to deploy for ninety days in ten minutes."

"Are you sure you're really a woman?" he demanded.

The humor left her face as abruptly as if he'd slapped it off her. He stared, startled. "Surely you know I was joking."

"Of course." Her lips moved and sound came out, but there wasn't even a hint of conviction in her words.

He wrapped his arms around her, drawing her close to him. She was so familiar to him, and yet it felt entirely strange to hold her like this in the privacy of a bedroom. This was real. He kissed her gently. At least at first. As always when they kissed each other, the room quickly disappeared and nothing was left but the two of them straining toward one another, lost in their own world of passion and blinding need.

He murmured against her lips, "I've never met another woman remotely like you. You're a warrior by day and all woman by night. You're smart and capable and take charge in a crisis, but you cuddle against me like a kitten and make me feel like the king of the world when you do. You're as at ease with a gun in your hand as a mascara brush."

"Makeup brushes terrify me," she mumbled against his neck.

He smiled back. "You laugh in situations that most women would fall apart in."

"Yeah, but I fall apart in situations most women would sail through, so it all evens out."

He drew back enough to gaze down at her. "Like when?"

"Like every time we came back to your hotel room after kissing and groping each other all evening. I didn't have the slightest clue how to tell you how much I wished it could continue behind closed doors."

"You wanted to be with me?" he demanded. "Why on earth didn't you say so? I thought you hated my guts after I needed to be alone that first night in Nice."

"What was that all about anyway?" she demanded back.

"Things were moving so fast with us. I was messed up in the head. Had to sort a few things out."

"Like what?"

"Like whether or not I was developing real feelings for you."

She said nothing. Most women would jump all over a comment like that and want to know what he'd decided. But she was not most women. "Don't you want to know what I figured out?" he asked.

"Do you want to tell me?"

"I have real feelings for you," he announced.

"Oh."

He frowned. "Is that all you've got to say to my big declaration?"

"A big declaration of what? So you have feelings for me. They could be feelings of dislike and distaste."

"Difficult woman," he grumbled. He exhaled hard. "I think I'm falling in love with you, for crying out loud."

"Oh." A pause. "Oh!"

He felt slightly better. She at least had the good grace to appear shocked.

"Are you sure?" she asked.

"I'm not sure about anything. I've never done this before. I don't have any idea what falling in love feels like. But I can't sleep at night for wanting to be with you. I can't wait to see your face when I get up in the morning. I want to know what you're doing and thinking and feeling all the time. I feel…empty…whenever we're apart, and I only feel like myself when we're together. You tell me. Is that love?"

She contemplated him thoughtfully. "I don't know. Could just be a bad case of infatuation."

Frustration soared in his gut. "Why are you fighting this?" he demanded. "Aren't you supposed to be happy when someone tells you they love you? And then you declare your feelings back?"

Her detached facade cracked. She said in a small voice, "Mostly, I'm scared to death. This has so much potential to go wrong. And I don't want to get hurt again."

He replied, "Don't all the poets and playwrights say you have to be courageous to risk love? You're the most courageous woman I've ever met, so what's the holdup?"

"I'm a fraud. I'm as scared as the next person. I just know how to mask it better than most."

"You're no fraud. And I'm as scared as you," he said.

She smiled sadly. "We're some pair, aren't we? Most people would be thrilled to discover they're falling in love and rush headlong into it. And here we are, hesitating like complete cowards."

"I'll jump if you will," he said quietly.

She stared at him a long time. And he held his breath for endless seconds. Finally, she said slowly, "Maybe after the mission. When I'm not working with you. When your family's out of danger..."

"You're procrastinating," he accused. "Avoiding the real issue."

Her gaze slid away from his.

"For the record, I'm planning to fight for you," he announced. "And we've already established that I don't fight fair."

That made her look at him warily. "What do you have in mind?"

"A warrior never reveals his tactics to the enemy," he replied grimly.

"Please don't mess with my career," she blurted. "I've worked too hard to get to where I am. Sacrificed too much—"

"Like love? Personal happiness?" he challenged.

Her gaze met his reluctantly. "Yes. Exactly."

"Why can't you have both a career and happiness?"

"That would take a man who fully understands and accepts my work. Who is willing to share me with my career until it has run its course. And with all due respect, Hake, you were raised in a culture where women's needs don't take center stage. I have a hard time believing you're going to be okay with my work at the end of the day."

That gave him serious pause. Finally he said, "You forget I was raised with twelve sisters and a European mother. I was raised to remember to think about the woman."

"Right. And that's why you've been hopping in and out of bed with them by the hundreds. Because you're so committed to their emotional well-being."

"That's not fair!"

"Are you sure it's not?" she challenged.

He paused to consider the accusation. He fought to set aside his defensive reaction. "I was always honest with them. I told them up front that I don't do long-term relationships and not to expect anything more out of me than the moment."

"And yet you wonder why I hesitate to dive into a relationship with you," she retorted drily.

"Things are different between us," he responded with a hint of desperation.

"Because we've nearly died together a time or two? That's just another day at the office in my world, Hake. It's not the basis for lasting love."

"Then what is?" he demanded.

She sighed. "I don't know. I don't have the answers."

He felt everything he'd ever wanted and not known he'd wanted until he met her slipping away from him. "Promise me you'll look for the answers with me. Let's figure this thing out together. Don't close me out until you've given us a chance."

"I don't know—"

"Just don't say no. Withhold a final answer until this thing with the terrorists is over." God, he hated negotiating for his life like this. He was sorely tempted to sweep her into his arms and kiss away her doubts, but he sensed that winning over her mind was every bit as crucial as winning over her body in this fight.

She frowned at him.

"Please. It's not too much to ask." It felt supremely strange to beg. It was not a thing he'd done often—or ever, really, truth be told—in his life.

She sighed. "All right. Fine. I won't decide anything until the mission is wrapped up."

He knew her well enough to believe that she would keep her word at all costs. She was honorable that way. Hence his next request. "Promise me?"

She commented reflectively, "You're getting to know me well if you know to ask that question." She studied him for an endless moment. Sighed. And then said, "Fine. I promise I won't make any decisions about us until the mission's over."

Chapter 15

Casey swore at herself under her breath. Every time her shoulder rubbed against Hake's, her breath caught in the back of her throat. She had to stop reacting to him like this! They were firmly back in her world, on a military transport plane headed for Bhoukar and a showdown with a group of deadly terrorists.

The rules of engagement were entirely different now. She wasn't playing the floozy girlfriend anymore. She was back to being the professional soldier, currently acting as a bodyguard for an extremely important asset. This was a no-fail mission, which meant she and her teammates were under orders to do whatever…*whatever*…it took not to fail. Up to and including killing. Or dying. This was no time to be making goo-goo eyes at Hake.

Although how she was supposed to turn off her feelings and pretend there was nothing between them was beyond her. He was in love with her? *Her?* The thought boggled her mind and did funny things to her stomach every time it occurred to her. She was pretty well head over heels for him herself. She hadn't the slightest idea what to do about it, however.

Ever since the terse teleconference in the apartment where Vanessa ordered them to bring Hake and the milling machine to Bhoukar, a tornado of activity had kept her from thinking about Hake's declaration to her. But now a ten-hour plane ride stretched before her. Hake sat strapped in a web seat in the cargo compartment on her left, and her Medusa team stretched away to her right. The big machine that was the cause of this whole mess sat in a wooden cargo crate at the rear of the aircraft. She shifted in the uncomfortable seat, and her shoulder brushed against Hake's yet again. Her breath caught, and she rolled her eyes in disgust at herself. She was hopeless.

Thankfully, Hake stretched out his muscular legs, crossed him arms over his chest, and closed his eyes. It was easier to think without his steady, warm gaze on her every move.

Roxi leaned close to her. "Chica, roll up your tongue and tuck it back in your mouth, eh?"

She turned to her teammate sharply. "What are you talking about?"

"You can't look at the man without lighting up like a tracer flare. Your whole face glows."

"Crap." She looked glumly at her friend. "What am I supposed to do?"

"Get the job done, and then drag that man to bed and don't get up for a week."

"I don't think a week would be enough between us."

Roxi laughed. "You may be right. He looks at you like he's planning to eat you alive. I knew he was hot for you, but I had no idea."

Casey sighed. "Thing is, you and I both know I can't just dive into the sack with him. Vanessa would have my head on a platter."

"If you two were to become involved seriously, you know, in a real relationship, the boss lady couldn't say much about it. You are allowed to have a personal life after all."

Casey rolled her eyes. "Hake El Aran serious about one woman? How likely is that?"

"I don't know. He looks pretty darned serious about you."

"That's just because I'm so different than a normal woman. I'm still a new and exotic flavor to him."

"Only way to know if that's all it is may be to let him have a good, long taste of you," Roxi said sagely.

Casey glared at her teammate. "Are you advising me to have a torrid affair with him to see if what we have is real?"

Roxi watched at her for a long time. Then she said, "What say you, ladies?"

Casey looked down accusingly at the microphone velcroed around Roxi's throat. "Were we on hot mike with the rest of the team this whole time?" she demanded, appalled.

"That would be an affirmative."

Casey groaned. Crap, crap, crap. Her entire team knew exactly how she felt about Hake now? She glared at Roxi. "You had no right—"

"I had every right. It impacts the mission, hence they needed to know." Roxi glared back until Casey's gaze faltered and fell away.

Casey touched her throat mike and transmitted, "All right. Fine. What do the rest of you nosy, pushy pests think about my private life?"

To their credit, her teammates didn't razz her. They seemed to understand the depth of her mortification and dilemma. Interestingly enough, it was Monica—the hard-core man-hater on the team—who finally answered quietly, "Casey, if you think there's a chance you and Hake could have something long-term, it's worth exploring. Don't walk away from the real thing if you two have it. Just wait until after this mission is over to find out, eh?"

Casey glanced down the row of her teammates and they all nodded in agreement. She sighed. "Easier said than done. Hake's prone to setting his own agenda. I may not control the timing of this thing between us. I'll do what I can."

Roxi spoke up soberly. "Promise me that if it's going to get in the way of the job you'll tell us what's going on between you two."

Casey closed her eyes in dismay. It was a reasonable request. But Lord, the humiliation of laying her love life out before her teammates like this. "Okay. Fine. I'll let you all know."

Roxi punched her lightly on the shoulder. "Chin up, kid. At least we're not demanding video."

Casey's gaze narrowed. "I'll kill anyone who tries to film us. I mean it."

The other women threw up their hands as one, laughing.

She caught up on her sleep and got thoroughly sick of the drone of jet engines before her ears finally started to pop, signaling their descent into Bhoukar. Compliments of the emir, they were exempted from clearing customs and hustled Hake straight off the jet and onto a U.S. Navy cargo helicopter, lent to them for the day by an aircraft carrier group in the Gulf of Oman.

Hake spent the short ride to his family's compound

staring pensively out a small, round window at the desert below. She'd never been to Bhoukar, but she'd seen plenty of mission footage from other Medusa forays into the tiny country. She knew exactly what the miles of endless sand below looked like.

The helicopter slowed to a hover and gradually lowered its bulk to the ground. The whop-whopping of the rotor blades began to wind down. Hake started to stand up, but Casey put a restraining hand on his thigh. His muscles went rock-hard beneath her hand and she looked up at him involuntarily. His gaze burned her alive as it met hers.

"We have to get an all-clear before we offload you," she murmured. "Medusa Team One is completing a security sweep of the perimeter as we speak."

"My sisters are going to love having all these girl commandos protecting Father and me. I'm never going to live it down."

She smiled. "It's better than being dead and not having to live it down at all."

"I'm just glad you're with me," he murmured.

Her gaze went to her teammates, but they were all occupied at the exit, checking for threats to their charge. She said back to him, "You and I need to talk. Alone. As soon as it can be arranged without raising any eyebrows."

"I'll see what I can do," he replied, sounding a little surprised.

And then Vanessa Blake's voice came over her earpiece, declaring the area secure and Hake clear to exit the aircraft. Tomas and his men went first, with the Medusas close behind. And then it was her turn to jump out of the helicopter's belly and to the ground, Hake beside her.

She was in Bhoukar.

With Hake. To meet his family. Her stomach clenched in apprehension. She reminded herself sternly that she was also here to keep Hake alive and catch a gang of violent terrorists. Priority number one.

Hake inhaled the familiar, acrid smell of the desert as a blast of hot, dry air slammed into him. He was definitely back in Bhoukar. Like it or not.

Casey touched his elbow and pointed at the massive building looming ahead. He nodded as they all took off jogging toward it. Tomas and his men flanked the front doors as Casey and the Medusas moved inside. Another half-dozen women in full combat gear joined them and the whole party piled into the foyer of his father's palace. They all took up only a small corner of the towering edifice.

Mosaic tiles of lapis lazuli and gold formed an intricate pattern overhead, and twin marble staircases curved upward in front of him. He'd always thought they looked like a woman's arms welcoming her lover.

"Wow," Casey breathed beside him.

He looked at her quickly. He didn't want her to be impressed. It was just a building. And he was just a man. Please, let her not be so dazzled by his family's wealth that she completely lost sight of him. He'd seen it happen more times than he could count. A servant he didn't recognize led them into the home, veering left into the public wing of the palace. To the right were his family's private quarters. It had been so long since he'd been here, he didn't know if he still had his own suite or not. He just wanted someplace he could be alone with Casey to…to what? Seduce her?

No. To court her.

Somewhere on the long flight, he'd come to terms with that shocking notion. He had no idea if things would work out between them or not. But he wanted to find out one way or the other and not let her walk away before they had a chance to explore this thing between them.

Vanessa Blake spoke ahead of them. "Mr. El Aran has been kind enough to allocate us space for our operations and quarters. It's next to his security center. We have plenty of room for you and your men, Tomas. Along with the El Aran family's permanent security personnel, we've established a hard perimeter and are keeping our presence minimal within the palace. Mr. El Aran has requested that we try not to make his home feel like a police state."

Vanessa veered down a hallway and the others followed her. Hake hung back, though, touching Casey on the elbow. She glanced over at him. "Come with me?" he murmured.

She looked up at her teammates. Roxi glanced back at her and nodded. Casey turned to Hake. "Lead on."

They peeled away from the others and soon were alone in the marble mausoleum his family called home. She commented lightly, "If this were my house, I'd have more furniture. Rugs. Maybe curtains on the windows. Some pictures. Something to make it feel a little more…"

"Homey?" he suggested.

She traded understanding glances with him.

He sighed. "It serves its purpose. It's a calculated display of wealth and power, establishing my father's position in society."

"You didn't need all of this to establish yourself as an important man in London. The financial markets took a measurable hit when people thought you were dead."

He smiled. "Oh, I'm not as important as all that. The markets were just worried about a shake-up in El Aran Industries. It is, without putting too fine a point on it, a big company."

"Not to be rude or anything, but where's your family? If the prodigal son came home at my house, there'd practically be a parade to meet him."

Hake glanced over at her, interested. "There's a prodigal son in your family? Does that mean you have a brother?"

She scowled back at him. "That's not the point."

Someday this woman was going to tell him everything about herself. Until then, he just had to be patient. He shrugged. "I may work with my father, but we are not... close. And the women in the family will not insult him by flocking to greet me before he does. He will greet me formally later."

"And you think having some belly dancer for a companion isn't going to insult the living heck out of him?" she replied gently.

Hake's gaze narrowed. "I am my own man. It's high time my father learned that."

She sighed. "Been there. Done that. Got that T-shirt. Thing is, he's your father. He loves you. He wants the best for you. Don't be so fast to shove me in his face."

Hake stared down at her, surprised. She was the last person he'd have expected to take his father's side. "If you're so determined to be his champion, what do you suggest I do?"

"Greet your father alone. Let me be introduced with the rest of my team as just another one of your guards. There's plenty of time later to make him aware of whatever else there may be between us."

Hake's jaw tightened. He despised her talking about their feelings for one another as if they were hypothetical. This thing between them was real, dammit. He'd done superficial and meaningless so many times he knew the difference.

"Where are we going?" she asked curiously.

"To see if I still have a room in this monstrosity for that private talk you requested. Plus, you can freshen up a little before you meet my family."

"In other words, I stink, huh?"

He laughed. "I suspect we both smell like jet fuel. And no, you don't stink, my dear. You're as lovely as always."

She smiled warmly at him. "That's one of the things I like best about you. You're always such a gentleman."

"I try. Although I'm not sure I always succeed."

She looped a hand in the crook of his arm. His gut tightened like it always did when she touched him. "Trust me. You succeed." And then she started as if just realizing she'd taken his arm and jerked her hand away.

He captured her fingers and put them back on his arm. "I like your hand there."

"I guess it became a habit when we were going out all the time. I don't want to offend anyone in your country, though."

"No one will be offended. Relax. It's just like being in London."

She appeared doubtful as they rode an elevator up to the third floor in silence. He led her down another impossibly long hall to a pair of gilded double doors. He threw them open, not sure what to expect.

His room was exactly as it had been the day he left a decade ago. The bed was made and fresh flowers stood in vases around the room, but it was still his space, complete with his books and maps and treasures collected from his boyhood travels.

"This room looks like you," Casey murmured.

"And how would that be?"

"Masculine. Elegant. Sophisticated."

"A bunch of books and trinkets are all that?" he commented in surprise.

She smiled. "Yes."

"May I offer you a long, hot soak in my Jacuzzi? There isn't one downstairs."

"You do know how to tempt a woman."

He grinned. "Go. Take your bath. I need to check in with my bankers, and their offices should be open in London by now."

She nodded and disappeared into his bathroom. It felt shockingly right for her to be here with him in this place. She was part of his life. Now, how to convince the lady of that? Time was running out on him.

Casey stepped out of the opulent marble tub, her heart heavy. She knew Hake was wealthy. But this was beyond her wildest imaginings. She would never fit into this world. She could handle Hake's yacht. And when she'd seen pictures in a magazine of his flat in London, which was spacious and chic, she hadn't freaked out. Heck, she'd ridden in the man's Rolls-Royce. But none of it had prepared her for this.

Reluctantly, she pulled on her desert beige BDUs and zipped up her combat boots. She strapped on her utility belt, and today it felt as if it weighed a hundred pounds, the pistol holstered at her right hip a block of lead.

With a sigh, she opened the door and stepped out into the main bedroom. Hake glanced up at her from the huge mahogany desk with a phone to his ear and did a quick double take, eyeing her uniform. But then he did the darnedest thing. He smiled at her. Just a smile. As if it was no big deal to him to see her decked out like a commando.

Shock flowed through her, followed closely by a wave a gratitude for his acceptance. Was it possible that he really might be okay with her career after all? He gestured for her to come sit with him, and she relaxed against his warmth as he took care of a few desultory financial transactions with his lawyer. It was a peaceful, domestic moment between them and she relished it far too much. No doubt about it. Letting go of this man would hurt. A lot.

He wound up the call and she rose to go, but he stood as well, taking her hands in his. He held them away from her sides as he looked her up and down again. "So, the soldier wins out over the woman today, does she?"

She shrugged. "Sorry. I'm on the job. It would look strange if I didn't dress like my teammates."

"You're still magnificent, darling," he murmured.

She smiled, but the expression felt brittle on her face. "This is who I am, Hake. Not that other person you think you know."

He frowned. "Why can't you be both?"

It was a hell of a good question. Why not, indeed? "You do have a way of cutting directly to the heart of a matter," she muttered.

"It's why I'm successful in business," he replied blandly. He leaned down and kissed her lightly on the cheek. "You're not fooling me. I still see the woman hiding beneath the trappings of a soldier. She's not gone under all that gear." He flipped one of her ammo pouches lightly.

She stared as he turned away and continued speaking as if he hadn't just stunned her speechless. "Your cell phone rang while you were in the bath, love. I took the liberty of answering it for you. Roxi asked me to have you call her back when you got out."

Uh-oh. Busted messing around with Hake and she hadn't been in Bhoukar an hour. Except she hadn't done anything with him…yet.

He was speaking again. "I'm going to jump into the shower myself while you make your call."

He disappeared into the dressing room and she dialed her phone reluctantly. "Hey, Roxi. What's up?"

"You two christened his room yet?"

Casey sighed. "There's been no hanky-panky between us, I swear."

"Why the heck not? The guy's smoking hot and so in lust with you he can hardly see straight."

"We've already been over this. I have to leave him alone until after the mission's over."

"Have you told him that?" Roxi demanded.

"Well, no. I was going to, though. It's why I agreed to come up to his room with him."

"We do have a little downtime at the moment. Can't do anything until the terrorists contact us. Maybe you should think of this visit to the palace as a break in the mission. Like halftime of a football game."

If only. Casey sighed. "Mama Viper already gave me the big lecture not to fool around on the job on this mission."

Roxi snorted. "Since when does any Medusa, including our ever-so-stern boss, follow the rules? How do you think she ended up married to her boss anyway? If you want the guy, go get him!"

"You're a bad influence, Roxi deLuco."

"Thank you. I try."

Casey rolled her eyes. "So was there a reason you called, or were you just trying to harass me and interfere with my love life?"

"Vanessa wanted to know where you were. She's scheduled a mission briefing in about five minutes. And she wants you here."

Casey sighed. So much for private time with Hake. "I'm on my way."

The water cut off as she called through the bathroom door, "I have to go to a briefing. I'll see you in a while."

The door opened and he stood there, his bronze skin dripping wet, with only a snow-white towel wrapped around his hips. Ho. Lee. Cow. Move over male cover models.

"I'm sorry. I didn't catch all of that," he said. His words were vague, coming to her as if from a long distance, such was the impact of his appearance on her befuddled brain.

"Uh. Briefing. Have to go."

"Me?" he asked. "They need me at a briefing?"

"Uh, no. Me," she mumbled.

A slow grin started to spread across his face. "Are you all right?"

"No. Not…no."

He reached out of sight beyond the door and came up with a second towel. He strolled forward, commencing to towel his hair. "Never seen a guy get out of a shower before?" he asked casually.

"No…uh…yes…but not…uh…you…"

He stepped close enough to her that she felt the humid heat rolling off his body. "You're cute when you're flustered," he said.

She opened and closed her mouth a few times and finally just shook her head. "This is so not going to work between us."

The towel came off his head. "Why not?" he demanded.

"You and I are from totally different worlds. This all—" she waved her hand to encompass his room "—it's too much. I don't belong in a palace. Everything about you is too—" she searched for a word and finally finished "—perfect."

Warm fingertips traced her jawline lightly and she inhaled sharply.

He said slowly, "Let me get this straight. You want to dump me because I'm too rich?"

"Well, sort of. I mean I don't want to dump you. But I don't see how I could ever learn to live with all of this."

A smile spread across his face and grew brighter and brighter until it nearly blinded her. Or maybe that was just lust blinding her. He said, "Just think of all the time it will take for the two of us to share our worlds with one another. Years. Decades, even. And every moment of it will be interesting and exciting and new for both of us. Tell me you'll give me and all of this a chance—"

She started to lean in to kiss him, mostly in desperation to stop him from completing the question and putting her horribly on the spot, but her phone vibrated in her pocket and saved the day. "I'm late. Gotta run."

She turned and fled without looking back. She was such a *coward*. She was too scared to admit to him just how hard she'd fallen for him, and way too scared to admit it to her teammates. Heck, she was barely able to admit it to herself. Any sane woman would've leaped all over the offer he'd made to her and done everything in her power to land this guy. But she…she was doing everything in her power to drive the guy away from her. What was *wrong* with her? And what on earth was she going to tell him when he lost patience and came right out and demanded to know her intentions toward him?

Chapter 16

Casey listened in dismay as Vanessa went over the details of her latest conversation with Geoffrey Birch. The terrorists had contacted him and were pushing to complete the sale immediately. Vanessa had advised the attorney to agree to the terrorists' terms. The transfer of funds would happen later today. Their teammates at H.O.T. Watch headquarters had a few hours to track the source of the monies and catch the terrorists that way. However, everyone agreed that the odds of the terrorists slipping up and making a mistake in hiding their money trail were extremely small.

Plan B was to go ahead with the transfer of the milling machine.

Tonight.

Casey's heart about fell out of her chest at that news. She and Hake were out of time. Worse, she wasn't mentally prepared for him to be exposed to danger. But unfortunately, the first condition the terrorists had set for the transfer of the machine was that Hake personally deliver it.

As H.O.T. Watch had anticipated, the terrorists expected to move the machine by sea, and they demanded that Hake drive it in a truck to an exact location they would give him later. The rendezvous point could lie anywhere along the coast of Bhoukar, which meant the Medusas would not have long tonight to scout out the meeting locale and get a team in place to protect Hake. For surely the terrorists expected to kill him once he'd delivered the goods. He'd had the gall to survive both of their earlier attempts to kill him; it would be a point of honor not to let him live out the night.

Once the hostiles had the machine, they would no doubt sail for the pirate-infested waters of the Gulf of Aden and the wild and wooly coast of east Africa where it would be easy for them to slip ashore and disappear with their prize.

"What about sabotaging the milling machine?" Casey asked, desperate to delay the handoff. "Is that done?"

Vanessa nodded. "Marat's engineers say it is. I'd like Naraya to take a look at their work herself and verify it, however."

The engineer on their team nodded briskly.

Vanessa diagrammed a rough plan of deployment. "We'll all ride in the truck with the machine, jump out as close to the meet as we can and work our way in on foot."

Roxi asked, "Is the Bhoukari Army going to insist on being there?"

Vanessa shook her head. "Our president and the Bhoukari emir share an extraordinarily close friendship, and the president has asked him, as a favor, to leave this operation entirely to us. Which is to say, the whole mission's on our shoulders, ladies."

Casey looked around the room. She couldn't think of a dozen other people in the entire world she'd rather have this mission depending upon. Forged in blood, sweat and tears, the Medusas had become a single, finely honed weapon, a seamless killing machine. They were tough, experienced and confident. Everything would go smoothly tonight.

Then why were her hands shaking and her innards threatening open revolt at any second? Hake. That was why. He was going to be out there, exposed to the very people who'd tried twice now to kill him.

"Casey, I want you on Hake."

She jerked at hearing her name and stared at her boss in surprise as Vanessa continued, "The terrorists know you. They think you're a bimbo—no offense intended—"

"None taken," Casey murmured.

"And we can use that to our advantage," Vanessa added. "They won't know why Hake brought you along and they won't like it, but they won't be worried by you. You did an excellent job getting yourself portrayed by the press as a harmless party girl."

Casey grimaced. "Gee. Thanks."

As chuckles passed around the table, Vanessa continued, "You'll need to find some sort of clothing that doesn't make you look like a professional bodyguard."

Casey nodded. "I'm sure someone around here can help me with that. What about Tomas and crew?"

"I don't want civilians in our field of fire, no matter how good they are," Vanessa replied briskly. "I'm assigning them to guard our retreat if things go bad. They'll lay down a volley of covering fire and open up an escape corridor if we need one."

Monica spoke up, "What if the terrorists get the machine onto their vessel and make it out of port?"

"That's actually the idea," Vanessa replied. "As soon as

they cross into international waters, the U.S. Navy will be waiting for them. We already have a submarine, a destroyer and three SEAL teams tasked to take these guys. They're loitering off the coast now and are under orders to sink the ship and make our terrorists disappear permanently. Ideally, they'll take a few prisoners for long-term interrogation, but the priority is to kill the ship. Our job is merely to drive the terrorists into their grasp."

Casey asked the obvious next question, "And if the terrorists stay in Bhoukari waters and don't go international?"

Vanessa grinned. "The emir assures us that it's very difficult for his navy to tell where invisible boundary lines in the water lie and he's quite fuzzy on the subject himself."

Vanessa spent the next half hour going over the operational plan for the handoff in excruciating detail. The whole plan centered around showing Hake to the terrorists as briefly as possible and then getting him the heck out of there before anyone could kill him.

Easy as pie. Then why was Casey's gut twisted into so many knots that she could hardly breathe?

Vanessa wrapped up with, "And while we wait for the call to come in, Mr. and Mrs. El Aran have invited us all to dine with them this evening. They're fine with our BDUs, but no weapons at the dinner table, please."

Casey gulped…and then prayed furiously that Hake took her advice and didn't make a scene about her tonight.

As the Medusas piled out of the briefing room and followed Vanessa to a massive dining room that already held nearly fifty people, apparently all of Hake's extended family, Casey made a point of blending into the middle of the pack of women soldiers.

She spotted Hake the instant the Medusas stepped

into the banquet hall. He was standing beside an older version of himself—that must be his father. And the elegant woman with them must be his mother. Even his parents were perfect and intimidating. But then Mr. El Aran smiled and welcomed them all so pleasantly that Casey's shoulders actually began to unhunch from around her ears. Mrs. El Aran, who spoke English with a light Italian accent, waved for them all to be seated and for the meal to be served. The crowd moved toward a giant table spanning the length of the room.

Mrs. El Aran gestured for Vanessa to sit beside her, and Casey was intensely relieved that her boss got diplomatic babysitting duty tonight.

But then Mr. El Aran's voice rang out clearly before Casey could slip into a nicely anonymous seat at the other end of the long table. "Which one of you is the dancer? The one who's been in all the tabloids with my son."

Oh, Lord. Her teammates flashed her sympathetic glances as Casey reluctantly stepped out of their protective midst. Hake's back was ramrod stiff and his jaw seemed about ready to shatter, he was so furious. This was going to turn ugly very fast and very soon.

She forced her feet to carry her toward Hake and his parents. Vanessa looked like a thundercloud beside them. She silently blessed her boss for taking offense at her reputation being questioned in any way. If only she deserved Vanessa's indignation. But she'd crossed the line with Hake, and no amount of scrambling now was going to change that.

Casey cleared her throat. "I would be the dancer, sir."

"Come closer. I want to speak with you, young lady."

Sighing, she calculated the odds of making it to the exit before one of her teammates tackled her and bodily dragged her to face Papa El Aran. Zilch. Maybe when his father was done with her, Hake would finally catch a clue and realize just how unsuited for his life she was.

In the meantime, she was a Medusa. She groveled for no man. Her heart might be breaking, but that didn't mean she was beaten. She lifted her chin and strode forward to face the music. The one thing she dared not do was look at Hake. She'd fall apart if she so much as glanced over at him.

Vanessa caught her gaze ever so briefly, and Casey thought she saw support and encouragement from her boss. Casey neared Hake and his parents, and she glued her attention on his father. The man was studying her intently, as if he were searching for something. "This is the same beauty I've seen splashed all over the newspapers?" he asked incredulously.

Casey blinked. "I beg your pardon, sir?"

"Remarkable. In this attire, you look just like the other lady soldiers. And you're the one who saved his life in that nightclub in London?"

Casey shrugged. "I shoved him under a table. Whether that saved his life or not, I couldn't say."

Hake interrupted. "Don't be modest, Casey." He turned to his father. "She threw herself on top of me to protect me. And she tackled me again yesterday with no regard for her own safety when the mines exploded at the polo field."

Mrs. El Aran startled Casey by stepping forward then and wrapping Casey, BDUs and all, in a hug. "Thank you so much for saving my son's life. How can we ever thank you?"

"No thanks are necessary," Casey mumbled. "I was just doing my job."

"Nonsense," Marat declared. "We are forever in your debt."

"In that case—" Hake started.

Casey cut him off with a glare. She turned to his mother and registered the woman looking back and forth between her and Hake in dawning amusement. Casey said politely, "In that case, Mr. and Mrs. El Aran, let's enjoy a pleasant dinner and you can tell me all about what a naughty child Hake was. After working with him for the past few weeks, I have no doubt he was a handful."

Mrs. El Aran laughed and commenced regaling Casey with stories of Hake's adventurous youth. Hake, who was seated across the table, rolled his eyes and put up with it, but clearly he was impatient with her. Too bad. Until the two of them had some idea of what was going on between them, the last thing they needed to do was involve his family. She was right, and he could just get over it.

Several times he tried to steer the conversation back to his relationship with Casey, and each time, Casey headed him off, smoothly turning the conversation to some other subject. And each time she did it, Hake's jaw clenched harder. She blandly ignored him as he stewed. If she wasn't mistaken, Mama El Aran's amusement was growing by the minute at Hake getting managed by a woman like this.

The food was delicious and the company pleasant, and no more was said of her and Hake's antics in France. But when the formal meal adjourned and everyone milled around chatting, Hake moved to her side and gripped her elbow tightly. He leaned down to growl in her ear, "My room. Ten minutes."

He strode out then, and she didn't watch him go. Really. She wasn't a silly teenager to engage in a secret rendezvous like this. However, almost ten minutes later, she asked one of Hake's sisters where a restroom was and the woman offered to show it to her. Casey smiled and accepted the guide.

The two women stepped out into the grand hallway and

Hake's sister murmured, "Take this elevator to the third floor and turn right when the door opens. Go all the way to the end, and it's on the left."

Casey stared.

"Go on," the woman murmured, smiling. "It's high time my brother found himself a woman who can stand up to him like you do. I haven't seen my parents so delighted in years. Good luck and go with the family's blessing."

The elevator doors closed and Casey stood there in shock. The family approved of her? The belly-dancing commando? No way. She felt like a high-wire performer who'd just had the net pulled out from underneath her in the middle of her show. She'd been so sure his family wouldn't tolerate her anywhere near Hake. Now what was she supposed to do?

Before she hardly knew what was happening, she was standing in front of Hake's bedroom door. What came next? She had no idea. But she did know one thing: she was a Medusa. And Medusas faced their fears head-on. She took a deep breath and pushed open his door.

As she walked in, Hake turned from where he stood by the bedroom window. She spoke sharply, "Unless that's bullet-resistant glass, you should get away from there. And even then, it's not good policy to expose yourself to a sniper. Sometimes they have gear that will punch through the best bullet-resistant materials."

"How do you soldiers say it...you can stand down now?"

"That's how we say it, but I'm not about to stand down. Your safety is my number one concern."

He strode forward, irritated. "Is that what you were doing at dinner? Protecting me? It was the perfect opportunity to tell my father about us. He was inclined to be generous with you and grant you a favor, and you wouldn't let me say a thing!"

"It was not the right time or place," she declared flatly.

"I am not accustomed to being told what to do," he snapped.

She laughed. "Then it must suck being around me and my teammates. Particularly when your life depends on following our orders."

He glared at her for a moment more, but then his irritation broke. He sighed. "I just don't like hiding my feelings for you like this." He commenced pacing, but well back from the wall of windows.

She leaned a hip on his desk. "I don't see anyone we need to hide from right now. Are there surveillance cameras in here I should know about?"

"Heavens, no. The family's private quarters would never be watched."

"Then relax already," she said softly. "You don't have to hide anything from me."

He stopped and stared at her. "I don't, do I?"

Their gazes met. A realization of just how far they'd come unfolded between them. Nervous, she murmured, "I have to brief you on the mission."

"The mission. It's always the mission with you. When are you going to admit to yourself that you're hiding behind all this soldiering stuff?"

She retorted, "When are you going to realize that a soldier is who I *am?*"

"I *am* a banker, but that doesn't mean I'm not a man, too. It doesn't mean I can't have a personal life."

"My work is different," she declared.

"Only if you let it be. You've chosen to let it consume

your life. To let it consume your identity and your femininity."

She glared at him and he glared back. Finally, she stated flatly, "We don't have time for this right now. I have to tell you about the mission." Ignoring his obvious frustration, she launched into a recitation of the plan as it currently stood.

He crossed his arms, plastered on an impassive look and listened.

"Oh, and one more thing," she added. "If they hit me, you have to let them."

That got a reaction out of him. A snort of contempt.

"I'm serious, Hake. These guys think women are worthless, and you need to appear to believe the same."

"Not happening. Nobody hits my woman and gets away with it."

A thrill shot through her that brought her up short. Okay, she was not supposed to get all fluttery over being protected by some man. But still…it felt good that he was protective of her like that. It took a moment for her to collect herself enough to say calmly, "Regardless, you must let them. My life will depend on it and yours, too. They have to believe I'm not important. That I can be ignored."

That garnered another snort from him. "I keep telling you. You're impossible to ignore. When will you get that through your head?"

Another thrill rippled through her. She couldn't think about that right now! Right now, she was a soldier. Not a woman. Why couldn't he see that?

"I have to go check my weapons and scare up some clothes for myself," she said grimly. "I'll be back to collect you when the terrorists call. In the meantime, you should try to get some rest. It could be a long night."

Roxi looked up sharply at her when she stomped

into their impromptu command center. "You all right, Scorpion?"

Casey scowled. She was emphatically not all right. Hake's insistence on reminding her that she was a sexy, desirable woman was distracting in the extreme. "I'll live," she grumbled.

"H.O.T. Watch sent us satellite imagery of the terrain along the coast. You might want to familiarize yourself with it," Roxi said neutrally.

Right. Terrain. She spent the next two hours going through the motions of final mission preparation, but she wasn't at all sure how much of it actually stuck in her head. Hopefully enough. The good news was that the rest of the Medusas would be with her and Hake. She felt perfectly safe in their care.

The call came in at midnight. Hake was to drive the large flatbed truck bearing the milling machine by a specified route to the coastal highway, departing within the next ten minutes, or the transfer was off.

Casey dialed Hake's cell phone. He picked up on the second ring. "It's me," she said briskly. "Time to rock and roll. We need to leave immediately."

"I'm on my way," he replied tersely.

She winced as she hung up. He sounded none too pleased with her. She supposed she couldn't blame him, but there was nothing she could do about it. She knew the mental, physical and emotional demands of a mission and he didn't. But he was about to learn.

Chapter 17

Hake stared in shock as Casey climbed up into the cab of the semitruck beside him. "What in the hell are you wearing?"

She was swathed in black, voluminous robes, her head covered by a matching black scarf that came down low on her forehead. Missing only was the draped scarf across her face. It was a shock to see her like that.

She replied, "Surely you recognize traditional Bhoukari dress. We left my face uncovered so the terrorists would recognize me. But I need the robes to cover my weapons. Remember, try to find a way to send me back to the truck after they've searched me, so I can fetch my toys."

"This is insane. I won't have you exposed to danger like this," he declared.

"What? And I'm supposed to sit home twiddling my thumbs while you charge headlong into the jaws of death?"

"Better me than you," he replied, supremely frustrated that a bunch of terrorists had forced him and everyone who mattered to him into this mess.

She replied soothingly, "I have years of the best training on earth for doing exactly this."

A metallic voice sounded inside his head, emanating from the tiny transceiver behind his last molars on the right. "Listen to her, Hake. She's right." That was Vanessa Blake if he wasn't mistaken. He swore under his breath. He didn't like this one bit. It was bad enough that he was probably driving straight into a trap. But to be forced to bring along the woman he loved…he swore again.

"Do you know how to drive this thing or do you need a crash course?" Casey asked.

"I spent a summer as a teenager driving delivery trucks for my father. He believed it was important for me to see our business from the ground up."

"Smart man," she commented.

"Everyone on board?" he murmured into his mouth-piece.

"We're ready to roll," came Vanessa's response. "And our ten minutes are almost up."

Hake shoved the lever behind the steering wheel, throwing the big truck into gear. "How will the terrorists know if I've left within their time limit?" he asked to fill the empty space between him and Casey.

"We think they're tracking your cell phone signal. Our telemetry shows nobody within the vicinity of the palace who could be doing eyes-on surveillance of you."

"Now what?" he asked.

"Head down the road they told you to."

He drove in silence. The truck's headlights lit a swath of tarmac before him, but everything else—the desert, the sky, the night blanketing them—was an enormous black void. It made a man feel incredibly small. The tension within the cab was palpable. Whether its source was the mission or the unresolved questions hanging between Casey and him, he didn't know. But either way, it was intensely uncomfortable. Finally, he burst out, "Look, if we're about to die, shouldn't we clear the air between us?"

She looked over at him but the scarf covered most of her expression. "I think we've pretty much said it all, don't you?"

"Not by a long shot," he burst out.

In the dim glow of the dashboard lights, she sent him a pleading look and pointed to her mouth and then her ear. He scowled. At this point, he didn't give a damn if her teammates heard everything the two of them said to each other. He was sick of not knowing where he stood with her.

She sighed. "Hake, if you truly want to be with me for the long-term, you need to see this side of me. Consider tonight an up-close-and-personal tour of my world. Let's just wait and see what you think after it's all over."

He considered for a moment. "Fair enough. But in return, I ask that you give my world a try." He added grimly, "With an open mind."

She stared at him for a long time. Finally, she nodded. All right, then. He could live with that. He sat back and concentrated on driving.

After about a half hour, a flurry of talking erupted inside his skull. Apparently the support team for the Medusas had picked up infrared satellite images of a cluster of people arrayed in what looked like an ambush formation a few miles ahead. Most of the chatter made little sense to him, but Casey went tense.

He eased off the accelerator.

"No!" she exclaimed. "Keep going the same speed. The

terrorists are tracking us. We can't signal them that we've spotted the trap or they'll know we're using sophisticated support."

Great. The terrorists were watching him. Her teammates were listening to him. Uncle Sam was looking down on him from space. It could give a guy a complex. The road began to climb and he downshifted to handle the grade. And then a sharp noise sounded from the seat beside him, making him jump violently. His cell phone was ringing.

"Pick it up," Casey said tightly.

He put the device to his ear. "Hello."

A male voice directed without preamble, "There's a bridge ahead. Drive across it and stop on the far side." The call disconnected before he could say anything.

"Got that?" Casey bit out.

"Roger," Vanessa replied. "We'll get out on this side of the bridge and make our way across the obstacle on foot."

An unidentified male voice—must be one of the H.O.T. Watch people—replied in Hake's head. "Negative, Viper. The bridge spans a gorge at least five-hundred-feet deep. Recommend you use the bridge to cross."

Vanessa spoke rapidly to her team. Apparently, they would decide when they saw the bridge whether to sneak across it topside or climb underneath the thing to cross the gorge. In the meantime, she ordered the Medusas to prepare to exit the truck. He looked at his speedometer in alarm. He was still going nearly thirty miles per hour.

"They're going to jump at this speed?" he asked Casey incredulously.

She replied, "It would help if you slowed down a little. Could you make it look like the truck's laboring up the slope a bit more?"

"Done." He downshifted again and the truck slowed to roughly twenty miles per hour.

"That's good," she commented.

As they neared the top of a rocky ridge, Vanessa ordered the Medusas to jump. He looked out his rearview mirrors, trying to spot them as they left, but he saw nothing. He listened to a quick check-in as all the Medusas reported in and regrouped to follow the truck to the bridge. He downshifted one more time, bringing his speed down to under fifteen miles per hour. It was the most he could do to buy the women behind him time to catch up.

The vehicle topped the ridge and Casey gasped. A massive gorge yawned before them. The bridge ahead looked sturdy enough, but the drop on either side of it was impressive.

Casey radioed, "Plan on going under the bridge. There's no superstructure at all to provide cover."

"Roger," Vanessa replied. The woman sounded a little out of breath. Must be running up the last bit of the slope behind them.

"Here goes nothing," he muttered as he guided the truck out onto the bridge. The tires bumped loudly across the steel joints. And then a funny thing happened. Casey seemed to relax beside him. Cool calm rolled off her.

"You all right?" he asked.

She merely nodded, scanning ahead of them. And then she murmured. "Rocky ridges at ten and two o'clock, range from the bridge, two hundred yards. Ideal cover for snipers. Open, flat clearing just beyond the bridge. Two SUVs parked. Four hostiles in sight."

The truck crossed the final few yards of the bridge. Hake applied the brakes and the vehicle came to a halt. He reached for the door handle.

"Don't get out," Casey breathed. "Force them to make the next move."

He nodded and subsided. All of a sudden, a massive flash lit up the night and an enormous impact of noise and concussion rocked the truck. He ducked instinctively, diving across the cab to protect Casey.

"Report!" she bit out frantically.

And then it hit him. The terrorists had just blown up the bridge. Were the Medusas already climbing under it when it went? Had all of her teammates died? And just as worrisome, had their support just been blown up? Were he and Casey completely alone with the terrorists?

Nobody answered her urgent radio call. Casey whispered again, more forcefully, "Report. Is anyone in the clear?"

Eventually, a voice—blessedly female—replied, "We just missed getting obliterated. Cho spotted the explosives and we backed off the bridge just before it blew. We're alive. But we're on the wrong side of the gorge."

His stomach fell like a brick. The two of them *were* alone and without backup. He looked across the cab at her grimly, and she returned the look, fully aware of their predicament.

Hake's cell phone rang. Thinking fast, he picked it up and said angrily, "What the hell are you people trying to do? Blow up your equipment before I can deliver it to you?"

"Get out of the truck. Hands on top of your head," the voice ordered.

"They want us outside. Hands on our heads," he murmured to Casey.

She replied low and fast, "Hit speed dial number nine, then put the phone in your pocket and don't disconnect it."

"Why?" He turned off the truck's ignition and reached for the door.

"I programmed H.O.T. Watch into your phone. They'll be able to monitor our conversation."

Damn, she was good. He did as she'd said and then opened the door. Across the cab, she did the same. He heard a series of ominous metallic clicks that sounded suspiciously like the noise of weapons being brought to bear and readied to fire.

"Did you have to drag me out here in the middle of nowhere, Hake?" Casey complained loudly. "And what on earth was that— Ohmigod! The bridge is gone!"

A man's voice called out, "Who is that? Kill—"

Hake called back, "I had to bring her along. My mother threw her out of the house. She's a belly dancer. She's of no importance."

Disgusted swearing met that announcement. He thought he heard a man say he recognized the girl. But Hake couldn't see a blessed thing. His night vision had been destroyed by that blindingly bright flash of light. He supposed that meant the bad guys couldn't see much better, though.

"All right, gentlemen," he announced. "Let's finish this thing and get you on your way before the army or someone else spots us."

Two men stepped forward, close enough for Hake to see the anger on their faces. "You were not told to bring anyone with you."

"I wasn't told not to," Hake shot back as a man stepped forward to frisk him. "Besides, your people surely know who she is."

The older man of the two looming before him with shotguns in their hands scowled. "You dare to bring that whore to us? How dare you insult us?"

Casey piped up indignantly as a man rudely ran his

hands all over her body beneath her robes. "I'm a dancer, not a whore."

The older man's hand whipped out and he slapped her across the face hard enough to drop her like a stone to the ground. Hake lurched, a snarl building in the back of his throat. But then something strong gripped his ankle and he jumped in surprise. Casey was squeezing his ankle tightly enough to make him grimace. He took a deep breath and released it slowly.

"Gentlemen," he said smoothly. "We are here to conduct a business transaction. Can we not do this in a civilized manner and then be on our way?"

The older man, clearly the leader of this bunch, stared at him assessingly. "Show me the machine."

"Of course." Hake led him to the back of the truck. Two of the terrorists jumped up on the flatbed, quickly unhooked the tarp covering the machine, and threw it back.

"Careful," Hake barked. "That's a piece of precision equipment. Watch it!"

"Show me how it works," the leader demanded.

Hake nodded and climbed up onto the truck bed. He risked a glance over at Casey as the leader joined him. She was back on her feet. Two more men had moved out of the shadows and were pointing guns at her. She seemed to be making conversation with them. At any rate, she had the men's undivided attention.

Hake turned back to the machine and the now eager man beside him. He gave the fellow a fast tour of how the machine worked. Hake used the most technical language he could muster in hopes that the terrorist wouldn't understand much of it.

"At any rate," Hake finished, "it's all in the instruction

manuals. They're in the truck. Cassandra, fetch the notebooks!"

She moved toward the truck and the terrorists let her. Apparently, they thought it perfectly normal to order the woman to do the manual labor. Their mistake. He'd glimpsed the arsenal she'd tucked under the front seat. She emerged from the truck, carrying a tall stack of binders.

"Where do you want these?" she asked humbly enough of one of the junior terrorists.

The fellow directed her to one of the SUVs and she dutifully trudged through the sand to the vehicle. She leaned into the passenger's seat, disappearing from view for a heartbeat too long. Hake suppressed a grin. She'd done something to the vehicle. She exited to the rear, passing behind the first vehicle and brushing past the other SUV. Knowing her, that had also been time enough to do something to the second vehicle. Hake was impressed. Aloud, he said, "My bankers tell me the money transfer is complete. If you'll tell me where we're going next, I'll drive the truck to our destination and load this thing onto your ship."

"We will take the machine from here," the elder terrorist replied sharply.

Hake shook his head in the negative. "This is a delicate piece of equipment. Load it improperly and you'll render it inoperative."

The terrorist scowled and pulled out a cell phone. He climbed down off the truck and moved away from Hake to make a call. Hake took the opportunity to move back to Casey's side. He murmured to her in English, "I told him they'll need me to load the machine onto their ship or they'll break it. He's calling his boss."

She murmured back, "When it's time, head for those rocks to the north. Their snipers are on the south ridge."

That was all they had time for before the senior terrorist strode toward them. "We will handle the loading. Give me the keys."

"A truck was not part of our deal," Hake replied evenly. "Are you prepared to pay for it or return it when you're done with it?"

The terrorist laughed shortly, without humor. "Sure. Whatever."

Hake didn't like the sound of that. These people were planning to kill him sooner rather than later. Had he not known Casey so well, he wouldn't have noticed the subtle tensing of her shoulders. But as it was, he had to consciously stop himself from bracing, too.

The older man stepped close and held his hand out for the truck keys. The sounds, two of them in quick succession, were no more than a gentle spit. A boy shooting a seed from between his front teeth. The terrorist, no more than arm's length from Hake, got a surprised look on his face. Stunned, Hake stepped forward fast and wrapped his arms around the man, staggering under his weight but preventing him from collapsing to the ground.

"Thank you for letting me and my family aid your holy cause," Hake said loudly enough for the other men to hear.

The other men started forward, but were confused enough by the abrupt embrace and declaration to hesitate. It was enough for Casey. She spun and fired from beneath her robe, six shockingly fast and deadly accurate spits. All three men dropped without firing a single round. Hake let his man slide to the ground.

Casey took off running, dodging behind the first SUV. Hake was on her heels. She paused just long enough to point at the ridge behind them. He nodded and they were off and running again, zigzagging low and fast. Casey pulled ahead of him by a few feet and dived over a boulder, disappearing. He mimicked the move, flying over the boulder, slamming into the ground and rolling until he fetched up hard against something warm.

Something pinged over his head and chips of rock flew past his face.

Casey swore softly. "I'd hoped to make the ridge before they pinned us down."

"Now what?" he murmured.

Her only answer was a grim glance. "Any chance I can get some backup in the next two minutes?" she asked whoever was listening to the other end of their radios.

A male voice came back. "Negative. We've got satellites on you and an unmanned aerial vehicle is en route. ETA fifteen minutes."

"That won't help us," she replied tersely.

Hake glanced behind them. Suddenly, the fifty or so feet of open ground before the first rise of the ridge looked miles wide. He peeked around the end of the boulder, trying to spot whoever was shooting at him. Dust flew up in front of him and he lurched backward. He didn't know much about military operations, but even he knew they would have to shoot their way out of this one.

"Have you got a spare weapon?" he asked quietly.

She glanced over at him. Silently, she passed him a pair of pistols from under her robes. "I've got limited ammo. How are you at crawling on your belly?"

Hake answered wryly, "I've never tried it. But if my life is going to depend on it, I'm pretty darned good at it."

The corner of her mouth curved up. "Put on my robe." She stripped the black garment and passed it to him.

As he pulled it over his head, the point of the exercise dawned on him. She wanted him to look like her. She expected the snipers to concentrate their fire on him, so she was trying to switch identities with him. He pulled the robe back off. "You wear it."

"Don't argue with me," she said warningly. "You agreed to follow my orders."

"I didn't agree to let you die for me," he retorted.

"Yes, you did. This is my job. Don't get in my way."

He ground out, "You're also the woman I love. I'm not letting you do this."

She glared at him. "We don't have time for this." She broke off to peek around her side of the boulder for a moment.

More rock flew and the male voice came back in his head. "Movement. Four hostiles. Range one-hundred-twenty yards. They're coming in cautious, staying under cover. One high-powered sniper rig. The other three are using medium-range, vintage rifles."

"Roger," Casey replied. "Best route of retreat?"

"Heading 0—1—0. But you will cross the hostile field of fire."

Hake frowned. That didn't sound good. Casey gave a quick affirmative, however, and didn't look fazed. He looked at her questioningly.

She answered his unspoken question. "Now we wait. We have to pull them in closer."

"Excuse me?" Hake retorted.

"We need a diversion, and I've got just the one. But I need the shooters to move toward us."

"Fake me being injured," Hake suggested.

She looked at him speculatively. "That's actually a good idea. But we're only doing it if you wear my robe."

He scowled. Sometimes in business, a man had to know how to give in gracefully. But he didn't have to like it. He yanked on the robe. "Fine. Now what?"

"I put my arm over your shoulder and we stand up just

enough to be seen trying to limp toward the ridge. Give it, say, three steps, and then hit the dirt. Got it?"

"Got it." She put her arm over his shoulder and he hoisted her to her feet. They hop-skipped a few steps while she pretended to drag a leg behind her, and then they dived together for the ground. Just in time, too, for the ground just ahead of them exploded with bullets hitting rock. They scrambled backward behind the cover of their original boulder.

"Well. That was fun," he panted.

H.O.T. Watch cut in, "Shooters moving fast in your direction."

Casey retorted, "Let me know when they reach the SUVs."

"Roger. SUVs in five…four…three…two…one…"

Boom.

Hake jumped, but was grinning before he landed back on the dirt. That was his girl. She'd managed to rig both vehicles to blow up without the terrorists spotting it. But then she yelled, "Run!" and he had no more time to think. He leaped up and took off running after her.

That fifty-foot open area took a dozen lifetimes to race across. With every step, the back of his neck braced for hot lead to rip through it. But then Casey took a running dive in front of him and he followed suit. He landed in a relatively soft patch of sand behind a low outcropping of sharp, volcanic rock.

Casey panted, "Catch your breath and then we'll start working our way up into the rocks. Maybe we'll get lucky and find a cave."

He nodded, too winded to speak.

Another voice intruded inside his head. The guy from H.O.T. Watch again. "We have movement in the south ridge opposite your position. Range three hundred yards. Eight hostiles moving on foot. Another dozen are circling wide to your left. Looks like they're planning to flank you and approach you from behind."

"Can we beat them over the ridge at our back?" Casey asked tersely.

"Negative."

"How much longer till that aerial drone gets here?" she demanded.

"Twelve minutes."

Hake frowned. It didn't take a military expert to know they were in trouble.

"Options?" Casey asked as she looked around, studying their position.

"Best bet is to hide," H.O.T. Watch replied.

Hake shook his head. "These are locals, if I had to bet. They'll know every nook and cranny of these mountains. It's likely the reason they chose this place for the handoff. We won't be able to hide from them."

Casey winced. "Unfortunately, Hake's right. How long until these guys are on top of us?"

The man replied, "Five to seven minutes at current speed. If you shoot at them, pin them down a little, you might stretch that to ten."

"Or they could just decide to run full-out at us and be here in three," she retorted.

She had a point. Hake looked around. They weren't in a good spot. Hostiles in front of them, a steep ridge about to be crawling with hostiles to their left and rear and only the gorge on their right. The gorge… "Casey, what if we go down instead of up?" he asked.

She frowned at him, then glanced at the gaping blackness on their right. "Go over the cliff? It's a thought. Let's have a look."

She took off crawling on her belly like an alligator, and

he imitated the movement. In about five seconds, his arms and back were protesting even though he was in pretty darned good shape. Meanwhile, Casey slithered along effortlessly in front of him. He caught up to her when she paused, her head jutting over the edge of a drop-off that made him light-headed to look at. The gorge yawned before him with nearly vertical walls. It might as well have been the Grand Canyon. No way could they climb down there.

"It's perfect," Casey announced.

He stared over at her. "Are you out of your mind? This is a sheer cliff. We'll kill ourselves if we try to climb it."

"That's why we're not climbing it. You'll jump."

"Are you mad?" he burst out.

She grinned. "Certifiably." As he stared in open disbelief, she added, "I've got a rappelling harness and cable. You'll put it on and go over the edge. I'll stay here and cover our position."

"I don't think so," he snapped. "You'll wear the harness and go over the edge, and I'll stay here to cover you."

"Hake, you're the civilian I'm here to protect. You're going down there. Besides, if I stay here, I can shoot at the bad guys until they take the truck and leave."

"I love you and take responsibility for you. I'll protect you."

She glared at him. "This isn't open to discussion."

"You're right," he replied grimly. "It's not."

Chapter 18

Casey stared at Hake in total exasperation. Did he have to go all macho and stubborn on her now? They didn't have time for this. She had to find a decent anchor point for her rappelling line, get him in the harness and make sure he knew how to use it. And she had about two minutes to make all of that happen.

"I'm not arguing with you about this—" she started.

He cut her off. "Good. Then don't. I'm done with you treating me like a helpless child you have to look after. I'm neither helpless nor a child. I knew what I was getting into when I came out here, and I was willing to do it to protect the people I love. And that includes you."

"I appreciate that, and I love you, too. But it doesn't change my mission parameters, which include protecting you."

The mission or her feelings for him—which was motivating her the most, she couldn't say. She supposed it didn't really matter. Either way, he was going over that cliff and she was staying behind.

"Listen to me, Casey. You've spent a good chunk of your adult life sacrificing your personal feelings for the job. And it's time to stop. You have a right to a life of your own. To happiness. Love. Quit being so damned noble and let me do this for you!"

"This is who I am," she ground out.

"And I love you for it. But part of loving someone is letting them love you back."

She stared at him, stunned. Was that her problem? She'd thought all along that she wasn't lovable. Not feminine enough or soft enough for any man. But was the problem really that she was incapable of letting anyone love her?

"Let me love you, Casey. I swear, it'll be worth the risk."

Risk. Now there was a word for it. Maybe she wasn't incapable of letting anyone love her. Maybe she was just afraid to. Terrified to the depths of her soul, in fact. Except this was Hake. He'd shown her over and over that he loved her and wanted to be with her, and she'd been too blinded by her own hang-ups to see it.

"What about you?" she challenged as she pulled her climbing gear out of her backpack and began untying it. "You're the one who keeps saying you don't do relationships. Why should I believe you?"

"People change. I've changed. Once I met you, I knew I'd be making the biggest mistake of my life if I let you get away from me. And I'm not a man who makes mistakes often."

"Why should I believe you?" Fear and denial swirled inside her, twisting around her heart like a pair of serpents.

"Because I love you. Because I want to spend the rest of my life with you. Because I'm asking you to marry me."

Marry him? Her entire being tumbled in confusion. He wanted to marry her? "But I'm a Hershey bar," she mumbled.

That damned voice from H.O.T. Watch intruded in her head again. "You're about to be a dead Hershey bar if you don't get moving."

He was right. She glared up at Hake. "We don't have time for this now. Put on this climbing harness." She shoved a jumble of webbing at him. "You step into these holes with your legs and buckle this part around your waist."

"I know how to use a climbing harness," he snapped. "And you're putting it on. You may ignore my marriage proposal, but you can't ignore the fact that I love you. I'd rather die than go on living without you." As she glared at him, he added implacably, "That's how I feel. Deal with it."

Damn him! Marriage and love and not living without her...it was heady stuff. Distracting stuff that would get them killed if she didn't get her mind back in the game and fast.

"How much do you weigh?" she asked abruptly.

"Two hundred pounds, give or take a couple. Why?"

"My cable's rated to two hundred fifty pounds. I weigh one-thirty. If I shed all my gear, we're eighty pounds over the max. That's about thirty percent. It might not work, but I'm willing to try us both riding down the cable."

He nodded briskly. "Done."

"You put on the harness. I'll ride on top of you," she ordered. "I'm lighter and have plenty of upper-body strength to hang on."

Thankfully, he grabbed the harness and yanked it over his feet.

"ETA on our hostiles?" she bit out.

H.O.T. Watch answered, "Three minutes. In about thirty seconds, the group at your twelve o'clock will come into the open. Suppression fire should be effective."

"Roger," she murmured. She pulled out her MP7 semi-automatic weapon and stretched out in a prone firing position. She began scanning the shadows before her.

"What can I do to help?" Hake asked quietly from beside her.

"You know how to shoot a weapon like this?" she asked.

"Yup. How about I provide cover fire while you tie off the rappelling cable."

"Perfect." She passed him the MP7. "Safety's off."

She inched backward, shocked to realize that she'd just entrusted him with a deadly weapon and her life and hadn't thought twice about it. He said he knew how to shoot and would cover her, and she believed him, no questions asked. Then why couldn't she believe him when he said he loved her and wanted to marry her?

She shoved the thought aside. They had to live through the next five minutes first, or the question would be moot. She looked around fast and spotted a solid-looking outcrop near the edge of the gorge. She made for it on her belly, catching a mouthful of dust and painful gravel down her shirt.

Bang! Hake had just shot behind her. Crud. The bad guys were almost here. As his pace of fire increased, she worked fast wedging crampons into crevices in the rocks and hammering them into place. She ran the end of the thin steel-and-titantium rappelling cable through all three tie-off points and secured it. If one crampon gave, the other two should hold. Assuming that any of this gear could take the extra thirty percent load they were about to put on it.

Bang! Bang, bang, bang. Hake was firing rapidly now, and H.O.T. Watch was calling out targets to him as fast as he could sight and fire at them.

"Hake!" she transmitted. "When I start firing, make your way over to me. Ready?"

"Yes," he grunted. "I'm almost out of ammo anyway."

"On my mark. Three…two…one…go!" she called as she started shooting her spare pistol at the moving shadows behind her. She ejected one clip and slammed in a second, resuming firing almost without pause. She had two more clips. Hake had to be at her side and ready to go by then, or they'd both die.

"Hurry," she gritted out as she continued firing grimly.

"Coming," he grunted, his voice strained with effort.

She slammed in her third clip. There seemed to be hostiles behind every rock out there, the muzzle flashes of their weapons pinpointing their positions. And then she caught a glimpse of something that made her blood run cold. More shadows swarming over the top of the ridge at her left.

Just a few more yards and Hake would reach her. She shoved in her last clip of ammo. But then she jumped as an explosion of noise erupted just in front of her. Hake was firing the MP7 one-handed as he crawled. It was actually damned hard to fire like that, but he sent a volley of lead up the slope, and the shadows momentarily stopped and ducked. She fired the last of her rounds over his back. Her pistol clicked. Empty.

"I'm out," he gasped.

She looked over her shoulder and swore. They still had a dozen feet of open space to cross prior to the cliff.

And then a new voice spoke in her head. "Need a little cover, Scorpion?"

Vanessa. And then her boss gave an order that warmed Casey all the way to her toes. "Fire at will, Medusas."

The night exploded into sound as a dozen high-powered weapons fired from across the gorge as expert markswomen unleashed hell's fury at the ridge behind her. "Time to go," she bit out.

She and Hake crawled low to the lip of the gorge. He lay down at the very edge of the cliff and she crawled on top of him, wrapping her arms tightly around his neck. Their gazes met in a moment of naked honesty that said it all. Fear, acceptance and, most of all, love passed between them in that instant.

The two of them had had a heck of a good run. If this was the end for both of them, there would be no regrets. Casey was stunned to see in his eyes the same gladness that he was here with her, like this. If he had to face death, he wanted to do it with her. Shockingly, she felt exactly the same way about him. And that was when she knew.

She truly loved him. This was the real deal.

He rolled to his side. Her legs came around his waist and she hung on to him for all she was worth.

"Don't you even think about letting go to sacrifice yourself for me," he muttered.

"Wouldn't dream of it."

His arms gripped her every bit as tightly as hers held him, and then they were falling, a sickening drop into space as the metal cable unwound from its holder with a metallic schwinging noise. They slammed into something hard, fetching up against the cliff face. She nearly lost her grip on Hake, but his arms tightened even more around her waist, crushing her against him.

They banged their way down the cliff face, tearing their clothes and getting scraped painfully. And then the cable tightened. The jerk of their fall breaking nearly dislodged her from Hake, despite both of them hanging on to each other with all their strength. Her legs came free, dangling in midair, and she scrabbled as her hands began to slip from around his neck, panicked. The abyss below beckoned.

"I've got you," he grunted, his arms tightening around her. She yanked her legs up and managed to get them wrapped around his waist once more. Thank God he was as big and strong as he was, or she'd have been a goner.

He leaned back in the harness, canting his body into a seated position within the webbing. She was able to rest much of her weight on his thighs as long as she maintained a good grip on him and kept her weight forward, close to his.

They spun in a slow circle, dangling under a small overhang.

"Seems like the cable's holding," he breathed.

"As long as the hostiles don't find our line and cut it, we might make it out of this," she breathed back.

Vanessa commented grimly, "Nobody's getting close to that line if I have anything to say about it. Report, Scorpion."

"So far so good," Casey replied.

The silence from above was nerve-wracking as she envisioned hostiles creeping toward the edge of the cliff to peer over. But then a faint sound reached her ears. Relief poured over her like a warm shower. That was the jet engine of an unmanned aerial vehicle. The drone was here.

"You are cleared to fire," the H.O.T. Watch controller announced after guiding the UAV to the far side of the ridge where the Medusas' weapons couldn't reach. A sound of automatic weapon fire erupted. *God bless the soldier on the other end of the drone's remote controller.* Shouts and the sounds of general chaos floated down into the gorge. Hake smiled at her, and she smiled back.

The drone made three passes overhead, and after the final one, another sound intruded upon the night. The engine of the truck Hake had brought to the meeting started up and the vehicle drove away. Silence fell once more.

"Did we make it?" Hake finally asked.

"We're not off this cable yet," she answered.

"Are we going to have to climb for it?" He looked doubtfully at the cliff behind them.

"We don't have the gear for a technical climb. A helicopter will have to come for us."

"How long is that going to take?" he asked.

She calculated the distance to the nearest U.S. Navy ship. "It could be an hour. Are you going to be okay for that long?"

"I'd hang here for a week if it meant you and me getting home alive," he declared.

She laid her head on his shoulder for a moment as the adrenaline of the immediate threat to their lives drained away, leaving her mostly tired and a lot scared. She knew the fear for what it was. Aftermath. Her mind was trained to hold off all emotions until the threat was over, and then, when the crisis was past, the feelings all came pouring in at once.

Except tonight, a host of other emotions came flooding in as well. Disbelief. Dismay. Joy. Exultation. Had Hake really proposed to her? Told her he'd rather die than live without her?

Caution—or maybe more of her same-old fear and unwillingness to let anyone get close to her—kicked in. Maybe that had just been Hake's adrenaline talking. He'd been facing death, and maybe he'd just blurted that stuff out by way of stress relief. She felt herself beginning to pull back emotionally. Dammit, she was going to lose him if she kept this up! She forcibly halted her retreat and asked in a small voice, "Did you mean what you said before?"

"About what?"

"About marrying me. And that stuff about preferring to die than go on without me?"

"Yes to both," he replied grimly. "For better or worse, that's how I feel."

"You're sure it wasn't just stress talking? I mean I'm fine if you just said all that to distract yourself from the fact that we were about to die."

"Casey, love?"

"What?"

"You think too much."

"I do not—"

He interrupted gently, "Yes, you do. Can't you just stop thinking for one minute and pay attention to how you feel?"

"Feelings are bad in my work."

"They happen to be an excellent thing in the rest of your life. Do you love me, Casey?"

"I…"

"Don't think about it. Just answer. Do you love me?" he challenged.

"Yes."

"Do you want to be with me?"

"Yes."

"Forever?"

"Yes."

"There, now. That wasn't so hard, was it?" he asked, laughing. "Someone will come get us off this rope and we'll go home, get married and live happily ever after."

"What?" she squawked. "I didn't say I'd marry you."

"Yes, you did. You said you love me and you want to be with me forever. What is marriage if it's not that?"

"But…you…me…*marriage?*" she squeaked.

"For a brave woman, you can sure be a giant chicken," he teased.

She stuck her tongue out at him. But he had a point. Love was a huge risk. It took courage. More than she had? And then she mentally snorted. She was a Medusa. Since when did a Medusa run from anything scary? Even if it was the prospect of handing her heart over into the keeping of a man? But not just any man. Hake. Did she trust him? Did she dare?

A faint thwocking noise became audible in the distance.

"I do believe our ride is here," Hake murmured.

More than a ride. The end of her mission. Return to her regularly scheduled life. She gazed at Hake, pained. He'd go back to his world of aggressive women and opulent excess, and she'd return to slogging around in jungles.

The thought left her completely, one-hundred-percent cold.

She jolted. Had he ruined her for ever being a Medusa again? A dark shape became visible, flying up down the gorge toward them.

If only she could have both—her military career and Hake. Then everything would be perfect. And that was when what he'd been trying to say to her all along hit her. She *could* have both. All she had to do was give herself permission.

The gunship made several passes out of sight, efficiently cleaning out the last resistance with its fifty-caliber machine gun. The helicopter came back one last time, easing into position overhead. She gripped Hake tightly as the rotor downwash did everything in its power to tear them apart. One last time, they clung to one another with all their strength.

A heavy hook swung tantalizingly beside them, and Hake reached out with one hand to snatch at it. It took him three hair-raising tries, but he finally grabbed it and hooked it onto his climbing harness. His arms went around her once more.

This was it. The end of the line. Literally and figuratively. Hake jolted beneath her and they began to rise.

"Fine!" she shouted. "I'll do it."

"Do what?" he shouted back.

"I'd rather jump off a cliff with you than lose you. How scary can marriage be after that?"

And that was how the two of them ended up tumbling onto the floor of the helicopter, tangled in one another's arms, kissing each other as if nothing else in the entire world existed but the two of them.

"I love you, Casey."

"And I love you, Hake."

"Are you ready for the adventure to begin?" he asked, grinning.

"I thought it just ended."

"Oh, no," he laughed. "We're just getting started."

* * * * *

HER SHEIKH PROTECTOR

BY
LINDA CONRAD

To Jo Ann Zimmerman, who lived one of the most
romantic stories of two people meeting that I
have ever read. Thanks for your story!
And to the amazing author and my dear friend
Karen Kendall. A special thanks for solving the
mystery for me. You're the greatest!

A bestselling author of more than twenty-five books,
Linda Conrad has received numerous industry awards,
among them the National Reader's Choice Award, the
Maggie, the Write Touch Readers' Award and the *RT
Book Reviews* Reviewers' Choice Award. To contact
Linda, read more about her books or to sign up for her
newsletter and/or contests, go to her website at www.
LindaConrad.com.

All the characters in this book have no existence outside the imagination of the author, and have no relation whatsoever to anyone bearing the same name or names. They are not even distantly inspired by any individual known or unknown to the author, and all the incidents are pure invention.

First published in Great Britain 2011
by Mills & Boon, an imprint of Harlequin (UK) Limited,
Eton House, 18-24 Paradise Road, Richmond, Surrey TW9 1SR

© Linda Lucas Sankpill 2010

ISBN: 978 0 263 88538 5

46-0711

Printed and bound in Spain
by Blackprint CPI, Barcelona

Prologue

Running late.
Rylie Hunt knew it was her own danged fault she
wouldn't be on time for the presentation. She'd foolishly
told her father she wasn't coming at all and then stormed
off in a huff. Oh, Lordy, how would she ever make it
up to him?

Finally locating a remote spot to park, she shut down
the engine of her snazzy red Corvette. The parking lot
of her family's newest oil-and-gas shipping facility
was packed to overflowing due to the grand-opening
celebration. The grand-opening celebration that her
father, CEO of Hunt Drilling, had originally intended
for her to officiate at as the vice president.

The mere idea of disappointing her dad gave her a sad
twinge. Everyone had always said she was "Daddy's little
girl with an attitude." But their last argument had been

too bitter and had gone way too far. She and Marshall "Red" Hunt were too much alike—even down to their auburn hair. They butted heads on nearly every subject. Today she was making herself crazy wild, worrying over exactly how mad her dad would be this time.

If she hadn't been late, Rylie would've stopped by the restaurant where she knew her mother was setting things up for the new board of directors' luncheon. Her mother could give her a clue as to Daddy's state of mind and to his reactions over the rather childish way she'd acted yesterday. With a wistful sigh, she prayed that her mom the peacemaker had already smoothed over this latest problem caused by Rylie's big fat mouth.

But she was running late and she hadn't taken the time to find out. She'd landed her little Diamond DA42 Twin Star at Executive Airport. Then she'd jumped into her car and raced toward the Houston Ship Channel, heading for the grand-opening celebration and her father. Eager to apologize, she couldn't wait to get this test of their normally loving relationship behind them.

After locking her car, she planted her feet on the hot and sticky surface of the asphalt parking lot. She jammed the keys into her jeans pocket, refusing to pay any heed to the weird vibes she was suddenly getting. Okay, maybe deep in her subconscious she knew something—somewhere—wasn't quite right.

The creepy sensation of being watched crawled down her arms, despite her attempts to shake it off. But Rylie was too late for the ceremony to pay attention. She made herself believe that the odd sensations were due only to guilt over the stupid argument with her father. Instead of looking for more trouble, she raced toward her family's new shipping facility and the big celebration.

Daddy was bound to forgive her. She hoped.

The heat off the asphalt rose around her in waves as she weaved through the massive lot full of cars. It seemed as if she'd had to park a mile away today. Every news team in the state must've turned out for this shindig.

I'm sorry, Daddy. You were right.

Well, half-right, anyway. Despite her many misgivings about Hunt Drilling taking on new partners, partners by the name of Kadir who owned a huge international conglomerate that included the biggest shipping line in the world, her father had been positive that this move would assure continued success for their firm.

Rylie hadn't given a rip about the Kadirs' power or money. She was more worried about the public relations aspect of a Texas company going into business with a Middle Eastern–based concern. Ever since 9/11, Americans in general had been highly suspicious of even the merest hint that terrorist-influenced groups were taking over U.S. enterprises. Congress had already blocked several attempts by Middle Eastern businesses to buy American companies or real estate, and especially the port facilities.

Given enough time, Rylie was sure she could've found another company to come to Hunt's aid, though she was well aware that few shipping firms flew an American flag these days.

Her dad remained firmly convinced he was right. He'd done his homework. The Kadirs were Bedouin, he'd said. For thousands of years they'd been nomads. Not connected to any politics, religion or particular country. They were definitely not terrorists or connected to terrorism in any sense, and they could do so much to promote Hunt Drilling.

Okay, Daddy, I've thought it over and agree. The PR might still be tricky, but you win. I agree the Kadirs aren't terrorists and we'll find a way to win over the hearts of Americans with the right media. She'd given up her stubborn stand, but hoped her father wouldn't rub it in. If she had been the one who'd won, she would have gloated, and her daddy knew that well. Chuckling, she remembered how he'd always claimed she'd given him his prematurely gray hair.

In her haste to pick up the pace and make up time, Rylie stumbled over a gravel rock and went down on her knees. Shoot!

She was up on her feet again in an instant, but then decided she should stop long enough to dust off her jeans. Bending over to brush at the worst of the gravel, she thought about how glad she was to be wearing her boots and denim today instead of a fancy pantsuit or even a dress. She'd considered changing, but...

At that moment, without any warning, the whole world came apart in a powerful cataclysm. Violent gusts of wind knocked Rylie down, putting her flat on her back and taking the breath from her lungs. A flash of heat rolled over her body, singeing uncovered skin. The back of her head banged hard against the pavement, while earsplitting explosions blew out her eardrums and turned everything eerily silent.

Mustering all her physical resources, Rylie lifted her head and looked around. Through a bleary haze she saw thick, black smoke and fire, rising over her like a towering volcano a hundred feet in the air. The smell of sulphur assaulted her nose.

Dazed and confused as she was, it took a moment to understand what she was seeing. The new shipping facility was gone. All gone.

That must mean… But what had happened to her coworkers and the local reporters? What had happened to the Kadir company officials and their guests?

Light-headed and suddenly sick to her stomach, Rylie closed her eyes and slowly formed the most important question yet. What had happened to the CEO of Hunt Drilling? Where in God's name was her father?

But before her wounded brain could even start processing those answers, reality began sinking away as everything in her immediate world turned from bruised purple to soggy gray—and in seconds went completely black.

Chapter 1

Six months later

"You don't have to do this, brother. Our cousins Ben and Karim are available and prepared. It would be best to let one of them attend the conference."

Darin Kadir listened over his shoulder to his brother but concentrated on readying himself for his first mission for the family. While Shakir argued his point from the other side of the room, Darin checked the cylinder on his Ruger SP101 .357 magnum. Hefting the small double-action weapon, he felt the weight of it like ten tons of responsibility.

Sighting down the satin-finished barrel but making sure to keep his finger off the trigger, Darin answered, "My job makes me the best one for this mission. After everything that's happened, I'm still considered the vice president of Kadir Shipping. It would've been my duty to attend the annual World Industry and Shipping conference before Uncle Sunnar was killed, and it might start rumors throughout the industry if someone else went in my place."

Shakir moved around the hotel suite, stopping to stand with his back to the balcony's glass doors, still not ready to concede. "If Uncle Sunnar hadn't died in that explosion in America, you would be preparing to take over as president of the shipping division upon his retirement. But things have changed—drastically. You're not ready for a field mission for the family, Darin. We need you at headquarters, strategizing and planning."

Darin finally glanced over at his younger brother, dressed in camo fatigues and silhouetted against the stunning views of Lake Geneva and beyond to the Swiss Alps. "And let my brothers and cousins have all the fun?"

The look of sober dismay on Shakir's face was a reflection of Darin's own feelings. He pocketed the Ruger and put a steadying hand on his brother's shoulder.

"We don't know for sure if the Taj Zabbar family will send a representative to the conference." He locked his gaze with Shakir's and forced him to pay attention. "If they don't, then I'm the best one to seek out information about them from our competitors in the industry. Remember, I've been working in the shipping world for the past ten years. I know the people who come to these conferences. No one else would have their confidence the way I do."

Shakir dropped his gaze to stare at the floor, but Darin did not release the firm grip he held on his younger brother's shoulder. He remembered a time when Shakir wouldn't have questioned his big brother's decisions, though Darin had only beena couple years older. In fact for much of his life, Darin had been the father figure for his two younger brothers. At the time of their mother's death, Shakir, a ten-year-old stutterer and in particular need of help, had depended on his brother for lessons on how to develop the intense loyalty of the Kadir clan.

"I'm proud of you and Tarik," Darin told Shakir gently. "Proud of the way you both have stepped up to the challenges our family must face. I'm aware you two have far more experience in the field than I do. But that doesn't mean I can't be of service to the family by obtaining covert information."

Tarik and Shakir had both spent their adult lives in military training, Shakir for the English paratroopers and Tarik for the American Special Forces. Neither had been interested in entering the family businesses after college. Unlike Darin, who'd been eager to climb the ranks of the family's shipping company after receiving his master's degree in business at Columbia University.

But despite his business ambitions, Darin had spent the six months since the explosion secretly mastering the darker arts of weaponry and self-defense. Their father had not yet called upon him to take the lead in forming the family's new offensive line against their ancient enemy, but Darin wanted to be ready.

He thought back to right after the explosion. Ignoring their grief over losing one of their own, his father and the other elders of the Kadir clan spent considerable time debating whether the incident could have been a first volley in an undeclared war. No one had taken responsibility for the explosion, but the centuries-old legends of the Kadir–Taj Zabbar family feud were recalled and retold by the Kadirs. Recent changes in the status of the Taj Zabbar family's financial and political positions were studied in detail. Internet gossip was combed through. Then, and only then, had the Kadirs slowly conceded the possibility of the worst.

Shakir slipped out from under Darin's hand. "You take our old legends too seriously, brother. Yes, the elders have decided not to promote you to president of the shipping line yet—for fear of repercussions or another attack. But this is the twenty-first century…not the sixteenth. You can't seriously believe the Taj Zabbar might want to destroy our entire clan for something that happened between the two families centuries ago?"

"No, of course I don't." Darin straightened his tie and practically stood at attention. "But we can't overlook the possibility that when the Kadir family sided with the country of Kasht fifty years ago at the time of the first Taj Zabbar uprising, we cemented our position as their sworn enemies."

"But Kasht gave us the shipping rights and port facilities in Taj Zabbar territory that allowed our family business to rise to global dominance in three short decades." Shakir held his hands out, palms up. "The Taj Zabbar would never have let us in."

All true statements—as far as they went.

Darin rubbed the back of his neck while he thought of what he wanted to say. "Right. And our father was the leader who brought the Kadir family to prominence after his father made the original deal with Kasht. Out of duty and loyalty to him and to the other elders, I feel my obligation is to gather as much information as possible.

"The Taj Zabbar have sworn to get even with us." Darin kept talking, wanting to impress hard truth on his brother. "We must make intelligent—and safe—decisions. We must be prepared before we act."

Using the power of his voice to make Shakir understand, Darin swallowed when his words sounded as rusty as an old scuttled ship. "You and Tarik have sacrificed for the family's sake. Just look at what you've done to date. You've put a hold on the security firm you and your buddies were trying to get off the ground. And Tarik. Tarik has resigned his commission from the U.S. Army."

Shakir shrugged, not looking directly at him but shifting his gaze to the windows. "We were both in good positions to lend our specialized knowledge to the family's efforts. You..." He let his words die as he waved a hand in Darin's direction.

"I am an expert in gaining information," Darin reiterated. "It's what I do for Kadir Shipping. I'm the one who investigates other firms for financial stability prior to takeover. I search through both public and private documents for authenticity. It's only fair that I share my expertise with the family as have my brothers."

Shakir threw up his hands. "Information retrieval is not fieldwork. Don't you see? You can help us the most by remaining at headquarters and leading the efforts at planning."

Darin knew Shakir was only worried for his safety, but he was done arguing. "Enough. I want to be reasonable, but my mind is made up. I'm the best person for this job and as the older brother, I am finished discussing it. And I'm late."

Darin pulled the conservative gray suit coat on over

his long-sleeved blue shirt and shot the cuffs. "Stick around if you want and back me up. But don't be too obvious about it."

He headed for the hotel-suite door but threw one last bit of sarcasm over his shoulder, the way he would have done during their teenage years. "Do you need me to remind you of covert protocols, little bro? If you do decide to stay and want to show up at the conference, play it smarter than most of your hoorah paratrooper buddies, will you? And…at the very least change your shirt."

Grinning to himself, Darin never turned around when he heard the crash of glass hitting the back of the door—at the exact moment as he'd stepped through and closed it. He picked up his pace and walked in haste to the elevator.

Rylie felt both tired and jet-lagged. The jet lag was new. The exhaustion was not.

She stepped off the public tram at a corner and took a few steps onto the wide boulevard known as Quai du Mont Blanc at the edge of Lake Geneva. Turning, she looked up the hill toward the city center twinkling at dusk with festive lights. Her old friend Marie Claire had given her directions for reaching the Presidents Hotel, where tonight's reception for the World Industry and Shipping conference was being held. But Marie Claire had also said it would be a lot easier to take a taxi. Rylie no longer had the cab fare to throw around.

Once again in her relatively short lifetime, Rylie Ann Hunt was reduced to taking public transportation. Coach airfare and buses. The sides of her mouth automatically turned up with the heartbroken memory as she thought about the delighted look on her mother's face the first time they'd taken a New York City shopping trip together after her daddy had hit it big. Rylie had suggested a cab.

"The Hunts no longer travel second-class, Rylie Ann," her mother said with a giddy laugh as she'd dragged her daughter into a limo. "It's first-class or nothing for these Texas gals from now on."

Remembering her mother in happier times, a more current picture formed in Rylie's mind. She knew exactly where her mama was today. Back in Midland in her tiny rental condo, sitting in an old borrowed rocker behind closed curtains, afraid to venture outside. Not a single smile had graced her mother's lips for six inconsolable months.

Rylie could not imagine what would've happened to her mother during the long days while Rylie was in the hospital, floating in and out of a drug-induced haze, if not for a few of her dad's old friends. And those friends would not let circumstances dissuade them, either, as they continued their care right up until today despite her mother's objections. There'd been a time when it was her mother who cared for others. But that same woman had aged twenty years practically overnight since the day of the explosion. She'd become a recluse. A broken spirit.

A chilly wind blew across the lake and hit Riley on the back of her neck. When that life-changing day of six months ago sneaked back into her mind, guilt lifted its nasty hand and smacked Rylie right across the face.

Even while good friends tried to make a difference, her mother had lost her lovely home and preferred to be isolated and alone rather than face the whispers and the possibility of bankruptcy. Riley, too, felt she was all alone no matter where she was. Alone to think. Alone to grieve…and to deal with her sorrow.

Daddy was dead. Riley still couldn't quite come to grips with the idea. But not one day went by that she didn't relive the explosion—and both her self-reproach and her anger grew.

Wrapping her arms around her middle and ignoring the ringing in her ears that occasionally returned when she was tired, Rylie trudged up the city street away from the lake, still going over in her mind what she could've done differently. The police and the insurance companies had said the explosion was an unfortunate accident caused by someone's carelessness at Hunt Drilling. She knew that wasn't true. So far the insurance investigators hadn't been able to prove their claims, either. Not one dime had been either paid out or denied yet.

Whether their company's fault or not, Rylie and her mother refused their lawyers' advice to wait until they were sued. In an effort to take care of the families of victims affected by the explosion who didn't have the benefit of insurance proceeds, Rylie and her mother chose to sell off everything they had and to liquidate much of their company to pay for things like funerals and hospital bills. Yet many debts still remained. Worse, through all of it, all the selling of her family's beloved things and all the pain of her burns and burst eardrums, Rylie's guilt about living when many others hadn't refused to die inside her and only gained power with each passing day.

The Kadir family must be responsible for the explosion and all this pain. It had to be them. Who else?

Perhaps their motive was insurance money. For whatever reason, they'd reduced her to nothing more than a lump of regret. The only thing keeping her going, keeping her plodding up this hill, was the need to prove them responsible for the explosion.

She would, too. Rylie was no less determined than a police dog on the scent and would find a way to prove the Kadirs were somehow connected. She couldn't find any other reason why a brand-new storage facility that had recently been safety checked and rechecked would suddenly explode.

In her quest for truth, Rylie had done her homework. Kadir Shipping always sent a representative to the World Industry and Shipping conference in Geneva. If the shipping business was anything like the drilling business, and she knew it would be, gossip was easy to come by at the conferences. After a day of long, boring speeches, attendees of these things normally let their hair down and drank too much at the evening get-togethers before having to confront another gruelling day.

A few questions. A couple of come-hither looks. Riley was ready to do anything to get what she wanted. What she must have. Proof. For this first party tonight, she could accept getting her hands on only a rumor—*if* that rumor would take her to the next step toward obtaining enough proof to accuse the Kadirs in public.

She'd been trying to swallow down her anger, but it was slowly taking over her soul as the months went by. She wouldn't readily admit it, but deep down she knew. The carefree young girl she had once been—the one who used to love everyone and needed everyone to love her in return—had changed forever. Her heart was quickly filling with hatred and her mind turning inward toward revenge. If she had looked in a mirror right then, Rylie wouldn't even have recognized herself through the grief and rage.

"Certainly, mademoiselle," the Frenchman politely told Rylie an hour later. "I am familiar with all Kadir Shipping representatives. A member of the Kadir family has been coming to our conferences for many years."

The middle-aged man in the navy wool suit smelling of mothballs turned in a half circle. "Yes, yes, I see Darin Kadir now."

He gestured to a small group of men nearby. "There, with several other gentlemen who also attend every year."

"Um, which one is he?"

Staring at her as if she were a bug who'd crawled up on the food table, the Frenchman gave her the once-over. Rylie knew she must look like she'd been sent through the spin cycle. Her singed hair, cut short after the explosion, had grown back in crazy curls, far beyond anyone's help. Her black dress was on loan from Marie Claire and too big. And her shoes were discount-store specials she'd bought right before leaving Texas.

Once upon a time, at her five-nine height, men had given her the once-over with a question mark, their gawking gradually evolving into lusty leers. But now that she had lost so much weight, she'd seen those same looks contorting into indifference or pity. And sure enough, the expression on the conference concierge's face when his glance landed on her loose dress and then popped back to her eyes turned to anxious concern.

"Are you all right, mademoiselle?"

She swiveled to study the group of men standing nearby. A Kadir family member was actually close enough to touch. At last she would start getting answers. But with her eagerness also came light-headedness as the colors in the room began bleeding together. Conversations ran down the walls like water.

Suddenly unsteady on her feet, Rylie nevertheless straightened her shoulders. "Yes, I'm fine. Just a little jet-lagged. Now which one was Mr. Kadir?"

After he pointed out a rather distinguished-looking younger man in a well-tailored suit, the concierge excused himself and wandered off. Rylie tried thinking of a way to wangle an introduction.

She leaned against the hors d'oeuvre table, reaching for calm and at the same time studying her enemy. The ringing in her ears began again in earnest. Starting at midlevel with the man's dark gray suit, she let her gaze roam up Darin Kadir's body to take in the wide shoulders. He must be well over six foot two. A good four or five inches taller than she was. She noted the expensive maroon tie knotted perfectly at his throat and above it the hard, square-cut jaw. The skin on his face, hands and throat had a golden glow that to her seemed far too dashing in the dim cocktail-party lights. His hair was that shiny raven color she'd never before believed could be for real. But on him…well, it was all too real.

He flicked a glance in her direction. She caught sight of midnight-black eyes, scrutinizing the party with keen intellect and a sensual but cold sort of perusal that many women would die for. He looked like a raptor about to pounce on prey. Rylie's knees wobbled as she put her hand out to grab on to the table like a lifeline.

Darin Kadir had the uncomfortable feeling that someone was watching him as his business associates began leaving his side, searching for the drink table. *Was someone from the Taj Zabbar family close by?* He absently touched the gun hidden under the suit coat at his back before glancing around the room once again.

He'd already learned the Taj Zabbar had sent family and business representatives to the conference this year. But so far, he had not run into any of them.

Catching sight of a tall woman standing at the food table watching him, he tried to decide if she was someone he had met before. She was obviously not part of the Taj Zabbar. Not with that curly dark red hair and fair complexion. But she did look vaguely familiar.

At that moment the woman's eyes closed and her legs appeared to give out. She went limp, slowly slipping toward the floor. He was at her side in an instant. Before he knew it, his arms were around her waist. He'd grabbed her intimately without as much as asking her permission.

She mumbled something he couldn't understand.

"Are you unwell? Can you stand on your own?"

She felt too insubstantial in his arms. All bones and skin and only a few bumps and curves in the right places to prove she was a woman. Not liking this forced involvement with a complete stranger, he nevertheless held on, hoping she would soon take charge of her own body.

"I…I guess I need to sit down." Her voice was as weak as a day-old tea bag.

Darin half carried and half dragged her to a quiet corner where a small overstuffed sofa sat vacant. He would rather the dwindling crowds at tonight's reception

did not see this situation unfolding. He wanted no
rumours. No questions. He'd been trying to blend in.
In his opinion, rescuing a woman who was probably
drunk would not be the best way of staying in covert
mode and gaining information about the Taj Zabbar.

He tried to drop the deadweight of her body to the soft
cushions, hoping to leave her in a comfortable position
while he went to seek out the concierge. Someone else
should take charge of her situation. But before he could
let go and step back, she threw her arms around his neck
and dragged him down beside her.

She clung to his arm like seaweed on the rocks during
a squall. "You're Darin Kadir?"

Blinking at him frantically and then pinching her
lips, she gazed over at him with singularly bright blue
eyes. The color of the Mediterranean on a cloudless
day, they bore into his with an expression that at once
seemed dazed, confused and questioning. But as he
looked again, he noted another, more shadowed emotion
in those oceans that he could only guess at as rage—
seething and deep. And directed at him?

Darin flinched and snapped his arm away from her
biting fingers. Gazing into her face, he expected to have
a hint of recognition. If she knew him, he must know
her, too. He didn't. But what he did recognize was an
unexpected kick of lust. Fascinated, he noticed she was
beautiful, even considering the sharp angles of her too-
thin cheeks.

"Yes. I'm Darin Kadir. Do I know you?"

"No." She spoke with more strength than he would've
thought her capable of. "But you should. I'm your
partner."

"Partner?" He sifted through his memory, trying to

come up with his connection to this stunning but strange woman. "Sorry, you need to fill me in. What's your name?"

"The name is Hunt, Kadir. Rylie Ann Hunt. I'm the new president of Hunt Drilling." Her eyes pinned him with a look that could've burned through stainless steel—incongruously making him think of superhuman strength.

As her name was beginning to register, she spat out a much stronger sentiment, sending a swift punch of regret directly to his gut. "At least what's left of it after you tried to blow us all straight to hell."

Chapter 2

Horrified by her own lack of self-control, Rylie pressed trembling fingertips to her lips, wishing she could take back the words. Why had she said that? She'd meant to be cool and conceal her true feelings. At least until she could coerce information from this man.

The festering bitterness boiling inside her was suddenly out there for the entire world to see. Her infamous impatience left her wide open. Would she never learn?

Darin leaned away from her, and his expression changed from what had appeared to be mild interest to a pucker of pure displeasure. "Miss Hunt, have you had too much to drink?"

Only a minute ago her overactive mouth was spouting off too much, and now she couldn't seem to get a word out. She shook her head fiercely and swallowed several times.

"No? Then I suggest you choose your words with more care." He stood, towering over her.

If looks could kill as easily as a chemical explosion, she would already be dead and in her grave.

"I am sorry for your loss," he said, dragging his sentence out on a harsh hiss. "But why would you say…"

Letting the words die in his mouth, he quickly glanced around the room and then tilted his head toward her. "Red Hunt was a well-respected oilman. He will be missed by the industry and his business associates. But as you must be aware, Kadir Shipping has already sent a team of attorneys to America to sort out the many claims, *and* to review our respective companies' currently complicated business association."

Rubbing a hand over his mouth, he looked as though he were choosing his words carefully. "In the meantime, I would recommend you refrain from making any statements to either a Kadir representative or to anyone else—especially in public—that you may regret in the future."

Struggling with both the light-headedness and the almost overpowering need to choke a confession out of this asshole, she screwed up her nerve and got to her feet. In league with terrorists or not, she needed Darin Kadir. Without him, Rylie knew she would never dig out the truth.

But once on her feet, her body swayed and she was forced to reach out and take his arm or else fall flat on her face. "Wait…"

His other hand closed around her biceps, keeping her from an embarrassing tumble but pulling her close against his chest instead. When she gazed into his eyes, her emotions began a roller-coaster ride. Deep within those coal-black irises she caught sight of a flash of—need.

Need? Hell's bells. In the eyes of an arrogant terrorist? Or perhaps she'd been all wrong, and he was only a businessman who had no scruples and was trying to scam the insurance companies for big bucks. Either way, *need* was the last thing she'd expected to see in his eyes.

Taking a step back and planting her feet, she held his gaze, searching for any reason why she should find herself in such sudden turmoil over a man she had vowed to unmask as a murderer. In the next instant, she could swear she sensed loneliness in him—and a glint of something else. Something much deeper she couldn't put a name to, coming from the same hidden recesses of his steady stare.

Then the moment was gone and his blank eyes were devoid of any expression save for irritation. But Rylie was shaken by what she'd seen.

As usual during times of stress, babbling words began spewing from her too-loud mouth. "I think I must be jet-lagged. I didn't mean... I apologize, Mr. Kadir... uh...Darin."

He let go of her arm and a wary look crept into his eyes. Not good. She didn't want him to be on guard. Now she would have to start all over again and figure out ways to make him trust her.

Her knees wobbled once more, and she decided any information-gathering efforts would have to wait for another day. "I could stand some sleep, but I would like to talk to you when I can make more sense. How about tomorrow? Can we set up a time to get together?" Teetering on her narrow heels, she hung on to his arm.

He shook his head slowly and she knew he was about to turn her down. "I have a heavy conference agenda all day tomorrow." Taking her by the shoulders, he eased her backward and helped her sit down on the couch. "But perhaps we could find a few free minutes after the workshops and before the evening banquet. Shall I plan to come to your hotel around five?"

Well, what do you know? Amazed by his sudden change of heart, she was too thrilled to ask why and take the chance of messing things up.

"Uh, no, not to my place." She wasn't registered at a hotel but didn't want him to know she was staying on Marie Claire's couch. "How about we meet at your hotel? Where are you staying?"

Tight lines formed around his eyes. "Let's compromise. There's a club...pub...bar, I guess Americans would say, called Arthur's Rive Gauche. It's rather more elegant than I would normally choose for conversation and it's wildly popular, but I'm sure we can find a quiet corner. Why don't I meet you there at half past five?"

"That'll be fine. Great." She made a move to rise, wanting to show him she could be perfectly civilized by shaking his hand. But she hadn't even made it to her feet before the dizziness returned and threw her back into the cushions.

"Stay seated," he insisted. "I'll search out the concierge and have him bring you a plate of food. Eating may give you a much-needed temporary energy boost. However, I have no hope of it stilling your temper or mouth." He cocked his head and waited for her to make a comment.

When she didn't, he added, "A little sustenance might at least provide you with enough strength to take a cab back to your hotel. Allow me to arrange it, Miss Hunt?"

She closed her eyes and leaned back—for only a moment. "All right, but please call me Rylie. And thanks."

"You must be joking, brother." Shakir lounged in one of the club chairs of their hotel suite several hours later, with a bottle of dark ale in his hand and a smirk across his face. "Rylie Hunt had the nerve to accost you and bloody well accuse you of murder?"

"You should've seen the look in her eyes," Darin told him. "It was enough to raise the hairs on the back of even your tough paratrooper's leather neck."

Shakir sat up straighter. "You don't think she could be some kind of spy or lookout for the Taj Zabbar family, do you? It would make a kind of perverse sense. I know if I was into subterfuge and covert warfare, using a woman who has reason to hate the world would be perfect. Who knows what lies they could've told her in an effort to make her bend to their will."

Darin gave it a moment's consideration and quickly discarded the idea. "Not this woman. I have the feeling she could spot a liar from a mile away, and I doubt anyone on earth could bend her to their will. But I've agreed to meet with her. I need to uncover what she already knows."

"Bad move." Shakir screwed up his mouth. "You can't seriously mean to get close to this woman. She could be dangerous. Why would you agree to do such a thing?"

"I felt sorry for her." But that wasn't strictly the truth.

He'd felt something, all right. But the something was pure, unrefined and nearly uncontrollable…lust.

Theoretically, his sudden all-consuming erotic need should've been tempered by his empathy for her situation. After all, his life had been altered irrevocably with that explosion the same as hers. But the trouble with theories was they weren't real life. In reality, despite what he should have felt, he'd searched his memory and couldn't come up with a time when a stranger, or anyone at all, had affected him with quite this much seething passion.

He wasn't sure why, either. She was a little too tall, a little too thin and a little too loud for his taste. Her overall appearance reminded him of what he'd always considered the looks of a spoiled girl from America's western lands. Over-the-top—in every way. Not in the least his normal type of companion when it came to the opposite sex.

His brother was still seated, staring absently at the half-empty beer bottle in his hand. "This is not a good idea." Shakir shook his head forcefully. "Even if she isn't working with the Taj Zabbar, let's suppose one of them spots the two of you together. That might give rise to a lot of false assumptions. False assumptions that could be life-threatening—to her or to you."

"Don't worry," Darin told him, letting his voice carry a cavalier tone he was certainly not feeling. "I've suggested our meeting take place in a pub that's popular with the locals but is out of the way for conference attendees. No one will spot us there."

Later that same night in the dimly lit lobby bar of Darin's hotel, Sheik Newaf Bin Hamad Taj Zabbar hung up his satellite phone when he spotted his distant cousin Samman Taweel walking his way. The young, hollow-eyed fellow weaved past several empty tables heading straight for him.

"Sit." Sheik Hamad gestured to the chair across from him with the glowing tip of his Cuban Cohiba Behike. "I assume you left a compatriot to watch Darin Kadir. Is this so?"

"Yes, my sheik. The target you asked me to watch has seemingly retired to his room for the evening. One of the other men you hired is watching his door."

"Very well. Then tell me what you observed of our target's behavior at the conference reception."

This distant cousin was far from brilliant. But Hamad had not hesitated to employ the dull but desperate man, because desperate men follow instructions exactly. Since the Taj Zabbar clan was finally on the cusp of exacting their ultimate revenge for the subjugation and humiliation they'd endured for centuries, he needed men like this one. Hamad knew better than to take a chance on hiring outsiders when his clan was close to their goals. The money was flowing. Let the retribution begin.

But patience was the key. For now, his goal was to detect new ways of embarrassing and humiliating three of the most important young Kadir men, the sons of the most powerful Kadir elder. Three of the Taj Zabbar's greatest enemies.

Hamad wasn't worried. Like this cousin, those rising Kadir stars didn't seem like any great geniuses. And Hamad would accept nothing less than full capitulation from them in the end. He had little doubt his clan's retribution would come to pass exactly as he'd planned.

The entire Kadir clan would soon suffer in the same ways as the Taj Zabbar had suffered throughout hundreds of miserable years. He was counting on it.

Cousin Taweel's hoarse yet respectful voice broke into his thoughts. "At the reception the target approached a pretty young woman and the two sat down together. They spoke for several minutes and then, before abandoning her, our target arranged with a concierge to see to the woman's comfort. Food and taxi service back to her hotel."

Hamad thought such behavior unexpected for the disciplined and rigid eldest Kadir son, and all exceptions from the ordinary worried him. "Did Kadir and this woman seem to be close friends? Did you find out who she was?"

"They appeared to be on most intimate terms, my sheik." As he spoke, a tic appeared near an eyebrow, telling Hamad of his conservative cousin's obvious disapproval.

Hamad didn't consider either the disapproval or Kadir's behavior important.

"I was told the name of the woman is Hunt. From America."

Hunt. What would one of the Hunts be doing at a shipping conference? Hamad did not care for the idea. Had Darin Kadir invited the woman here to share information?

The Taj Zabbar elders had decided on temporary surveillance of the Kadir brothers rather than an outright attack. Extreme secrecy was essential for their revenge to succeed. Plans still had to be finalized and everything had to remain undercover until it was too late for their enemies to stop the schemes. But if it were true that

Darin Kadir already suspected the Texas explosion was not an accident, his life would shortly come crashing to an abrupt end. It was Hamad's duty to make it so.

Leaning back, Hamad tried easing his tension by chewing on the cigar. He felt positive that each detail in Texas had been dealt with cleverly, that nothing had been left to chance. The shipping facility explosion had been judged an accident, exactly the way Hamad planned it. Of course, he had anticipated the blame for the *accident* to accrue to Kadir Shipping instead of to Hunt Drilling the way their foolish American law enforcement believed. But the results were nearly the same. Kadir business interests had taken a loss, both financially and in reputation. All in all, it had been an excellent first shot in the Taj Zabbar's war of retribution.

Hunt Drilling was only unfortunate collateral damage, as the Americans would say. His sources told him the Hunt organization had been fatally weakened and that the remaining Hunt family felt extraordinary anger toward the Kadirs. Had that changed?

Hamad needed to understand this new development. His plans could well depend on finding out what the Hunt woman knew—or thought she knew.

The flame had gone out of his cigar and he used the tip to make his point to the cousin. "I want to talk to this Hunt woman. Is it possible to find out where she is staying? Can you question her taxi driver?"

The young Taweel lowered his eyelids and shook his head slowly.

Growing impatient, Hamad tapped his cigar against the tabletop. "I will put out a few requests. Perhaps we can locate her hotel yet tonight. In the meantime, you are to remain with Darin Kadir. When he leaves his rooms, do not let him out of your sight. If he meets with that woman again, I want to be notified. And then, bring her to me."

"You may be requesting an impossible task, my sheik. What if the woman does not wish to come?"

The cigar tip tapped rapidly against the table as Hamad held frustration in check. "Then you must insist. Or…" Tap. Tap. Tap. "Just see that you bring her to me."

It was nearing 2:00 a.m. when Hamad Taj Zabbar placed his last phone call of the night. Frustration had decimated his posture since he had sent his cousin away an hour earlier. His shoulders were strung tight from the strain.

The Hunt woman was not registered in any hotel in the city. Due to the late hour, Hamad had been forced to give up his search. It was possible she'd registered at any number of inns, bed-and-breakfasts or hostels, and he would never be able to hunt through every one.

Unaccustomed to not winning each skirmish he entered, Hamad rubbed his temple, vowing that his failure to locate the Hunt woman right away would be only a minor setback.

Hamad felt confident that even his dull cousin could bring her to him at the first opportunity.

Taweel had better.

The next morning Darin rolled his feet out of bed and hung his head in his hands. What a long night it had been.

Dreams of drowning in vibrant blue-green eyes had kept him tossing for hours on end. He'd been lost in luxurious layers of auburn curls. Soft and shiny, so smooth against his skin. Like a bath in velvet.

What a fool he was. The urge to pound his fists into his empty head drove him to stand. Perhaps a shower would help. As he walked to the bath, it became clear he had better dredge up some of his infamous impassivity. It should come easy for him, as he'd been accused of being aloof and detached for most of his life.

Right now he could use some of that lethal remoteness. He'd not needed anyone, save for his two brothers, since his mother's death. Women were friends, business associates and overnight flings, and this was no time for his libido to begin overruling his head. The middle of his first covert operation for the family would be the worst time to undertake a romantic relationship with a woman he barely knew.

While cranking the cold water on high, Darin thought of a brilliant plan. As soon as he stepped from the shower, he would find out as much as he could about Rylie Hunt's background. No one could withstand his kind of scrutiny. No one. He was positive that the more he learned about Rylie the more this crazy obsession of his would wane.

Yes, a good plan. Such a good plan that he began to whistle. Until…he stepped into the shower and a shot of freezing water hit him flat in the chest.

As he swore, the first image that came into his mind was Rylie's. Completely naked and lingering under the shower with him. Hell. Perhaps no plan would be good enough to rid him of his passion.

"Rylie, you asked me to wake you while it was still early. I've made a pot of tea."

Marie Claire's lilting voice caused Rylie to lift

her scratchy eyelids and rouse herself from a fitful morning's dream. She managed to sit up and put her feet on the rose-patterned carpet, but her T-shirt was wet with sweat. Her bones were still stiff from tossing and turning. Her mind still reeling from another night of seeing fire and smoke in her dreams.

Yawning, she glanced toward the rain oozing down a windowpane. Unlike Texas gully-washers, the wetness here seemed damp and depressing without being cleansing. Only enough mist and fog to frizz the hair and muddy the boots.

"Did you get enough rest?" Marie Claire sat in the one other chair in the room and began pouring them both cups of fragrant tea. "I'm not sure my sofa is comfortable. No one has ever stayed the night on it before and it's too short for someone of your height."

"The sofa was fine." Rylie lied to her old college roommate as she reached for her tea cup. "I appreciate your hospitality. I'm not sure what I would've done if you hadn't invited me to stay."

Marie Claire gave her an I-know-you-and-you-would've-found-a-way look before blowing on her own steaming cup and glancing at Rylie over the rim. "I was searching the Internet for info on the Kadir family this morning. You seem convinced that they're the bad guys and I can't quite figure out why. I wanted to know more about them."

Rylie felt the muscles in her face soften. Her dear friend had given up free time to help with Rylie's important mission.

"I could've told you most of their background information if you'd asked. Between the original lawyers for our business merger and my own private investigators,

I'm sure I know everything worth knowing about the Kadirs."

Sitting back in her chair, Marie Claire's lips pursed, making her look like a pixie with a secret. "Oh really? Then will you tell me more about the Kadir–Taj Zabbar family feud? Start all the way back in the fifteen hundreds, okay?"

A sudden swallow of hot tea burned Rylie's tongue and left her sputtering. "What feud? And who are the Taj Zabbar?"

"The reason I was asking is because I couldn't find an explanation for the feud online." Marie Claire shrugged a freckled shoulder. "Just a mention of the Taj Zabbar holding their grudge for a long time. I do know a little about the Taj Zabbar clan, though. They live in a desolate place in the Middle East called Zabbaran. For centuries their territory was ruled by neighboring countries. One neighbor, Kasht, took over their land about a hundred years ago. The Taj Zabbar mounted a couple of rebellions along the way, but they never could break free.

"Then about two years ago, the Taj Zabbar managed to liberate themselves from Kasht, shaking off their oppressors with help from the world community." Marie Claire took a sip of tea before raising her eyebrows. "Now it seems the Taj Zabbar family is suddenly rich. An ocean of oil has been discovered under their land."

Dang. Marie Claire had sprung this new twist on her without warning. Rylie took pride in her information-gathering ability and had thought she'd been prepared.

Well…looked like maybe not so much. She'd apparently missed something important. An ancient feud and gushers of money made it sound as if the Kadir–Taj Zabbar situation could be potentially dangerous to not only Hunt Drilling but the rest of the world.

Still Rylie couldn't put all the pieces together. She was still missing something. Why? What was behind the feud, and could it have something to do with an explosion as far away as Texas?

Chapter 3

Looking over the busy club at masses of people, Darin caught a glimpse of wild auburn hair in a far corner. Meeting Rylie here had sounded like a good idea yesterday. But now that it was happy hour and the place was packed with young professionals, he wasn't so sure.

He made his way through the boisterous bodies, still wondering if tonight's meeting was smart. It was possible his brother had been right last night. Despite his erotic dreams of her, Rylie Hunt could be in the employ of the Taj Zabbar, and talking to her might be dangerous. After all, he was a businessman. What did he really know about covert operations?

He knew one thing for sure: Rylie was who she said she was. He'd found pictures on the Internet of Red Hunt's daughter in accounts of the explosion. But was she also a gorgeous and deadly spy? He couldn't know that for certain unless he talked to her.

He'd asked around about her this morning and checked with others back at his office. He now knew that she'd spent weeks in the hospital after the explosion. Since her release, she'd also taken a few altruistic business steps above and beyond what Darin considered reasonable.

Admirable? Perhaps. Foolhardy? Very likely.

Did that necessarily mean she was not also involved with the Taj Zabbar? He had to coerce her into opening up to him in order to find out.

Her table was located in an alcove and seemed relatively quiet. As he arrived, she glanced over at him and froze. Even in the inadequate lighting, he noted that her pupils were dilated and her expression frazzled. Her face was a deathly shade of gray that seemed more pronounced in proximity to her black denim jacket and jeans. Her lips tensed and she crossed her arms tightly against her chest. Shrunken in on herself, she looked like a housefly suddenly caught up in a sticky web and docilely expecting the spider.

His heart thumped once and went out to her. If she was as innocent as she appeared, Rylie Hunt had no reason to fear a Kadir.

He simply could not put the picture she made sitting there, her whole body trembling, together in his mind with a Taj Zabbar spy.

When he got closer, two bloodred spots appeared on her cheeks and tears backed up in her eyes. For a moment Darin's only thoughts were of calming her by taking her in his arms. Instead, he slid into the lone empty chair at her table with his back to the corner.

But it was all he could do not to reach out and cover her quivering hands with his own.

"Hello," she said in a shaky voice. "I wondered if you would really show up."

"I'm here." He nodded at the waiter to get his attention and ordered himself a sparkling water and Rylie a glass of pinot grigio, hoping the lighter drink would calm her nerves without sending her into some alcoholic stupor.

After the waiter acknowledged the order and left, all was quiet at their table and Darin took a moment to look around the club. Rylie had put them in the best possible spot for quiet conversation. No one around them was paying any attention.

A couple of young lovebirds at the closest table, who might have been near enough to hear what was being said, were kissing and whispering with their foreheads touching together and their hands touching everywhere else. Impervious to all around them. Darin was almost jealous of the way they blocked out the world. His relationships were never so intense.

Bringing himself back to his immediate surroundings, Darin felt confident enough that he and Rylie were isolated in the middle of a crowd. They could talk freely.

"Why?" Her voice was a bit stronger, a bit lower than yesterday.

Shaking his head at the out-of-place question, he was beginning to wonder if that explosion had affected her mind.

"Why are you here?" she blurted before he could say anything. "I wouldn't think a Kadir would be willing to talk to a Hunt."

Surprised by the question, but interested in where she was going with this line, he chuckled and gave her a polite nod. "Now it's my turn to ask—why not? You don't have plans to do me harm, do you?"

She didn't answer, but before the lull in the conversation dragged into an embarrassing void, her wine and his water arrived. Her lack of a response, to both his question and his companionable attitude, did nothing to fill him with confidence. He had expected either a lie or an accusation. She confused him with a simple blank stare.

Rylie took a sip of wine and kept on staring at him. He felt as though he were a rat being studied in a scientific experiment, and he wasn't crazy about the idea. Being too closely scrutinized had to be bad for covert operations. The longer she stared, the more he wondered if she was, in fact, working for the Taj Zabbar.

A spark appeared in her eyes. But before Darin could figure out if that spark meant a change of mood or something more dangerous, she asked, "Would you mind telling me about the Kadir and Taj Zabbar feud?"

In the middle of lifting his water to his lips, Darin choked, spilling the drink down the front of his button-down shirt.

"What did you say?" he sputtered. "Who told you anything about the Taj Zabbar?"

Leaning in toward him, she hurriedly dabbed at his chest with a paper napkin. Tiny smile lines appeared at the corners of her eyes. It was the first easy expression he'd seen on her face and the casualness of it made her glow. How beautiful would she be if she ever actually laughed?

He couldn't imagine, but the mere idea made him want to see for himself.

Before Darin could give her an automatic grin, he ordered up the covert operative inside him and brushed her hands away. "Forget the shirt. The water will dry. Tell me what you know about the Taj Zabbar."

"All I know is what a friend read on the Internet." She sat back in her chair and looked as though she was poised to run. "The Taj Zabbar is in control of their own country again after nearly five hundred years of being oppressed by neighbors. And they apparently hate the Kadir family for some reason, but I can't find out why."

When he said nothing, she continued, "I do know the Kadirs weren't the ones who enslaved them. You folks don't even have your own country, do you? Why would they carry a grudge against your family?"

Under her shower of questions, Darin felt his jaw and shoulders tightening. He tried to relax. Beyond the obvious lust, what was it about her that so intrigued him?

If this was some kind of game, he would play along until he was satisfied she wasn't working for the enemy.

"I suppose I can tell you the family legends of the Taj Zabbar feud. But then I have a question or two for you. Do you promise to answer truthfully?"

"Why should I?"

"Because otherwise this conversation is over. I have business matters that need attention."

Her lip jutted out and her eyes narrowed. "Okay. Maybe. But I reserve the right not to answer."

She frustrated him beyond belief. "We'll see about

that." He tried to find some emotion he could pin down in her eyes, but all he found was hunger.

"Wait a second." He lifted a hand, palm out. "I've decided there is one more condition. I'm going to order something for you to eat and I want you to eat every bite—or else no more conversation."

Her mouth gaped open. "What is with you and the compulsion to feed me?"

"It's just your tough luck that you picked this Kadir to harass. I won't be responsible for you collapsing from hunger while you're with me. And you look like you could be blown over by a light breeze. Is it a deal?"

"Fine," she muttered. "Do you think this place serves salads?" She rolled her eyes. "Don't I look like I need to diet?"

Nearly done chowing down on the huge bowl of pasta and seafood Darin had insisted she order, Rylie was trying to calm her racing mind. For the last thirty minutes, Darin had been almost overly polite. Talking casually about the chill in the air or the newly budded spring blossoms on the trees seemed bizarre. The evening was starting to feel like a date, except that his eyes kept darting around the room as if he were expecting someone else to show up.

Somehow over the last twenty-four hours, Rylie's anger toward the Kadirs—or at least toward this Kadir—seemed to have subsided. She tried to dredge up a chunk of that old hatred, but all she came up with was curiosity.

She dropped her fork and blotted her mouth with a napkin. "Done. Will you—please—tell me the story of the feud now?"

"It isn't a true feud. Feuds take two parties. The Kadirs have not held a grudge against the Taj Zabbar—in the past."

The way he added that last part was curious. She made a mental note to ask about it later. But in the meantime, Darin sat back in his chair and sipped his sparkling water as if he was done talking. Like hell.

When she glared at him and fisted her hands on the table, he lifted the corners of his mouth and rolled his eyes. "All right. I guess I did promise. There's an old legend about the family's first encounter with the Taj Zabbar—over five centuries ago. Is that what you want?"

"To start."

"Yes, well… For nearly a thousand years the Kadir clan have been nomads and traders. Originally we traveled the Spice Route in ten-mile-long caravans, staying for a time with the various peoples we met along the way. Our clan never claimed any lands as our own but would rely on the kindness of those who would allow us to pitch our tents on their land."

Rylie leaned back in her chair and listened to him speak in that dreamy voice of his. As he spoke, she thought about the Arabian Nights tales. His hushed words tied her in a web of romance, destiny and mystic promise. Visions of sandstorms and camels and dark sheiks riding across dunes on horseback swam in her mind.

"At around sixteen hundred AD," he went on, "the Kadir caravan arrived in a new territory. A land of vast, isolated deserts and rough mountain terrain. A land with easily accessible coastlines for commerce. The Kadirs found the territory was inhabited by a fierce warrior tribe called the Taj Zabbar."

Darin was finally getting down to the legend. "The Kadirs have always come and gone in peace, no matter where they've traveled." Shooting a quick glance around at the thinning crowds in the bar, he continued. "But the Taj Zabbar wanted no trade and no peace. Our people were preparing to move on when the caravan was attacked. Taj Zabbar warriors robbed, raped and murdered many of our people before the Kadirs could mount a defense."

He'd stopped talking and a faraway look appeared in his eyes. Rylie wondered if the magic of the legend was affecting him the same way it did her.

"Don't stop now. What happened next?"

"What? Oh, sorry." He suddenly looked annoyed and Rylie was about to ask why when he said, "Do you see anyone watching us?"

She pivoted in her chair and checked around the bar. "Nope. Why?"

His lips narrowed into a grimace. "Nothing. It's just…

"Never mind. Where was I?"

"Your ancestors defending themselves against attack."

She couldn't quite name the expression in his eyes, but in a moment he began his story once more.

"The Kadirs successfully defended themselves. But by then the caravan was destroyed. It would've been impossible for them to move on in the shape they were in. They were compelled to settle down where they were for long enough to repopulate their herds of camels and horses and to construct new tents. A second generation of our people had been born before the caravan was ready to travel again."

"Wow. So, like, years, then? What about the Taj Zabbar during that time?"

"Yes, it was many years. And the Taj Zabbar continued their raids on our people." Darin's voice dropped to a near whisper and she was forced to lean forward to hear what he was saying. "Finally, in desperation, the Kadir elders decided they had no choice but to fight back. They rounded up as many of the Taj Zabbar as they could, executing the worst of the murderers and dispersing the rest."

Rylie felt a whiff of air on the back of her neck at that moment and looked around to see if someone had opened a door behind her. She found the bar crowds had thinned considerably, and the door was firmly shut against the night air. She could barely believe she'd been so entranced by the story that she hadn't even noticed the time.

Darin kept talking and she whipped her head back to hear what he was saying. "After the Kadir clan left their territory for good, the Taj Zabbar rulers and warriors had been so decimated that they couldn't defend themselves. Their neighbors swarmed over their lands and enslaved what was left of the tribe." Darin shook his head at his own words, which seemed a little strange to her.

"The Taj Zabbar never forgot or forgave the Kadirs, I suppose."

"No. Not for the following five hundred years."

"But it's over now, isn't it?" she demanded. "I mean, the Taj Zabbar finally got their territory back a couple of years ago. All the problems between your clans were long ago."

"Not exactly."

She thought about what he'd said at the start of his story.… *Our first encounter with the Taj Zabbar—*

"Something else has happened since? What?"

Darin raised his eyebrows. "Sorry. It's my turn to ask the questions."

"But…"

"Uh-uh." His face lit up like he'd been given a special present. "A promise is a promise."

He was right about that. She believed in honoring a promise, too.

But she didn't have to like it. "Fine," she grumbled. "What do want to know?"

Taking his time, Darin raised his glass and swallowed the last of his wine. "First, I would like an explanation of why you threw that accusation around last night about me causing the explosion?"

Struck, as if by his hand across her face, Rylie drew in a breath. "I didn't mean *you* exactly. I was talking about…"

"My family?" he suggested. "But even that doesn't make any sense. My uncle was killed in the explosion the same as your father. Thinking logically, why would the Kadirs kill a member of their family and cost their own company untold amounts of trouble and aggravation?"

"I…" It did sound ridiculous now hearing him say it. How would she explain herself?

The ugly truth was all she had to offer, but she vowed to take the punishing embarrassment that came with it like her father's daughter should. "I wasn't thinking clearly, I guess. Maybe I thought the explosion was some sort of suicide bombing."

"Terrorism? You thought we…" He stopped talking and the strangest look crossed his face.

His shoulders raised and straightened as he glared at her. "Certainly an educated person wouldn't let prejudice cloud their mind in such dark ways. You seem too sophisticated for racial profiling."

"I am." She heard the desperation in her voice and wondered why this man's opinion of her had suddenly become so important. "I mean, I don't really believe any of that stuff. But my judgment has been impaired since the explosion—since the death of my father. I…I haven't been completely well. Obviously."

It took him a second, but the hard expression in his eyes finally softened to sympathy as he said, "Which brings me to my next question. Why are you here? You should be home with your family and running what's left of your company."

She tightened her lips and glared at him, not ready to discuss this yet.

"I learned this morning that you have nearly bankrupted yourself and the entire Hunt firm," he continued. "All in an effort to lessen the suffering for victims of the explosion—every one of them, and not only Hunt employees. That may be admirable, but what good are you doing them or yourself by coming here?"

The question made her stop and think. Why was she here? What had she hoped to accomplish?

"Justice." Once she'd spoken the word aloud, it made sense. "I want to give the dead and injured justice. I am positive that explosion wasn't caused by any accident. It was deliberate. And I intend to find out who caused it and why."

* * *

Still stunned by a couple of things Rylie had said, Darin ignored the creepy sensation of being watched as he paid their bill and ushered her outside. He'd checked out every person remaining in the club before they left, but he couldn't pinpoint anyone who appeared to be spying on them.

He wasn't the kind of person who ordinarily gave himself over to fantasy. But he thought perhaps it was the strong sense of responsibility toward Rylie that he'd been experiencing that was making him paranoid on her behalf.

Her mention of justice had stopped him. He understood her sentiments and her loyalty to her father. Justice went along with honor and family loyalty. But on the other hand, for centuries the Taj Zabbar had used their quest for justice as an excuse for threats and dishonest behavior toward his family.

Justice was not a concept he took lightly. Over the last hour, he'd begun to reconsider some of the steps that the Kadirs had already taken against the Taj Zabbar—without any proof. Where was the justice in building a defensive line and spying operations without knowing for sure that the Taj Zabbar were already at war?

One thing would definitely be different for him after tonight. Darin felt confident Rylie was not involved with the Taj Zabbar in any way. She was merely a grieving victim, trying to make sense out of the nonsensical.

Death had a way of turning normally smart people into hysterical idiots. He knew that because he'd been there himself at least once. When his mother died, Darin had been ready to blame anyone and everyone—except the cancer that killed her.

Those thoughts made him wonder if the death of one of their own hadn't also sent the Kadir elders into that same spiral of frantic paranoia. Both he and Rylie might be better off to quit their respective witch hunts and go back to work.

Gently laying a hand at her waist to help guide her through the doorway and outside to the walkway, Darin thought back on the other stunning thing she'd said tonight. Or perhaps it wasn't what she'd said but the way she'd said it.

She had been wrapped up in the tale of his family when she'd looked up at him and demanded he finish the story. He'd gotten a good look at her eyes. Those eyes with their oceans of emotions had totally lost their anger. Instead, he spotted something else in them that he hadn't expected.

Destiny. Preordained and undeniable. One day soon, they were fated to be together. Whether for one night, one week or forever, he could not say. But he was as sure of her as he was of the rising sun in the morning.

"I think I can manage to make it back on my own," she said as her voice broke through his thoughts. "Thank you for the dinner and the history lesson."

Not a chance. He wasn't letting her go anywhere alone.

Before he could tell her that, a man appeared at the curb directly in front of her. A Middle Eastern man in the clan keffiyeh of the Taj Zabbar held his palms out as if pleading with her to understand. Rylie came to an abrupt halt and Darin could sense her tension in the way she held her body.

His own body was as tight as the skin on a conga drum. Sweat trickled at his temple. He prepared himself for defense, trying desperately to remember everything he had learned.

"Excuse me," the man muttered in hesitant English. "Miss Hunt, my employer wishes to speak with you. You will come now?"

"How do you know my name?"

The man gave a tentative glance over her shoulder toward Darin. "You will come now, please. My employer insists." He reached out and took her by the arm.

And for Darin, everything changed.

Chapter 4

Damn it. Just when she was starting to like Darin, it turned out he'd been lying. How stupid could she be?

Letting him lead her right into a trap.

Rylie ripped her arm out of the stranger's grasp and stomped down hard on the man's foot. As the guy yelled and danced around in pain, she rounded on Darin. But before she could rear back and jam her knee to his groin, Darin shot out of her reach. Next thing she knew, he was punching the strange man dressed in Middle Eastern garb and knocking him off his feet. With one smooth motion, Darin whirled and grabbed her around the waist, lifting her off her feet. He half dragged and half carried her down the mist-dampened sidewalk in the opposite direction of the man lying in the street.

"Move," he growled in her ear.

"I'm not going anywhere. Not with that guy and

not with you." Balling her fists, she tried smacking Darin's face.

Her efforts were ineffective because her feet were dangling in midair and she couldn't get adequate force behind her swings. Darin never missed a step on the slick, uneven cobblestones. She gave a good show of kicking him, but he was moving too fast and her toes were still barely touching the ground.

They made it around the next three city street corners using the same combined running and crablike moves before Darin finally slowed, turned and checked behind them. He never loosened his hold on her, not even a little.

"Let me go." She gulped in air while her heartbeat raced like a motorcycle engine.

"You were terrific back there," Darin whispered, breathing hard. "Quit fighting me. If you act stupid now, he'll catch up to us again. I think there's a small hotel in the next block. I'm sure we can make it that far, and we'll have the doorman summon a taxi and be long gone before your assailant ever comes to his senses."

She'd heard real respect for her actions in the tone of his voice and it helped to put a stopper in her fear. "Let me down," she said calmly. "I can run faster if you'll let me go."

Rylie had no intention of going anywhere with Darin, but together they would have a better shot at getting away. She could give him the slip later. Right this minute, he was the devil she knew.

Darin loosened his grip and lowered her to her feet. She was amazed he had actually believed what she'd said and her mouth dropped open. For a moment she stared into his trusting eyes. Then she turned and ran.

"Split up and double back," she hollered over her shoulder. "I'll meet you—"

She never had a chance to finish the thought because Darin caught her from behind, gripped her arm and kept up the momentum she'd begun as the two of them dashed down the half-lit sidewalks hand in hand. He might be trusting, but it seemed he wasn't stupid.

Out of breath, they made it to the doorstep of an inn. Banging on the locked door with one fist, Darin kept his other hand glued tightly to hers. Apparently he was also familiar with the concept behind the saying "Fool me once…"

A particularly grumpy innkeeper finally let them in after Darin explained their circumstances in the man's native French. Rylie wasn't sure, but the memory of her old college French led her to believe Darin had also mentioned a bonus for calling them a cab.

Within a few minutes, money had changed hands and she was safely tucked into the backseat of a beat-up Mercedes taxicab.

Suddenly exhausted, Rylie leaned her body against the strength of Darin's shoulder. "Where are we going? To the police?"

No answer.

A sneaky thought of betrayal crept into her mind. Could he be one of the bad guys after all?

"Okay," she said in a meek tone…at least it sounded meek considering that the tone came from her own loud mouth. "No police. Then at least tell me where we're headed. I kinda thought you and I were beginning a real friendship back at the bar. You owe me…"

"Friends don't lie to each other."

"When did I lie? You were the one who lied to me."

She forced this new white lie out with an indignant groan as if she'd meant it, but that was the best she could muster. Of course she'd lied in the middle of trying to escape. She wasn't a fool, and she would have done anything to get away. But if he pushed her too hard, she might crumble in a heap on the cab floor and beg for his forgiveness now that he'd saved her life.

"I do not lie." His tone was hurt instead of incensed, and she felt a very real pang of regret.

"Okay…" Suddenly needing to find a little backbone and a lot of pride, she steadied her voice. "Then who was that guy? And I want the truth."

"I have never seen the man before."

Screwing up her mouth for a few well-chosen words, she was about to let them loose when he continued, "But I did recognize him as Taj Zabbar. He wore the purple-checked head cloth of their modern-day businessmen."

"Businessman? Bull. That assailant, as you called him, was far more interested in kidnapping than business."

The next thought came out of her mouth much too easily. "Hey. Talking about kidnapping, he was after *me,* not you. What the heck would the Taj Zabbar want with me, anyway?"

Her words lingered in the stale air of the backseat as the cab jerked around corners and then over one of the Rhône River bridges. Interesting question, wasn't it? She could almost feel Darin mulling the same idea over in his head.

"If you're not lying again," he began in a sober tone, "then that's something we must learn together."

His voice was rigid, unyielding, but as he spoke he

gently folded her hand in his. He glanced over at her, and if she'd been talking, his expression would've surprised her speechless. Instead of a glare of suspicion, his eyes plainly said he thought she was the most exquisite and priceless creature he had ever beheld. A tiny shiver ran to the base of her spine at the sensual look in his eyes. This was not the gaze of a man who wanted only friendship and truth.

Rylie was unsure of what she wanted, so she left her hand right where it was. The idea of kissing him…and more…was certainly appealing. Being this close to a man as exotic and enticing as this one was driving fire through her veins.

Still, she didn't know him. Not really. And someone—maybe someone he knew well—was trying to kidnap her.

Darin spoke to the cabbie in French and the driver made a couple of quick left turns, heading for the expensive part of town. A few more minutes of riding in quiet and the cab pulled up in front of the Geneva Four Seasons Hotel, a spendy and trendy joint that was far above Rylie's current circumstances. She looked up at the bright lights and marbled entry and wondered how much this place could possibly cost per night—and then couldn't help thinking how many hospital bills she could've paid with all that money.

The cab stopped, Darin threw a wad of Swiss francs at the driver and then eased her out with a nod to the doorman holding the open cab door.

When Rylie put her none-too-steady feet on the pavement, Darin reached for her. He pulled her close and took a moment to study her under the light. She knew she must look a mess, all sweaty and disheveled.

Trying to break free, her only thought was getting away from both his intensity and the harsh light.

But Darin held her fast. Using the pad of his thumb, he gently touched a spot on her cheek while his lips turned down in a deep frown. The hurt look in his eyes made Rylie wonder if he what he was rubbing was dirt or a bruise. As far as she could tell she was nothing but one big bruise.

"Come on," Darin said in soft tones. "It's time you met some of my family."

Family? The first crazy thoughts to enter her mind were how sweaty she was and how much she needed a shower before being presentable enough to meet his loved ones. But her very next thought quickly changed channels back to the reality show of her current life.

Darin was still looking at her as if he would love to eat her for breakfast, much like a man on a first date who was smitten. But their situation seemed to her to be more a life-and-death matter and not much like any date.

Still seething, Hamad Taj Zabbar sat back on the hotel's settee and threw a final instruction to his idiot cousin. "This time, catch up to her without one of the Kadirs nearby. And I don't care how you arrange it, but I expect you to make it look like an accident or a generic kidnapping. And for Allah's sake, take off that damned Taj Zabbar head scarf. I don't want any bystanders putting two and two together. Got it?"

The cousin visibly trembled but stood at attention. "Yes, my sheik. I will not fail again."

At that moment, Hamad received a new satellite call, coming from one of the other Taj Zabbar elders.

Predicting this call would not add a lot to his frustration level, he knew the coming conversation was bound to annoy him in far different ways.

He waved off his dullard of a cousin and waited until the man headed for the elevators. They had already decided Darin Kadir must eventually return to his rooms, and the best plan was to continue following him. He would lead them once again to the woman.

As soon as the cousin was out of sight, Hamad acknowledged the caller.

"A communiqué is being couriered to you," the elder, Mugrin Bin Abdul Taj Zabbar, told him over the line. "Information within the document is classified and vital. Much too vital to send via any modern communication system. Telephones and computers are inadequate. No one must be allowed to waylay these secrets."

The elder paused after speaking, breathing hard into the phone line until he could whisper once again. "We have written the message down using ancient family codes. You will have no trouble translating, I'm sure."

Hamad refused to let any hesitation show in his voice, at least not in the way paranoia clearly showed in the elder's voice. The elder Mugrin could someday be his rival for power. But upon further reflection, that seemed not highly likely. This particular elder was part of the old guard and refused to accept modern technology. How quaint, and yet how annoying.

"No trouble," Hamad said to calm the old man and make him believe all was well. "And will it be left in the usual place and in the usual manner?"

"Of course." Mugrin Bin Abdul sounded worried, and that made their conversation disturbing. Hamad felt certain the elder was concerned about losing his position of power. The man was weak.

Bidding goodbye to the elder Mugrin, Hamad swallowed the dregs of his bitter Middle Eastern coffee, then rose from his shadowed corner spot in the hotel lobby. As he moved, he made slight adjustments to the plans in his mind. He still had time before daybreak to issue new orders.

These new orders would mean a couple of stops and a new final destination for his not-too-bright cousin. But Hamad was certain even Taweel should be able to follow revised instructions. After all, the cousin knew he had but one chance left to make things right, or there would be no chances left for him to have a future. Hamad did not have time to coddle inept employees.

"But why did you bring her here?" Shakir set his jaw and flicked his thumb toward the closed bathroom door where the noise of running water made it clear Rylie was taking a shower. "She could be leading the enemy right to us."

Darin wanted to say that he would never leave her out in the cold and unprotected—this woman of his obsession. He wanted to tell Shakir that nothing his family could say, and certainly nothing she could possibly do, would change their destiny. It was written in the stars.

But he didn't mention any of that. "She's an innocent bystander, bro. The Taj Zabbar came after her, and I think we need to find out why."

"Innocent my ass." Shakir jammed his fists on his hips and the muscles around his eyebrows tensed. "I'm not buying that. What's she doing here in Geneva, anyway?"

Darin turned his back on his middle brother and walked to the sitting room bar. "You won't believe it. She says she came to find out who is responsible for that explosion in Houston. She doesn't think it was an accident. Sound familiar?"

"I bloody well don't accept such a ridiculous excuse. And I can't believe you could be so gullible. What has she done to you?"

Darin straightened his spine without turning around. "She hasn't done anything to me. But you should've seen her take on that Taj Zabbar gorilla without as much as pepper spray to defend herself. She was magnificent."

"Oh?"

Darin felt the air rustling and knew his brother had moved close behind him. He busied his hands with pouring them both drinks, unready to put on his I'm-not-infatuated face. Shakir was the one brother of the three who had been in love, and it had ended badly nearly four years ago. Since then, Shakir had soured on love and women in general.

"I'm calling Tarik," Shakir said through gritted teeth when he reached his side. "When it comes to spy work, he's the most knowledgeable. He can be here by tomorrow evening. Then we'll see what he thinks of all this."

Darin turned and offered Shakir a shot of Blue Goose vodka on the rocks. Though he seldom drank alcohol, his own drink was twenty-year-old scotch. Both of them needed a moment.

Shakir swallowed his down in two huge gulps, then set his ice-filled glass back down on the counter with a slap. "This is the first time any of us has as much as set eyes on one of the Taj Zabbar. I think it must prove the elders have been right all along. We *are* in an undeclared war with them. And you uncovered the truth. You can be proud, brother."

Darin heard the *but* coming loud and clear. "And…?" He urged Shakir to finish the thought.

Shakir lifted a shoulder, dropped it and his chin and glared down at his empty glass on the counter. "And I think it's time you went back to headquarters and began strategizing in earnest. I'm sure the Kadir elders will want you to head up the family's defense systems from now on. Let Tarik and me take care of this first skirmish."

Chuckling into his own drink, Darin lowered his glass and said, "And what do you propose I do with Rylie? Pack her off to America with a pat on the head and no explanations?"

"Works for me. Why not?"

"Because you don't know her. She would never accept leaving without learning the real reason for the attack."

Shakir swiveled to face him. "Oh, and you know her so well after a mere twenty-four hours?"

His brother might have had a point if he'd been dealing in real time. But to Darin, Rylie was the embodiment of the best of his past and his dream of the future. However, he was not ready to voice those feelings, especially not to this brother.

"I think she's in real danger, Shakir. What's to stop them from coming after her in America or anywhere else?"

"Why?" Shakir grumbled under his breath. "The

Taj Zabbar have no quarrel with the Hunts. Last night's attack, if it was for real, and the one in Houston, too, had to be because of us. Because a Kadir was in the vicinity. Have you considered that if she's as innocent as you say, she might be better off—safer—if she stayed away from the Kadirs altogether?"

The idea had crossed his mind but he'd pushed it away.

"She is innocent." No question at all and no room for debate. "And she needs protection. I'm not losing sight of her until we figure out what it is the Taj Zabbar wants.

"You and Tarik do what you do best," Darin continued. "And Rylie and I will see what we can find out on our own."

Shakir looked as if he was about to argue, so Darin cut him off. "Don't worry about me, brother. Together, she and I will be invincible."

Rylie awoke with a start. Something, somewhere, had jerked her from the first sound sleep she'd had in months. Rolling on her side, she was surprised to see it was still dark outside the full wall of windows in Darin's hotel bedroom. The lighted dial on the bedside clock read 5:00 a.m., but she was done sleeping for the night. Peace would never come while thoughts and questions stalked through her mind in brilliant colors and scattered pieces.

She dragged herself out of bed and tried to get her bearings, carefully making her way to the bathroom in the dark. Most of last night remained a blur in her mind. She distinctly remembered the run-in with her assailant, giving him the slip and then coming back here with Darin. And she vaguely remembered Darin treating her like some kind of fragile doll, insisting that she take his king-size bed while he slept on the pull-out couch in the sitting room.

Flipping on the overhead light in his bathroom, Rylie winced against the glare and wished she hadn't been looking in the mirror when the room lit up like a night game at the baseball stadium. Her hair was standing straight up on its curly ends. Her eyes had a sunken-in and bruised appearance. What a mess. Had she looked like this last night when she'd met Darin's brother?

No wonder Shakir had treated her so suspiciously. Who could blame him? It would be hard to trust anyone who looked as disreputable as she did at the moment.

She hadn't gotten a good read on Shakir, other than he was loyal to his brother. And that he was big, bigger than Darin—and mean-looking. Or maybe those mean glances were because he seemed convinced she was one of the bad guys. Her. As if.

She pulled Darin's T-shirt up over her head, grateful that he'd offered it after her shower. Her underpants were still hanging over the shower rod, and she was pleased to find them mostly dry when she slipped them on. After splashing water on her face, she squeezed a dab of toothpaste onto her finger and swished it around in her mouth. One of the men's spray deodorant cans sat on a nearby shelf, and Rylie didn't hesitate to use it on her underarms.

Feeling moderately better, she went back to the bedroom but left the lights there turned off. Forced to feel around until she found her clothes and trusty traveling purse over the back of a chair, she sat down to slide her feet into her jeans and boots. A hairbrush would've been a godsend right about then. But as she hadn't been able to cram one into her tiny purse with the passport, phone and wallet, she ran her fingers through her hair and patted it down the best she could.

Rylie took a second to think about what her next move should be. Darin had made a comment at the end of last night about the two of them working together to solve some mystery. But in her mind, the only mystery was whether she should trust the Kadirs. Every time a Hunt found themselves too near a Kadir, all hell broke loose.

Would she dare try it again?

Maybe. Maybe she could try again at some point—just to prove to herself this magic she felt with Darin was for real. It had been a long time since her body had responded to the touch of a man. And it had been even longer…as in never…that she'd wanted a man to hold her and protect her through a long, sleepless night.

Darin Kadir was special. All of a sudden she'd been thinking about a future instead of wishing she had died in that explosion along with her father.

But before they could talk about any kind of future, she had to learn all his secrets. Was he dangerous? Potentially evil? A part of her wanted to wait and ask him for the explanations, trusting him beyond what seemed reasonable for someone she had recently met. But a bigger part, a more thoughtful part, was afraid he could tell her anything and she would never know that he'd lied until it was too late.

Nope. Rylie knew she had to find out about his past, his family's secrets, all on her own. Then when she asked him and he told her the truth, she could be sure he wasn't spinning fancy tales.

With that settled in her head, the only thing left for her to do was to slip out of his hotel suite without being noticed.

Chapter 5

Arms crossed under his head and lying flat on his back on the sofa, Darin stared into the night while lights coming through the glass doors bounced off the ceiling like tiny, ghostly bats. He'd heard the water running in the bathroom and knew it had to be Rylie because Shakir had ducked out at about 3:00 a.m. Grinning absently into the blackness of the room like an idiot, he wondered if it was normal for her to wake at such an early hour.

Everything about her was unknown and fresh. What did she like to eat for breakfast? What kind of scented soap did she prefer? He couldn't wait to begin peeling back the layers and discovering the real Rylie Hunt.

He'd only managed a couple of hours of sleep, but that's all he usually needed. During most nights, his mind raced with plans and schemes—for making money or finding other ways to get ahead in business. Not sleeping through the night wasn't out of the ordinary.

What felt unusual tonight was the way his thoughts had centered on a single woman. He'd never seriously considered becoming involved before. And yet tonight, all he could think about was how to convince Rylie that they should give romance a try.

He wanted to know her—every detail—both mind and body. He wanted to slip into her soul. He wanted to stand beside her during rough times and console her during the darkest nights.

What was the matter with him? Was the woman a witch? In such a short time, how could he be this sure she was what he wanted?

Yes, it was true he loved the way that burnt-cinnamon hair of hers curled lazily upon her neck. And yes, his hands itched to touch her skin every single time they came within ten feet of one another. But were those good enough reasons to make him want to change his whole life?

Logically, no. But nothing about his obsession seemed logical, and that was the rub. He was a man of thoughts, not passions. He was a planner. A man with lists and goals and tomorrows never in doubt. It was bad enough that the Taj Zabbar had unleashed their war of retribution at a critical time in his business life, disturbing his goals. But he'd had no choice in the matter.

He did have a choice with Rylie. He could send her away as Shakir suggested, and perhaps that would be the best for everyone involved. But oh, no, not him. He couldn't even entertain the idea. Not when she needed both his protection and his basic knowledge of the Taj

Zabbar—and not until he found out why he'd become this obsessed.

The last time any emotional subject had captured his entire attention was when he'd been twelve and his mother left. Stopping to shake his head at the wrong choice of word, Darin quickly corrected his thoughts. She had not left—voluntarily. She'd died. The two were not the same thing, though to his twelve-year-old mind they'd felt similar.

Somehow the situation with Rylie felt the same. He remembered only too well the frustration he'd experienced when he hadn't been able to save his mother from the cancer that consumed her. Now his frustration was mounting again as he tried to find the right words to say to Rylie. Words he could say that would be convincing enough for her to let him provide the protection needed to save her life.

The water stopped and Darin wondered if she would be going back to bed or coming out here to the sitting room. He could make a pot of coffee if she wanted to talk.

He hoped she wanted to talk. The thought of seeing her again. Of sitting next to her. Of hearing her voice speaking to him was enthralling. The nervous excitement was almost more than he could stand.

Sitting up abruptly, he chastised himself. Weren't those the sort of thoughts a lovesick schoolboy might have? The adult inside him felt embarrassingly absurd at the idea of such a childish obsession.

Still, ridiculous or not, Darin found he was holding his breath and waiting for her appearance.

In a few seconds the bedroom door opened. But instead

of lights and the sound of Rylie's voice whispering to him and asking if he was awake yet, nothing happened. Then he heard the rustle of her moving through the room and wondered what came next.

Next was the sound of the suite's hallway door being opened from inside. She was sneaking out? Leaving without him?

He rose to his feet and started to call out when the door shut with a quiet snick.

Hurt but determined that she would not rush into possible danger without his protection, Darin quickly slipped a polo shirt on over his head and shoved his arms into his jacket, grateful he still had on his jeans. He grabbed up his passport, money, phone and the gun from the coffee table where he'd dumped them last night. Meanwhile, he'd shoved his feet into his shoes.

By the time he made it to the hallway, the elevator doors were already closing. His suite was on the twelfth floor and Darin headed for the emergency stairs at a run. Fury and fear were equal partners in his chest as he banged down the stairs and, out of breath, crashed through a door into an alcove off the lobby. Checking every square inch of the grand lobby, bar and alcoves in one fluid glance, he turned to the elevators. Soon he realized she must have arrived first and already left through the front door.

But why? And where was she going?

He still refused to accept the idea that she was involved with the Taj Zabbar. Shakir had been dead wrong about that. He had to be.

Arguing the point in his mind, Darin all but flew across the lobby to the main entrance. Outside, the sky ran in streaks of Halloween colors as daybreak made a memorable entrance across the Alps.

"Can I be of assistance, sir?" The uniformed doorman crossed the pavement, coming in his direction. "Will you need a taxi? It's early but…"

"Did a woman just come out and order a taxi? Did you see her?"

The doorman studied him for a second. "You are Monsieur Kadir, yes?"

"Yes. Did you see her?"

"A pretty young woman left the hotel a moment ago, sir, but she did not request a taxi. She asked for directions to the nearest tram stop. I told her that Geneva trams do not run for another hour, but she insisted."

Darin still had a chance to catch up to her. "Which way did she go?"

The doorman pointed and gave him curt directions to the proper corner. Darin threw bills toward him and was gone with the man's thank-you still resounding in his ears.

As his feet pounded down the sidewalk, Darin tried to imagine what would've made her leave without a word. The answer came from a voice in his head, a surprising voice sounding very much like his dead mother's.

Fear would make a woman run. Rylie was afraid. Afraid of what the Taj Zabbar wanted with her, of course. But he also suddenly understood that she was probably a little afraid of him, too. After all, he'd used his usual detached-father-figure attitude. And what did she know of him really?

Don't be afraid.

He wouldn't hurt her, or let anyone else hurt her.

But she had to listen before he could make her understand that.

Give me a chance, Rylie. I'll make everything okay.

Rylie froze in place when she heard footsteps coming from behind her. Shifting to the side, she went into fight-or-flight mode, flattening her back against the nearby building before finally turning to look that way.

Nothing.

Nothing back there but empty shadows cast by dawn's first light. Not one soul was on the street at this hour. Nevertheless, the skin on her arms swam with imaginary insects while her heart raced wildly in her chest. Maybe she'd been unwise to insist on the tram instead of a cab this time.

Fighting off the strong adrenaline rush that had nearly blinded her, Rylie worked to calm her nerves by taking deep breaths. Now that she'd convinced herself no one was really there and it had all been in her mind, she figured it was senseless to worry about being followed at such an early-morning hour. How would anyone know where to look? She had told no one but Marie Claire that she would be staying overnight in Darin's hotel suite.

Grateful that Darin hadn't awoken when she'd sneaked out, Rylie still felt sorry that she hadn't at least said goodbye. She owed him a thank-you for helping to save her from a would-be kidnapper and for giving her a place to crash afterward. Though truthfully, she could've handled the whole situation on her own without anyone's interference, thank you very much.

Sighing, Rylie gave in, knowing she would take time to thank Darin. In person. As soon as she found out more about him and the whole of the Kadir family's history.

She continued her walk down the sidewalk in the growing light, heading for the tram stop and a ride back to the safety of Marie Claire's apartment. Rylie looked up and realized she only had another block to go, then it would be right around the corner to the stop. She was close. Too close to be worried over nothing.

Gazing down the hill between the buildings, she caught sight of the lake bathed in the lavender color of early-morning light. Streaks of gold shone against the water as streams of mist rose like tiny, spewing geysers across a cloud-filled fountain. The unusual sight reminded her how strange the last thirty-six hours had been.

Something odd was happening inside her. She felt different from when she'd first arrived in Geneva.

Rylie took a quick inventory of her feelings while she walked. Grief, her familiar best friend, still hung around her shoulders, quietly threatening at any moment to bring her stumbling to her knees. And the dogged determination to find truth continued its own kind of bubbling irritation unabated in her chest. Sometimes that stubborn determination made it difficult for her to breathe. But at least those two things remained the same.

So what felt different?

As she continued the debate in her mind, Rylie turned the final corner—and ran smack into a bulky, bug-eyed man with a huge frigging knife in his hand.

Ohmygod. Ohmygod. Ohmygod.

Her feet were stuck to the concrete. Her tongue

swelled up to twice its size. Terrified, she couldn't run or scream.

"You will come now, Miss Hunt." It was the same voice. The same man from before but without the head scarf.

Rylie had never in her memory been at a loss for words. But this time, when she opened her mouth to either scream or demand the man tell her why he was doing this, nothing came out but a strangled gurgle.

All she could do was stare down at the biggest knife she had ever seen. The damned thing had to be at least eighteen inches long, with a double-edged blade, a leather hilt and what looked like some kind of animal head carved into the metal of the handle. Holy moly. It was an antique dagger, for heaven's sake. Lethal, hooked at the tip and pointed straight at her gut.

She had to do something or die. Screaming was out. Even if she could've managed, there wasn't anyone around to hear.

After taking another quick breath to fill her lungs with fortifying air, Rylie brought to mind the promise she'd made to her father. And the many workouts she'd undertaken in order to be able to take care of herself. Her daddy had seen to it that she knew how.

"Nobody is going to coddle you, little girl," Red Hunt had said as he'd dragged her to self-defense classes and taught her how to shoot a gun. "And nobody will ever take care of you the way you can take care of yourself. Be strong, Rylie Ann. You're a Hunt. We take care of others. We don't wait to be rescued."

But, Daddy, this knife is huge.

"Please seat yourself in the auto, miss," the man

muttered in a deep, gruff tone, scaring her almost beyond her wits.

The devil's words rang terrifying alarm bells in her ears. She turned her head and saw that a car with a driver sat at the curb with its motor running.

Two assailants.

Oh, man. Rylie figured if she was ever going to get out of this, big fat knife or not, it would have to be while she was still outside the car with only one attacker and not two. She remembered learning that your first escape is always your best. *Never get into the car.*

"All right. All right. I'm going." At least she'd managed those words. And they hadn't sounded as horrified as she'd felt. Silently promising her daddy to do her best, she readied her body by going into fight mode in the way she had been taught.

Gathering up every ounce of adrenaline she could, Rylie pretended to turn toward the car while secretly rebalancing her weight. Her legs were shaking, but other than that she felt ready.

When she turned, her assailant turned, too, and put himself at a disadvantage. Now or die.

Her feet exploded from under her body as she kicked out at his knees with such force that she took both of them to the ground. He grunted as he fell on his back, and the knife dropped from his hands.

All Rylie wanted to do was get the hell out of there. She tried scrambling out of his reach. But before she could crawl to safety and get to her feet, he grabbed her with an iron grip around the waist.

She scratched and kicked, trying for the eyes or groin. But he must've had a good forty pounds on her. Out of the chaos, she heard him call to his comrade in a language she didn't understand. But she understood the sentiment. Her assailant was calling for reinforcements.

Oh, Lordy. When it came to two against one, she wouldn't stand a chance.

Darin had been jogging down the sidewalk toward the tram stop, hoping to get there before Rylie boarded a tram and was out of sight. But right before he came to the last corner, he slowed his steps, hesitating to scare her by flying around it blind.

Despite his brother's declarations about her being nothing but trouble, Darin was positive that on the contrary she was *in* trouble and needed his help. It made him wonder what he could possibly say to make her understand.

Rylie had an independent nature. Perhaps too independent for her own good. But in a way, he appreciated that about her. No whining or clinging and begging for help from that woman. And he knew her situation back in the States was dire. But she had never even considered asking for his help.

As he took a few slow steps toward the last corner, he knew that's how he would approach her. They could work together, he would say. They could…

He heard the commotion before he jerked past the building on the corner and could see the worst. Rylie. On the ground and being dragged around by another assailant. Momentarily stunned, he thought perhaps this was the same man as last night. But this time he also saw a second man exiting the driver's seat of a car at the curb and yelling toward his comrade in the Taj Zabbar language.

Fighting hard, Rylie was holding her own with the

bigger man for the moment. His first instinct to run to her assistance would've been all wrong. Right then the second man came around the front of the car, and he had a gun in his hand.

The second guy was so absorbed with the vision of Rylie and her attacker on the ground that Darin had a moment to reach for his own weapon without anyone noticing. He drew the gun from under his jacket and then wasn't sure what to do with it. If he shot at the second man and missed, Rylie might be killed.

Frustrated by indecision, Darin started yelling, raised his weapon and began shooting above the second man's head. With the first gunshot, everyone stopped dead, frozen in their places and staring at him.

That instantaneous silence didn't last long, however. The man standing raised his own gun and turned, pointing it directly at Darin. Looking down the deadly end of a monster gun barrel, Darin knew he had no choice. He dropped his arm and fired before the other guy got off a single shot.

The man with the gun stumbled back when the bullet hit him in the middle of the chest. A bloodstain blossomed at the entry point. So much blood. The man's arms flailed and his fingers loosened from around his gun. He gurgled something incoherent and then crumbled to the ground, his gun skittering off into a gutter.

Stunned by what he had done, Darin was a little slow to turn around, transfixed by a man taking his last breaths. Then a scream broke through his fog. Rylie.

Swinging around, he pointed his weapon at the ground where Rylie and her assailant had last been tumbling together. But Rylie alone remained on the sidewalk. She was screaming at the other man, who was running like his life depended on it and just about to disappear at the end of the block.

"Go after him," she demanded.

Darin shook his head and slid his finger off the trigger. "Let the Geneva police department handle it. Someone is sure to have called them by now.

"Are you all right?" He started toward her but she was on her feet and dusting herself off before he could take two steps in her direction.

"I'm okay. Did you kill that man?" She pointed at the second assailant lying crumpled in the street, and then she went back to brushing off her jeans.

He hadn't wanted to think about that yet. But Darin forced himself to turn and go to the prone man's side. He touched the pulse point found at the base of the neck and felt nothing. Next he leaned in close to the man's face, hoping to feel even a small breath of air coming from his nose. Nothing.

The truth poked its nasty finger in Darin's chest. He had killed a man. A member of the Taj Zabbar clan, most probably. But dead was dead, and the idea pushed reality right in Darin's face with a resounding thud.

Then he spotted something beside the man. Whatever it was that caught his eye gleamed through the last shadows of dawn. The shiny thing had apparently dropped from the dead man's jacket pocket and was glinting irreverently in the first rays of the sun.

Darin reached out and picked it up, wanting closer study. It was a key—with an attached tag and writing in French. The lighting wasn't good enough for Darin to read all the words, but he saw enough to sense that this was a key to a lockbox or locker.

Palming it, he decided it must be important and he wanted to get a better look at it in a good light. Some sixth sense was telling him this key could provide the Kadirs with a few answers. And he wasn't about to let loose of it until he found out what.

"Did you find something?" Rylie tilted her head, and when he didn't answer right away, began walking toward him.

Vibrating sounds of Swiss police sirens began jangling, interrupting the still morning air. Both of them stopped and turned their heads to the noise. Judging from how loud it sounded, the police would be there any second.

Darin looked over at Rylie. He was torn, but knew the police could take good care of her. Nothing bad would happen if he followed his hunch now and left her behind.

It wouldn't be forever. He vowed to catch up to her later in the day. They still had much to discuss.

Backing down the sidewalk in the other direction, he yelled, "I need to run this down." Then he picked up his pace. "You stay and talk to the police. Tell them the truth. I'll let you know what I find out."

With that, he turned, darted across the street and disappeared around a corner before she could utter the first word.

Be safe, Rylie. I will see you soon.

Chapter 6

It took Rylie a moment to close her gaping mouth. Darin left. He actually ran off and left her with a dead body, the police on the way and with no real explanations for what had taken place.

"Tell them the truth," he'd said.

Dang it. What truth? That one man had attacked her and then disappeared? And that another man saved her and then he, too, disappeared? Not cool. She could end up spending the rest of the year in a Geneva jail before it was all straightened out.

She turned her head, blankly looking in the direction of the screaming sirens. Indecision wrapped her in a blanket of anger.

How could he leave? And what did he find that was important enough for him to, quote: "Run this down"?

Not a chance in hell you're leaving me behind, pal.

Taking a quick look around at the scene, Rylie made sure her travel purse was still under her shirt before considering both the knife and the dead man's gun. But she had no place to carry either one. So, throwing up her hands and cursing all men under her breath, she took off in the same direction as she'd seen Darin run.

She had always been a fast runner. On the track team in high school, and she'd placed in the state college finals in the one hundred. She figured Darin's leather-soled shoes would slow him down on the still-damp streets.

When she first rounded the corner, Rylie discovered she was right. And lucky. She spotted him as he was dashing around another corner on the next block up.

With sounds of sirens blaring in her ears, Rylie ran to that corner without hearing a single sound that resembled a bystander's shout. Regulating her breathing in preparation for another sprint, she prayed no one had spotted her leaving the scene. But it was too late now for any such regret. Her decision to leave was already made.

Ducking into the shadows of the same deserted alley where Darin had disappeared, she had to slow her steps and hug the building the moment she spotted him standing in the sunshine of the upcoming street corner. Should she confront him now? Maybe not. She decided against it for the time being because she was afraid he would only give her the slip again.

He was paying her no mind and seemed to be concentrating on something in his hand. No doubt the object he'd found near the dead man. What was it?

Once again, she found herself cursing him under her

breath. He'd said he wanted to protect her. That the two of them could work together. Well, hell. Leaving her to fend off the police on her own and then taking a potential clue with him to study didn't seem like ways for someone to earn trust.

Who was this guy, anyway? One second he was all responsible and proper. The next friendly and sexy. Now he was acting like a double agent in a spy movie. The man was driving her crazy.

Dying to run him down and demand answers, she held back. She could no doubt catch him again if he took off. But maybe she should stay here a moment and then follow, see where he went?

He reached into his pocket right then, pulled out his cell phone and made a call. And in the end it was curiosity that decided her question. He promptly hung up and checked around as if he were trying to get his bearings and make sure no one was following.

Where to now, Darin "the Sneaky"?

Glancing over his shoulder, he apparently decided he was in the clear and turned down a street that was now steeped in brilliant sunlight. Rylie wasn't about to lose him after everything that had happened. She ran full out until she, too, hit sunshine. Then she came to a screeching halt, looking in every direction for which way he'd gone.

But he was nowhere in sight.

Rylie pushed off, hoping she'd guessed right and moving as fast as she dared on the suddenly crowded sidewalks. Morning traffic and pedestrians heading for work all conspired against her. She excused herself as she tripped over an older woman who had stopped to gaze in a window. Then Rylie had to step into the busy street in order to get out of the way of a baby stroller being pushed by a heavyset woman.

Growing rash, Rylie deliberately landed in the street and began jogging down the gutter. If Darin had gone the other way or turned off somewhere, it might be hopeless trying to find him in the bustling city. But try she would.

Stopping at the next street corner to catch her breath, she looked up—and there he was. She'd only had a glimpse but was sure that had been his polo shirt she'd spotted as he'd turned into one of the stores or apartments in the next block.

Rylie waited for a bus to pass by, then walked swiftly to within ten feet of the same spot where she'd last seen him. She was beginning to feel like a really bad covert operative. Nevertheless, she flattened herself to the wall before easing her head around the corner to check it out. She found an entrance to a stairwell. It held open stairs leading up to offices above the stores.

And the stairwell was empty. Narrow stone stairs led up into the darkness above. Checking out a posted sign-board at the bottom of the stairs, she tried to guess which office would be the one where he'd been headed.

Her French was so poor that she couldn't make out the meanings on a couple of the signs. But she felt sure one of them was listed as a doctor's office. Another sign read: Émigré Europe Ltd. And in smaller letters below that, it said something about business services for foreigners. Darin was a foreigner here.

But had he gone to that office? Or maybe to the doctor? And if so, why?

Unsure what to do next, Rylie came to the conclusion that her best bet would be to wait. Find a place close by where she could stake out the sidewalk entrance and hang around there until he came out. She would give him an hour, no more. Then she would go upstairs and start pounding on doors until someone told her something—or until someone called the police.

Wishing he had more knowledge about covert operations, Darin wondered how to charm the middle-aged woman behind the counter. She was making every effort to speak in English, though Darin would have preferred French to her broken, stilted, one-sided conversation.

"*Oui,* monsieur. We pride ourselves on our security. No one would be allowed access to your depository box but you yourself."

In the strictest terms, she was not correct, since in truth this wasn't Darin's box at all. Nor had the woman's statement been an answer to his original question. But he was not about to force understanding on this woman when she was trying so hard to be accommodating.

Murmuring a thank-you in both languages, he bowed slightly and made his way, at her invitation, behind the counter to a half-hidden row of safety boxes located in the back alcove of the divided room. Émigré Europe Ltd., as written on the key, had turned out to be a moving and forwarding company, with offices located all over Europe. They helped businessmen and their families relocate to various cities on the Continent.

Not only did they provide furniture and possessions moving and storage for corporate employees on a temporary basis, they also served as a mail-forwarding concern. And the key he'd picked up was for one of their lockboxes. Émigré Europe did not seem to have an adequate security system in place to ensure the right person picked up mail.

Using the key he'd found to open the matching numbered box, he withdrew a medium-size leather portfolio. The tooled leather was quite old. Several centuries old, if Darin was any judge. He noticed a unique symbol in the pattern etched into the leather. The panther. The ancient Taj Zabbar family symbol, meant to signify any marked object as belonging to their clan leaders.

Checking over his shoulder to see if anyone was watching, Darin carefully opened the portfolio. Inside, he discovered a five-by-six packet of papers, all strung together like a notebook and then secured with twine. Interesting. He sneaked a peek at what was written on the pages but couldn't make out the language at first glance. Besides the packet, he also found a half-page note, handwritten in the Taj Zabbar language, and two one-way tickets on this afternoon's train to Milan.

Torn between replacing the portfolio in the box and waiting to see who might come to pick it up or instead taking the whole portfolio with him for further study, Darin decided the better choice was to get the hell out of there as fast as possible. He was too curious to hang around. Plus, getting caught here would, more than likely, not be good for his health.

He jammed all the contents back into the portfolio, relocked the box and left with the whole leather packet under his arm. Once outside he would find a quiet place to give everything another look.

The moment Darin hit the sidewalk at the bottom of the stairs, he heard police sirens—and they seemed to be coming in his direction. Had someone turned him in for the shooting? How would they have found him? For security's sake, Darin never hesitated. He took off at a dead run, brushing past noonday shoppers and crashing through lunchtime crowds.

Ten blocks later he was out of breath, but the sirens had long since faded into the city's bustle. Luckily, he found an empty table in an out-of-the-way open-air café. Sitting, he ordered bottled water and surreptitiously checked the people sitting at other tables drinking morning coffee. He had that same strange feeling that someone was watching him again. But he couldn't find anyone staring, or even glancing in his direction.

After his water arrived, Darin felt a little calmer. No one could possibly be following him. He had been careful.

Opening the portfolio and spreading the contents on the table, he fingered the paper pamphlet and flipped through its pages. What sort of language was this? It looked like some kind of ancient Sanskrit writing, but Darin didn't believe that could be true. The paper was modern. Cheap. Bought at any store.

Certainly someone in the Kadir family organization would be able to translate this. Perhaps his cousin Karim would like to take a stab at it. Karim was the computer genius in the family, and also an amateur cryptologist. He should have no trouble figuring out the meaning of these words—if they were real words.

Darin put down the pamphlet and opened the note, handwritten in the Taj Zabbar language. He'd been taught the language as a boy and wondered if he remembered enough of their grammar to translate this message.

The writing on the note was scratchy, hurried. But he made out enough of the words to understand. It was clearly a note from one of the Taj Zabbar elders to an underling.

After bumbling through a few more passages, Darin could see he would need help—and now. Pulling out his satellite phone, he dialed his brother Tarik, who answered before the first ring.

Quickly telling his youngest brother the gist of what he'd been through thus far, Darin went on to add the facts of what he now had in his possession.

"Bring it to headquarters," Tarik said gruffly. "I hope that pamphlet is as important as it seems. We could stand a break in our covert war of innuendo with the Taj Zabbar. Plus, you should be off the streets and out of sight as soon as possible."

Tarik cleared his throat and added, "You've never had to kill a man before, have you?" Not a real question, as Tarik already knew the answer. "Maybe you need to talk about that with someone. Taking a life can lead to serious personality and emotional changes. Come back to headquarters and…"

"I'm all right. I don't need any help." Though Darin did feel changed. "There's too much to do here. I'll go back there in a few days when all this calms down." And after he'd had a chance to explore his obsession with Rylie.

"Not in a few days," Tarik demanded. "Now. I suspect you have the Geneva police, the Taj Zabbar *and* that Hunt woman all looking for you. Get off the streets now."

Darin wasn't quite ready to hide. "I will. But I sincerely believe someone should follow up on this note first. It appears to be an order for one of the Taj Zabbar soldiers to bring both the pamphlet and Rylie to an address in Milan by tomorrow afternoon for a meeting. Two tickets for the sightseeing train leaving Geneva CFF station in an hour were included. I want to be on it."

"You? No. You bring us the papers and we'll take it from there." Tarik's American-accented words were spoken with a hoarse rasp, and Darin heard his sincerity through the receiver. It seemed his baby brother was every bit as concerned for his safety as Shakir had been.

When Darin didn't respond, Tarik became all the more insistent. "Why the need to travel by train? I can fly to Milan and be there by noon tomorrow with skilled men and covert equipment. Let us handle this the right way."

Darin held the phone between his shoulder and his ear, checking the time and waving at the waiter, yet still trying to make his brother understand. "I'd be willing to bet a cool grand that Taj Zabbar henchman, the one who ran away after this morning's assault attempt, may still try to make the train. Or maybe, at least make the meeting tomorrow in Milan.

"And, brother," Darin added, "let me tell you that I can't wait for another opportunity to question that son of a snake."

Still seeing in his mind's eye the man with his hands all over Rylie, Darin drew in a breath and made another urgent request of his baby brother. "Send someone to the Geneva police to rescue Rylie as soon as you can, will you? The Kadirs' fight with the Taj Zabbar has nothing to do with her. But I will find out what they wanted with her. Tell her I'll take care of it, and that I'll contact her as soon as I can."

Through the phone, he could hear Tarik grinding

his teeth before he said, "Listen, I'll make a few calls on Rylie's behalf, but I can't shuffle anyone to Geneva in time to take that train today. Though I promise to personally be at that meeting in Milan tomorrow.

"You got us a decent lead there, oh brother of mine," Tarik said with real appreciation in his voice. "Just don't screw things up now, and don't take any unnecessary chances. Stay off that train. Pocket the pamphlet and leave Geneva on the first flight out."

The waiter arrived with his check, and Darin threw a few bills on the table as he dashed to the curb to hail a taxi, still holding the phone to his ear. "Sorry, you're fading in and out," he lied. "I'm going to Milan. Take care of Rylie for me."

Before Tarik could remind him that satellite phones did not fade, Darin shut down his phone and slipped into a waiting taxi.

Rylie had to run full out from her hiding place beyond the potted plants in order to catch up to Darin. But he was in a cab and gone before she could get his attention. She'd wanted to wait until he was off the phone and then appear out of the crowds at his table side and demand to know what was going on.

Terrified at the thought of losing sight of him before she could badger him into explaining, she hailed a cab and got lucky for once as one stopped at her feet.

"Can you follow that cab?" she asked the driver while diving into the backseat.

Unfortunately, her luck flew right back out the window and landed in the midst of the busy streams of traffic on the street ahead as the driver said, *"Je ne comprends pas ce mot."*

Oh, no. "You don't speak English?"

"*Oui,* mademoiselle. I speak a little."

Rifling through her memory for the right words became nearly impossible when every nerve ending was urging her to be on the way before Darin's cab disappeared. "*Suivre!*"

Hoping she'd used the verb "to follow" and not a way of saying "I'm on a diet," she frantically threw her arms toward Darin's cab and simply ignored any possible embarrassment. "*Je te suis…uh…le taxi!*"

The driver turned to stare where she pointed and pointed himself. "*Ce taxi?*"

"Yes. Please. *Dépêches-toi!*" Wow. Some of her French had come back. The phrase to say "hurry up!" must've been stuck in her mind for all these years. How about that?

The driver nodded, turned back to his steering wheel and eased into traffic about three vehicles behind Darin's cab. She prayed her luck would keep holding for long enough that they wouldn't lose him—and that the driver really understood what she wanted him to do.

She leaned her elbows over the back of the front seat and tried to keep Darin's cab in sight. Fortunately, the traffic was traveling at a snail's pace.

After a few minutes, her driver followed the other cab and turned left onto a street she recognized. Rue de Lausanne was a fairly big street in the downtown section of Geneva and she'd already been here a couple of times in the last forty-eight hours.

The driver made a right turn then and commented in French about something, but she didn't catch his meaning. "Pardon?"

"It goes…*le train,* mademoiselle."

What? "Oh, you mean the taxi is going to the train station?"

"*Oui.*"

What in the heck was Darin up to? She knew he had found or taken something from that office back there. She'd seen him carrying a package that looked like an envelope under his arm. And then he'd been studying something at the café before he made that phone call.

Curiosity was driving her to distraction. She could barely keep her mind on where she was and what she was doing.

Her cabbie pulled in close behind Darin's, already stopped at the curb in front of the station. Rylie fumbled around in her waist purse, digging out enough in traveler's checks to pay her fare. By the time she was done, Darin's cab was pulling away from the curb and Darin was nowhere in sight.

Oh, no. She couldn't lose him now. Taking off at a dead run, she headed for the station's ticket booth. Darin would have to buy a ticket if he was going anywhere, wouldn't he?

But when she finally located the ticket seller, Darin was still out of sight. Now what?

Still breathing hard from her run, she began a slow turn, trying to glance in every corner of the station at once. Halfway around, she came to a dead halt.

"Hi." Darin stood right behind her. Close enough for her nose to almost touch his chin, a giant grin creasing his normally sober face.

Speechless, she reached out and touched him to be sure he was really there.

The moment her hand landed on his chest, Darin pulled her closer, bent his head and planted his lips on hers. Hard and demanding at first, his kiss soon became slow and urgent as she opened for him and their tongues met and tangled. She molded herself to him, their legs aligned and his already hard erection settled in against her belly. Her hands went to his hair. Flames of sensual need licked at her mind, making her totally brainless.

She lost track of time and place. Nothing mattered but the sweet sugar of his mouth and the pure heaven of the hot, wet way he made her feel.

Then a noise came from somewhere outside her fog. She heard someone cough behind her, and the foreign sound broke the mood and pulled her out of Darin's arms fast.

Words came tumbling out of her mouth in a rush. "What do you think you're doing?" As far as smart retorts went, that one left a lot to be desired. But it was far better than either the cuss words *or* the words of desire backing up on her tongue.

A dazed look came and went in his eyes. Finally he said, "I might ask you the same thing. Why are you following me? And what happened with the Geneva police?"

Gulping in air and willing her racing heart to slow, Rylie fought with her own anger and embarrassment and promised not to smack him upside the head for being stupid. "I didn't wait for the cops to show up. Why did you leave me back there and run away?" And where were the words she needed to hear about that spectacular kiss?

His pleased expression, the one similar to the fox who'd just made off with the eggs, disappeared and was replaced by flaring nostrils. "I didn't *run away*. I told you I needed to check something out. And I was concerned that explanations to the police would be too long and complicated."

"Exactly. That's why I followed you. I didn't want to stay, either. And do what? Try explaining a dead body with a gunshot wound, no shooter—and also no gun." Dang Darin's ornery hide anyway.

"You…followed me? All day?" Darin's face flushed red and his eyes narrowed as they shot darts of fury in her direction. "But I stopped a couple of times. Why didn't you say something? Why did the cab driver have to tell me your cab was following us before I knew you were anywhere around?"

"I tried. Or at least I thought about trying a couple of times. But you…"

An announcement of train schedules came across a loudspeaker at that moment. First in French and then again in English and Italian.

"I have a train to catch," Darin told her when the announcement was finished. "Go home, Rylie. All the way home to Texas. My family will help you reach there safely. I'll contact you first chance I get and we'll talk. Explanations can wait till then."

He was shooing her away? Like a fly? And after just kissing her breathless?

"Not a chance, pal. Where you go, I go. Get used to it."

Chapter 7

"Turn back. This is no game." Darin folded his arms across his chest and tried his best glare. He couldn't let her set foot on the train. It was far too dangerous.

Rylie flicked her wrist at him. "Don't be such a jerk. If you're taking the train, so am I." She punctuated each word with a wave of her hand. "I want to know what's really going on."

His brother's warning had been repeating in his head for the last two hours: *"…if she's as innocent as you say, she might be better off—safer—if she stayed away from the Kadirs altogether."*

As obsessed with her as he was, he still couldn't allow her to follow him into a potential trap. And he *was* obsessed. No doubt about it. He'd been positive that kissing her would break the spell. But no. The kiss had only made things worse. He hadn't wanted to stop.

He would have given anything, including his life, for a chance to continue on with that kiss.

Now he would give anything to run away with her to some far corner of the earth. The two of them could explore each other at their leisure. Time. They needed more time.

But they had no time. And at this moment, nothing on earth mattered as much as keeping her safe. Not a covert war. Not his extended family—or even his brothers. Nothing.

She stood there, hands on hips and blue eyes flaring. Magnificent. Her whole body radiated unleashed energy. He'd foolishly indulged himself with that one kiss as a spur-of-the-moment thing. But he hadn't been able to help himself. Her face had been flushed from running, her chest heaving, and his mind had gone blank. The draw of her lips had been a magnet pulling on his libido.

His mind was perfectly clear now. She was in danger, and yet all he wanted to do was kiss her again. To lose himself and all his family's troubles in the depths of her rosy mouth and soft body.

He dug his fingers through his hair. "Rylie, listen to me, please." His own voice was thick with need and shook with fear—for her. "I'm trying to save your life. I could be walking into a trap. The Taj Zabbar…" What could he say to make her understand that all he wanted was her safety?

Those beautiful blue eyes went dark, then shot dangerous daggers of fire in his direction. "Just one minute, bub. After everything we've been through in the last couple of days, do I strike you as the timid type? As some kind of fragile flower?"

She fisted her hands; opened and closed them. It was as if he could read her frustration. He could see that she was strung tight with it and her tenuous control matched his own. The idea of them being so much in tune was sensual. Almost erotic. The sight of her bouncing on her toes, ready to fight, made him weak in the knees.

She punched him square in the chest. "Well, not *this* Texas Rose. If you're danged determined to take a train, you'd better get aboard. I'll be right behind you. We can talk there."

He opened his mouth to try again. Or to demand that she pay attention to his warnings. Or to...

Right then something in a far corner of the station caught his eye. A man. Standing half-hidden behind a pillar and watching them. The thing that had first caught Darin's attention from across the room—the one thing he most feared—was a purple-checked head scarf of the Taj Zabbar.

Hell.

That changed everything. Darin couldn't possibly leave her here now. At their mercy? And all alone?

"Fine," he said gruffly as he grabbed her by the wrist and twisted them both in the direction of the distant train platform. "Let's go."

Racing for the huffing train, he pulled a stunned Rylie in his wake like a water-skier. The Taj Zabbar had spotted her. Nowhere was safe from their threat anymore. Darin came to a quick decision. Real safety for her would come only if the two of them stayed together.

His original impulse had been the correct one. The two of them had to be attached at the hip from now on.

Regardless of the consequences to his body and soul.

Hunched down on the tufted and cushioned bench of their luxury first-class cabin, Rylie listened to the clack, clack, clack of the train's wheels against the rails. She'd been staring at the quilted wallpaper and sulking since they'd pulled out of the station. Meanwhile, Darin was feigning sleep in the seat beside her.

The package he'd been carrying most of the morning, the envelope or whatever, was nowhere in sight. She'd tried to see if he had the thing on him still, but he never let her get close enough.

He hadn't told her anything so far, either. He'd hustled them onto the train and into his reserved cabin. Next thing she knew, he'd closed his eyes and was snoring. She wasn't even positive she knew where they were headed, let alone the reason for this unexpected trip—or for Darin's sudden change of heart about letting her come.

But she'd taken notice of how he carefully locked the door to their cabin as the train pulled out of the station. Rylie didn't think she could ever forget the look of pure fear that had crossed Darin's face as he'd changed his mind and dragged her across the train station's concrete floor at a sprint. Something—or someone—had scared him into bringing her along.

Squirming in her seat, she turned to look at his profile. His act of sleeping peacefully only incensed her. Just look at that stunning, stubbled jaw of his. At the perfection of his Roman nose and the long black lashes that lazily touched those sculpted cheekbones. Damn him for making the butterflies churn in her stomach.

Her gaze dropped to the mouth that had already shown he knew more than most about great sex. An urge to kiss those fantastic lips of his again curled tightly inside her belly. But in the nick of time, she remembered that his mouth also knew how to tell great lies.

Darin knew more than he was saying about the explosion that had changed her life. Okay, so she was pretty sure he had not been involved directly. But he *knew* who was and he'd been keeping the information from her.

Rylie leaned over and poked him hard in the ribs with her elbow. "Stop pretending to sleep. Get up and talk to me."

"Huh?"

"Don't you *huh* me, Darin Kadir. You're not sleeping for real, and I have a lot of questions. The first one is—where are we headed?"

Darin had the nerve to yawn. "Um…this train is the sightseeing train that travels over the Alps to Milan, Italy. We should be there by midmorning."

"Overnight sightseeing? What can you see in the dark?"

He straightened up. "Wait until you see the beautiful sunsets and sunrises in the Alps this time of year. And the train makes stopovers in Bellinzona and Morithy. Both splendid places for sightseeing. Even in the early morning."

Pursing her lips and narrowing one eye, she said, "Okay, then. But why? Why the heck are we taking a perfectly *splendid* train ride right now?"

"We had the tickets."

Argh. Heaven save her from smart-assed men.

"Can we just talk for a while?" Maybe casual conversation would get to the truth. "My nerves are shot after that assault this morning and from chasing you around all day. I need to settle down."

"Why don't you try a nap?"

Frustrated, she poked him the ribs again. "I can't sleep yet. And neither can you. Don't lie."

He mumbled something she was glad not to hear and then breathed a deep, mournful sigh. "Fine. What do you want to talk about?"

She wanted to ask about the object he'd found, or talk about that horrible, life-changing explosion. But she knew he would only feed her a bunch of bull about those things. So she tried a different tack.

"It was nice meeting your brother. I don't have any siblings myself. Do you have other brothers and sisters?"

"Nice? Shakir would hate being called nice." Darin chuckled and a loving gleam entered his eyes. "I have two brothers. Shakir, whom you met, and our baby brother, Tarik. Only, Tarik would have my head if he heard me referring to him as anything but a tough ex American Special Forces officer."

"Ex? What does he do for a living now? Tell me about him. Tell me about both of them."

Darin cleared his throat. "They're family." His sentence had ended abruptly, as if that was all that needed saying.

But as she was about to ask another question, Darin continued, "Our mother died when I was twelve. Shakir was ten then, and Tarik was five years old. Our father... our father is a very busy man. Besides being head of the board of directors for most of the Kadir family holdings, he is also the titular head of elders in our extended family."

"You mean like a king?"

"Not exactly. I come from a long line of traders and nomads, remember. Because we have no country of our own, the modern Kadir family holds together like a corporation. We own property in various places throughout the world. We own businesses and homes, hospitals and schools. But we don't claim any territory, and we communicate through family reunions and conferences instead of through edicts."

Darin stood, checked the lock on the door, then he sat back down.

"Tell me more about your brothers." She thought about Shakir. At least six-four, he had a quiet intensity about him and an underlying strength that seemed almost chilling.

"I had to step in to be a father figure for them. But I'm afraid I was not in good enough psychological shape at that point to even help myself. Our mother's death hit us all hard.

"Shakir maybe worst of all." Darin shook his head as painful emotions fluttered in his eyes. "Before six months had passed, Shakir began to stutter. He quit his athletic endeavors and buried himself in books."

Rylie had seen something quite different in Shakir from the shy bookworm his brother was describing. A lethal intelligence gleamed in Shakir's eyes, true. But the looks he gave her were more those of a deadly assassin. A man with no morals. A man who would sooner slit your throat than look at you twice.

"If it hadn't been for our maternal grandfather

taking him under his wing," Darin went on, "I'm afraid Shakir might never have broken out of his self-imposed cocoon."

"Oh? I'm glad the rest of the family stepped in to help."

Darin shook his head sharply. "Don't be so quick. Our grandfather was not a man you would've liked to meet in a dark alley. My mother came from a tribe of savage desert warriors, and her father was determined to turn at least one grandson out like his ancestors. Shakir was vulnerable to the mind-bending lessons he received in fierce warfare. He learned a great deal, but none of it is particularly helpful in civilized society."

"He seemed civilized." Just barely.

"Shakir attended a proper English university when he came of age. But then he joined an English paratrooper regiment and spent several years fighting in the isolated mountains of Afghanistan. If he seemed civilized to you, it's only a veneer. Underneath...I'm not too sure what lurks underneath that thin veneer these days.

"But I love my brother," Darin added with a cheerless smile. "Both of them. And the Kadir family is nothing if not loyal. We would all give our lives for each other."

Darin stood again and paced the small cabin. Rylie folded her hands in her lap. This wasn't getting her any closer to finding out what the object was that Darin had found or why they were on this train.

"What about your other brother? You said his name is Tarik?"

"Yes, the baby of the family." This time it was a genuine smile that spread cheer across Darin's face. "When Mother died, Tarik had to compete for attention. He quickly learned the lesson about catching more flies with sweetness than with bitter vinegar. He became the clown of the family. Or...perhaps a better description is the family's chameleon.

"My youngest brother is a master at hiding his true feelings behind a grin." Darin paused his pacing and stared out the window at the passing scenery for a moment before continuing. "You'd like him. Everyone does."

"You said he'd been in the U.S. Army? Special Forces? What's he doing now?"

Instead of answering her questions, Darin turned to look at her. Really look at her for the first time since they'd been on this train. She came to her feet, not knowing why exactly. But it felt important for her to be closer to him.

He took a step and picked up her hands, tenderly holding them both in his own. "Rylie, we only had our suspicions until the happenings of the last couple of days. But now it looks like the Kadir elders were right."

He winced, as though what he had to say would hurt them both. "Apparently, now that the Taj Zabbar have endless pools of money, they've decided to take revenge on the Kadirs. For real. We're fairly sure now they're taking secretive steps to ruin us. And my father believes if they can't ruin our businesses and reputations, they intend to kill us."

Rylie was shocked, almost speechless. "All this over something that happened five hundred years ago or more. Not really?"

"No," he answered softly. "Not really. It's true that old fight probably didn't make us terribly popular among the Taj Zabbar, but grudges can be hard to hold for centuries. In more modern times, about fifty years ago, the Taj Zabbar began mounting a revolt against their Kasht oppressors. They pleaded with world leaders for help, but…"

Darin's hesitation said more than any words. He didn't want to finish telling her his tale.

"Go ahead. This all happened long before either of us was born. I'm listening."

He gently squeezed her hands. "The Kadir elders of that time were working to spread their influences throughout the world. They had made a deal with the country of Kasht for control of a profitable deep-water port—located in Zabbaran territory."

Darin closed his eyes but he never let go of her hands. "It was greed. Pure and simple. Well, and maybe a little desperation. It's not easy becoming a world shipping power without having your own territory.

"Nevertheless," he went on after opening his glazed eyes, "the Kadir elders used bribery, blackmail and whatever other underhanded tricks they had at their disposal to make sure world leaders ignored the Taj Zabbar's pleas for help."

Dropping her hands, Darin turned his back and finished speaking over his shoulder. "The country of Kasht put down the minor Taj Zabbar revolt with iron fists. Many Taj Zabbar died or were thrown into horrific prison camps. It took them nearly fifty years to recover. So you see, the Taj Zabbar have good reason to hate Kadirs."

He was embarrassed. Chagrined over the poor image he'd had to leave concerning his family. Her heart hurt for him in return.

She took a step and touched his arm. "Darin. Please

look at me. None of this was your doing. It all took place a long time—"

"You shouldn't have come." He spun around in one fast move. "If anything happens to you, I'll never forgive myself."

Before Rylie could catch her breath, Darin took her in his arms and lasered a fierce kiss across her lips.

Hunger. Desperation. Sorrow. Humiliation.

Every combined response from both of them registered with her in that moment. And then he took the kiss deeper, and nothing but the two of them and the searing heat mattered at all.

Darin put everything he had into the kiss. All the obsession. All the anger and fear. He plundered her mouth. Punishing, pleading and devouring at the same time.

Go away, he thought in his mind. *Stay forever,* his heart begged. Kissing her long and hard, and with a demand for possession that scared the hell out of him, he felt her whole being returning the sentiment.

And that scared him even more.

Releasing her, he staggered back, his head reeling and his breath coming in erratic bursts. He stared at her through eyes that had misted over. Her own blue eyes were sharp with emotions and questions. Questions he had no answers for at the moment.

"What was that?" she asked in a raspy voice. "It wasn't…it wasn't just…" She stopped, waving her hand like he should be able to fill in the blanks.

He could. But he wouldn't.

"…a kiss. That was not a simple kiss."

She was right. But he could do nothing more than

stand there like a rooted tree while the sound of the train rumbling against the tracks grew louder in his ears.

"Say something," she demanded. "Tell me I'm right. Or—" she narrowed her eyes at him "—tell me I'm wrong. What the hell is happening between us?"

He couldn't give her an answer. He couldn't even give himself an answer. Not while she was in danger. Not while he didn't know if tomorrow his entire family might be blown off the face of the earth.

Finally he opened his mouth, and the weakest thing he had ever said flew from his lips. "Later. We'll have to talk about this much later."

"But…"

At that moment a faint thud came from right outside the door. Darin put his hand over her mouth and shook his head to keep her quiet.

The door's handle squeaked. Another more metallic sound clanked through the silence.

Darin braced himself and pushed Rylie to the back of the cabin. Holding his breath, he positioned his body at the side of the door. Whoever this was would get a big surprise from him.

And then the handle slowly turned—and the door opened just a crack.

Chapter 8

Aware of his weapon, the weight of it heavy where it sat lodged at his back, Darin opted not to draw it and take any chances with Rylie's life. He could hear her turbulent breathing behind him. Could almost feel the erratic pounding of her heart, beating together with his in double-time.

No, this kind of close-range surprise situation called for the hand-to-hand-type combat he'd learned in defense classes. But it became more than he could manage to stand motionless, waiting while the door slowly opened wider. Adrenaline surges crashed inside his head like waves upon a stormy shore.

In the span between two seconds, Darin made his move. Whirling, he kicked the door open and pinned his assailant. Shoulder driven into the intruder's chest and elbow jammed into his windpipe, Darin drew his knife and rammed it up hard under the man's upraised chin, almost piercing the skin.

"What do you want with us?" he growled in a voice not sounding like his own.

The man choked out an answer that Darin didn't understand. Jerking his elbow from the man's Adam's apple, Darin grabbed one flailing wrist and twisted the assailant around. He drew the man's arm up and pressed that wrist solidly between his shoulder blades, thrusting the man's nose into the wall in the process.

"Ow." The cry came out more like a whimper than a war whoop. "Monsieur. Monsieur. Please don't hurt me. Sorry to disturb you. I…I am ze porter."

"Darin, stop! Don't." Rylie's pleas filtered through the fog of rolling hormones zinging around in his mind.

Dropping his hands and lowering the knife, Darin sank backward and fell against the cushioned bench. "What have I done?"

"It's okay. Everything's okay." Rylie filled her lungs with air and went to the unfortunate porter slumped against the open door. "You're not hurt, are you?"

"No, mademoiselle. I…" The man touched his red nose, straightened his jacket and squared his shoulders. "It was my fault. My responsibility is to knock. But I did not think you were in residence."

The man's Italian accent mixed with his stilted French words and covered most of his shaky tones. Rylie was amazed. If this had been America, the guy would've already been lawyering up and screaming about his rights.

"But we locked the door. Didn't we? How'd you get in?"

The man smoothed his finger across his mustache and

cleared his throat. "There is...how you say? Ze porter's key? If you wish not to be disturbed, you must adjust ze sign which tells to all *occupée*. Yes?" He pointed out a sliding button next to the door.

"I came to make up ze bedding," the porter continued as if nothing had happened and everything was in perfect order. "But I will return later. Do mademoiselle and monsieur wish to view a menu?"

Darin came to his feet, eyes suddenly alert. "No food, but a question. I heard a thudding noise out in the corridor right before you came in. Did you see someone else out there?"

"I passed a gentleman as I entered ze car, signor. Another passenger, perhaps."

"What did he look like?"

"Just a man."

Darin looked frustrated. "But was he dressed differently? Anything outstanding that you remember?"

The porter pursed his lips in thought. Finally he said, "Ze gentleman was dressed like a member of a sheik's party." The porter touched a hand to his bare head and lifted his eyebrows.

"With a keffiyeh? The head scarf? What color? Was it purple?" Darin peppered his questions at the man.

The porter withstood the assault of words and made another curt nod in his direction. "*Sì. Ze colore* it was *porpora*."

Darin shoved a handful of Swiss francs at the porter and sent him on his way. Then Darin picked up the long, stiletto-style knife from where it lay on the floor, flipped it closed and returned it to his pocket.

"Where'd you get something like that?" Rylie asked

as the sharpest frigging blade that she'd ever seen disappeared.

"My brother." He hadn't said which brother, but Rylie was guessing something like that could only belong to Shakir.

Darin's eyes were feverish, glazed. Rylie wanted to help him. She eased down onto the bench and lifted her palm, wordlessly pleading for him to join her.

He sat down beside her, but she could feel the nervous tension stringing his body tight with electric charges.

"Talk to me," she said, using as calm and collected a tone as she could muster.

"About what?"

"Finish telling me what your family is doing about the Taj Zabbar threat."

Darin stared at her a long minute, as though he couldn't believe she would be asking such a thing.

But as she was about ready to say something else, he said, "My brothers and I have taken leave of our professions in order to flush out the truth. Our family must be prepared for the worst." His voice was rough, hoarse, but finally quiet.

"The Taj Zabbar are known to be secretive," he went on. "Few people in the world know for sure what they're up to, and that's been their operating style for centuries."

She was almost sorry she'd asked. He looked so distraught. So guilty—for no good reason she could see.

"We've also recently learned they're covertly trading in a variety of illegal enterprises." Darin shifted and ran his hands down his arms as if he were cold. "The legitimate money they've made in oil seems to be financing more criminal-style activities with the potential for bigger profit yet. Drugs. Arms dealing and weapons of mass destruction. Human trafficking and slavery. A whole plethora of dirty activities."

When Rylie gasped and widened her eyes at the idea of such nasty and deadly dealings, Darin dropped his chin and stared at the carpeted floor. "I know. It sounds bad. But now that we're sure they're conducting a war of retribution against the Kadirs, I'm afraid my next accusation will sound much worse."

This time it was Rylie who picked up one of his hands and grasped it tenderly between her own. "Go on. Whatever it is, I can take it."

"They're coming after our family like a python, using stealth and power to bring us to our knees and choke the life out of our businesses and destroy our families. The explosion that killed your father and my uncle, nearly ruining Hunt Drilling, must've been a tentative first round in their war against the Kadirs."

"I knew that explosion wasn't any accident."

Darin looked into her eyes, anguish clear in his face. "I'm sorry your family got caught up in something so terrible. But my brothers and I will find the person responsible and make it right. I promise."

"You and your family are trying to uncover the Taj Zabbar's next moves. What will you do then?"

"Turn the information over to the international authorities. The United States. The United Nations. If we make the snake public, we remove the worst of its bite."

"I want to help." Her own words surprised her, but she didn't intend to take them back. "I want to let the whole world know who caused that accident and who should be stopped by whatever means necessary."

Shaking his head, Darin whispered, "It's too dangerous. You shouldn't even be anywhere near us. I'm sure that's why the Taj Zabbar has already tried to kidnap you. Because you've been seen with me.

"You have to stay out of this, Rylie," he pleaded. "It's not your war. Let us do what we must. I promise I'll let the world know the explosion was no accident and who it was that caused it. Give me a little time."

"Let me help." Again she surprised herself with such fervent determination. She would help, she realized. Nothing could stop her now that she knew the whole story.

"No. You have to stay safe. Away from the Kadirs and their enemies. Away from me."

She began to argue. "I'm tougher than you…" But then she looked into his eyes. Really looked. The man was terrified—for her sake. No one but her father had ever been concerned for her welfare. The idea was powerful and potentially life-changing.

She interrupted her revolutionary thoughts to turn the subject around with a coy smile. "Let's talk about all this later. Right now I'm too hungry to continue this discussion. Feed me."

After a quick stop in the compartment's tiny toilet to freshen up, Darin ushered Rylie to the dining car. Eager to go in search of the Taj Zabbar assailant whom he felt sure had boarded the train with them, Darin frantically ran through ideas in his head for a way to keep her safe in the meantime.

"Oh, look at the golden eagle." Rylie pointed out the

window to a large bird, soaring in and out of sunset's shadows on the springtime updrafts.

The waiter seated them at a small table set with white tablecloth and sterling utensils. Rylie still didn't take her eyes off the picturesque sight out the window.

"I never believed anything could be this beautiful."

The train was climbing higher, moving slowly past mountain pines and dwarf spruce. Up ahead the ice-covered Alps with their rose-colored peaks were brushed in a golden glow of the setting sun. They stood like a line of sentinels guarding the Swiss-Italian border.

"Would you like me to order a bottle of wine?" he asked to recapture her attention. "A nice Tuscan cabernet or perhaps one of the Masseto merlots?" Maybe with enough alcohol in her system, she would become sleepy and he could lock her safely in their compartment while he searched the cars for their assailant. Or perhaps the porter could scare up a couple of sleeping pills.

"I'd better not. I don't suppose they have sweet iced tea on this train?"

"I'm sure they don't." His chances of locking her away for safety appeared to be more and more remote.

"My ears just popped."

"It's the altitude. We'll be traveling through the Gotthard Pass a little after midnight and dropping into the Ticino valley a couple of hours later. You'll probably experience the effects of more altitude changes by then."

They ordered dinner and ate a meal of spring veal and gnocchi. Whie she was drinking the espresso he hadn't wanted her to order, Darin realized it had grown late and they were the sole occupants of the car. Maybe it was time to try putting a scare into her. That could make her stay out of his way.

He withdrew the Taj Zabbar letter from his pocket. "Do you see this letter?"

She jerked it from his hand and frowned at what must have looked like jibberish to her. "Is this what you found today? A letter? In the Taj Zabbar language? What's it say?"

"It's an order from one of their elders to one of their soldiers. An order demanding the capture and transportation of you—or your body—to a meeting place in Milan tomorrow."

"Me?" She actually had the nerve to beam at him. "Think of that. I wonder how I got to be so important."

This was not the reaction he had anticipated.

"It's nothing to joke about. They want you dead. These men are beyond dangerous, Rylie. You need to give them a wide berth. We've intercepted messages from them before that tell about torture and seduction of young women for both profit—and for fun. Stay out of their line of sight."

She casually shrugged a shoulder and studied her fingernails.

Finally she glanced up at him. "But what if I *let* them capture me? Couldn't your family use someone on the inside? I could listen for…"

"Not one chance in a thousand hells of that happening."

Rylie folded her arms over her chest. "Maybe we should ask your brothers for their vote."

"That's it." Darin threw his napkin on the table and stood, pulling her along by the elbow.

"You're going back to the sleeping compartment to wait for me. I'm on this train to find that bastard who attacked you. He boarded with us and I intend to capture him and make him talk."

"But…"

"No buts." Darin had had enough. "You can have the gun. And I'll slip the porter money to keep an eye on the corridor and on your door. You should be safe enough."

He inched his arm around her waist and began shuffling her out of the dining car. But the moment her body was pressed to his, their combined heat raced along his veins and landed hot and erotic at the base of his spine.

Impossible. *Not now.* He eased his grip on her and backed away to a more respectable distance. But he kept them both moving forward through the passenger cars.

Rylie never spoke a word. When he gave her the gun and final instructions on how to use it, she glared up at him with a look that could've set fire to a glacier.

"Stay safe," he reiterated while turning his back on that gorgeous but furious face. "And be here when I return."

He took a deep breath and walked out the door, praying all the while that by leaving her alone he wasn't making one of the biggest mistakes of his whole life.

Rylie stared at the back of the closed door, still waiting for Darin's return and to hear him say he needed her help. Ten seconds. Forty. One minute. Two.

Well, dang it.

Okay, she got that he was worried about her. Really

she did. But she'd also hoped he was coming to know the person she was inside. The person who could never in a million years wait around in safety, sitting on her hands while someone she cared about worked to save her life.

Uh-uh. So not going to happen, Darin.

It was amazing how close she felt to him after such a short time. How well she knew the real him even with few words spoken between them. How could he care about her and not know her any better than he apparently did?

And he did care for her, she was absolutely positive. Um, maybe his emotions were based mostly around lust, but he did care. She could easily see that in the way he looked at her and in the way he kept demanding that she stay safe.

Her insides were already jumping, raring to follow after him. But she would sit here for one more minute first. To be sure he didn't turn her around in the corridor and find a way to lock her inside their cabin.

Images churned in her mind as she perched a foot over one knee, flapping it up and down in midair with nervous energy. She cared about him, too. More than cared. In fact, what she'd been feeling verged on a once-in-a-lifetime thing.

But was it real? Her emotions had been on such a roller-coaster ride since she'd first set eyes on him that she hardly knew what to think. It had started out with her being sure she hated him. Positive he'd had a hand in murdering her father. Now she knew he was no murderer. Taking a life in self-defense had all but killed him, too.

As the days and hours had gone by, she'd been

experiencing many other feelings toward him. Some she couldn't even name. Lust was right up there on top, of course. But there was so much more.

That last kiss had been...special. It was the kind of kiss that spoke of millions of tomorrows. The extraordinary sort of kiss that brought to mind knights in shining armor about to give up their lives for the woman they loved. A kiss like nothing in her experience.

Love? Not a remote possibility in their case. Darin didn't even know the true her. And would he still care as much if he did? Maybe not. Maybe they came from such differing backgrounds that he would never be able to respect a strong woman. A woman who wanted to stand beside her man and not behind him as they faced life together. A woman like her.

And how did she feel about him deep down? She knew there was a lump in her chest whenever she thought about him. A lump in her chest and a wildly crazy heat at her core. The man seriously turned her on.

Hmm. Perhaps that could be the answer for all her questions. The two of them needed to have sex. That would clear both their minds of any infatuation and prove once and for all if their differing backgrounds could ever be overcome.

Rylie found it easy to imagine that whatever lust Darin had been feeling for her would quickly disappear in a puff of smokin' hormones after one roll in the hay. She'd seen it happen to men before. But she wasn't going to push him into having sex for his sake alone. She wasn't that horny. No, she had come to the conclusion that the two of them should have sex for her *own* enlightenment. She was the one who needed to discover how becoming intimate with a person so different from herself would affect her emotional well-being.

Would she want more? Or would she run screaming from his arms and fly all the way home, glad to be free? She would never know until she tried.

Yep. That was all settled. Having sex was the plan.

But first she had to make sure he stayed alive.

Two hours later Rylie's ears were popping again as she crept through the quiet corridors looking for any sign of Darin or the Taj Zabbar kidnapper. The train must be heading lower, going in the direction of the lake below the mountains. Rylie could almost feel gravity pulling her downward.

She must've been just missing Darin and the kidnapper while she searched. It was possible they had ducked into a cabin or hidden behind a closed door when she'd gone by. But she had traveled the length of this train twice, looking. Now she wasn't sure what was left to...

The train rounded a steep U-curve right then, and Rylie got a good view through the windows into another corridor as the snaking cars doubled back on themselves. There, maybe only two or three train-car lengths ahead, she saw two men locked in mortal combat in the well-lit corridor of a sleeping car.

Darin.

Blasting out of her own corridor at a dead run, Rylie swore under her breath. She should be covering his back. She was the one with the gun, after all.

She pushed through pressurized door locks and tramped across the little vestibules that connected two cars. Through one car. Then into the next.

By the time she hit the third empty corridor in a row she was breathing hard and very confused. She'd seen them. Clearly. It hadn't been a dream.

Then she heard a noise coming from the end of the car. It sounded as though someone had momentarily gone through the pressurized door onto the next vestibule. Shoving hard to open the door, she blinked at sudden air movement and turned her head in that direction.

To her amazement, she saw shoes as they disappeared up a ladder that she'd never noticed before. A ladder to the roof of the train? Why?

After she heard a distant shout, sounding for all the world like Darin's voice, the why didn't seem too important. If he could chase someone to the roof of a train, she could follow.

She carefully checked to be sure the gun was secure in her waistband. Then, shaking her head at the craziness of the whole idea, she began to climb.

A cold blast of wind whipped prickles of ice at her body as she neared the roof's edge. But that didn't stop her. Nothing could've stopped her until she found out what was going on up above.

Peeking over the edge of the roof, she saw a sight that took her breath. Darin and the Taj Zabbar would-be kidnapper battling with each other. One swung wildly and then the other did the same. Both had knives drawn and were swearing at each other in different languages.

Rylie eased her body onto the roof and lay there spread-eagle, wondering if she had the nerve to stand up while the train was traveling on a twenty-degree incline. Then the car leveled out some while the train rolled across a well-lit trestle above a deep, glacial-cut ravine.

She watched as the kidnapper struck out at Darin's hand and his knife flew free. Darin whirled in a defensive move and the kidnapper's knife went sailing, too.

Sucking up courage, Rylie pulled the gun free and came up on her knees and elbows. Pointing the weapon at the kidnapper, she screamed over the roar of the wind.

"Stop! Stand still. I've got you covered."

When Darin turned his head toward her, his face went deathly pale. Before she could blink, he dove in her direction and tried to shield her with his body.

"Here." She thrust the gun at him.

He turned it on the kidnapper, but the man was close and scrambling toward both of them with desperation in his eyes.

Everything seemed to happen at once after that.

Darin fired. Ducking, the kidnapper slipped on a patch of ice and started sliding. Darin reached out, trying to give the man a hand. Rylie watched in horror as the man's fingernails scratched deep grooves in the paint with his futile attempts to stay in place.

And then, without a noise, without any sound at all above the howling winds, the Taj Zabbar kidnapper was gone.

Vanished into the nothingness of the dark night.

Chapter 9

Back in their cabin, Darin and Rylie sat together in silence on the newly made-up bed. Both of them waiting for their heart rates to settle. Grasping her hand to assure himself that she was truly alive, Darin couldn't believe how close he had come to losing her for good.

What was he going to do with her? Part of him was fascinated with her independence and that amazing self-confidence in her own abilities. She stirred something in him in a place that no one had ever reached before.

But another part of him, the more rational and coherent part, was horrified at the chances she took. He could never keep her safe if she kept undermining his efforts at every turn.

But how would he ever manage to talk her into walking away from a fight that was not her own? Darin feared he was partially to blame. He had been keen to keep her close. Secretly dying for a chance of the two of them becoming intimate. He had been positive that having sex with her would disabuse him of his powerful obsession.

A nearly fatal mistake on his side.

He must change all of that—and quickly. His obsession would have to be buried now, without the benefit of seeking out an answer to his questions of why. The real truth to the matter was that they were obviously unsuited. A committed relationship between them would be out of the question. This whole obsession thing had to have been born out of pure lust. And lust could always be conquered by the power of the mind. Or buried by the power of determination.

Yes, things must change. He would find a way to send her away by feigning disinterest. Now that her would-be kidnapper was gone for good, Darin could pretend to be more interested in the Taj Zabbar war and in his family business than in her. He could stop mooning over her and treat her in a rude and perhaps even crude manner. He searched his mind for an example—and came up with his father's attitude toward women.

Darin wasn't sure he could even playact such arrogance. But he could try.

"You were lucky," he said in as cold a voice as he could remember his father using. He dropped her hand and slid a short distance away. "But foolish. Next time do as I tell you."

Her head came up and she glared at him. The exact reaction he had hoped she would have.

"Don't give me that." She folded her arms around her waist, as though he had delivered a blow. "You're alive because I brought you the gun. Just say thanks and be grateful I didn't follow your *orders*."

She had slipped right back into the wrong attitude. He would have to keep trying. Opening his mouth to deliver the next hit, he froze in midthought when a knock sounded at their door. Both of them jumped up and stared at the back of the door as if the knock had been a hiss from a poisonous viper.

"What'll we do?" she whispered.

He reached out toward the handle. "We'll answer and find out who it is."

When he opened the door, the porter was on the other side and a small commotion could be heard going on down the corridor. "*Pardon.* May I speak to monsieur and mademoiselle for a moment?"

"Certainly." Darin brought the man inside the cabin, but he stuck his head out past the threshold, trying to find out what was happening.

He turned around, shutting the door behind him. "What's going on?" he asked the porter.

"Ah, yes. The reason why I must speak with you. It is feared a terrible accident has occurred."

"An accident? What kind of accident?"

"A man has reportedly fallen off the train to his death."

Darin's blood pressure blew off the charts, but he forced a mild, surprised look instead of the guilt he was feeling. "Oh? What makes anyone think that?"

The porter lowered his voice conspiratorially. "A couple, older I believe, say they saw ze man fall. They were standing in a darkened compartment, staring out ze window, when zis form of a body passed by their view."

"Really? That seems odd. Are they sure?" Darin lowered his voice to match the other man's.

The porter nodded. "*Sì*. They say they were awakened by sounds—" he pointed above his head "—on ze roof. When they looked out...*le voilà!*"

Darin shot Rylie a look. She was pale, and he imagined he saw her trembling, but she pursed her lips and held herself together.

"What's happening now?" Darin asked the porter.

"The train staff, we are checking each compartment. We match tickets to passengers." He shook his head and rolled his eyes as if to say he did not believe their search would find anything. "If a man is missing, we will find out."

"Then what?" Rylie's voice was shaky, but Darin could hear her trying to stay strong.

"We arrive at ze town of Bellinzona momentarily. Ze Swiss police, they will question all passengers."

Darin's mind rifled through ideas. He couldn't speak to the police. He was no good at lying. Not like Tarik was.

When nothing else came to mind, he said, "Oh. But we were counting on resting at Bellinzona. And seeing the sights. My—" he gestured to Rylie "—my friend is not feeling too well. A little motion sickness, I think. Can't you help us out?"

While the man hesitated, Darin could feel the train slowing. Heard the slight screech of brakes against the rails. It was now or never.

Darin put his hand in his pocket and withdrew a wad of francs. He began peeling off bills, one at a time, and handing them over.

"*Sì,*" the man said as he shot a fast look at the closed

door behind him. "You are already checked by me, no? When ze train stops, I will lower steps from zis car for easy exit. You will go to the inn of my cousin. Unfortunately, not many hotels are to be found in Bellinzona. But La Villa di Ticino will be comfortable for the mademoiselle. Yes?"

Rylie put out her hand and gently touched the man's arm. "Thank you."

The porter bowed his head, his eyes twinkling with concern for her in return. *"Sì. Sì."* He patted her hand. "The train, it will stop for several hours, mademoiselle. You may rest easy at the villa."

Maybe Rylie would rest easy. But Darin wouldn't rest at all until she was on her way out of the country, out of Europe and away from both the danger—and from him.

Fifty miles away in Milan, Sheikh Newaf Bin Hamad Taj Zabbar prepared for a mourning ritual by donning the ceremonial white tunic and red sash. The colors of innocence and blood.

In his mind he chanted the ancient rituals. Rituals based on the unique mysticism of a historical militant sect. These teachings, brought from across the centuries via the god of Time, were given to Taj Zabbar elders by their tutors and guardians—the early Assassins.

Their one true belief, the foremost revelation by the Sheik of the Mountain, was clear to everyone who followed. *All that matters is action.* Action, along with total loyalty to the master.

According to the teachings, a loyal warrior's suicide and martyrdom shall lead to the Assassins' paradise in the Shadow of Swords. But Hamad had read the historical facts and knew that the original sect of Assassins, called the Nizari, had built a model paradise in a valley near Persia. They had wished to fool their followers into devoting their lives and deaths to the sect.

The Assassins' very real paradise on earth was described in detail centuries ago by the great Marco Polo after he was brought to the valley by the original Imams.

> In a beautiful valley…lies a luxurious garden stored with every delicious fruit and every fragrant shrub.… Palaces of various sizes are to be found, ornamented with works of gold, with paintings and with furniture of rich silks. By means of small conduits…streams of wine, milk, honey and some of pure water were seen to flow in every direction.… Elegant and beautiful damsels, accomplished in the arts of singing, playing upon all sorts of musical instruments, dancing, and especially those of dalliance and amorous allurement were seen continually sporting and amusing themselves in the garden.…

Such a description of paradise might be enough to lure some into martyrdom, but Hamad preferred to find his own paradise in life first. He vowed to maintain at least one of the teachings of his ancestors: *death and blood shall bring followers the reward of eternal life.* As part of that doctrine, Hamad would use the mourning ritual to assist his foolish cousin Taweel forward to his death's reward.

Hamad could've predicted such an end to his not-terribly-bright employee. The man was not a snake, as his ancestors demanded of their followers. Nor was he fit to wield the poisonous dagger.

The Taj Zabbar were descended from the best of the Assassins. And Hamad believed he was the best of the best. Deadly—of course. But smart, too. Smart enough to use modern means to rid himself of both enemies and unworthy friends. He had been informed of the exact instant when his cousin's life had expired. The computer chip implanted in his chest had showed the time of death with an immediate transmission to Hamad's computers. A great cheer had gone up among the men at Taweel's martyrdom.

"Pardon the interruption, my sheik." Another of Hamad's men entered his private chamber after a quick knock. "You asked to be informed about the progress of the train. It has stopped at Bellinzona and will be searched by the Swiss police."

"And the whereabouts of the coded communiqué sent by the elder Mugrin?" Hamad was still annoyed over the elder's stupid and dangerous choice of writing his message down on paper. Certainly, that elder would have to be eliminated sooner rather than later after this move.

"It is believed the Kadir son known as Darin still has it in his possession, my sheik."

"And do we also believe the Hunt woman continues to travel with Darin Kadir?"

"Yes, Excellency."

This news might be good. Hamad could bring down several threats with one throw of his dagger.

"I want a team of our best trained men—men trained in the ways of our ancestors. Send them to the train and waste no time bringing the communiqué back to me."

"What about the woman?"

It took a few seconds for Hamad to make a decision about the woman. "If it is possible, bring the woman alive, as well. We have profitable uses for a beautiful woman such as that one."

"And if it is not possible?"

Fuming over too many questions about a subject that should be clear, Hamad narrowed his eyes at his assistant. "It is the communiqué that is all-important. It must not be allowed to be decoded by the Kadirs. Do whatever you think necessary to bring it to me. I don't really care what you do with either the man or the woman to accomplish this task. The Taj Zabbar war of retribution has been uncovered. The Kadirs now know the truth. There is no need for further secrecy."

"Yes, my sheik." The man backed out of the room and quietly shut the door.

Hamad bowed to the makeshift altar before him. Gingerly picking up the ceremonial dagger, he used the blade to slice a line across his wrist. Bloodred droplets spattered onto the stark-white linen cloth.

A Taj Zabbar warrior must be honored and assisted to his paradise. Revenge for his death would be had later—all in due time. Hamad recited the seven mystical laws based on personal concentration and supreme loyalty, clearing the way for cousin Taweel to his paradise.

"Enjoy your reward for the effort you expended, my cousin." Hamad whispered the chants against the roar of time moving forward and then added a personal postscript. "Darin Kadir shall join you on your journey, cousin, before the sun sets over Zabbaran once more. I swear to it."

"Come on." Rylie swung back around, urging Darin to follow her down the train tracks and into the old town of Bellinzona. "What's wrong with you? I thought you were the one who wanted to sneak away from the train until the cops were finished questioning people."

Darin stood, staring at something on the outside of the car they had exited—but finally he turned. "Huh? Oh, yes. Let's go."

He was certainly acting strange. Almost as if he were trying to memorize which car they'd left. But why?

She grabbed hold of his shirtsleeve and dragged him along beside her. When they rounded the end car of the train, they had to make a dash for the dark shelter of an alley between the edge of the station and the old rock buildings beyond.

La Villa di Ticino was six long blocks away. Rylie wouldn't feel really safe until they made it there.

Considering all the commotion at the train station, the town itself seemed fairly quiet. A few street vendors were selling their wares along the sidewalks closest to the station. But at dawn, not many other people seemed to be out and about.

"Hold on a minute." Darin dragged his feet, tugged against her hand and brought her back toward him.

He pointed to a large black shawl hanging over a street vendor's wagon. Within seconds Darin had negotiated a price with the vendor and was draping the handmade treasure around her head and body. It almost covered her completely from head to toe in black knit. And after being put into place, the shawl left her practically suffocating and nearly blind.

"That should help keep us from being discovered while we travel these streets," Darin told her as he threw his arm around her shoulders and helped her navigate the cobblestone walks.

"You think we look like a local couple now?"

"Not to the locals. But hopefully to the national police, at least from a distance."

Rylie shifted enough inside the shawl so that she could see out. They raced past five-hundred-year-old castles and a few even older churches that had been made entirely out of rough-cut stone. She worked hard not to trip on the uneven terrain.

The medieval architecture and the quiet morning should've been enough to bring her peace—and maybe would some other time. But right this moment her heart was pounding and her palms sweating as they hurried along toward the inn.

At last they came to the side street where La Villa di Ticino was located. A small sign swinging over an old wooden door was the only marker. As she was about to knock, the door opened.

"Buon giorno! Vieni dentro." A stout, middle-aged woman beamed at them as she dragged them over the threshold and into a small reception area.

"Did you know we were coming?"

"Sì. The nephew of my husband…the porter from your train…he calls to say you need refuge. *Benvenuti al nostro albergo.* Welcome to our inn."

"Thanks," Darin said gruffly as he slid a protective arm around Rylie's waist and moved in closer. "Can you just show us to a room, please?"

Rylie knew exactly what he was feeling. This woman seemed too friendly. Too outgoing. Too glad to see them.

Relieved when they were finally alone and locked inside a Spartan room, Rylie collapsed on the one queen-size bed. "I didn't think we would make it."

"I didn't, either. But I'm not sure I like the feel of this place. Something in my gut says it's not right."

She nodded. "Yeah. Have you checked the windows?"

Darin made a quick trip around the room to assess where they had found themselves. Then he went into the bathroom, came back and closed and locked windows, knocked on walls and looked behind the two paintings on display. Finally he spent a little time in the closet, checking out the walls in there in case of any false doors.

"Actually, this place is made like a fortress," he said when he was back beside her. "The walls are thick. I'm guessing several feet thick and made from solid stone. See there?" He pointed to the wires dangling from the ceiling. "They've had to string cords around the room in order to bring in electricity and modernize the place. The two windows in here have interior wood shutters that I've shut and locked. We're closed up enough now that we could be in a cave—or a fortress."

Darin was the one who was closed up. They had to stay put for the next few hours, and if he kept this nervous tension up he could have a meltdown or a heart attack by the time it was safe to leave. He had taken on the entire responsibility for keeping them from harm, and it wasn't fair. Rylie wanted to say something, do something that would help him relax.

"We've managed to get rather filthy in the last couple of days, don't you think?" She took a few steps toward the bathroom. "How're the facilities? Can we catch a couple of quick showers while we wait for the police to finish?"

Darin stared at her as though she'd lost her mind.

"Yeah, I know our lives are at stake. Believe me, I know. But we're stuck here for the next few hours at least. What else can we do? Besides, I feel sticky."

She stuck her head in the small room off the bedroom. A tiny sink with an even tinier mirror above it hung at an awkward angle against one wall. A small claw-footed tub had been squeezed against the other wall. And a miniature toilet with hardly enough room to sit down was wedged into a corner and was the only other thing in the small space.

She'd hoped for an oversize tub made for two. But no such luck. Well, she wasn't sure she could've talked Darin into the tub with her anyway. Though after the two of them were cleaned up, she fully intended to wrangle him into that nice big bed. This was as good a time as any to test her theory about the tension between them dissolving as soon as their raging lust was satiated.

"We could talk." Darin gazed at her with a sober, bruised look. Those dark-as-midnight eyes still held in deep, dark secrets.

"You mean *you* could talk and I could listen? No thanks. Not while we both stink. The showers come first."

And after that—the sex. Talking could wait.

"Go right ahead and hop in," he told her. "I want to call my brother. And maybe I'll speak to the innkeeper about breakfast while I'm at it. Are you hungry?"

Not for food. "Coffee and a roll might be nice."

"Okay, I'll take care of it. Don't rush. I'll clean up, myself, after you're done."

Yes, you will, Darin Kadir, she thought. *Today is the day when we'll clean up our lives, both physically and emotionally. We'll push away all the secrets so at last we can figure out where we stand.*

You can count on that.

Chapter 10

"No need to drive to Bellinzona," Darin assured his brother over the phone. "We've met a train porter who will be sure we reach the Milan station safely."

"Of course he will." Tarik's skepticism came through in his voice, even over the sound of running water as Rylie took her shower not ten feet away. "You will hand over the coded document the minute you reach the Milan station. Right? One of our men will fly it and Rylie to headquarters." Tarik didn't sound too crazy about the idea, but it was a plan.

"I'd prefer it if you would use one of our own jets to fly Rylie home to Texas. And make her as comfortable as possible."

"You're sure she'll be willing to leave?" Tarik's tone mocked him. "Shakir tells me she seemed pretty determined to stay until she has all the facts concerning that explosion in Houston."

Darin lowered his voice, though he was positive no one could hear him. "She already knows the Taj Zabbar were responsible. And I intend to make sure she's ready to go by the time we reach Milan. Leave her to me."

Tarik's low chuckle was loud enough to be heard even through his sat phone. "Yeah, and you've always been so great at convincing the ladies to do anything. Listen, maybe I should…"

"No thanks, baby brother." Darin worked to release his tight jaw as he reached over for his coffee cup. "You take care of getting your men ready for an assault on that Milan address I found. I'll be in time to join you at the takedown. I want to be there when we learn what they're planning—and their identities. Wait for me to arrive before you move in, will you?"

"As you wish. You deserve to be in on this first skirmish, Darin. But I won't be a bit surprised if your lady friend shows up there, too. Make sure she stays out of our way."

It was all Darin could do not to hurl his cup at a wall. "Shut up, bro. You do your job and I'll see to it she makes it on that plane."

Without waiting for another snide remark, Darin closed his phone and set it on the bedside table. Except for that annoying conversation with his brother, Darin was feeling a lot more relaxed about being stuck at this inn for the next few hours. The signora had delivered up strong coffee and fresh pastries without any complaints. She'd brought warm bath towels and a replacement travel kit, containing shampoo, toothpaste, a brush and razor, to replace the one Rylie was using in the bathroom.

Cheerful, much like her cousin the porter, the innkeeper had even volunteered to launder their clothes while they caught a couple hours of sleep.

She'd come by to collect Rylie's things along with his pullover shirt and zip-up jacket, leaving him naked to the waist. But he'd decided Rylie had been right. It would be a real pleasure to arrive in Milan clean and pressed.

While he'd waited for Rylie to finish in the shower, Darin had come up with another plan to get rid of her. As smart as she was, the woman seemed to have some kind of death wish. And he would be damned if Rylie was going to kill herself while he was standing nearby.

This time around, he'd decided the plan needed to use friendship and loyalty as a hook for pleading his case with her about doing the right thing. She was certain to understand what was honorable. He knew they at least had that much in common. In fact, Darin himself felt somewhat desperate, for once in his life, to do the right thing by a woman he cared about.

Sure that he understood Rylie rather well by this point in their relationship, Darin knew she would value friendship above any small matters of pride. And that was but one way they were alike in their thinking.

He thought back to what she'd done in the name of honor, for instance. Maybe she'd gone about it wrong, but Rylie had been trying to honor her family's name by selling off their assets and taking care of the victims of the explosion. Darin was also empathetic to her compulsion to honor her father's memory by proving that Red Hunt had not been the cause of the explosion. Rylie now understood that truth the same way that Darin knew the truth of the Taj Zabbar's covert war against his family.

Yes, the two of them had similar views and opinions on several subjects. This was no small matter in the big scheme of things. They shared views about right and honor and putting family first. Her safety seemed to be their one big sticking point.

The bathroom door opened and Rylie stepped into the bedroom, halfway disappearing in the cloud of steam that accompanied her. Darin nearly swallowed his tongue. Her hair was wrapped in one towel and her body was wrapped in another. He knew she didn't have on a single thing underneath.

Waiting a beat for his pulse to settle, he pointed at the coffee and rolls because he couldn't utter a word.

"Where are all my clothes?"

He cleared his throat. "The signora is laundering them. She just brought in the coffee."

"I don't even have any underwear to put on?"

Shaking his head, he tried for a look of chagrin. But he couldn't pretend to be overwrought about her problem. Not when his veins were sizzling and his libido was taking too much notice.

Rylie gave him a most unusual glance. He had a feeling she was thinking of something else, something he should've been able to figure out. But he was having trouble thinking at all. His brain had fogged over at the first sight of her.

It was time to back away while he still could. "My turn in the shower?"

"Yes. But hurry back."

He made a hasty retreat and eased the door shut

behind him. How had he gotten himself into this situation?

Could he still do the right thing? Silently laughing at his own sudden uncertainty, Darin discovered he could barely even speak, let alone convince her to leave for her own safety and his piece of mind.

But he wasn't some randy teenager stunned by his first sight of a naked woman. He was thirty-two, the vice CEO of a multinational business, and experienced in the sensual ways of womankind. Furthermore, he was strong-willed—and strong-minded. He could do anything if he concentrated hard enough.

Gathering his wits and promising to banish erotic thoughts and any hesitation, he stepped into the shower and flipped the water all the way to cold. Maybe if he stayed in here long enough, he could convince himself that even while talking to the naked woman in the next room he could still manage to do the right thing.

When the water from the faucet slowed to a trickle, Darin quickly shaved and dried off. After stepping back into his slacks, he stood with his hand on the doorknob, building up his nerve to face her again.

Taking a deep breath, he threw open the door with a flourish. While striding into the room like he knew what he was doing, Darin tried to think up some clever way to begin their conversation.

But he stopped midstride, astonished to find her sprawled across the bed with the black shawl covering all her important parts. Asleep.

He'd known she was exhausted. They hadn't had any restful sleep in over thirty-six hours. But he had been all set for their talk. Grateful for a reprieve, he glanced down at her face. So peaceful and beautiful. She needed sleep more than she needed a conversation about hard truths. Perhaps he would be better off to slip on his shoes and go have a nice long, boring conversation with the innkeeper instead.

Good idea. Still, Darin couldn't take his eyes off the figure in the bed. Noticing that her shawl had slipped, revealing the swell of one creamy breast, he leaned over to push it back in place. But when his fingers touched the warmth of her skin, she opened her eyes.

"Hi," she murmured with a lazy drawl. "All done in the shower?"

"Mmm." He coughed and then added, "Go back to sleep. I thought I'd go visiting, maybe make another telephone call."

She reached out to him. "Stay. Come lie down with me."

What his body urged him to do at that moment was as far from the right thing as he could imagine. "You don't want this, Rylie."

He sat at the very edge of the bed when she said nothing. "I've been thinking about your future. A lot. My family is about to embark on what has the potential to be a long, drawn-out mission. A mission fraught with danger at every turn. You, on the other hand, must go back to Texas and honor your family and their business. They need you to make things right."

"Darin…"

He shook his head. "Just listen. You and I have found each other despite the most outrageous of circumstances. I'd like to think that in only a few days we've formed a bond…a friendship that can last a lifetime. But if we do this—"

It was all he could do not to beg to do exactly what she was suggesting.

Straightening his shoulders, he took her hand. "We can't. It could ruin everything between us."

She shook her head. "Not *everything*. Don't you trust me? I trust you."

"If you mean, do I trust that you have no illnesses and have taken care of yourself—of course I do. You may trust me on that account, too. But becoming intimate too soon destroys relationships. I don't want that to happen to you and me. We shouldn't."

Rylie sat up, ignoring the shawl as it slid down to her waist. "We should. And maybe it will ruin things, or maybe it will provide us some interesting answers instead."

Darin was dying a thousand deaths, wishing he could simply take her in his arms. The sight of her naked to the waist had left him panting.

"You…you're so beautiful, Rylie. And I *do* want you, but…"

"What *I* want—" she pulled herself up on her knees, the shawl pooling on the bed, and then reached out to him "—is for you to touch me…hold me…make me forget about families and wars and death. Make love to me, Darin. Now. We only have a little while."

That did it. He surrendered. Darin could never turn away from her while she begged, even if it was the right thing to do.

When he touched her—when he drew her into his arms—it felt less like a surrender and more like an awakening. This was good—right. Being here with this strong woman, who clearly wanted him, was turning into exactly what *he* needed to make things right.

Darin had never been with a woman before who wanted him quite as much. Nor with one who could turn him into a quivering mass of expectation as Rylie had done. Something about this whole spur-of-the-moment thing suddenly felt big—huge.

He experienced a moment of pure panic. Then Rylie leaned in close and kissed him.

Whispering against his mouth, she said, "You have too much on." She rubbed her breasts against his bare chest, creating the most exquisite friction, while she reached for his zipper.

"Careful. Things are already tight down there, and becoming more dangerous by the moment." He stood, disposing of the slacks himself.

The look on her face as he stood before her in all his glory was priceless. He would never forget it.

Her skin was flushed. Her eyes glazed. The budded tips of her breasts jutted up toward him. Smiling, she carefully took his erection in both her hands, gently caressing his swollen flesh. He couldn't move—could barely speak.

She bent her head, but halted at the last moment and gazed up at him.

His knees buckled and he sucked in air. "Rylie," he gasped. "Wait."

She let her eyes do all the smiling as she flicked her tongue over his sensitive tip. "I'm done waiting."

Lowering her chin, she closed in enough to plant a baby-soft kiss against the part of him pulsing in expectation. He called out her name—and then promptly forgot his own.

Rylie was on her knees before him in a submissive position, but she wasn't fooled. Pleased with herself, she knew she held all the power. She took him hard into her mouth.

All the power. The idea was an aphrodisiac, spurring her on as he dug his fingers though her hair and moaned. His pleasure became her pleasure. She took him higher, closer to an edge, then backed away. Tasting. Licking. Controlling.

The more he trusted her to set the pace, the more intense was her gratification. She heard her own moans coming from someplace deep within her throat as they ramped up the friction. Wrapping her arms around his hips, she captured him in the most intimate of embraces. The idea of a total possession, in both body and mind, flicked across her consciousness…right before she fully gave up to the insanity.

Crazed with dizzying power and need, as soon as Darin drew back she went with him and collapsed in a heap on the bed. But she cautioned herself to hold off. For one heartbeat she waited, intent on finding out if he would insist on controlling their new positions. To her amazement, he rolled on his back and pulled her up his body, inviting her to decide where to go from here—and giving her the freedom to do as she wanted.

And she wanted. Oh, how she wanted.

Straddling his hips, she pressed her palms to his shoulders and grinned down at him. "Gotcha. Right where I want you. You are my prisoner."

"Do with me what you will," he teased, but in a dazed voice. "I am at your command."

Absolutely positive that there had never been a better sexual fantasy in the history of the world, Rylie leaned over and offered her breasts by brushing them across his lips. He licked and stroked each until he finally lifted his head off the bed enough to fully capture one in his mouth.

Even though she was on top, it soon became a question of who was tempting whom. Drawing the sensitive tip into his mouth with a greedy gulp, he alternately sucked and soothed. Tormenting her until she issued a sensual moan from somewhere deep inside her, he nipped at each nipple. And with each small pain came a resulting electric shock of pleasure.

Wet and slick, and so hungry to feel him inside her that she was wild with the desire for it, she lifted her hips and positioned herself over the head of his erection. Darin put his hands at the sides of her hips to help guide her, and she felt his whole body tense with anticipation.

Her heart pounded. Her muscles tightened along with his.

She had never been so sure of anything in her whole life.

Unbelievable heat. Wet. Hot. Tight.

As Rylie slowly lowered her body down to cover him, Darin's last coherent thought was again of surrender. He had thought he'd given himself over to her hands. Yet now they were both giving and taking and rejoicing in each other's needs. Neither one had given in. Both had succumbed.

Gripping her hips as she lifted her bottom, he helped her rise up, inch by incredible inch. He waited, holding his breath until she hesitated at the very tip, and then he rammed his hips up at the same time as she brought hers down with a hard slam.

His breath exploded from his lungs on a sharp rush.

Her breathing became labored as he continued guiding her up and down. Between one lungful of air and the next, they began moving as one. The pressure built. The pace increased.

They worked together in a frenzied motion that belied how he felt. He wanted this to last forever, yet he was racing toward the finish line. It was too much. It was not nearly enough.

He gazed up at her, watching as her chest rose and fell. Watching as she fought her release. He couldn't help himself. He pinched her nipples between thumb and forefinger. Once. Twice. Her eyes opened wide in her pleasure.

"Keep your eyes open," he begged her. "Look at me."

Higher and higher they climbed toward the peak. But she did as he asked and locked onto his gaze.

In one of the most erotic moments of his entire life, he watched her eyes as he reached down between them and rubbed a thumb against her sensitive nub. He felt the electric shock as it careened through her body. Her eyes rolled back in her head.

She finally gave in to it and came on a long, delicious shudder. Her internal muscles sucked and milked at him like a dangerous undertow. The sheer power of it brought him to his own release.

Too soon the astounding sensations totally consumed and inflamed him with majesty and euphoria. The enormous explosion of heat and fire seemed to go on and on.

He rolled with it, let it arc over them both. She collapsed against his chest, melted and boneless. Both of them gasped for air, hearts pounding and sweat pouring. His arms cocooned her against the outside world as he let her fall asleep in that position.

There would be no sleep for him. It took a moment for his head to clear. But when it did, thoughts zinged around his brain.

This woman was his. Had to be his.

Embarrassing emotions he had ducked his entire life leaked out of his heart right along with the tears leaking quietly from his eyes. When she shifted in his arms and breathed against his chest, he knew his obsession was going to be a lifetime curse.

How had this happened? He'd never wanted anyone to become this important. This necessary to his very existence.

The last time anyone had meant this much, she'd died. His mother had died. And he had failed her.

Darin knew he'd failed her because his father had always acted as though he believed it to be true. Believed that his sons had contributed to their mother's demise. Crazy or not, Darin had done everything he could to make up for it. To prove he was strong and smart—and worthy of a father's love.

Now here was yet another person whom he felt he should prove something to. Whom he could not fail. Darin's only mission in life from now on was to protect Rylie. Keep her from any harm. It was no longer a choice but a command that came from somewhere so deeply buried that he would never admit that he recognized it for what it truly was.

Love.

Looking down at her peaceful face and her thick

auburn lashes lying quietly against her cheek, Darin knew only one thing. Felt the certainty of only one thing.

Mine to cherish, he thought. *Mine* to always protect.

Chapter 11

Rylie woke up groggy and disoriented. She'd just had the sexiest dream imaginable.

Trying to roll over, she found herself entangled in broad, buff arms and pinned down by heavy, muscular thighs. Darin. Not a dream at all, but the most sensual experience of her entire life. Without thinking, she almost turned into him, ready to show him how much what they'd shared had mattered to her.

Damn it. She froze, her mind reeling over exactly how much being with Darin *had* really mattered. Now what was she supposed to do?

She'd been counting on having so-so sex with the man. Instead, he'd turned her whole theory about them being incompatible on its head. She had pushed him and teased him, sure he would never give her the mutual respect she knew she must have.

And what did he do? He gave her magic.

Damn it. She'd seen a whole new side to Darin, and it scared the hell out of her.

Torn now, with one part of her wanting to wake him up with kisses and declaring her undying love. And the other part of her wanting to sneak out of the room without waking him so she could run like hell. Rylie was on the verge of becoming unglued.

Damn it. And damn him for making her want to believe in happily-ever-afters for the first time in her life.

How crazy must she be? Crazy enough to be stupid, that's what. They'd known each other for a grand total of what? Three whole days? Lifetime commitments didn't come in such neat little packages. Her parents had known each other for most of their lives when they'd finally gotten married. Her mother said it took that long to develop respect and deep regard for another's feelings. Besides, every quickie overnight affair Rylie had ever heard of had ended sooner rather than later. And had ended badly to boot.

Yet all of her knowledge, all of her warnings to herself, meant exactly nothing when she thought about how he'd gazed into her eyes. With looks that seemed to say he wanted her to be his Cinderella. The more she thought about it, the more she went into panic mode. She'd been playing at some kind of crazy, stupid game and now it looked like she would get burned as a booby prize.

Trying to quiet her traitorous pounding heart, Rylie searched her mind for sensible reasons for why she should be feeling this way about him. Was it simply a matter of an adrenaline letdown? She'd read about how people who had been in life-and-death situations sometimes needed to have a sexual encounter in order to prove to themselves that they were really alive.

That might be true in some cases, but it was not applicable here. Surely they were safe. At least for a while. Furthermore, it had been all her idea long before they'd done that scary top-of-the-train balancing act.

Well, dang. Where did any of that leave her?

Falling in love?

But she didn't want that. Could. Not. Have. That. Not with a man whose family took part in international espionage and covert wars of retribution with centuries-old enemies. It was crazy—stupid!

Again she asked the question: *Where did that leave her?*

The answer came into her head loud and clear. It left her running for her life. As soon as she could get dressed and find her way back to Geneva.

She tried to slide out from under his arm, but Darin only tightened his grip around her.

"Hi," he said in a rough voice. "I don't guess we have enough time for a repeat performance?"

She twisted out of his embrace and sat up, dragging the shawl around her chest as she went. "No way. In fact, I'm beginning to worry about our clothes being ready in time for us to catch the train. Can you check on them while I clean up a little?"

She wasn't going to talk to him about splitting up at the train station and each going their own way. Not yet. One glance at Darin told her he was already staring at her like she'd slapped him.

Not ready to face any after-the-fact discussions, Rylie scurried from the bed, still trailing the shawl. How could she talk to him about something when she hadn't even settled it in her own mind yet? She took two steps toward the bathroom before he spoke.

"Aren't we…can't we talk first?"

She refused to turn around. "Talk about what? Everything's all set, right? I mean with your brothers and the Taj Zabbar."

"Yes, that part is all set. That's not what I want to talk about."

"Oh?" She bounced on her toes, ready to make a mad dash into the bathroom. "What did you want to say?"

"I wanted to talk about what just happened to us in this bed." Now his voice was sounding all edgy and pissy.

Well, too bad. She did not have time for either recriminations or regrets. "Um… It was great. Really. Best sex ever. But you know we can't take a chance of missing that train. Please go check on our clothes."

"Great sex?" The sound of his voice was…hurt…and it made her finally turn around.

"Darin, I don't know what you want from me. It was really, *really* terrific sex. But we can't be late."

He turned away from her to step into his slacks, though first she'd seen the most heart-wrenching look pass over his face. What had he wanted her to say? Obviously something she hadn't given him. Now Rylie was totally confused. She certainly hadn't meant to hurt him.

"Get ready," he told her as he opened the door to the hall. "I'll get our clothes from the innkeeper. Be back in a minute."

Twenty minutes later, Rylie still felt a little crazy-stupid. Neither she nor Darin had spoken one word since he'd left to pick up their clothes. But at this point, the two of them were dressed and nearly ready to leave for the station.

Darin was pocketing his things. He'd stored his weapon, passport, phone and cash in the nightstand's drawer alongside her waist purse. A casual thought occurred to her out of the blue. Where was the leather portfolio that he'd been carrying? She hadn't seen anything of it since before they'd gotten on the train. Had he left it in Geneva? She thought about asking, but it was time to go.

Darin seemed satisfied that everything was stashed and after giving the room one last going over, he turned to her. "Ready?"

His eyes were still brooding, sad. Rylie couldn't manage to say a word for fear she would break down entirely and spill words that she hadn't had the time to consider.

She nodded. He turned the doorknob and stood aside to let her go first.

Stepping across the threshold, Rylie felt as if she were leaving behind a special place. And a special time. For one second she wished they could go backward for a few hours. She turned to give the room one last glance and caught Darin's gaze.

He was watching her closely, and it seemed to her that he was blinking back a sheen of wetness. She opened her mouth to say something, anything, when all of a sudden his gaze flicked away to glance at something over her shoulder. Before she could judge whether this new look was one of anger or terror, she was roughly grabbed from behind and shoved hard.

Darin reached for the gun at his back, but a deeply

accented voice came from right behind her. "Don't try it, Kadir. Not if you want her to live."

A strong arm, clothed in rough cloth, came around her throat. Immediately she was pulled up tightly against the solid wall of the man's chest. A man whom she had yet to see.

Darin took a step forward. "Don't hurt her."

Rylie felt the sharp edge of a knife blade digging into her throat. She squeaked when the blade broke her skin.

Darin raised his hands, offered up his weapon and stepped back. "Okay. Okay. Stop! I'll do whatever you say."

The shadow of a man dressed in Middle Eastern–style robes brushed past her and disarmed Darin. After pocketing the gun, the fellow casually slammed his fist into Darin's face. Hard. Darin's body stumbled backward and hit the wall beside the bed.

Rylie could do nothing but whimper.

Then a third man, a great bear of a guy, stepped around the man who was holding on to her. This third, huge man had his fist wrapped around the throat of a much smaller man, and he was dragging the poor little fellow beside him.

Rylie was stunned to realize the smaller man was their porter from the train. Blood trickled from the porter's ear and he was crying.

Instead of feeling panic, Rylie became angry at such injustice and furious over the treatment they and the porter were receiving from these thugs. But she was in no position to help. So she silently swore to get even as soon as she could get the chance.

The Middle Easterner grabbed the front of Darin's

shirt and pulled him forward to spit in his face. "You have property that does not belong to you, Kadir dog," he snarled.

Darin started to shake his head, but he never got the chance. The big bear of a guy dropped the half-conscious porter in a heap on the floor like a rag doll. Then he reached out and raised Darin off his feet, using only a two-fisted grip. Slamming Darin down hard again, bear-guy held on to him with one enormous hand while ripping Darin's jacket right off his body with the other. As Darin's arms were yanked from his sleeves, Rylie swore she could hear popping sounds as if his shoulders were being pulled from their sockets.

Darin winced and tried to fight, but bear-guy backhanded him and rocked a fist into his gut with such force she was surprised when it didn't rip his body in half.

Oh, Darin.

Rylie tried to inch out of the hold she was caught up in, but with her first move, the man behind her tightened his grip and pushed the blade farther into her skin. She felt blood leaking down her neck and realized she had no choice but to stay quiet and watch as Darin was stripped, frisked and beaten.

When he lay moaning on the floor, minus all clothing except for his slacks, the Middle Eastern–looking man turned to her. "Are you carrying our property, whore?"

She was afraid to speak. Couldn't even move enough to shake her head.

Everything was mostly a blur after that. She remembered the big man moving into her space and roughly patting down her body. When he felt her travel purse, bear-guy stopped, and in a move so swift it shocked her stupid, he tore the T-shirt up and over her head. Standing there with only her bra for cover from the waist up, she began to shake. The next thing Rylie saw coming at her was the tip of a sharp, slender knife.

In the background, she heard Darin calling out for them to stop, but the knife's arc never halted. She cried out, sure she was about to die. With one long downward slice, bear-guy cut the purse right off her body, leaving an angry-looking gash down her rib cage.

Too hysterical to cry, Rylie bent over and grabbed her shirt from the floor while bear-guy stayed busy demolishing her purse and tearing into her passport and cell phone. Next thing she knew, the Middle Eastern–looking man nodded at bear guy. Rylie was afraid of what came next.

The bigger man proceeded to tear the room apart, using both the knife and his bare hands. He ripped the mattress to shreds. The nightstand was turned over and smashed to bits. It occurred to her that all this commotion should bring the innkeeper—or the police. But all remained silent.

Trembling, but not being held at knifepoint at the moment, Rylie slipped on her shirt again and went to kneel at Darin's side.

"How badly are you hurt?" she whispered.

He turned his head and tried to wink at her out of an eye already swollen and blue. "I'm okay. Stay alive, Rylie. No matter what else happens. You stay alive."

"I will, Darin, I promise.…"

At that moment, the big man stopped tearing up the room, reached down and yanked Darin to his feet. Darin swayed but stayed upright.

"Once more, Kadir," the Middle Eastern man began.

"Where is our property?" Then he turned and grabbed Rylie by the hair, jerking her up beside him.

He placed a long-barrelled gun to her temple. "Quick. Tell me or she is dead."

"It's on the train. I swear I left it in our sleeping car."

The Middle Eastern man exploded in a voice at once low yet loud in his throat. "Liar! We checked that car."

Silently, bear-guy put his big, meaty hands around Darin's throat and began to squeeze. Darin tried to fight him off, but the other man was at least twice his size.

Rylie closed her eyes so she couldn't see down the barrel of the gun and held her breath, waiting for her end to come. *I'm sorry, Darin. I tried to stay alive.*

She expected to hear the last click and explosion she would ever hear coming from a gun before it was all over and everything went black. Instead, Rylie could hardly believe what she heard. The Middle Eastern man began speaking a few soft words to his comrades in an odd language. Her eyes popped open and she saw bear-guy drop a still-breathing Darin like a hot rock. The Middle Eastern–looking guy, apparently the boss, was now holding a phone to his ear and not a gun to her head.

Ohmygod. Both she and Darin were still alive. And if she could stay alive like she'd promised him, there was always a chance of clocking these dudes. Of showing them a little Texas justice.

Rylie bit down on her tongue to keep her mouth shut and bided her time until she could make a move against them. And oh man, she couldn't wait.

* * *

Hamad Taj Zabbar was seething as his hired man tried to explain the situation over the phone. "The communiqué!" he shouted into the speaker. "We must have it."

"We have searched both the train car and the entire villa, master. And we have searched the persons of the man and woman. The communiqué is not to be found."

Never trust a subordinate to do what you should do yourself. "Is the man still alive? What has he told you?"

"Yes, he is alive. The Kadir dog swore he left the papers on the train. But we searched. It is not so."

Hamad hesitated over his next move, wishing he knew more about this particular Kadir brother.

His assassin-trained employee spoke up out of turn. "Shall we kill them both, my sheik?"

"No, you fool. Kadir is the only one who knows where he put the papers." Hamad quickly sifted through what little he knew of Darin Kadir. "You found the man and woman together in a room at the villa. Is that right?"

"This is true."

Then without question, Hamad knew what he must do. "Bring them both here to me. Keep them alive."

"Yes, master. Shall we eliminate their conspirators?"

"You mean the porter and the innkeeper? It is not necessary. Tie them and leave them. It is very possible we may yet need them alive."

Hamad felt certain the porter had no knowledge of the whereabouts of the communiqué. The man had fallen apart with only minor torture and quickly disclosed everything he'd known. Yet if the Hunt woman did not prove to be the impetus for obtaining the truth from Darin Kadir, then the porter's life might be worth using in trade.

"How long will it take to bring Kadir and the Hunt woman here to Milan?"

"We must drive, my sheik. The train left Bellinzona an hour ago."

"A couple of hours, then. Very well. Keep them both hidden, and hurry."

Tarik Kadir stood on a siding at the Milan train station, hands on his hips and questions burning in his brain. "And you are sure this is the sleeping car where my brother and the Hunt woman were passengers?"

"Yes, sir." One of Tarik's Italian investigators stood beside him in the warm sun as the two stared up at the uncoupled car. "The Swiss police gave it a quick once-over in Bellinzona during their search for the missing man.

"But somewhere between there and here," the investigator continued, "your brother's compartment was tossed. Cushions and mattresses were slashed and storage bins broken apart. The porter, your brother and his friend are missing. The Italian police have set the car aside here and mean to go over it again tomorrow for evidence."

"I need a few minutes inside first. Is that possible?"

"Yes, of course. Not a problem. The Italian police are your friends." The investigator casually waved a hand toward the car's steps, inviting Tarik aboard.

Tarik had been trying to reach Darin for the last

couple of hours with no luck. But he hadn't been overly concerned with his brother's lack of communication until his man called a while ago, announcing that Darin had failed to arrive at the Milan station. Tarik already had a couple of men on their way to Bellinzona, the last place Darin had made contact. But he had little hope of locating his older brother there.

As he took the steps up to the sleeping car, a memory of a young Darin, trying his best to console his two little brothers after their mother's death, crept into Tarik's mind. Without Darin, Tarik never would've made it to adulthood. He owed his oldest brother his life.

Damn Darin anyway. He had no business playing at being an investigator with a group as dangerous as the Taj Zabbar. Tarik's heart ached at the real possibility of losing his big brother.

But Tarik would not let that happen, despite the difficult circumstances. Their mission had already been complicated when his team surrounded the apartment where the Taj Zabbar leader was supposedly having a meeting, only to find the place empty.

Walking down the train corridor, Tarik headed for his brother's former compartment. It was worth a look.

After that, Tarik would make use of his nervous energy and do what he did best. Locate the bad guys—and then locate his brother.

Darin had better still be alive or there would be hell to pay. The Taj Zabbar thought they were at war now? Ha! They had no idea what a real war of retribution could look like.

Chapter 12

Rylie stared mournfully through the dirty piece of glass next to her head at the traffic driving by. Too bad it wasn't a true roll-down window but only a filthy, stationary sheet of glass. Not that she could've done much had it been a real window. Being hog-tied the way she was left little room for movement.

Sighing at the frustration of her situation, she let her head roll back on the cracked leather seat. Their three attackers took up most of the room in this old European car. Most of the air, too. She'd found herself squished into a tiny corner of the backseat, trying to keep at least a few inches between her body and big bear-guy's rolls of fat. Middle Eastern man was riding shotgun, and the third mysterious man drove.

It felt like they'd been riding on these crummy cobblestone streets for hours. But she was fairly sure it hadn't really been that long. Still, with each interminable second, all she could think about was Darin, locked in the trunk. Could he breathe back there? Was he bleeding? Throwing up?

With every bump, her heart broke. With every stop, she held her breath and listened for any sound.

Since they were now driving into Milan's city proper, her hopes had built that one of the hundreds of pedestrians milling about would recognize her distress and come to the rescue. She didn't want to think about the remoteness of such a possibility. But every street-corner cop they passed was like a symbol giving her false hope.

That hope dwindled more and more with every mile.

She closed her eyes and imagined talking to Darin in the trunk. *You are the one who needs to stay alive now. Promise me.*

A lone tear tried to escape from the corner of her eye. But Rylie never cried. Not even as a little girl. No amount of physical pain had ever been enough to bring her to tears. She had never once in her life cried over a man, either. Emotional crying seemed silly and useless. She hadn't even cried at her own father's funeral.

Sniffing back the single tear, she bit down on the inside of her cheek and thought again about the man in the trunk. *I'll find a way for us to get free if you stay alive, Darin. Trust me and hang in there. I know that as long as we're together we'll be able to master these idiots in one way or the other.*

Together.

How could she be so sure they would be able to work

together? It wasn't logical. But she was as sure of that as she was about the afternoon's sun setting in the west.

Rylie had discovered herself desperately in love for the first time in her life. Unfortunately, that life had been passing before her eyes for the last couple of hours—the way they said it did when you were about to die. Being on the edge of death had made the truth of her feelings become clear and sharp.

It didn't matter how long she and Darin had known each other. It didn't matter that they came from different parts of the world, or had vastly different backgrounds.

She loved Darin Kadir. Would always love him. Right to the last breath she ever took.

Exhaling on the prayer that she and Darin would have many more breaths to come, Rylie opened her eyes. Their car had stopped in the middle of a traffic jam. She glanced out the glass beside her and saw a man in the next car studying her. He wasn't anyone she had ever seen before, though the man seemed to recognize her.

Rylie widened her eyes and mouthed the word *help!* But what else could she do to make him understand? She let her eyes plead with him for comprehension. Then she inched her hands up to the glass to show him the ties.

Middle Eastern man in the front seat must've noticed something amiss because he spoke to bear-guy right then in a voice that sounded like a growl. The large man suddenly wrapped a beefy arm around her head and pulled her away from the window, muttering something under his breath.

With her head locked between his biceps and dense chest, she couldn't breathe and struggled for freedom. But nothing she did made a bit of difference against the wall of tubby flesh holding her tight. As she was about to pass out, the car rolled forward and bear-guy released her.

Sucking in air, she leaned back and sneaked a peek out the window. Both the man and his car were gone. Had she only dreamed them? Maybe she'd been wishing for help badly enough that any curious stranger was starting to look like a rescuer.

Their car made two more quick turns and within moments pulled into an alley behind an old four-story apartment house. Car doors opened and fresh air streamed in. Bear-guy jerked her out of the backseat and hustled her into the building.

What about Darin? She dug in her heels, trying to hang back and see if he came out of the trunk alive. But bear-guy dragged her behind him up the stairs. When she slipped once on the rough concrete steps, he just lifted her over one shoulder and thumped up the four flights with no trouble.

Next thing she knew, she was unceremoniously thrown into a tall, dark wardrobe. The door slammed shut behind her, locking the light out and her in.

Fruitlessly, she banged a fist against the wood, crying dry, silent tears for the man she loved.

Darin. Oh, Darin. Please be alive!

Darin came out of the car's trunk dizzy from the carbon monoxide and blinded by the bright sunlight. His knees buckled when he tried to stand, but one of the kidnappers wrapped a firm hand around his arm and held him upright.

Gulping in fresh air, Darin fought to clear both his lungs and his eyes. His first thought was of Rylie, and as he came to his senses, he scanned the area looking for her.

"Inside, dog. Our employer wishes to speak to you."

He tried to jerk his arm free, but received a hand across the face for his trouble. Still, he was able to scan the area around him and check out the parked car. It was empty now.

Darin experienced perhaps the worst moment of terror in his entire life. Had they killed Rylie in Bellinzona and left her body behind?

His shoulders slumped at the thought. If Rylie was gone, there would be no reason left for him to live. Let the Taj Zabbar torture him. But if he died, he would be taking a few more Taj Zabbar pigs along with him.

The henchman who'd yet to speak dragged Darin into an old building. Judging from the size of the buildings around him, the city had to be Milan. There weren't any other cities as large in all of northern Italy, and Darin knew he hadn't been driven around in that airless trunk for more than a couple of hours. In fact, another half an hour locked inside there and he might not have emerged alive at all.

"Up the stairs, Kadir." The man dressed in robes, who seemed to be in charge, held a gun to his side.

These were not regular Taj Zabbar warriors. They did not wear the Taj Zabbar colors. He and Rylie had been assaulted by a specially trained set of agents. True, they spoke in a Taj Zabbar dialect, but it was one he did not recognize.

By the fourth flight of stairs, Darin was practically crawling. Every square inch of his body hurt, but he lacked the will to care.

Rylie. They had never gotten the chance to talk. He'd never told her how much his time with her had meant. How changed he felt by knowing her. If she were really dead and a way could be found to take revenge against her killers, Darin would stay alive long enough to take it.

Did he have any hope of that? He thought of his brothers. He thought of Tarik, the undercover expert, and suddenly he could actually feel his brother's presence nearby.

He had hope.

At the top of the stairs, Darin was shoved through the door to an apartment larger than he would have thought possible from the outside. He landed on his knees on a dusty flower-patterned carpet.

The shoes of a large man appeared by his side. When he glanced up, he was looking at the visage of one of the Taj Zabbar's most important elders. Darin wasn't sure of the man's name, but he recognized him from pictures. Besides, there could be no mistaking his position from the clothes he wore. The expensive suit. The purple-checked head scarf. Even the tie imprinted with the Taj Zabbar snake and staff said this man was a leader.

"Put him in a chair," the elder ordered. "Tie him and then fetch water. We want him able to communicate, don't we?"

When his orders had been carried out, the elder stood towering over him with his hands on his hips. "You are in the presence of Sheik Newaf Bin Hamad Taj Zabbar, elder of clan Zabbar and wizeer to thousands. And you are known as Darin Kadir, eldest son of the chicken thief called Khalid Ben Shareef Kadir. No need for further introductions between us. I have come to know you well over the last few days, Kadir."

"What have you done with Rylie Hunt?"

Hamad Taj Zabbar put his hand to his chin in thought. "I can see that you are concerned. The woman is safe— temporarily. But I wish to have a calm discussion with you before the two of you are reunited. Agree?"

Rylie was still alive. Relief poured out of his pores like sweat.

Darin raised his chin and nodded sharply.

"Fine. Then the first question concerns the Hunt woman. Why did she come to Geneva? Are you and she in a…relationship…as they say in America?"

Darin wasn't sure of the right answer. Yes, of course they were in a relationship, and chances were good that the Taj Zabbar intelligence already knew it. But then why the question?

"Yes, we are in a relationship," he told Hamad, the elder. "Why have you been trying to kidnap her?"

Lights twinkled in the elder's eyes for an instant. Then he waggled a finger at Darin.

"*My* questions, Kadir. Not yours."

Hamad looked away a moment and brushed at an imaginary piece of lint on his sleeve. "You are apparently a master at covert relationships. There was not a breath of scandal about the two of you before Geneva. I am impressed."

So. The Taj Zabbar had been keeping tabs on the Kadirs. Or at least on him. Interesting.

Darin shrugged and kept his mouth shut.

"Now for the most important question. Where did you hide the Taj Zabbar property you stole?"

Darin shrugged again and fought a grin.

"No answer?" Hamad turned and gestured to one of his men. "Well then, let's see if we can make a trade. Your people take great pride in being traders, do they not?"

The elder's henchman disappeared through a door into another room. Darin heard a slight commotion coming from that direction and then a soft feminine cry.

Rylie!

He twisted in his chair, struggling against his bonds. "Don't touch her, you pig!"

The corners of Hamad's lips came up in an evil approximation of a wry smile. But the elder said nothing more until his man dragged Rylie, kicking and screaming, into the room.

"Quiet down, Miss Hunt. Your companion would like to see you."

"Darin!" Rylie's struggles turned frantic but the silent henchman held her arms and kept her steady at about ten feet away. "You're alive. Are you hurt?"

Blood had crusted over the wound on her neck and a rust-colored stain had dried on the shirt over her rib cage. It was all Darin could do not to cry out for vengeance.

Instead, he tempered his voice and spoke quietly, gently. "Shush, my darling. Say nothing. Remember your promise and trust me."

Rylie bit her lip and her eyes clouded over.

"How touchingly romantic."

At the sound of Hamad's voice, Darin turned his head to find the elder had produced an ancient Taj Zabbar dagger with a panther carved into the hilt. Its silver tip gleamed in the sunlight streaming through the glass panels of a floor-to-ceiling door out to a tiny balcony.

Hamad waved the sharp blade closer to Rylie, while her narrowed eyes were shooting daggers of hatred right back at him. "Have no fear, Miss Hunt. It is not necessary for you to learn the true significance of the Taj Zabbar Panther of Death. Our business is with the Kadir dog."

"Don't touch her," Darin growled.

No matter what it took, Darin vowed to kill this elder for causing Rylie pain. His brain churned with ideas for escape.

The elder touched the point of his blade to Rylie's cheek. "Pretty skin. It would be a shame to mar such perfection."

"I thought we were going to trade," Darin said, hoping to bring the elder's attention back to him.

"Oh, but we are trading. I am offering to keep Miss Hunt's skin in one piece in trade for the return of my own property. More than fair, don't you think?"

"Don't give him anything, Darin." Rylie was whispering, but her meaning was loud and clear. "He's going to kill us both anyway."

Darin couldn't look at her. He needed to stay strong—for her sake.

"Not if he wants his property back intact." Darin stared into Hamad's rage-filled eyes. "Okay, here's the deal I'm willing to make. I will go alone to pick up your papers. After I have them in hand, you will let Miss Hunt go in a public place of my choosing. When I see that she is safe, I will return them to you."

"Darin, no! He'll kill you."

Hamad ignored Rylie's outburst. Darin knew the elder

was no fool. He must understand that Darin was offering to sacrifice himself to save her.

"Almost a deal, Kadir. With a few minor adjustments in my favor."

The elder Hamad glanced over his shoulder to the bank of computers set up in the next room, then returned his attention to Darin. "One of my men will accompany you. You did not think I should be stupid enough to set you free to roam around Italy and contact police?

"My man will carry a phone with a camera built inside. He will take a photo of one of the pages you recover and send it to me. When I am satisfied that it is indeed my property, you may accompany him back here for the trade."

"Darin, no."

Darin shook his head at Rylie but never took his eyes off Hamad. "Not quite." Darin knew Hamad's offer had only been a first round and the man was waiting for a new bid. "Your man can come with me. But I will carry the phone. I will send a photo *and* directions for where we shall make the exchange once you send a return photo showing that Rylie is still safe and in one piece."

"I assume my property is in Milan and in a public place, yes?"

"Yes. It's still on the train like I told your idiot employees. A member of the Kadir clan does not lie."

Hamad's eyes filled with rage for a second, but he let it pass. "Very well. We will do it your way. But do not try to swindle me, dog. At the first sign of anything wrong, your lady here will begin losing body parts. A little skin. An ear. Then perhaps a finger or a few toes."

Hamad glared, clearly hoping to force Darin into a mistake. But Darin never flinched.

"If you so much as cause her one more moment's pain," Darin began with calm promise ringing in his words, "I shall never rest until you are a dead man. Nothing will stop me from hunting you down. You will pay here, or I promise I will make you pay throughout all eternity. I swear it by my ancestors."

Leaving Rylie behind with that bastard was the hardest thing Darin had ever done. Swallowing back his fear for her, he listened intently while Hamad's men spoke to each other in their odd dialect and prepared themselves for this mission to recover their boss's property. As difficult as it was to translate their speech, Darin hoped he'd learned enough to be prepared.

All three men who had assaulted them in Bellinzona pushed a still-tied Darin down the stairs out in front until they reached the alley. He understood that one of the men would accompany him as promised. But he also knew the other two would be tailing them, ready to attack if anything went awry.

"Are we taking the car? Shall I do the driving?" Darin wanted to push these men as far as possible, hoping for any mistake on their part.

The same man who'd seemed to be the leader of this trio in Bellinzona took a knife from his robes and slashed the ties binding Darin's hands. "You will remember that both your whore's life and her beauty are on the line as we travel through the city, Kadir."

He thrust the camera phone at Darin. "We will be taking a taxi to the train station and you shall not make one sound of protest on the trip. Do not hope to use that phone for any reason other than your bargain with our master."

Darin nodded, but said nothing. He could feel watchful eyes following his every move from the shadows in the alley. But instead of fear, he felt comforted. He was as sure of Tarik's presence nearby as he was of his growing hatred for Hamad.

Two of the Taj Zabbar men stayed behind as Darin had known they would. Their leader walked Darin to the corner and hailed a taxicab. Darin felt sure the other two men would be jumping into the parked car to follow them as soon as the taxi was out of sight.

The main street was oddly deserted at dusk. Seemingly out of nowhere, a lone taxi pulled up to the curb and Darin was unceremoniously shoved into the backseat.

As the taxi took off again, Darin straightened out and raised his head. He was surprised to see a man sitting in the front passenger seat. The man's body was turned around to face the backseat and he was holding a powerful gun in his hand. Even more surprisingly, the barrel of that weapon was pointed not at Darin but at the Taj Zabbar henchman.

That's when Darin spotted a very familiar profile sitting in the driver's seat. "Tarik. I knew you weren't too far away."

The Taj Zabbar assassin jerked and reached into his robes. But the deadly click of a safety being released in the front seat had him raising his empty hands in the air instead.

"Don't kill him," Darin warned the other two men. "I believe there's a GPS-type chip embedded under his skin that not only tells the Taj Zabbar of his location but also whether he remains alive or not."

The man in the front seat nodded and released his finger from the trigger. But he kept his weapon trained at the Taj Zabbar gunman's head.

"Good intelligence work, brother," Tarik told him. "But I guess that means your intentions are to try saving Miss Hunt. Otherwise, it wouldn't matter at all if we killed these assassins quickly and then blew away their Taj Zabbar leader with a few well-placed bombs. Dying in an explosion would bring justice for Uncle Sunnar, after all."

"As soon as Rylie is safe, you can do anything you want with these assassins. But Hamad Taj Zabbar is mine."

Tarik said nothing to that but kept his eyes on the road ahead.

"How'd you locate us?"

"The Taj Zabbar use ordinary cell-phone technology." Tarik shook his head at the thought. "Not the brightest move for people who are supposedly familiar with technology."

Tarik shrugged and went on. "We intercepted their calls with little trouble. Then when we had their location pinned down within a mile or two, I sent out as many men as I could find to scour the area. One of them spotted Miss Hunt riding in the backseat of their car and we followed it to their new headquarters. I have to hand it to her, she is both brave and smart."

"Drive to the train station as fast as you can," Darin quickly interjected. "I need to recover those Taj Zabbar papers and get back here in a hurry to save her."

Tarik turned the taxi down a side street, pulled to

the curb and let it idle. "Not necessary. I've already recovered the Taj Zabbar's papers. Good work on hiding them, by the way."

"How did you find them behind the padded wallpaper in our sleeping car?" Darin was astounded. "I'm absolutely positive they couldn't be spotted. I even used toothpaste to glue the quilting back down good and tight so no one would notice it had been disturbed. Not even the Taj Zabbar's best men would ever have found them there."

"Like I said," Tarik said with a chuckle, "good work. But remember it was me who taught you that trick. Those papers are on their way to headquarters right now. We'll have them decoded within days. You're a hero."

"What?" Darin felt a thrust of real panic for the first time since he'd known Tarik had come to their rescue. "Those papers aren't in Milan? How fast can you get them back here?"

"They've been in the air for a good hour. So at least that long. Maybe an hour more for the return trip. Why?"

"You may have just sealed Rylie's fate. Without those papers, she's as good as dead."

Chapter 13

"Are you comfortable?" Hamad stood beside Rylie, close enough that she could smell his spicy aftershave.

The stink made her gag. He'd had her shoved into a back bedroom and tied to a chair the same way he'd done to Darin.

"Oh, fine and dandy, thanks." Her neck wound was beginning to itch. The ties binding her hands behind her back were too flippin' tight. She was hot and hungry and nearly hysterical with worry over Darin. But she would never give this bastard the satisfaction of saying so.

"You think I am asking only to be mean? You think I am evil?" A look of concern crossed his face. "Not true, Miss Hunt. I have a proposition to make, and I believe you must be clearheaded to consider what I say."

"What kind of a proposition?"

Hamad pulled another chair close and sat down

beside her. "You are a smart woman, which is easy to see. And may I say, very beautiful, too. You could do many things in your lifetime. Profitable things."

Rylie glared at him, wondering what came next.

"It would be a shame to see your life cut short and all that potential destroyed."

"I couldn't agree more."

Hamad's leer widened. A little drool began dripping from the corner of one lip. "See there? Smart. Not like your friend the Kadir dog. He and his kind are not smart. And they shall perish for their stupidity."

It was all she could do not to spit in his face. But she didn't figure making the man mad would get her anywhere. Hamad seemed ready to propose some kind of deal. Perhaps another bid for freedom for her and Darin? Whatever it was, it could mean a chance to get out of here.

That's all Rylie wanted. A chance to free herself and save Darin. So she kept her mouth shut and listened.

"We both know that your friend will not live to see another sunrise."

"But you made him a deal," she blurted. "Why should I believe anything you have to say if you're just going to lie?"

Hamad gave her another leer along with a low chuckle. "The deal I made with him was for your life—not his. But I never had any intention of harming you." He reached over and tenderly drew his finger down her cheek.

Disgusted, she jerked her head away from his hand.

"Well, yes, perhaps you are right," he said with a

shake of his head. "It is never wise to play with your work."

"What's your proposition?" Rylie's stomach churned as the bile rose in her throat.

"I have business partners and wealthy clients, men of both integrity and power, who are in the market for a wife. Your beauty and brains would fit their requirements quite nicely."

"You want to sell me?" This bastard's gall was beyond belief. "Are you nuts? Why would I ever agree to become someone's sex slave?"

Hamad tsked at her. "Do not be so hasty. No one said anything about slavery. Let me give you a few names and you'll see what I mean by powerful."

He ticked off a half a dozen names. She recognized some as leaders of third-world countries, others as major international industrialists.

Rylie could barely sit still. She fidgeted in her seat, tugged on her ties and pursed her lips. "All right. Go on."

"I propose we hold a marriage auction. Bids to start at…say…twenty million U.S. dollars. Proceeds from the auction will be split between us."

The man wanted to auction her off to the highest bidder? He was insane. But she still needed to humor him. She had to get free, and this might provide her best chance.

"What good would that much money do for me if I ended up a slave anyway?" She could barely speak in a civil voice.

"Stop talking about slavery. Leave it to me to choose the bidders wisely. None of my clients would harm you. In fact, we would make them sign a marital contract in advance. A contract giving you both considerable freedom and a generous portion of their estate."

Estates? Now Rylie was beginning to get the picture.

"So," she began as her mind put two and two together. "If something were to happen to my new husband. Say for instance, if he died suddenly after the marriage…"

"Then you would be a very wealthy and powerful woman."

"And terribly grateful to you for putting me in that position?"

"Of course."

One of Hamad's men stuck his head in the room then and spoke in that dialect Darin had said was the Taj Zabbar language.

Hamad spit out what seemed like a curse, and then turned back to her. "You must pardon me for a few minutes, Miss Hunt. It appears that excuse for a man you find so attractive is trying a double cross. His taxi has stopped on a side street. I would guess that he is trying to bribe my employee. However, the dog will be sorely surprised on that account."

"You don't think your employee can be bribed?"

Hamad actually grinned. "Someday I will explain the special training my employees receive. They are known as assassins and fanatics, and they would rather cut off their appendages than go against their master. Each of them has already lost a toe or a finger to prove their loyalty. So, no, Miss Hunt. I am sure that my employee will not be bribed by a Kadir."

"They cut off their own fingers and toes?" Ewww. Rylie was horrified at the notion.

"I can be a most appreciative master for such loyalty."

He withdrew his knife, stepped behind her and cut the ties binding her hands. "See how kind I can be? I want you to think about our partnership without discomfort."

Hamad started to leave, but turned back at the door. "Please take this time to consider my offer. I have ordered a pleasant supper if you would be generous enough to join me. The food should arrive in about an hour—after your friend has retrieved my property and met his end. We shall talk further about our partnership then."

With those horrid words, Hamad left the room and shut the door behind him. Rylie rubbed at her arms to force the circulation back into limbs that had fallen asleep.

In a few seconds, she tried standing and shook out the kinks in her legs. The next thing she did was run to the window to look for a way out. The glass doors of the window ran from the floor almost to the ceiling and she could fling them wide-open for air. But that would be as far as she could go. The window was four flights straight up. Below was a narrow residential side street with cars parallel-parked down one side. Clearly there wouldn't be any escaping that way.

Turning a full three-sixty, she studied every inch of the room where she was being held a prisoner. One window. One door. One bed. Two chairs, a lighted wall sconce and a table. Nothing to help her escape, or that could be used to attack her jailer.

She felt useless. Tied without ropes. Nothing to use as a weapon.

With at least three large Taj Zabbar men, she was outnumbered and overpowered physically. Her brains were all she had left with which to defend herself. And right this minute she couldn't think of anything that might help. Darin was the one and only thought occupying her mind. She might get out of here in one piece by using her wits, but what about him? Damn it. They were a team now. He couldn't die. How could she let that happen?

Standing at the open window, she kicked furiously and hit nothing but air. Sighing, she looked out over the Milan rooflines, just beginning to disappear in the dusk settling over the labyrinth of city buildings. From here she caught a glimpse of the Castello Sforzesco. A place she knew as a historic castle, located on a marvelous piazza that made for good photographs. Rylie remembered it from having been in Milan once before with her parents—years ago as a teenage tourist.

The fleeting thought of her parents brought a familiar ache. Her father would've known how to get out of a mess like this. But Rylie was stumped. Aware that for the first time in her life she was in a situation that she couldn't control, Rylie sank down on the bed.

She thought of Darin. The first man she had ever truly loved with her whole heart. The only man other than her father that she could envision as a partner. But in Darin's case, it was as a partner for life.

Rylie yearned for him. The two of them had never gotten their chance to talk. Or to just be together. And now she had no way of helping him, either. He was out there somewhere, fighting to save her life. And here she was, a useless puppet with no way out. She had always been a fighter, and the frustration of being boxed in weighed heavily on her chest.

Staring bleakly out at the first of the evening stars,

she had to swipe at her cheeks as tears began to roll. Useless. Out of control. Boxed in.

She thought of her mother. Of the others back at home who still needed her help when she couldn't even help herself. More tears threatened. Defeat settled in around her shoulders like a shawl.

Finally she threw herself across the bed and sobbed. A fountain of liquid pain erupted from somewhere deep inside. Her tears appeared at first because of the frustrating situation. But they quickly turned into a waterfall of the unshed grief that she had refused to express for the last six months.

Oh, Daddy, I miss you. I'm so sorry to let you down but I can't do this one alone. For the first time ever, I admit I need help and now no one is there to come save me.

Below the window, standing in the growing shadows, Darin and his brother looked up at the light as Rylie's image had moved in and then back out of view.

"Miss Hunt doesn't look much like a prisoner to me." Tarik spoke in soft voice.

"She is." Darin could feel Rylie's frustration and desperation in the same way as he had felt Tarik's presence earlier.

Speaking quietly to his brother over his shoulder, he said, "Are you sure that assassin is still alive and on his way to the train station?" Darin was smart enough to match Tarik's low whispers.

"Positive. As we tied him and put him in the taxi's trunk, he attempted suicide, but we were too quick for him. We also took care of his pals, the ones in the car following the taxi."

"We have to get Rylie out of there soon." Darin's anxiety was growing as the minutes ticked by. "Before Hamad realizes I don't have access to his papers."

Tarik turned to face him. "I've had a thought about that, bro. There might be another trick that'll give us the few extra minutes we need to form a rescue plan."

It was all Darin could do to drag his gaze away from the fourth-story window where he knew Rylie was being held. "What is it? We don't have a lot of time for preparations. That taxi will be pulling in to the train station at any moment."

"No need for long, drawn-out preparations." Tarik was studying his face in the low light coming from a nearby second-story window. "We only need your ability to carry out a covert story line. How are you at lying?"

A flash of his earlier smart-assed reply to Hamad about Kadirs not lying ran through Darin's mind. But the thought was quickly replaced by a picture of Rylie's face in the throes of passion. What if he could never see that spectacular look of pleasure ever again? Hell, he couldn't lose her now. That she'd landed in this mess in the first place was all his fault.

"I can lie when necessary," he said slowly.

"Uh-huh."

"Tell me what you want me to do, Tarik. I'll do anything."

Tarik sighed. "You really love her, don't you? I've never seen you respond to a woman this way before."

"Tell me."

Tarik was carrying a high-tech toy in a pocket and it buzzed twice, then stopped. "That's the signal. The taxi has arrived at the station. You have to do this now. Put in a call to Hamad like you promised. But tell him the train is surrounded by cops and you can't reach the sleeping car. Tell him he has to give you more time. Another hour so that you can find a way past the police."

It might work and was worth a try.

Darin took a deep breath and pulled Hamad's cell phone from his pocket. "He doesn't have a way of locating me from this phone, does he?"

Tarik chuckled. "Naw. I pulled the GPS chip, put it in a throwaway cell and put it in the taxi. These Taj dudes are seriously screwy. It's like they have one foot in the twenty-first century and one foot in the Middle Ages. Make the call."

Darin punched the single phone button like Hamad had shown him. When the bastard answered, Darin gave him the lie and even managed to bluff a line about why there wasn't any background noise in the train station.

After he hung up, Darin didn't feel as elated over making Hamad believe the story as he'd thought he should. He hadn't been able to talk to Rylie, and they still needed a plan to free her. He wasn't going to feel anything good until she was back by his side.

"Nice work, brother."

The new voice had Darin whirling around. "Shakir! How did you sneak up on me? What are you doing here?"

"I move quietly." Shakir's understatement almost made Darin grin. "And you don't think I would let my two brothers have all the fun, do you?"

"I'm not sure *fun* would be the word for attacking a Taj Zabbar stronghold."

Shakir patted him on the shoulder. "Now, now. Thus far, I've been enjoying myself immensely. I took down the three outside Taj Zabbar guards a few moments ago. Well, with help from one of Tarik's men. And I found that action to be bloody brilliant."

Shakir rubbed his hands together. "So, what's the plan for reaching the fourth floor?"

Tarik had been speaking softly into a hidden mouthpiece, but at his brother's question, he turned back. "Our intel shows there's possibly three more guards inside the apartment, along with Hamad and the girl. We don't have a plan yet."

"And you're sure we can't just blow up the whole freakin' building?" Shakir looked gleeful at the idea.

Darin rolled his eyes and ignored the comment. "We have to go with what we know. We know Rylie is in that back bedroom. A few moments ago, she was alone. I can reach her room from the roof. While I'm doing that…"

"Hold it." Tarik held up his palms. "What exactly do you mean by 'reach her room from the roof'?"

Both of his brothers were staring at him as if he'd suddenly sprouted angel wings.

"It's not that big a distance from the roof to the top of her open window. Maybe one of Tarik's men can lower me down with some kind of makeshift rope."

"You're crazy, Darin." Tarik was shaking his head.

"Lovesick is more like it." Shakir's head was rolling side to side, as well.

"Nonsense," Darin insisted. "This can work. You two attack through the front door and make a big commotion. Use flash bangs or something. Everyone's attention will be drawn your way while I climb down and protect Rylie until the attack is over and the Taj Zabbar are finished."

"I thought you wanted to be the one to kill Hamad Taj Zabbar?" Tarik was looking at him thoughtfully.

"Rylie's safety is more important."

Tarik looked to Shakir. The two of them shrugged and then released their breaths as one.

"Okay, Darin, we'll go with your plan. But one of my men will cover you from the roof across the street. In case."

Darin started to argue with Tarik that it wasn't necessary, but the determined looks on his brothers' faces made him shut his mouth. He knew to quit while he was ahead.

What he didn't know was how Rylie was holding up. Fighting terror-filled images and dreadful thoughts of what Hamad was doing to her, Darin prepared himself to be her savior. But what kind of shape would she be in when he came to her rescue?

Rylie forced down another bite of filet mignon, but her stomach was churning with acid already. Light-headed and suddenly too warm, she twisted around to check that the bedroom window was still open. It was, but not a breath of air stirred in the room.

"The food is good, yes?" Hamad sat across the table from her and had been silently concentrating on his meal for the last ten minutes. "I must apologize again for the unforeseen problems keeping us from discussing our plans over this excellent meal. Though I completely understand. Certainly you would not feel free to contemplate a future while your *friend* is still breathing.

"But do not overly concern yourself," he added

flippantly. "That little detail should be rectified shortly."

Hamad took another sip of his burgundy wine and stared at her over the two-person table he'd had erected in the bedroom, allowing them to eat in private. "I'm sure it will be only a matter of an hour, more or less. Perhaps the announcement of his end shall arrive while we're having brandy. And then we can be free to discuss our partnership."

Rylie shifted the steak knife into her right hand and pretended to use it to cut her meat like the Europeans. As far as weapons went, the little knife wasn't much. Certainly no match for Hamad's antique dagger or his bodyguards' guns. She would have to get too close to an opponent for it to do any good.

Still, she didn't feel nearly as helpless with a knife in her hand as she had without one. The mere sight of it had been one of the reasons she had agreed to sit down at this table with a person who seemed mad.

Relieved to find out Darin was still alive, she would have agreed to almost anything when Hamad suggested they should eat the meal he'd had prepared while they waited to hear something more from the train station. Since then, her mind had raced with escape plans as she listened to Hamad sounding more and more deranged.

He talked to her as if they were having a business meeting. As if the two of them were on the same side. And as if Darin's life was only a stubborn detail to be negotiated between them.

Hmm. Was that a possibility?

"Sheik Hamad, may I ask a question?"

He waved a good-natured hand in her direction. "Of course."

"You said before that people who were loyal to you could expect your appreciation. Would that be true of me, as well?"

Nodding, he stuffed his mouth with creamy pasta.

"What if I agreed to every one of your ideas, and in addition signed a contract letting you manage all my money from now on? Would you consider me a loyal partner then?"

He dropped his fork and grinned, ignoring the ring of Alfredo-style sauce around his mouth. "You would make me ecstatically happy, my dear. And could expect me to be most appreciative."

She steeled herself for his reaction to her next statement. "I will do all that as fast as it can be arranged. Tonight if possible. But in return, I would need your promise that Darin Kadir will be kept alive."

Hamad pushed back from the table and stood. "Whore! You try to trick me?"

Rylie also stood. But she rose on shaky legs and backed up a few steps.

"It's n-not a trick," she stuttered. "Only a business deal."

"The Kadir clan must all die. *All.* Darin Kadir cannot be an exception. It is preordained." Hamad took his dagger from an inside pocket and shook it menacingly as he came in her direction. "No more talking. I will ask for your decision once again after the Kadir dog is dead. By then we'll see what you have to say."

Hanging on to her steak knife like a lifeline, Rylie expected to feel the blade of Hamad's dagger at any moment. But if the cut came, she swore to do her own damage in return.

All of a sudden Hamad's eyes grew wide as he stared

over her shoulder toward the window at her back. She hesitated to turn around for fear he would stab her from behind.

"Stop. Or I will cut her." Hamad raised his dagger over his head.

A big arm came around her waist then and dragged her sideways into a solid, masculine chest. Without looking, Rylie immediately knew it was Darin. Her heart started up again. It hadn't really been beating since she'd last seen him. Now she could breathe. He was alive.

Darin pulled her backward until they hit a solid wall. "Stay away from the window," he whispered in her ear.

Something whizzed through the window next to her. A bullet? But it missed the agitated Hamad, who was stepping from side to side.

At that very moment, a huge commotion began in the next room. Explosions rang out. Men shouted. The door opened and one of Hamad's men ran into the room brandishing a firearm and shouting curses in his own language. Then the assassin fired a wild shot and screamed like a banshee.

Darin stepped in front of her and used his body as a shield. But she didn't want his protection. She wanted to work with him to take out Hamad and get free. They were a team.

Smoke filled the room, and Rylie lost track of things in the confusion. She slid out from behind Darin and came face-to-face with Hamad's bodyguard.

His huge knife gleamed at her through the haze. Darin yelled something Rylie couldn't understand. She wanted to turn and ask him for a better weapon than her silly steak knife, but she was afraid to lose sight of their attacker.

The assassin kept coming—closer and closer to both her and Darin. By now all she could see through the smoky haze was their attacker's yellowed teeth. It was surreal.

And Rylie knew that meant they didn't have much time left.

Chapter 14

The smoke from his brothers' flash bangs grew thicker. Darin could see that Tarik's sniper wouldn't be able to get off another clear shot while smoke poured from the window. Good thing, because Rylie had disappeared into obscurity somewhere near that same window. He should've known Rylie wouldn't cower behind him in a fight.

But how was he supposed to protect her when she wouldn't stand still? He suddenly caught sight of her through the haze. And his heart stopped. On hold—along with his breathing. She had a small knife in her hand and was waving it slowly in front of her as though the puny blade would be a major deterrent to any attacker.

"Rylie, duck and cover." He tried to get her attention, but she seemed frozen in the midst of chaos.

She wasn't too far away from him. But smoke blew

between them again and she disappeared. He took a couple of steps forward, hoping that she would still be in the same spot.

Darin pulled his weapon but was terrified to use it for fear of hitting Rylie—or maybe of hitting one of his brothers. Where were his brothers? Perhaps they had run into more trouble than they'd expected in the front room.

The smoke began lifting. But it still flowed out the window, obscuring the sniper's clear shot from across the street.

"No!" That was Hamad's voice, suddenly ringing out loud and clear. "Not her. Do not harm that one."

Darin finally saw Rylie, turning to the sound of shouting. With his heart bursting in his chest, Darin turned his head, too, and saw Hamad standing on the opposite side of a dinner table with his back to the door. The Taj elder must've closed and locked the door between the bedroom and the front room to let the smoke clear. But Darin knew that wouldn't slow his Kadir brothers down for long.

He swung back to find Rylie. She stood not far away with her back to him. She was facing one of Hamad's assassins. The man appeared to be stalking her with dagger in hand.

"Rylie!"

Hamad started screaming orders once again. "That one! Kill the man. Kill the Kadir dog!"

Things seemed to happen in slow motion from then on. Both the assassin and Rylie lifted their heads to look for Darin. Meanwhile, Darin took a step or two closer to them.

The assassin reared his arm back and let his dagger

fly. Rylie screamed, dropped her knife and threw herself at Darin—stepping right into the flight path of the dagger.

Darin could visualize what was going to happen before the dagger ever hit her in the back. But he was helpless to do anything. Time stopped. It was like the worst horror show he had ever seen, and he knew it would haunt his nightmares forever.

Rylie's eyes opened wide as the knife buried itself deep in her flesh. She took another step forward and hesitated. A look of confusion crossed her face. Darin caught her up with his one free arm.

"No. You idiot! Kill the Kadir!" Hamad was still shouting but he didn't move from his spot of safety across the room.

Darin turned, pointed and fired his gun, hitting Hamad right in the forehead. The look of shock on the Taj Zabbar elder's face was priceless. He opened his mouth automatically but then puffed out his lips and looked like a fish out of water, gulping for air. The very next instant, Hamad dropped to the floor like a heap of trash.

Still holding on to Rylie, Darin turned his gun and pointed it at the assassin. The startled man stared at his boss on the floor for a split second. Then the assassin pulled a stiletto from his own shoe. With his pulse beating wildly, Darin once again prepared to fire.

But the assassin was quicker. Without a second's hesitation, he used the knife to slit his own throat. A horrific sight. Blood spouted like a fountain from the man's neck, and it was over before Darin could pull the trigger.

"Is it finished? Are we safe?" Rylie managed to

speak in a weak voice. But when Darin nodded, her legs collapsed from under her.

"I knew we made a good team." Rylie's eyes closed as she grew limp against him. Letting loose of his weapon, he pulled her into his arms and together they sank to the carpet.

"Hang on, Rylie. Just hang on." Trembling, Darin rocked her in his arms.

Hold on, my love. She couldn't die now. It would kill him to know another woman he loved had died because of him. If she died, he died.

Tarik and Shakir broke through the door.

"Hey, bro, no fair. You managed all this without us. Where's the fun in that?"

"You're sure she's going to live?" Darin had asked that same question of various doctors at least a thousand times over the last three days.

"Miss Hunt was extremely lucky." Rylie's newest specialist spoke in one of those serious doctor's voices everyone always hated.

But as the specialist turned to her in the bed, he offered up a bit of genuine cheer. "The knife blade missed most of your vital organs but just nicked your liver. You're going to be with us for a while, but when you leave the hospital you should be able to resume your regular activities."

It was all Darin could do not to kiss the man. The warm flow of relief poured through his body all at once, forcing him to sit down. He leaned his elbows on his knees and put his head in his hands.

When the doctor said his goodbyes and left them alone, Rylie spoke. "Are you feeling okay, Darin? You don't look well. You're sure you don't have any internal injuries?"

He raised his head and looked over at her. "I'm sure. The doctors tell me I have a bruised kidney, but that I should heal with no trouble. Other than that, I guess I look worse than I feel."

"Purple and green splotches seem to suit you."

She was making jokes. He felt as though the end of the world was right around the corner and she was making jokes.

Standing, he went to her bedside and gazed down on her. "Yeah? Well, you look beautiful, too. All quiet and regal lying in that bed. Like a sleeping beauty."

She did look beautiful. Beautiful and fragile and slightly shell-shocked over what they'd been through. He hadn't seen her looking this vulnerable since the night they'd met when she'd been jet-lagged and scared.

He'd done that to her. Made her vulnerable again.

Everything that had happened to her, brushing her with death and this hospital stay was his fault. He felt helpless again.

Rylie reached out, her hand encumbered by needles and wires, and touched him. He gently took her fingers with his own. Their connection was immediate.

He experienced her warmth. Her gentleness. The spark of life that still burned strongly within her heart.

His obsession with her was as vivid as ever. He longed to hold her. To make love to her. To keep her with him always.

But every time he looked at her, he also remembered the stark terror he'd felt when she came toward him—the hilt of that huge dagger sticking out of her back. He would *never* forget it.

Darin couldn't keep doing this. He couldn't stay here and potentially be the reason for her coming to more harm. The Taj Zabbar were not finished with their war. They still intended to kill the Kadirs. And the next time, she might not…

"Have you talked to my mother? And to my friend Marie Claire? Do they know I'm all right?"

Swallowing down the hard lump in his throat, he said, "Your friend telephoned your mother last night and told her a story about you visiting a spa for a few days. We didn't want to worry your mother too much. You can call and talk to her yourself as soon as you're feeling well enough."

He tried a smile, but knew immediately that it was a dismal failure. "Marie Claire is taking time off from work to come visit with you while you're here. She says she wants to see for herself that you're really okay."

"It'll be nice to assure Marie Claire—and to be able to cheer up my mother again." A ghost of a smile lingered around Rylie's mouth.

Hell. This woman was amazing. She was thinking about everyone but herself.

All he could think about was how close she'd come to dying. Tears burned the backs of his eyes.

"What…" Rylie stopped to clear her throat. "What happened with the Milan police? All those…dead bodies."

Darin squeezed her fingers to let her know he understood what was going on inside her head. How seeing men die could affect you for the rest of your life.

"Don't worry. Tarik has friends in high places here in Milan. He's taking care of it."

Rylie tried to shift her body and grimaced with the effort.

"Want to sit up a little more? Here, let me adjust the bed." He used the remote to raise the head of the bed and then showed her how it worked.

"Thanks," she said when she was settled again. "Actually, thanks for everything. I wouldn't have made it out alive if not for you."

He shook his head. "Don't say that." *Please don't even think that. Without me, you wouldn't have been in the line of fire in the first place.*

"You're a strong, independent woman," he said instead of what he was thinking. "Nobody can get you down."

Her eyes clouded over with sadness. "Can you do me one more favor?"

He nodded and held his breath.

"Can you check on Hunt Drilling while I'm stuck in this hospital? See how the company is doing and how the victims of the explosion are faring. I should be there. I shouldn't have…I shouldn't have left them the way I did."

This one was easy. "I've already talked to my attorneys in Houston. Kadir Shipping will be paying all the bills related to that explosion at the Houston shipping facility. We're setting up a victims' fund, as well. I know it doesn't make up for the suffering." He shrugged but couldn't manage a smile. "Anything we can do."

"But the explosion wasn't the fault of Kadir Shipping."

If only that were true. "The Taj Zabbar would never

have noticed Hunt Drilling if not for Kadir Shipping. It's our fault and we will make amends."

Darin wished he could put her mind more at ease about her father's firm. "I've decided to publicly break our ties with Hunt Drilling. I want you and the company off the Taj Zabbar radar. But if you'd be willing, Kadir Shipping will become your company's silent partner. We'll funnel you anything you need to bring Hunt Drilling back to a place of prominence. Money. Expertise. Anything."

A light moved into her eyes for the first time since she'd been stabbed. "Thank you—again. Uh, so what you're saying is that you believe the Taj Zabbar will continue trying to kill your people, even though Hamad is dead?"

"He was only one man. Now he's a martyr. They have many that would gladly die like him if it meant doing harm to the Kadirs."

She tilted her head in thought the way he'd seen her do before. He tried to memorize the movement for the coming endless nights without her.

"Then you and your brothers intend to continue with your secret actions in order to stop the Taj Zabbar?" she asked at last. "You still plan on proving to the international community that they're the bad guys."

"Yes, certainly. Nothing has really changed."

"You know," she began, sounding almost coy. "Hamad gave me information regarding his operation. I could potentially be a big help in your investigations."

And there it was. Exactly what he had been dreading. Her first move to talk about their future.

He didn't know what kind of story would be the best way to go, but he wanted to let her down gently. Should he pretend he didn't care? Shrug her off and say, "It's been fun, but…"

Rylie would never buy that. She was far too smart, and he had been far too open about how much she meant to him.

No, he had no choice but to stay with who he was. Stay with the honest truth.

He steeled himself, drew in a deep breath and began, "Rylie, my life has become—complicated. Dangerous. Far too dangerous to be starting any new…uh… relationships. At every turn, I run the risk of being killed. By a sniper—a knife attack—or by an explosion."

Her face paled at the mention of explosions, but he was in too deep to stop now. "I can't afford to take on any obligations at this point. It's not…"

"But we're a team," she said softly. "I'm not an obligation. I can help. I want to help. The Taj Zabbar are truly evil and they need to be stopped."

"Not by you." The words came rushing out of his mouth too harshly, but he was becoming frustrated. Frustrated and devastated.

"Look," he began again after composing himself. "Your company needs you. Go back and take over. I'll send Tarik here to the hospital to take your statement before you leave. Tell him what you know. And let us do the rest. Stay away from the Taj Zabbar."

"Darin, please." Her voice wavered, cracking as she spoke his name.

Turning his head rather than look at her didn't help.

She insisted, "You know what I'm asking. I realize we've only known each other for a week, but what about us? I thought we had…a thing. Where do we go from here?"

"We don't go anywhere." He hung his head, still unable to look her in the eye. "At the risk of sounding clichéd, there is no *we*. You don't have any idea what you're asking. There can't be anything between us as long as the Taj Zabbar continues their war against the Kadirs."

"But…"

He couldn't take any more. Knowing he was hurting her was killing him.

"I'd better let you get some rest." He moved toward the door without turning to face her.

"You're not coming back, are you?"

He stopped, hesitated, but knew he couldn't weaken now. "You're going to be fine. Your girlfriend should arrive in a couple of hours. You two sure don't need me hanging around."

"Darin, wait…" Her words were interrupted by the saddest-sounding sob he had ever heard.

And without ever turning around, Darin did the hardest thing he had ever done in his entire life. He walked out the door.

"Damn, but it's bloody dark in this place." Shakir walked to the window and threw open the drapes. "And your apartment is utterly disgusting. Where the hell have you been, brother? We haven't even seen your shadow for weeks."

"I needed some time off." Darin slammed down his beer bottle and put his feet up on the desk. "And I don't remember asking for your opinion about my housekeeping, little brother."

Shakir walked to the sofa, brushed aside the empty liquor bottles and remnants of peanut shells, and sat down. "Bugger that. You never needed a vacation before."

Picking up a half-empty bottle, Shakir stared as liquid pooled on the carpeting. "Why the sudden need for booze? You seldom drink."

"I do now." Darin looked over at his brother and shook his head. "You and Tarik have been talking about me, haven't you?"

"We might have." Shakir put the bottle on the table and rested his elbows on his knees. He leaned forward, ready to have his say while looking sincere.

Oh, no. Here came the "get your act together" speech. Darin turned his back and stared out the window at the sun shining against the crystal-blue Mediterranean. How he hated that sight. The color reminded him of the sexy eyes that had been haunting his dreams. That's why he'd closed the damned drapes in the first place.

"Well, get on with it." Darin let the irritation show in his tone. "Tell me why I need to go back to work. Give me the lecture about supporting the Kadir cause."

Darin needed something, certainly. Maybe he needed his brother to kick a bit of sense into him. Darin was itching to hit something. Or pound on someone. But he was too annoyed with the world at the moment to make a move. That made him an asshole.

And his brothers were bigger asses for caring.

"No need," Shakir said. "You've got all the answers."

Darin wished he had all the answers. Or an Aladdin's lamp to give him what he wanted the most. He'd spent days drowning in his own self-pity, wishing that the Taj Zabbar would disappear off the face of the earth.

"I suppose all this—" Shakir waved a hand over the

mess in the apartment "—has something to do with Rylie Hunt. Want to talk about her?"

"Not much." He hadn't heard a word from her since the day he'd turned his back and walked out.

But what had he expected? He'd apparently done a terrific job of driving home his point. She'd be better off if she stayed thousands of miles away from him.

And yes, it hurt to think he would never see her again. So what? Love always hurt. One way or the other. But better hurt than dead.

"Tarik went to see her." Shakir sat back and Darin could feel him looking for a reaction. "Says she's real smart. She gave us several leads to follow. But we… need someone to analyze those leads."

"Was she all right?"

Shakir slowly breathed in and out until he finally said, "She was being dismissed from the hospital. Heading back to Texas as I understand."

Suddenly Darin had a terrible thought. "What if the Taj Zabbar decide to seek retribution against her for Hamad's death?" Why hadn't he been smart enough to see this possibility before?

Shakir raised his eyebrows, but spoke softly. "Something like that is always possible, but…"

"No, seriously. The Kadirs can't be in any more trouble with the Taj Zabbar than they already have been for centuries. But what about Rylie? They must know she participated in Hamad's death."

Breathing deep, Shakir shook his head. "This is war, Darin. Covert war, but war, nevertheless. You have heard the saying, 'War is hell'? No one can be one hundred percent safe in times like these."

"But she has to be safe. She has to be."

Darin stood and began to pace. He kicked out at the newspapers and books littering his floor. *Think.*

But his thinking was hampered by the amount of alcohol in his system. He turned to his brother for help.

"Shakir, we have to protect her. She didn't ask for this. It isn't her war."

"It seems to me that our war is her war now." Shakir calmly folded his hands and followed Darin's movements with his eyes. "She stepped into it willingly. Didn't she come to Geneva looking for answers? Well, she got them."

No! Darin couldn't accept that. Wouldn't.

Feeling more useless than he ever had been in his life, Darin slumped down on a chair. "Help me. Please. Someone has to watch over her. Make sure she's not in danger."

"Someone?"

Chapter 15

Rylie threw a quick look over her shoulder and dashed for the stairs leading to her second-floor condo. *Who was that man?* There'd been a dark figure lingering at the edge of the parking lot, smoking a cigarette—and watching her.

Ohmygod.

With her heart pounding out a beat like a high-stepping marching band, she took the stairs two at a time. Grateful for having her keys already in hand, by the time Rylie hit the second-floor hallway she was already punching her house key toward the lock.

Shaking badly as she reached the door, she dropped her set of keys and had to scramble around to pick them up. Then she held her breath, unlocked the door and was inside in a blink.

Letting loose of her gym bag, she turned back,

relocked the door and set the chain. Then she leaned her head against the closed door, drew in a deep breath and listened for any out-of-place noise. Were those footsteps on the stairs? Movement just outside her door?

Rylie squeezed her eyes shut and regulated her breathing. It was okay. She was okay.

Most probably the danger had all been in her head. Still, she would be glad when tomorrow arrived and they installed the new alarm system she'd ordered.

As her heart rate slowed, she thought back to her discussion with Tarik right before she'd left the hospital. He was the one who'd put thoughts in her head of the Taj Zabbar coming after her for retribution. It had come from an offhanded comment of his. A single phrase about watching her back.

But after considering the idea for the last couple of weeks, she had to agree that it was a possibility. So possible that after getting settled back at home, she'd gone out and bought herself a new handgun. Then she'd signed up for target practice, ordered the alarm system and returned to her self-defense classes in earnest.

She sighed and figured she was being silly to worry about some strange man in the parking lot. Throwing her gym bag on the couch and heading to the kitchen, she turned on all the lights. Deciding she needed something stronger than bottled water when she opened the fridge, she dug out a diet cola. Not that she really needed to diet.

However, if she were totally being truthful, she had put on a few pounds since her return to the States. Still, no one would call her chubby. But she did figure that the carbonation in the cola would settle her still-trembling stomach and nerves.

She held the cold unopened can to her forehead and stared blankly into the fridge. Being a little frightened now and then was good for a person. Would keep her on her toes.

And working on bettering her own self-defense skills was something to do besides sitting around worrying about Darin and feeling sorry for herself. She certainly wasn't in demand at Hunt Drilling these days.

By the time she'd been released from the hospital and made it back to Midland, Darin's people had already convinced the federal investigators that the shipping-facility explosion was an act of terrorism against both Hunt Drilling and Kadir Shipping. The word had spread that Hunt's employees and executives had done nothing wrong and were victims themselves. Business was booming again from people who wanted to show their support. Not surprisingly, the loyal, longtime employees at Hunt had also stepped up in her absence, and the company had been running smoothly even before her return.

No one needed her at work anymore.

Even her mother was blooming again and didn't seem to need her much, either. True to his word, Darin's attorneys had set up a victims' assistance fund and then had called upon her mother to administer the money in the name of her deceased husband. Rachel Hunt was in her element, working long hours visiting invalids, paying off hospital bills and approving no-interest loans.

The last thing Rachel needed at this point was a mopey daughter hanging around.

Her phone jangled suddenly, causing Rylie to drop the can, just missing her toes. Squeaking, she slammed the refrigerator door and picked up the receiver while searching for calm.

"Rylie, this is Tarik Kadir. Is everything all right?"

"Tarik? Has something happened to Darin?" Her pulse stood at a standstill. Her mind blanked.

"He's fine. Maybe a little pathetic, but he's slowly coming around."

She swallowed hard, trying to keep the melancholy sound out of her voice. "What can I do for you? Why are you calling?"

"I wanted to tell you that we intercepted a Taj Zabbar directive today. They've put out a contract on your life, Rylie. They want you dead for taking part in the killing of Hamad. I've been afraid of this."

Gasping, she nearly dropped the phone. She gripped the receiver as if it were her only lifeline and listened as Tarik spoke in even tones.

"You should be okay," he added. He sounded so sure of himself that her heart rate evened out. "I've had a couple of our men watching out for you for the last week to ten days. Just in case. They tell me you're taking some smart steps toward your own safety. That's good. And, uh…"

He hesitated for only a second and then finished the thought. "Uh…I also thought you should know Darin is on his way to the States to help you with further safety precautions."

"I…see." She leaned against the counter for support instead of crumbling to her knees.

"You haven't given up on him, have you?" Tarik's voice was full of worry. "My brother, well, Darin's personality and background have given him a handicap when it comes to relationships. You should talk to him about it sometime."

She almost smiled. "You would have no way of knowing this, Tarik, but I intend to talk to him, and I don't give up easily."

"Actually, I do know about you not giving up," he admitted. "I've been checking you out. I think you might be a great addition to my investigations team. If you're interested. And if your business can stand to lose you for a while."

Chuckling at the very idea of being on a Kadir team, she asked, "Does Darin know about this?"

"Not yet. I thought I'd let you find the best way to tell him after you've thought it through and made a decision."

Rylie thanked Darin's brother for the job offer and agreed to give the idea serious consideration. It might be just the thing she'd been looking for. Especially now that she had a price on her head.

Relieved to find out that the scary guy watching her from the parking lot had been one of Tarik's men, she turned her thoughts to the other man she'd been trying to forget for weeks. *Darin* was on his way.

Wondering whether he would be coming in tonight or waiting until tomorrow morning, she decided that either way a shower was in order. She'd better wash her hair and maybe even shave her legs.

Rylie dragged her T-shirt up and over her head, leaving the sports bra for last. Moving through the condo, she grabbed her gym bag and started down the hall, turning on lights as she went.

Halfway there she thought about how heavy the gym bag had grown recently. She'd taken to carrying her twenty-pound weights in order to do some light lifting, keeping in shape at home. And it had been working.

Smiling, she wondered if Darin would appreciate how strong she'd made herself. She would have to ask him when he arrived. Of course, if she had any say in the matter, they would be doing a lot more than talking. Sex seemed to be the way they communicated the best.

The idea made her warm all over. She couldn't wait.

Ready to hit the shower, she skipped the rest of the way down the hall and pushed open her bedroom door. A Taj Zabbar assassin stood on the other side, his gigantic dagger gleaming at her in the hall's light.

Darin tried to stay under the speed limit, but the car his man had provided at the Midland airport seemed to jump right out from under him at every turn. Or maybe that was due to his lead foot and jumpy nerves making him press ever harder on the accelerator.

He couldn't tell if he was more worried about Rylie's immediate safety or about having to face her again. There might be some serious backpedaling going on the next time he saw her. He should never have left her on her own. Now he owed her a major apology.

When he'd first landed at the Midland two hours ago and cleared customs, he'd considered checking into the hotel and then going to Rylie's in the morning when they were both fresh. But something urged him to see her tonight. To finish with the apologies and start on plans for her safety.

She wasn't going to like having to hide out, moving around from one safe house to the next, maybe even changing her name. That wasn't Rylie's style. But he was here to make sure it happened. Even if she hated him for it.

Stopping for a traffic light, Darin thought about calling her. His men had reported that they'd tailed her from the gym to her apartment a little while ago. He knew she was home. But maybe she was expecting company tonight.

That errant thought did not make him very happy. He had never given a moment's consideration to the chance that she might find someone else. And he didn't like the image in his mind of her with anyone new.

But he wasn't here as her date. He was here for her safety.

He'd better call ahead. Punching in the number he had memorized but never used, Darin listened to it ring. Perhaps he would invite her out to dinner. She wouldn't feel uncomfortable about talking to him alone in a restaurant. He didn't want to push her.

Yes, the more he thought about that idea the more he liked it. They could find a nice, quiet restaurant where he would explain all the ramifications of her new status as a Taj Zabbar target for death. She couldn't become too mad in a public place, could she?

Her answering machine picked up. He left a short message and hung up. But then he suddenly knew something wasn't right. He called one of the men he had watching her place.

"Yes sir, Mr. Kadir," the guard assured him. "She went inside her condo about twenty minutes ago and she hasn't come out. Miss Hunt turned on a lot of lights and they're all still on. Maybe she's in the shower and that's why she isn't picking up her phone."

Darin swallowed back his terror long enough to tell

the man to meet him in her parking lot. Then he checked his GPS. Five more minutes to her door. He decided to make it in two.

Be safe, Rylie. I'm on the way.

When the phone rang and startled them both, Rylie flipped around and flew down the hall away from the assassin. Running in a zigzag pattern, she worked hard to avoid the repeat horror of a knife being thrust into her back. But the heavy footsteps in the carpeting right behind her said she didn't stand a chance. Her assailant apparently wasn't trying for a clear shot. This man seemed to want his assault up close and personal.

Adrenaline surged through her veins as she hit the end of the hallway and dashed around the couch in the living room, trying to put some distance between herself and the attacker. Sweating profusely, she ran faster, wanting a lead that would allow her to unlock and escape out the front door.

Too late.

On the next step, her hair was grabbed roughly from behind. The surprise move yanked her head backward and made her stop in her tracks. Ignoring the pain, she planted her feet and twisted her slick, sweaty hair free of his grasp. As she jerked and turned, she swung the gym bag as hard as she could with both hands.

Her quick move surprised the assassin, and he stumbled back a step while his dagger went sailing. She would've tried to retrieve his blade but getting out was her first impulse. The front-door locks would take too long. Heading for the utility room back door, she scrambled into the kitchen, moving her feet faster than she'd ever thought humanly possible.

But her attacker was almost as quick. She rounded the kitchen counter, heart crashing inside her chest and her goal in sight. But she wasn't watching her feet. Tripping over the cola can, she slipped on the tile. Down she went and slid headfirst into a cabinet. Pain drove through her shoulder, but she forced herself onto her knees and then blindly came to her feet.

Too late again. Her assailant had her cornered against the kitchen cabinets. The edges of his mouth came up in a terrifying grin while he withdrew a long, silken cord from his coat pocket. Pulling the cord taut between his two hands, the assassin came in her direction.

She tried to fight him off, digging her fingers at his eyes and kneeing him in the groin. But he was way too big. Overpowering.

Before she could slip away, he whipped the cord around her neck and drew it tight. Wildly thrashing about, trying to find something to use as a weapon, Rylie fought with everything she had. She used her nails against his hands, kicked backward at his knees and punched at his head. If she could plant her feet again, she might be able to leverage him over her shoulder. But her time was running out. She was already getting light-headed.

Out of nowhere the doorbell rang, once again startling the assassin as he turned his head toward the noise. Rylie used the momentary lapse to her best advantage.

She leaned closer to a drawer, ripped it open and pulled out a carving knife. Gasping for air, Rylie forced her arm straight out for leverage and then shoved the blade above her head as hard as she could.

Not being able to judge where she'd been thrusting, she still knew she'd hit something. The assassin screamed and the cord around her neck loosened. Just enough.

Wrenching herself from his grip, she withdrew the blade as she whipped around to face him. The assailant was holding his neck with both hands. Blood was spurting everywhere.

Horrified by what she saw, Rylie dropped the knife. When she did, the wounded man lunged toward her. His eyes were wide with pain, but the fury inside them scared her more than all the blood.

Screaming with her own rage and fear, she pushed off and shoved at his chest as hard as she could. But her blow knocked him back only momentarily. He righted himself and started for her again. But with his first step, he, too, slipped on the cola can and fell backward, hitting his head on the edge of the counter. All the air rushed out of his lungs in one big whoosh and his body spiralled to the floor like a shooting star.

Panting, gasping for air, Rylie stared down at his inert body. He wasn't moving and she was alive.

Somewhere through the blurry haze of her mind, she realized the doorbell was still ringing and now the phone was going off, too.

Numb, Rylie stumbled to the front door. Without thinking at all, she opened the locks and threw open the door.

"Rylie...darling. What the hell happened?"

"Darin." Flying into his arms, she began to cry.

She sank into him, sobbing and kissing his face.

"You're okay." His voice was steady—safe. "I've got you."

Yes, he did, she thought. For good.

But unfortunately that was her last coherent thought, as everything else around her went dark.

The woman was amazing. Darin backed out of the hotel's bedroom while Rylie headed for the shower. She swore she would be okay alone.

She'd handled a Taj Zabbar assassin. Then she'd calmly given a statement to the police. And she'd insisted she was fine when the paramedics wanted to take her to the E.R. after hearing that she'd fainted.

He guessed she could take a hot shower by herself after all that.

As for Darin, he couldn't stop shaking.

Since her condo was still a crime scene, he'd brought her here to a long-term-stay hotel where he had a reservation. When he reached the sitting room, Darin pulled out his sat phone and called Tarik. He spent a few frustrating moments trying to explain how the men had totally missed checking on Rylie's utility door and how that was the way her assailant had entered.

"You're sure she's okay?" Tarik asked again for the tenth time.

"She will be." Darin decided right then that she would be seeing the same psychologist that he'd been seeing for post-traumatic stress.

"All right. You two had better get some sleep. This time my men will not miss anything, and they have that hotel covered. You can relax."

Darin hung up but knew he would not be relaxing or sleeping.

He could have lost her for good.

Despite his and his brother's best efforts.

She could've died.

Drawing in a ragged breath, he collapsed on the sofa as tears filled his eyes and ran over to his cheeks. He snuffled. Ran a rough hand across his eyes. Then he tried to stem the tide by biting his tongue.

But nothing worked. Frustrated, he gave in to it, curled into a tight ball and cried like he never had as a child.

Rylie sneaked out of the bathroom after her shower, expecting to find Darin asleep on the king-size bed.

"Feeling better?" He sat in the dark, the only light coming in from the open bathroom door behind her.

He was magnificent. The mere sight of him reminded her that she was alive. His features were so strong. His shoulders so broad. He was vital. Vital and totally alive.

Sitting there, he looked relaxed with his shirt and shoes off. It seemed as if he'd been thinking the same thing as she had. She had been dying to feel the warmth of his arms once again. To have him surround her, keeping her safe.

"Much better. But I'm exhausted. I don't feel sleepy yet, but I'm so tired I can barely continue standing here."

"Go ahead. Climb in. Sleep will do you good." He waved at the wide stretch of clean, crisp linen, but he didn't seem to have any intention of joining her.

Dropping her towel, she hoped the sight of her naked body would induce him—seduce him. She slid between the sheets and sighed. Loudly. In her best come-hither tones.

But Darin didn't make a move.

She gave him a few moments and then said, "Aren't you coming, too?"

"I'll sit right here, making sure you're okay. You'll be able to sleep more soundly if you don't have to worry about anyone sneaking up on you."

"Darin, please." She patted the empty spot beside her. "I need you to hold me for a while. Maybe…maybe we can talk until I stop seeing that assassin in my mind."

She didn't have to ask him twice. But he came into the bed still dressed in his slacks. Instead of slipping in beside her, he stiffly placed his back against the headboard.

Rylie cuddled closer and laid her cheek against his bare chest. When she was settled, he put his arms around her.

"You're going to be safe from now on," he whispered. "Something like this will never happen again."

"You can't promise that. I know the Taj Zabbar still have a price on my head."

Darin felt good to her. So warm. She listened to the steady beat of his heart under her ear and it anchored her to the room. To life itself.

"Your whole life must change drastically from here forward. You know that."

"Yes, I know. I couldn't go back to that condo now even if I thought it was safe. I would keep seeing all that blood. I'll have to move."

"Rylie," he began again in the most somber tone she had ever heard him use. "It's more than that. Much more.

"I'm sorry I left you alone in the hospital," he confessed. "I was being an ass. But I've changed. Nearly losing you for good has changed me."

She wanted to ask how, or to put in her own opinion on his leaving. But she could tell he had a lot more to say. So she kept her mouth shut, held her breath and listened.

"I won't ever leave again. From now on I'll be your shadow."

"Oh, Darin…"

"Wait. There's more. I want you to move out of the States and come to the island of Lakkion where the Kadirs have their headquarters. We can keep you safer there."

"Hmm." She had a feeling she knew what was next, but she wanted him to take the lead. "You make a Greek island in the Mediterranean sound like a prison. What would I do there?"

"Relax. Breathe in freedom. Know you are safe."

She grinned against his skin but wasn't going to let him off the hook. "Do you know that Tarik offered me a place on his covert investigations team?"

"What? No. You can't. It's too dangerous. I'll give you a job on my…"

"Team?" she offered. It was all she could do to hold back the giddy chuckle.

He wanted her. This wasn't only about keeping her safe. But he didn't know how to say it. Rylie wasn't sure what she truly wanted and couldn't help him.

Darin took her by the shoulders and moved her back a little, letting him get a good look at her expression. "Maybe you would be safer if you changed your name. How does Rylie Kadir sound?"

"You think Kadir sounds safer than Hunt? You're crazy."

He bent his head and took her lips in one of the

wildest kisses she had ever known. She responded, reveling in the sensation of being wanted so desperately. But she wanted him, too, and her eyes were wet with tears by the time they came up for air.

"Marry me."

Gasping for air and feeling powerful, she grinned. "No."

"No? But…I thought…" His eyes welled up and her teasing mood disappeared.

She needed to take a stand for what was right. "I'll gladly move to Lakkion with you, Darin. I'll work beside you, and I'll sleep beside you. But I won't marry you."

"Why not?"

"We don't know each other well enough yet. We need to have a lot of long talks. Ask me again in six months."

He captured her lips, showing her how he felt about that. This time, the kiss was all about need. Possession.

"Just be with me, then," he finally whispered against her lips. "I'll change your mind."

With that, he flipped her over and tucked her beneath him. Showing her exactly how he would change her mind and at the same time making sure she felt safe.

Rylie squeezed her eyes shut while the two of them went off into their own world. She absorbed his strength and gave him her own.

And not too long afterward, Rylie had a vision of the future. Despite not knowing each other well, she was sure what she and Darin had between them was going to last.

Maybe forever.

Epilogue

Six months later

"I call." Tarik shoved his chips to the center of the table. "Show your cards, brother."

Darin fanned out his cards and waited while the rest of the table groaned. His inside straight beat everyone else's hands—without question.

Shakir and his two cousins scooted back from the table and stood to stretch.

"It's late and I'm busted," Shakir said. "Besides, I want to go check on that new intel Rylie found this afternoon."

Gathering the cards for another deal, Rylie glanced over at Shakir, her face contorted with concern. "You really think that list we came across of women being held for sale in Zabbaran contains a name you know?"

Shakir nodded. "Unfortunately, yes. That's what I need to find out for sure. I'll see you all in the morning."

Their cousins mumbled excuses and left the table, too. That left Rylie and him—and Tarik. Darin turned his attention to his brother and glared meaningfully.

"Oh." Tarik raised his eyebrows and was obviously fighting to keep the grin off his face. Damn him.

Yawning, Tarik drawled, "Well, I guess I'd better turn in, too."

"Wait a second, Tarik," Rylie said. "I wanted to know more about that operation we were talking about. Specifically, what did you find out after Karim finished decoding those Taj Zabbar papers Darin found in Geneva?"

Tarik stood but stayed next to the table. "For one thing, the Taj Zabbar suspected we'd been infiltrating their operation in Turkey." He grinned. "We had. But we got our man out before they ever pinned him down. What they don't know yet is that we're infiltrating many more of their operations. I've even put a couple of men straight into Taj Zabbar."

Rylie smiled at him but spoke softly. "Be careful. I know you think they're stupid. Behind the times. But they are still extremely dangerous."

Tarik reached over and patted her shoulder. "Don't worry. I wouldn't underestimate anyone with the kind of friends the Taj Zabbar has. Good night, all." He finally left the room and closed the door behind him.

"One more hand?" Darin held his breath and prayed Rylie would say yes.

She stretched, in the that ultrasexy way of hers.

"Okay. But I'm almost out of chips. What'll I use to place a bet?"

"If I win," he began casually, "you'll have to do whatever I say."

Rylie laughed and shrugged. "Oh boy. Now, what naughty things do you have in that mind of yours?"

When he only raised and lowered his eyebrows, she laughed again. "Okay. It might be fun. But if I win, you have to fix all the meals for a week."

"Deal."

She dealt the cards and he came up with three aces. He drew two more cards and found the fourth. Tarik had promised to fix the cards for him. Guess he'd been good as his word.

When the hand was over and she'd admitted he'd won easily, Rylie heaved a heavy sigh. "You win. Do I dare ask what you have in mind for me?"

He stood, moved closer and knelt at her feet.

She began to giggle. "Right here? You're sure?"

Then he pulled the jeweler's box from his pocket and her expression changed. "Oh."

"Marry me."

He opened the box and her eyes went wide. She took one look at the ten-carat diamond and began to cry.

"You don't like it." He tried to hide his disappointment. "I wanted something substantial. Like you are. I wanted something crystal clear and multifaceted. Like you. When I saw it, I was sure you'd love it, too. But you don't. We'll take it back."

Tears poured down her cheeks, making his heart ache.

He took her in his arms and patted her back, hoping to stem her tears. "The ring doesn't matter. What matters is

I love you and I think you love me. It's been six months. We've talked and talked until I think I'm talked out."

Darin had never said so much to anyone. He'd told her about feeling guilty over his mother's death. Rylie had told him about her guilt over her father. They'd cried together and vowed to keep talking for as long as they stayed together.

Now he would be sure they stayed together forever. "And I won the bet, love. You have to marry me."

Rylie reared back and stared at him through shining eyes. "Do you realize that's the first time you've ever said you love me?" She reached for the box. "Of course I want the ring, silly. You picked it out. It's perfect."

He put the ring on her finger and she started to cry harder.

"I've been trying to figure out how to ask *you*," she said through her tears. "I thought you'd changed your mind about getting married. Or that maybe you'd forgotten your promise."

"I will never forget any of it." He held her close and closed his eyes. "And I will always love you."

How amazing it was that their lives had changed so dramatically. She'd once been a grief-stricken woman who couldn't ask for help. And he had once been a detached bastard who'd needed both his ass kicked— and a big hug.

Now, after admitting they weren't perfect, they would be able to keep each other safe. Safe and loved.

Always.

* * * * *

2 FREE BOOKS
AND A SURPRISE GIFT

We would like to take this opportunity to thank you for reading this Mills & Boon® book by offering you the chance to take TWO more specially selected books from the Intrigue series absolutely FREE! We're also making this offer to introduce you to the benefits of the Mills & Boon® Book Club™—

- **FREE home delivery**
- **FREE gifts and competitions**
- **FREE monthly Newsletter**
- **Exclusive Mills & Boon Book Club offers**
- **Books available before they're in the shops**

Accepting these FREE books and gift places you under no obligation to buy, you may cancel at any time, even after receiving your free books. Simply complete your details below and return the entire page to the address below. You don't even need a stamp!

YES Please send me 2 free Intrigue books and a surprise gift. I understand that unless you hear from me, I will receive 5 superb new stories every month, including two 2-in-1 books priced at £5.30 each and a single book priced at £3.30, postage and packing free. I am under no obligation to purchase any books and may cancel my subscription at any time. The free books and gift will be mine to keep in any case.

Ms/Mrs/Miss/Mr _____ Initials _____

Surname _____

Address _____

_____ Postcode _____

E-mail _____

Send this whole page to: Mills & Boon Book Club, Free Book Offer, FREEPOST NAT 10298, Richmond, TW9 1BR